Through
the
Third Eye

Lynn Boston

Metrix Source – Publisher
Phoenix, Arizona, USA

First Print Edition – March 2012

ISBN-13: 978-0-983841-61-6
ISBN-10: 0983841616

Previous Editions:
First eBook versions – July 2011
Second eBook versions – November 2011

Metrix Source – Publisher
Phoenix, Arizona, USA
publisher@metrixsource.com

Author:
www.lynnbostonbooks.com
email: lynn@lynnbostonbooks.com

Front Cover Design by Tyler LaRocque
Cover Finished by Az Publishing Services, LLC

Author's Preface

This is a work of fiction. But depending upon personal beliefs, the topic of reincarnation and past life regression is a fringe area between reality and science fiction. Readers may have to move to one side or the other to enjoy the adventure. Through the experience of regressions, the novel deals head-on with many sensitive and controversial subjects. Characters and events portrayed in the storyline are for the most part fictitious. Even though most of the historical figures and events described in the regressions were real or probable, some historical events portrayed are purely fictitious. It is for the reader to determine which historical "facts" were fabricated. Many of the topics in this novel may appear politically insensitive or prejudiced toward certain genders, races, religions, beliefs or cultures in the historical setting. There was no intent to offend any groups. However, this controversy may provide a foundation for healthy debates between readers. By the end of the book the reader may have many unanswered questions about our place in the world. Those questions could be answered in the next book of the Third Eye series.

To set the reader's expectations:

- Chapters 1-3 set the stage.

- Part I – Search of the Past: Chapters 4-28:

  History Channel and Science Channel addicts will not be able to turn off this channel.

- Part II – Quest of the Present: Chapters 29-61:

  Indian Jones and Da Vinci Code lovers may finish the book in one sitting from here.

- Part III – Forging into the Future: Chapters 62-79:

  At this point, reader debates will turn to arguments over what is real and what is fiction.

At the back of this book is a list of many of the historical figures represented from the characters' past life regression sessions. It also includes some of the interesting terms or artifacts referenced in the book. This list might be helpful when looking up on the Internet or in the library. Perhaps then you can ascertain what is real or fiction … or can you?

Look for Books 2 and 3. Please enjoy and send me your constructive feedback. See About the Author at the back of the book.

Lynn Boston

* * * ~~~ * * *

Chapter 1

Amman, Jordan

Shali pulled back her long black hair, revealing her smooth, golden-brown Indian complexion. She glanced over at the out-of-place, middle-aged American man strolling beside her. "Do you think we'll get the right Iqbal today?"

Clay responded, "I don't know. We've done Iqbal Al-Subari and Iqbal Al-Suwari, but neither were the right target. They had the wrong name, wrong incarnation, wrong soul. It sure would be nice to get more precise information on our subjects, but no such luck this time."

"We obviously didn't get an accurate family name for our Iqbal from the regression of the woman in Jakarta. She had that lisp, which threw off my transcription of the name. As you've said, we are bound by the body through which we see the world, so we were limited by her impaired pronunciation of the name."

Clay and Shali continued walking down the busy main street in Amman toward their rustic hotel in the old section of town. The early morning air was crisp and pungent with the sharp smell of cooking spices and fried breads. Having just finished breakfast at their favorite side-street cafe, they were returning to set up the hotel suite for the morning's past-life regression session.

Clay said, "If today's Iqbal isn't the right one, we've got three more Iqbal Al-Subari-Suwari-Suhari's in their mid-twenties to go through. But today, I feel positive."

"The problem with today's Iqbal is that he is only giving us one session. We've got three days of regression work to cram into one day, so we'll have a problem if he *is* the right guy."

"We'll just have to move fast," Clay said, quickly adding, "You've got to keep us on track."

Shali replied, "Or we pay him more to get another day of regressions."

"Hey, I'll triple his fee if he is the one we're looking for. Quadruple."

"If we find those secret treasures you believe exist, then money shouldn't be a problem."

Clay hesitated for a moment as they walked into the hotel lobby. He looked at Shali and said, "But you know it's not about money. I already made my millions doing this regression stuff. I could make many millions more. I'm just after those secrets. I want them for what they are, or might be - not for some monetary value. But at this point we don't even know what they are exactly, and we certainly don't know what they are worth. If the secrets really are some kind of advanced knowledge, we need to bring them out to better this world we live in. It could sure use some help."

Shali nodded her head in acknowledgment as they walked up the stairs to the second floor hall that led to their suite. With Clay behind her, she unlocked the door to the suite. Suddenly there was a crashing sound in the room. As she pushed open the door, they saw a man dressed in local Arab garb dashing across the dimly lit room.

Realizing they were being robbed, Clay pushed Shali aside and darted towards the dark figure. He tackled the thief mid-waist, several feet from the open balcony door where the man had been attempting to make his escape. The two tumbled and rolled across the floor, slugging and beating each other like grade-school bullies.

Shali flicked on the lights and screamed down the hallway for help, using several Middle Eastern languages. Clay was on top of the perpetrator, swinging as hard as he could at his opponent's face. His years of training in the Army helped him gain the edge, but that training was not able to stop the knee that sharply jabbed into his crotch. He let out a loud yelp and leaped almost straight into the air before buckling and falling on top of the man.

Shali grabbed a metal floor lamp and slashed it across the thief's shoulder as he pushed out from under Clay. The bloodied thief let out his own yelp and scrambled on his knees towards the open balcony with Shali swinging the lamp in close pursuit. He turned back to Shali and yelled out in a Middle-Eastern tongue.

Clay moaned and tried to get back on his feet, as the thief and Shali remained at a stand-off. She stood firm with a wildly swinging floor lamp while the perpetrator stood on the edge of the balcony lecturing her as if the entire episode was her fault.

The thief suddenly turned and vaulted over the balcony onto the hood of a parked car below. As the car's alarm blared with ear-piercing beeps, Shali dropped the lamp and pulled Clay back to his feet. Both ran to the edge of the balcony and watched with adrenaline-pumped tremors as the thief ran off down the street, still looking back to yell his chastisements.

In less than a minute, the hotel security guards and manager ran into their suite, expressing concern and promising action. Clay and Shali surveyed their equipment and materials but found nothing missing. Clay discussed the matter with the hotel manager, and they agreed not to involve the local authorities at this time. That would only complicate their stay. However, the manager agreed to post two twenty-four-hour security guards--one in the street below and one in the hallway outside their room - for the remainder of their stay. While they were speaking, two maids arrived to clean up the broken lamp, tables and glasses.

Shali and Clay freshened up in their own rooms and then met back at the suite. After pouring a cup of sweet, spiced tea for each of them, Clay said, "Our Iqbal shows up in thirty minutes. Considering what just happened, should we be doing this regression today?"

"If you're OK, then I think we'll be alright," Shali responded. "We're only going to get one shot at him, and he has already taken the day off of work. We can't risk losing him, so let's just do it."

Clay sat for a moment sipping his tea and finally said, "Fortunately, we must have walked in on this thief shortly after he got into the room. He didn't have a chance to take anything."

She gave Clay a look of contemplation. "I don't think he was here to steal anything."

"What do you mean? He was going to rob us."

"I don't think so. I think he just wanted to know what we were up to."

Looking puzzled, Clay said, "How do you know? What was he was yelling at you?"

Shali took a deep breath. "It was confusing. He was yelling in Hebrew, but he had a heavy Palestinian - or maybe an ethnic Jordanian - accent. I couldn't tell for sure."

"But did you catch what he was saying?"

She seemed solemn. "He said something like, 'You don't know what you are doing' or 'You don't know who you are dealing with. You are asking for trouble.' Or something like that."

"So if this guy wasn't a thief, why would he care what we are doing? Or did someone else send him here?"

Looking through the corner of her eyes, Shali replied in a facetious tone, "I couldn't get the guy on the couch for a hypnosis session, Chief, so I have no idea what was going on in his head."

"Fair enough."

Her face mutated to a teasing smirk. She nodded her head at Clay's crotch, which had been battered during the scuffle. "How're you doing ... you know ... down there?"

Clay snorted. "It'll be alright after a little physical therapy. Maybe you can help out."

Shali giggled lightly and replied, "It ain't gonna happen, Charlie - not by me. You know what happened last time. I'll call room service for a bag of ice. That ought to cool you down."

The two laughed at the joint jabs, remembering how history had played out between them.

Chapter 2

A large, full-reclining chaise-lounge chair sat in the center of their regression suite. On one side was a chair and small table, and on the opposite side was a table with a computer-equipment set-up akin to a small TV studio.. Shali turned on the equipment on the table, while Clay turned on another computer in the adjoining room.

He called out from the far room, "He's supposed to be here at eight-thirty, so we don't have much time."

"We'll be OK if we don't hit any snags. You ready to test the audio?"

"Give me a minute."

On the table next to the computer in the main room was a large, shielded microphone box with a baseball-sized hole in the front. The contraptions were designed to protect against high levels of electromagnetic radiation that could be emitted during a regression. The heavy microphone box was lined with sheets of lead and copper grounding mesh. Recessed inside the opening was the high-quality directional microphone. As long as they kept the hole pointed at their subject, the whole session would be recorded on the computer in next room.

Shali checked the thirty-foot cables that ran from one room to the other. When she got to his room, she said, "It's such a pain to haul these heavy-assed cables every place we go around the world."

"Heavy-assed cables?" Clay laughed.

"Sorry. Blame my step-dad – you know, talk like a sailor."

Clay thought back to her descriptions of her stepfather, the Portuguese ship captain. He still pictured Shali as being culturally constrained, despite knowing that her Indian mother from New

Delhi rebelled after the pre-mature death of Shali's very conservative Hindu father.

"So, do we really need all this stuff? We haven't had any problems in the last two years."

"I'm not sure if all the precautions are necessary, but they are part of the protocol and help protect against high levels of electromagnetic radiation. The specs for the PLR protocols are very specific. Anyway, I've never had a failed recording in over five years of regressions, so those scientists must have known something."

"So when are we going to get some interesting lives? So many past lives seem so boring."

"Now, come on. Once in a while we get some interesting characters. I've verified a lot of actual previous lives, but I never got any really famous people." He continued his tinkering with the equipment. "So, what's this particular Iqbal's background again?"

"He's a twenty-three year old Palestinian - a junior accountant at a construction company and a recent finance-graduate from Al-Ahliyya Amman University. There's nothing significant or different about him; he's just an ordinary young buck with aspirations for a fruitful and productive life. Did you see him trying to hit on me when we interviewed him last week?"

Clay snickered. "Yes. And you're what, ten - or is it fifteen years his senior?"

"Hey, can't a girl have a little privacy or maybe even an ego boost in her personal life?"

"We're paying him more Jordanian dinar for an eight-hour session than he makes in two weeks at his bean-counting job. He needs to focus on what we hired him to do, not hit on a fine-looking Indian babe trying to regress him."

Shali gave him a smile of gratitude for the jealousy-laced compliment.

"No, today our Iqbal needs to relax," he said in a melodic tone, "and go for a hypnotic ride back into his soul's history. Maybe he'll get to see that hot cave-lady from twenty thousand years ago. He could knock her in the head with a club and drag her back to his cave."

"Maybe he *was* the cave-lady," Shali fired back with a grin. "He won't remember a damn thing when it's over, anyway. Have you ever used those protocols where subjects can actually remember their past lives?"

Ever since Shali had worked with him, he had used PLR Protocol 75, which kept the subjects from remembering anything about the secrets, should they find them. This was a precaution, because if the subjects remembered they might join the race to find the hidden treasures.

"A few times, but any head shrink can do that with hypnosis," he replied. "But I'm not really interested in all that anyway. I'm looking for specific things. If they want to remember their boring past lives, they should be paying me - not me paying them."

"But they could never track down the soul pods or soul mates on their own."

"Maybe. Being in the same soul pod, they seem to know where other mates are at any point in time and space. The challenge is to coax out details before the souls or their guides get suspicious about what we're up to; otherwise, they clam up. The guides are protective of those souls in their trust and don't often reveal where other souls may be incarnated. If a shrink can do that or if the person gets good at regressing themselves, it's possible to identify their soul pod."

"I've never had any bad regressions since we've been working together. Have you ever seen any bad ones in the years before that? You know, blow outs during or after a session?"

"Nah, not really." Clay looked back at her and said, "The secret government studies say that attempts to access or confront previous lives could have emotional or psychological effect, but it is usually beneficial. It's basically the same as what shrinks do when they try to fix people's problems with hypnosis. But PLR Protocol 75 shields them from any knowledge of their previous lives anyway."

Shali said, "I'm ready to test the headphones."

Clay turned some dials and clicked the keyboard. "OK. Are you getting it?"

Shali pulled back her long, silky black hair and lifted the headphones to her right ear. "Good." She could hear the sound-generator pumping low, throbbing Alpha wave frequency pulses to her brain. The pulses helped drive brain waves down to a low frequency where regressions were optimized.

Shali lifted the futuristic looking goggles to her eyes. "Give me a check on the goggles." Clay clicked more buttons and purplish colors flashed rapid sequences in sync with the headphone Alpha waves. She picked up a small skull cap with its attached electrodes and set it on the back of the chair, waiting for their regression subject. The cap would send magnetic pulses to the right and left sides of the brain at different times during the regression to help manage the subconscious mind. Shali knew PLR was heavily influenced by sensory control over the mind. She recalled Clay's jest that they should also have a smell gadget in case someone wanted hot buttered popcorn during their regression.

Shali then laid out a set of EKG-like skin pulse pads with dangling electrodes. The micro-pulse generator was a key component to the protocol. The pads sent micro-frequency pulses to shock several critical points on the body at various times. The pulses were not automatic but act more like a cattle prod when they wanted to stimulate the subject's soul to respond.

Shali put a pair of the pads on the large shoulder muscles on either side of her neck. "I'm ready for the first pad test. Hit the shoulders." Clay pressed some buttons. Her neck and shoulders twisted in slight convulsion. "Whew. Good." The shoulder pulses were used to slap the soul around to get their attention.

She put another pair of pads on her forearms. "Hit the foot pads." When Clay pressed more buttons, her arms jerked back against her body. These pads were placed on the balls of the feet under a pair of wool socks. The foot pads stimulated the subject into progressing forward through the regression if they hesitated. Shali picked up the fifth, smaller single micro-pulse pad and moved it toward her forehead. She paused, then moved the pad to her forearm. "Hit the Third Eye." Clay pressed a button. Shali's arm jerked and she let out a small "Whoa. A little too hot." Clay made an adjustment and tried again. "Perfect. We should be ready."

She looked over to Clay and raised her eyebrows in inquiry. "I know it seems to work, but do you really think the Third Eye pulse makes a difference? And don't bull me, I was raised a Hindu, you know. My mom still wears her dot on the Third Eye."

"At first, I had trouble accepting this Third Eye aspect of the protocol," Clay admitted. "Yeah, I knew of its spiritual significance in Hindu, Buddhist and Kabbalah traditions, and even in yoga, chi gong, karate, meditation and martial arts, but I still couldn't see its value. Then I read translations of some seven-hundred-year-old Rosicrucian documents. That's when I saw a physiological connection between the Third Eye and the pituitary and pineal glands. By stimulating the Third Eye with the pulses, I suspect the human body is induced to a higher state of focus through an injection of natural chemicals into the nervous system. I don't really understand it, but the scientists who developed it at Stanford Research Institute were a lot smarter than I am."

Shali responded, "I must have watched hundreds of past-life regression videos on YouTube. Every once in a while I'd see the PLR hypnotist lean over and push the subject's forehead when they wanted the subject to focus or dig deeper."

"You got it: pop the third eye. That's all we're doing."

A few minutes later, their Iqbal knocked on the hotel suite door. After introductions and a ten minute orientation in Arabic by Shali, they got him settled in the lounge chair. She then wired up the goggles, ear phones and micro-pulse pads. Clay positioned himself five feet from the young accountant and began pressing buttons on a laptop control panel. The colored bars, lights and digital readouts flickered on and off in scanning, pulsing sequences.

Chapter 3

Shali sat three feet to the side of the young subject, waiting for Clay's cue. Because the PLR sessions were conducted all over the globe, her prodigal fluency in seven languages proved invaluable.

Shali glanced at Clay and nodded. "Everything is in place. He seems comfortable and says he is ready to go."

Clay threw a switch and the control-panel light labeled "RECORD" turned red.

"Test… one, two …" Strong signal readings displayed on the control panel sound meters. Bar graphs and meters on the laptop computer recording system in the next room pulsed alive with every spoken word.

"This is Clay Barton. It is eight fifty-two a.m. in Amman, Jordan, on the second of February. The subject for this past-life regression is Iqbal Al-Suhari, subject KC8273-VD5532; suspected soul is ID number SE49-5433. I am assisted by Shali Faisal as session facilitator and translator. The objective of the session is hypnosis and regression of the subject to previous lives. This will be followed by attempted transition to the life between lives realm for interaction with the soul. Because the subject has only agreed to one regression session, we will attempt direct interaction with the subject's soul, guide or other elder souls in the LBL of today's session. Subject is cooperative and understands the possible consequences of participating in this regression. PLR Protocol 75 is being used, as pre-regression hypnotic examination using PLR Protocol 14 revealed easy adaptation to Protocol 75. There are no indications that the subject will experience adverse or lingering side effects from the regression."

Clay started up a sequence of computerized processes on his console. He monitored feedback meters on the control panel as the computer in the next room pumped out digital signals to the various gadgets wired up to the young Jordanian. The Alpha sounds, video flashes and micro-pulse generator made different parts of Iqbal's body twitch in planned sequences as the computer ran through its initial preparations.

Several minutes later, the meters showed that Iqbal had reached a proper state of readiness. Clay nodded to Shali to begin the first hypnotic script. She spoke to Iqbal in Arabic, using a script from the four-inch-thick protocol binder. Each section of the binder was carefully tabbed, sub-tabbed and indexed with a letter-number system. Shali's hypnotic directions to Iqbal were slow and monotone with several-second pauses between each statement.

"[قـ بلـ], أذت يـ شعر   أذت يـ سـ ترخي .ومريد حة أذا د أريد أذت أن"
"أذت يـ سـ ترخي كـامـلة جـ سمك, جزء واحدة [تـ يمـ أت] بـ ما   أذا   أذت"

"Iqbal, you are feeling very relaxed and comfortable. Relax your entire body, one part at a time, as I direct you. Start at the top of your head. You can sense your hair - every strand of hair. Your hair is completely relaxed, and now you feel a tingling sensation in your scalp. The skin on top of your entire head is tingling with relaxation. Experience and enjoy the wonderful sensation as your head relaxes and releases all stress and tension."

Shali paused five seconds. "Your forehead is now completely relaxed. Relax those wrinkles on your forehead and make the skin lay flat. The wrinkles are disappearing as you relax. The wrinkles on your forehead are now gone. You feel a slow rush of warmth and a tingling sensation flowing down the side of your head, across your temple, slowly down across your ears like a warm flowing liquid, relaxing your every muscle, relieving you of every concern in the world. You have no worries, no problems, no feelings, no emotions - simply total relaxation."

Clay noticed Iqbal sink back deep in the lounge chair, his head turning slightly to the left. His neck twisted a bit to the right and then to the left as he experienced sensations he had probably never experienced before. He entered a deep level of hypnotic trance. Clay reviewed the monitors, dials and digital readouts. Having done regressions for five years, he could tell Iqbal was a good subject. He nodded to Shali to proceed.

Shali continued with more than five minutes of standard hypnotic techniques, pushing Iqbal deeper and deeper into the trance. Clay finally looked up from the meters and gauges and made a slight slicing motion with his hand. Iqbal was deep enough. If Shali continued, he could fall into a deep sleep and then the session would be over.

Clay made small adjustments to the intensity of the stimulation points and monitored the feedback on the meters. He grinned in silence as the protocol sequence shot small electronic shocks into Iqbal's body parts, causing them to twitch. He motioned for Shali to move forward to the next set of scripts.

She continued the regression in Arabic. "Iqbal, you will remember nothing from this session. During the session, you will feel no pain despite anything terrible you may see, hear or experience. You will remember nothing. You will not be physically or mentally hurt or injured during this session. Do you understand this?"

"Yes," he mumbled in Arabic.

"After the session, you will remember nothing that was said or experienced during the session. Nothing. Do you understand?"

"Yes," he said in a more vibrant acknowledgment.

Clay watched the feeds anxiously. Within a few hours, they should know if this was the target he had been seeking for the last several years.

Part I – Search of the Past

Chapter 4

Clay motioned for Shali to continue, and in response she turned to the next tab in the script book.

"Iqbal, look ahead of you. You should see a very long hallway with doors on both sides. The hallway reaches as far as you can see. Each door leads to a different life you have lived before. One of those doors leads to a life that you lived almost two thousand years ago. Walk down the hallway until you reach that life. When you get to that door, I want you to stop and look at it." Shali paused and then said, "Are you in front of the door yet?"

"No."

Clay could tell where she was on the script and that Iqbal was having trouble moving down the imaginary hallway. He turned the knob for the micro-pulse to the balls of his feet and pressed a button. Iqbal's ankles and feet twitched as the pulse generator sent him small micro-shocks.

"Continue walking down the hall." Shali paused for five seconds, and then repeated, "Continue walking until you reach…"

"Yes. I am there, at the door."

"Good. Open the door and walk into the room. Look around and tell me what you see."

There was a long pause. Clay knew where Iqbal was and lifted his hand to signal Shali to wait. After another five seconds, he nodded his head for her to proceed again. As with any regression, Iqbal was at this moment experiencing a surrealistic dream-like state. His subconscious mind would be wondering if this was real or just his imagination. He was probably wondering whether he could have created an illusion from some late-night movie he had seen long ago on television.

"Tell me what you see. Look around slowly and tell me what is there."

Clay sent a small pulse to Iqbal's shoulder muscles to stimulate his motion.

Iqbal's shoulders shrugged upward and back toward his ears. He attempted to say something, but it was unintelligible, nearly inaudible. This was normal on a first regression for any subject. Clay and Shali both knew the subconscious mind got better after warming up on a few past lives. Successive regressed lives almost always got better and oftentimes became almost conversational.

Slowly, Iqbal responded in a drawl-like mumble, "Books, scrolls, manuscripts everywhere. What a mess. Piles of writings." His tone and speed picked up. "How can anybody find anything in this room?"

Shali looked over and smiled at Clay with a nod. "What year is it?" she asked.

Iqbal's head turned slightly to one side as if looking around the room. He inhaled a slow, deep breath through his nose. "Ahhh." He breathed in another breath. "Leather - smell of leather."

"Can you tell what year it is in this life with all of the books?"

Clay pressed the button for a micro-pulse shot to the Third Eye. There was some hesitation as Iqbal searched for a date in this picture. "220. 230.No, 226. Yes, 226."

"AD or BC?"

"AD," Iqbal shot right back.

Clay understood Arabic numbers and shook his head with disappointment. He whispered almost under his breath, "Damn, missed it by two hundred years."

Shali glanced up at Clay's comment but quickly refocused her attention on the regression scripts. Clay continued watching the intense yet barely perceptible expression on Iqbal's face. He nodded for Shali to prompt for more.

"Please go on," she said. "What else do you see in the room?"

"Large writing table. This is where I do my best work. The Empress, she is pleased with my work - and the Emperor, too."

"Which emperor and empress? What city are you in?"

"Italy. Rome. No, Athens, I think. No, I can't tell - one of those cities. I'm not outside, so I can't tell."

"That's OK. You can try later. Which empress and emperor?

"Emperor Severus, of course, and his wife the Empress."

Iqbal's tiny smile glowed with happiness and satisfaction. Shali knew they were starting to roll, now. At least they had a subject who knew some nobility.

She prompted, "Which empress? What is her name?"

"Domna. Empress Julia Domna. They are pleased with my writings. Oh, she has such a full and complete library. She allows me to use the library any time I wish. The books, the scrolls, are from so many philosophers. Such very wise men. She is such a beautiful and intelligent person; she is a wonderful philosopher, herself. I know. She does not hesitate to challenge my thinking, or anyone's thinking or words. But she welcomes debate even as the Empress of Rome. She is a great woman."

Iqbal paused for a few seconds as if collecting his thoughts. Then he started again without any prompt, this time with a scowl on his face. "But many of the others do not like her. These other people, they have much power, and they do not like her. They believe she is too philosophical; she challenges their authority, their power. She is a threat to them."

Shali probed, "Who are these other people?"

Iqbal scowled even more. He jerked his head quickly to the right. Shali and Clay looked at each other in puzzlement. Shali nodded and Clay pressed the button sending a micro-pulse to the Third Eye. No reply came back.

Iqbal's expression turned from a serious scowl back to a satisfied smile. He continued, totally ignoring Shali's question. "The debates we have in the atrium and the courtyards are so challenging, invigorating, absolutely exhilarating. This time is so wonderful. Yes."

There was a long sigh and pause as he languished in past memories. Shali quickly summarized the session for Clay. He shook his head again in disappointment at first, but then he lifted his eyebrows and nodded. "This is not exactly who we wanted to find," Clay whispered so as not to disturb Iqbal, "but we're close. I've done extensive research on this era and possible threads of lives. Even though we missed the target date by a couple of hundred years, Iqbal could still be the soul we're looking for. But I'll bet I know who this is anyways."

He signaled for Shali to move to the script in the next section. "What is your name in this life?" she asked.

Iqbal strained to pick up a name from many lives earlier and then finally drawled, "I can't tell exactly."

"Just try. What does it sound like?"

Iqbal struggled to pronounce a name he may not have spoken for nearly two thousand years. "Something like…"

Clay tipped his head back and looked at the ceiling, listening carefully.

"Filo … stratum."

Clay almost lip-synced under his breath in cadence with Iqbal: "Philostratus." With a huge gloating smile, he pumped his arm in victory and whispered, "Yes!"

Shali glanced at Clay, eyebrows squeezed inward in query. She leaned over and whispered, "Clay, give me a ten-second brief on this Philostratus."

He ran through a rapid-fire dissertation in hushed tones. "He was a famous Greek-Roman scholar and the author of many philosophical and historical books. He died in his mid-seventies about 250 AD. His most famous works were manuscripts on the Life of Apollonius of Tyana. We're looking for Apollonius, because I think he might know where the secrets are hidden. I heard Iqbal say 'Domna.' That must be the Roman Empress Julia Domna Severus, one of the most powerful women during the entire history of the Roman Empire. If I recall, she chartered Philostratus to write about Apollonius and had a huge library that preserved many of Philostratus' works for centuries after her death. However, the books had to be hidden to survive a series of political and religious purges. Almost every religious crusade for a thousand years tried to destroy books of any conflicting ideology, including her library."

"It wasn't just religions that did that. Look at Hitler's Kristallnacht and the Chinese Cultural Revolution in 1965. Anyway, do you think Domna's library is what we are looking for?"

"I'm not sure. It would seem too obvious. Historians think that in the six hundreds AD the hard-core Christian Emperor Justinian destroyed a lot of what the empress had collected. She strongly supported open philosophical discussion and posed a big threat to the Christians at that time. Nevertheless, she committed suicide about 217 AD after her son, the new emperor, was murdered in a purge of philosophy-loving rulers and leaders. What a waste."

"So do you think any of the writings survived?"

"Don't know, especially after the Catholic Pope Gregory tried to finish destroying them. According to the history books, four hundred years after her death he destroyed what was left of the empress' library. He called the writings 'philosophical chaff.' The Christian churches, particularly the Catholics, always seemed threatened by philosophies that challenged its authority, even if they didn't pose an immediate threat. A copy of Philostratus' book called *The Life of Apollonius*, managed to survive the Christian destruction. That book is still preserved today in the U.S. Library of Congress."

"If you think this might be Apollonius' soul, where do you want to go from here?"

"Philostratus lived about one hundred and fifty years after Apollonius. When we're done poking around Philostratus' life, try again to find out who was attempting to destroy the writings, and then we'll try to move backward one more life. If we're lucky, we might get Apollonius."

She moved forward through the regression scripts for fifteen minutes. Iqbal's soul, as Philostratus, reminisced about past lovers, philosophical rivals, obnoxious family members and confidants had he known during that life.

Chapter 5

Iqbal's soul began to ramble endlessly about its experiences in this life, so Clay and Shali left him to babble along while they stepped aside to talk about the next steps. Because the sessions were recorded, they knew they could pick up any missed details after transcription.

Clay leaned over to Shali and said, "Many historians believe that Philostratus escaped to Athens in his forties when the Empress Julia Domna died."

"Why? Was he in danger, or threatened?"

"Perhaps. He may have felt he was a target because of his association with the empress."

Clay began surfing his computer for more information on Philostratus. He searched Wikipedia and several university websites for any descriptions of Philostratus' life. "There was speculation he spent his last years in Tyre, a coastal city in Lebanon," he told Shali in a low voice as he read. "There are purported events but nothing definitive on his later years on how or where he died. Let's see if we can fill in the gaps in the history books."

They went back to Iqbal, and for the next fifteen minutes Shali continued to question him on events in this life that had been historically documented. They compared historical claims against what really happened, as described by Iqbal's soul. They joked at how documented history had distorted much of the subject's life.

"Shali, let's get to the end and find out how he really died. There is a lot of debate on that. The regression should clear it up."

Shali prompted Iqbal, "Move forward to the last moments of this life." She waited five seconds. "Are you there?"

There was a long pause. Clay pressed a shot of micro-pulse to the Third Eye, and the expression on Iqbal's face became serious. This reaction was normal for the first death or two experienced by any subject in a first regression session.

"Yes. Yes. I am there."

"Tell me what you see. Where are you located and who is with you?"

"I'm on the side of a hill. I am outside of Athens. I was walking, early in the morning. I only went for a walk in the hills ... No!" Iqbal shouted. "No! Ahhh!"

Shali quickly injected, "You will not be hurt by what you see. You will not feel pain or suffer in any way. You can float away from this body and look down on it at any time. If this becomes painful or concerns you, move out of the body and watch from above. Now, tell me what you see."

"I was walking, a simple walk early in the morning. I fell off the path in the hills. I was just taking a walk to the top of the hill to enjoy the view of Athens. I fell off of the side of the path and rolled down the hill. That was so stupid. My back, it hurts badly. I broke my back and my neck. It's broken, and I can't move. It doesn't hurt any more, but now I can't talk, I can't move, I can't feel anything. I cannot even yell for help. There is no pain now, but I cannot move. I can hear people walking on the path to the top of the hill, and I cannot call to them."

"How long are you there on the hill? Does anyone come or did anyone help you?"

"No. Two days, three days. I lay there three days - three very long days. No one can see me or hear me. I cannot move. My body is paralyzed. No one hears me. The nights are cold but it doesn't bother me because I cannot feel it. Only my face is cold at night. My mind is so full, so active. I have so much to say, so much to do, so much to write. I cannot tell anyone. No one can hear me. I do not want to be finished with this life yet."

Iqbal's facial expressions showed that he was not pleased with this experience. However, Protocol 75 would suppress this bad memory after the regression.

"You said you were in Athens. Are you sure you are in Athens and not Tyre?"

Iqbal smiled and laughed out loud in a muffled tone. "They think I am in Tyre; they did not know that I slipped away and came back to Athens. I had to hide from them for many years. I was safer hiding under their noses in Athens than living in Tyre." The smile turned to a grin that poked out of the corner of Iqbal's mouth despite the obvious stress he'd witnessed in his past life.

"Who are they?" Shali prompted tartly. "Who are you hiding from, and why do you have to hide?"

Iqbal did not answer. Again, he turned his head hard to the right, as if trying to hide.

Shali asked again, "Who are you are hiding from?"

Clay pressed the button for another micro-pulse the Third Eye.

After no response, Shali asked, "Are these Christians who are looking for you? Are they Greeks? Romans? Who are they?"

"They came to great power in the last fifty years. They do not like my writings or my words. I know what they did to the empress."

"What did they do to the empress? Did the empress kill herself, or did someone else kill her?" In a frustrated and commanding voice, Shali said, "Tell me who these people are; tell me now."

After a short pause, "Hmphh," was his only response. Iqbal's head suddenly reeled back in his chair, as if escaping from the regression. He ignored the question said, "I died. I left this body. It is over, and no one is there with me. But that body was old and sore anyway. I was ready to move on, ready to see my friends; I missed them. There is always the next life."

Shali looked at Clay and shrugged her shoulders. Iqbal's soul was obviously avoiding her questions. She leaned over to Clay and whispered, "Kind of a gruesome way to go on that hillside, huh?"

"Yes, but not as bad as cancer or diseases in the old days. Think of all the stories we have heard about different ways to die. Souls take sickness very differently than they take a sudden death like this. Some belabor the diseases."

"You've been doing this a lot longer than me. Do you ever get tired of all the death you see while doing regressions?"

Clay broke into a big, joking smile. "Nah. It's just part of life. Everybody dies. It's just that you and I get to see death firsthand, at the end of every regression. As soon as you let me regress you through a couple dozen deaths, you'll see. I'm telling you, it's no big deal. After re-experiencing your fourth or fifth death, it's pretty easy to take. After that, if you get to see some wildly violent war death or criminal death from your past, it's almost exciting, a bit like a movie. Remind me to tell you about the time I was nearly sliced in two in North Africa." Clay chuckled under his breath. "Damn Barbers."

Shali glared at him and snapped back in counter jest, "Clay, you're sick. You need a shrink, and maybe even a regression session to work out your underlying issues."

Smiling, Clay pointed to their subject in the lounger and nodded for Shali to continue. She turned and focused her attention on Iqbal. It was time to dig for soul mates. "You spoke about seeing friends. What friends? Who are they?"

"I don't know who they are or what they are. I just know that I will see them again, soon, after this death."

Shali leaned over to Clay. "This soul seems to be longing for his pod mates."

"That's good. We can look forward to the LBL phase; that's where we'll get the good stuff. If this soul is unencumbered by a weak and prejudiced human subconscious, it could be a gold mine. But we'll never get there without building some rapport first. Let's get on to the last of the script."

Shali turned to Iqbal, "What did you learn from this life?"

Iqbal slowly and deliberately responded. "That the teaching of others was my purpose for this life: to communicate ideas but not to push so hard as to alienate others. I learned that to be a teacher of new ideas, you must walk the fence of the lions' cage. You must keep your balance or the lions will feast. The one called Apollonius showed me the way. Apollonius could taunt the lions to frenzy but would not fall into the pit." Iqbal's face flashed a guilty grin. "I have fallen into the pit so many times before this life, but I gain more balance each time."

When Shali translated for Clay, he became hungry for more details. Clay slid forward in his chair and almost fell into the table of electronic gadgets.

Shali picked up on his curiosity and gave him a look of "What do I do next?"

Clay signaled she should keep digging.

She continued. "Tell me more about the lessons you learned."

No response. Five seconds later, Clay pressed the button to send a shot of micro-pulse to the Third Eye.

"Did you learn everything you were supposed to learn?"

No response. Clay leaned over to Shali. "We're not getting any further on this, so let's go to the scripts on the secrets."

Shali flipped to a section in the back of the script book and turned back to Iqbal. "Did you ever hear of hidden writings, secret writings, secrets of life, or secrets of the world?"

Clay gave another long hard micro-pulse shot to the Third Eye. After a few seconds, Iqbal responded, "Yes, there are secrets, but few people know about them. They are written, but they are hidden. The secrets are hidden in the words; the words are hidden in the hills. I do not know where. I do not know how. I just know…I just know."

Clay whispered, "I don't think this soul knows where the secrets are hidden, but keep pushing. There's a link here somewhere, so we have to get to his soul mates. We'll do that in the LBL."

Shali nodded and continued questioning Iqbal. "Do you know of anything that might be called a secret doctrine?"

He gave no answer.

"Have you heard of the seven keys or the seven secrets?"

No response.

"Do you know of the Chinese writing called Yih-Ching?"

No response.

"Do you know the source of Kabbalah?"

No response.

This closing script continued for five more minutes as Shali grasped at straws at the end of this life's session. Iqbal simply did not respond to her fishing expedition. Clay handwrote a quick note for Shali with several spontaneous unscripted questions.

"When you were an older man in this life, did you know or meet a young man named Plotinus? Perhaps you met him in Rome?"

"I have heard of him."

"What do you know about him? What have you heard?"

"I did not meet him. I was told that he was well-traveled, educated and knowledgeable. His was a Greek-Roman but he came from Egypt. He was educated in Alexandria, but he later traveled and battled in Persia. His ideas and thoughts were interesting, so I was told. I was hiding in Athens when he came back to Rome from Egypt, so I never met him. He was not popular among the powerful leaders either."

Shali translated for Clay, who wrote out more questions for her.

"Have you heard of a man named Ammonius Saccas? In Alexandria. Did you ever know him or hear of him?"

There was a long pause, but Shali finally got a reply. "Yes, Ammonius was an Egyptian; he lived in Alexandria. He was a well-known scholar and a very popular philosopher, but he did not write much. I did not know him. I only heard of him."

The back-and-forth questioning continued for another five minutes, but Iqbal gave no more responses. Clay knew Iqbal was finished talking about this life for now. It was time to take a short break and let Iqbal's mind roam in memorable reverie while they regrouped to prepare for another life of this soul.

Chapter 6

While Iqbal rested, Shali pulled Clay into the next room.

"Clay, what are you after with this Plotinus guy? You keep asking about him."

"I'm not really sure. I picked up his name several times in the regressions that got us to this point. Both Plotinus and Ammonius Saccas have a connection here, somewhere. A lot of these philosophers and scholars seem to be interlaced at the soul level."

Shali gave her partner an intense look. "If Iqbal has Apollonius' soul, I need to know more so I know what to dig for. You've got to fill me in on this guy and explain how you think he is connected to the secret writings."

"I really have no idea how. In fact, I don't even know that the secrets *are* writings. That was a speculation because they talk about knowledge. I figured knowledge has to be writings of some sort. I assume the soul of Apollonius knows what the secrets are, or perhaps where they are hidden. Even if his soul doesn't have first-hand information, maybe he can link us to one of his soul mates who may have the key. I'm counting on the fact that souls hang around in pods in between lives and experience many lives together as soul mates. We're getting close, Shali. If Iqbal's soul is not Apollonius, then I'll bet our good ol' Apollonius is in the same pod. Here in this chair lies the soul of Philostratus, the foremost authority on Apollonius. There *has* to be a connection, I know it. You're closing in."

"The eternal optimist, you are. OK, so we're close to Apollonius. That still doesn't help me ask the right questions. When we get to the LBL-phase and the guide opens the Akashic records, you know they are only going to give us what *they* want us to know. I have to coax it out of them almost every damn time. I know you've been holding back, but you've got to give me more details on the secrets. Where did you ever find out about them and who or what is leading you there? Oh, and by the way, who the hell do you think this guy is so afraid of?"

Clay paused for a moment to gather his thoughts. "First, I don't really know who he is afraid of, but we consistently see this when we get mention of the secrets. Somebody doesn't want the secrets to get out." Clay hesitated and sat back in his chair. "As to the details, I apologize for being so tight with the secrets since we've been together. I know I have to give you more to work with." Clay paused again. "Alright. You know I got my all my wealth by doing regressions for several years before we met. But you don't really know how I made that money."

"Yeah. No joke, Sherlock. You've been playing a mystery game with me for almost two years. You've held back, I know. I didn't want to push you, but I need to know more or I'm working half-blind, here. We've finally got a good lead. So, come on. Fess up."

"Well, when I first started, instead of playing the psychologist game and doing regressions to solve individual's personal problems, I did them to seek out lost or misplaced items from their past lives. You know, like finding buried treasure. I had a couple of big hits early on. I've found war booty, stolen gold bars from cargo shipments, stashed diamonds. That's why I use Protocol 75. I didn't want to compete with my subjects in running for the hidden treasures. Perhaps it was a bit selfish, but now that I've got plenty of money I can pursue treasures for the good of others. Sorry I haven't opened up before, but after what happened between us when we first got together, I just didn't know if I could completely trust you."

"I'll give you that. I could have ended up as your competition. So move on. But hidden treasures from past lives? What're the odds of finding that? I figure you'd have a better chance of winning the lottery."

"Oh, no, my dear lady, you'd be surprised. It seems like almost every soul has hidden something in a past life. They might forget about it while living or maybe they would die before recovering it. It must be impressionable on a soul to have hidden something in some earlier life without ever benefitting from it. During my early regressions, I'd just ask my subjects to go directly to a life where something like this happened to them."

"But there just aren't that many rich people in the world. How'd you get to the big money?"

"You're right. I'd get lots of little things, like a wooden toy that a child hid from his sibling in 300 BC. There was a small bag of coins a woman hid from her constantly drunk husband in 1300 AD, Russia. He killed her a few years later and that soul never got to retrieve the coins. Things like this are just not worth pursuing though. I waited for big ones."

Shali asked, "Like what? What were your big hits?"

"I had one regression on a subject in Australia. This woman's soul was once a member of a small band of Mexican bandits who robbed a bank in Flagstaff, in the Arizona Territory, in the late eighteen hundreds. The band fled south toward Phoenix with eleven saddlebags of gold coins - that's worth tens of millions of dollars today. That same night, they were ambushed by the Flagstaff Sheriff with an aggressive posse who killed most of the bandits in the gunfight. A few of the Mexicans escaped on horseback with ten bags of the gold, which they buried in the Arizona desert so they could dig it up later. They took off for Phoenix to let things cool down, but they were captured by US Marshals and hung a few weeks later. No one ever found the gold bags ... until I came along." Clay sat back and smiled. "This woman's soul was absolutely eager to tell someone where it was hidden. I only found nine bags, but that was enough to get me jump started: instant wealth. I sold the coins on eBay, a couple at a time." He smirked. "I am speaking to you in confidence, because I trust you, now, OK? I have several more good finds but I'll have to tell you those another time."

Shali kept pushing. "But how did you find out about these secrets that we're looking for - the supposed secrets of the universe, as you say?

"I don't know if they are secrets of the universe, but they are supposed to be something really big. Anyway, I got a bit greedy and started asking my regression subjects if they knew of any *huge* hidden secrets, bigger than anything imaginable. I was really looking for a big stash, like a lost shipment of jewels or maybe a proverbial king's ransom hidden deep in Nottingham Forest. However, all I got were consistent references to hidden secrets, not monetary treasures. Some of them would talk of hidden treasures but when I dug in deeper, they really meant secret knowledge of some kind. Most of the regressions came from lives that were lived between one thousand and two thousand years ago, and mostly in the Middle East, Western Asia and Europe. Only a few lives less than one thousand years old made reference to these hidden secrets. It was as if the secrets disappeared, or were forgotten about."

"Alright, now I sense that you don't know a whole lot more about the secrets than I do. So, what about Apollonius?"

"This is where Apollonius comes in. Several times I got references from regressed souls who pointed at Apollonius' soul as some kind of originator, collector or protector of the secrets. I don't have many more details because I couldn't get these souls to give me more than that. They kept talking about the secrets as if they were some kind of hidden writings or knowledge. Some called it a divine wisdom or referred to 'seven secrets.' The souls who referred to the secrets often talked about ancient Kabbalah or Zoroastrianism or Buddhism, but I could never get it pinned down. Some regressions to more recent lives made vague references to the Masons and the Theosophists in particular. Souls with older lives talked about linkages with the Abrahamic religious sects, Indian mahatmas, and yogis, and Buddhist high priests of some sort. I'd even gotten linkages to Chaldean Oracles from Babylonia in today's Iraq. Some spoke of Eastern Initiates or Ancients who were clear -the secrets should not be released to mankind. It's all a bit of a mish-mash, but the common thread is that there are some big secrets hidden out there, somewhere."

"Well at least you gave me more to go on. Now I know how you got the last sets of regression scripts."

"But I am certain there are a couple of copies of these secrets stashed out there. I got one lead that alluded to the Vatican having a copy of the secrets - but if that exists, it's unlikely anyone will ever see it. I don't think they would even acknowledge, let alone release, any secrets of the universe they might have."

"Ok, ok. Let's get back to the regression. If Iqbal's soul lived as Apollonius, hopefully we will find it a life or two earlier in time."

Chapter 7

They moved back to the regression room and settled into their positions on either side of Iqbal. Shali commenced with the next sequence of scripts and took Iqbal to the next life in the regression.

"You are back in the hall of doors. Walk down the hallway and find the door that goes to the life you lived just before Philostratus. Do you understand?"

"Yes."

Shali waited five seconds. "Do you see that door?"

Clay shot a micro-pulse to the balls of Iqbal's feet.

"Yes, I am there."

"Open the door, walk through it, and take several steps further. Look at everything around you. Look up and see if there is sky, or whether you are inside of a building. Now look to the left and then to the right. Look down at the ground, and at your feet and your legs. Look at your hands. Notice what type of clothes you are wearing. Now describe everything you see."

Iqbal took a long, slow, deep breath. Shali and Clay saw him slowly twist his body slightly. Ten seconds and still nothing happened. Clay gave a shot of micro-pulse to Iqbal's feet. His feet made a small but noticeable twitch. Clay then shot a boost of pulse to his shoulders. The back of Iqbal's neck contracted slightly, but another five seconds went by with no response. Then Clay shot a pulse to the Third Eye. Iqbal immediately tilted his head backward as his inner self was released from the subconscious mind.

"I see old stone buildings. The boys … the boys are playing. We're playing with sticks and a ball of some kind. It's like a leather ball. We are playing something like stick-ball. I like this. I miss this. I am happy now."

"How old are you?"

"I'm ten years old." A big smile comes across Iqbal's face. "I will soon be eleven. These are good times. My family is content; food is plentiful."

"What year is it? Can you tell what year this is?"

Iqbal took a large breath and hesitated a moment. Clay shot another short pulse to the Third Eye.

"100. The year is 101."

"BC or AD"

"101 BC."

"Where are you at? What is the name of the city or country that you are in? Can you tell what part of the world you are in?"

"Babylon. My home is Babylon. Oh, such a beautiful city."

"What is your name? What do people call you? What do your friends, the other boys, call you?"

"Allal, or Hallal. It is something like that."

Shali translated for Clay. An inquisitive look came across his face. He shrugged his shoulders and whispered, "We overshot. Apollonius was born about 40 AD, one hundred forty years after this boy was born. We have to move one more life forward in time - if, of course, there was a life there. But he seems to have liked this life, so let him experience it a bit before we try to move forward one. This will build trust that should help us with the Akashic records later."

Shali nodded. She walked Iqbal's soul through another ten minutes, re-living two different progressive ages in the life. All were pleasant and happy times for this soul, and he continued yammering about his life as a young adult until he suddenly exclaimed in a loud and excited voice, "חמים חומוס זהו אמא ,ואו! עברית!"

Shali broke out in a huge burst of laughter. Clay looked at her with puzzled eyes and asked, "Come on, what did he say? It had to be good."

Shali continued giggling as Iqbal excitedly rambled on. She glanced at Clay with a blushing smirk. "He just had a fling with a beautiful young woman. He exclaimed something like, 'Whoa momma, what a hot Hebe chick,' and then he went on to describe their intense, intimate sexual encounters in explicit detail." She paused as Iqbal continued replaying his previous life and then he laughed out loud again. Clay shook his head and smiled with a slight look of envy.

After five more minutes of excited descriptions, Iqbal slowed down his pace and paused. Shali moved him through two memorable periods in this particular life and then jumped ahead.

"Move forward to a time of significant importance to this life. Move forward as many years as you like and tell me what you see. Look around at your the surroundings. What do you see?"

Iqbal's shoulders rolled back in the chair. "Whoa. I am older now. I am sixty … no, sixty-five years old. I am a student." Then, with some hesitation and confusion, he asked, "How can I be a student? Yes, I am a student. I am not in Babylon. I am in Jerusalem, now, studying."

"What are you studying at that age?"

"The Bible. No, the Torah. I am studying the Torah. Well, no, not really. I have studied here for over twenty years, now. I am not really a student, but I see myself as a student. There is so much to learn."

"What else do you do besides study? What are you known for? What have you accomplished - or what do you plan to accomplish - with your knowledge?"

"I confronted the Sanhedrin. It was difficult and there was much conflict, but I showed them that they were wrong." Iqbal's expression became filled with anger, and his demeanor became almost violent. He clenched his fists and yelled, "You must put an end to this. It is wrong. You cannot please God by killing innocent people."

Shali touched Iqbal's hand and firmly said, "Do *not* go into that life. Only view that life from a distance. Tell me about it, but do not enter it. Do you understand?"

Iqbal's demeanor calmed. "Yes, I understand." After a brief pause, he continued. "It was a long debate … many years long. But I finally convinced them."

"Tell me more about this Sanhedrin. And what did you convince them of?"

"It's like a court. They are rabbis. Yes, they were like judges. It was a court of judges in Jerusalem. There were maybe twenty or twenty-five of them, all rabbi judges and all elders - wise and experienced elders. I convinced them to stop sacrificing humans. Human sacrifices are so wrong. They sacrificed humans for no reason, just on a whim. It served no purpose. After several years, they finally agreed with me, and they mandated to stop all human sacrifices."

Shali looked toward Clay and gave him a quick translation. A puzzled look came across his face. He bit the bottom right corner of his mouth as he went into a state of mental recall, and then he nodded for her to continue while he turned his attention to the laptop. He began searching the Internet for who this person might really be.

"Were you happy or proud about stopping the sacrifices of humans?"

"Yes, very much. But that is only the beginning. There is so much more to do."

"Tell me more about yourself."

"I was a happy man. I seldom got angry. I was very meek, very mild and peace-loving in this life. That was what I was known for."

Shali continued for several more minutes before she translated again, looking for guidance from Clay.

Clay whispered, "Let's move to the end of this life. Find out how he wrapped up the life and what his big lessons were. We've got something here, but I don't know what. I found a few people who this might be, but we'll have to see. Try to get his age and the year he died."

Shali nodded acknowledgment and started the wrap-up script. "Move forward in time to the last moments of this life." She waited. "Are you there?"

There was a long pause and the expression on Iqbal's face became calm and relaxed. He drew a deep breath of air and slowly exhaled, as if he was totally relaxed and complacent.

"Yes. I am near the end, now. I am at peace. It is so peaceful."

"Tell me what you see. Where are you located? And who is with you?"

"I am in a bed. My body is tired and old. It is time to leave this body." He paused. "There are many people with me here. My grandchildren and great-grandchildren and my great-great-grandchildren. But they are all so old. I do not understand. There are many rabbis here. They are so sad." Iqbal then spoke out loud, as if addressing an audience, "No, absolutely not. Do not be sad. No one is to be sad."

Shali asked, "How old are you? What year is it and what city are you in?"

Iqbal's present-day Islamic context poked itself into the view of this life. "Oh Allah, Allah, Allah, I am very old: one hundred eighteen or one hundred nineteen years old. That is so old. It is about 10 AD. I am in Jerusalem now. I've been a leader for the Jewish people, or at least that is how they see me."

Clay slowly grew a huge smile of satisfaction. He nodded as Iqbal continued.

"They like my sayings, my phrases. I am quoted by many people. We are joking, now. My rabbi friends are telling me jokes about the sayings that I have made famous. I am laughing hard, but it hurts my chest when I laugh. My chest hurts, even though I like to laugh." Iqbal actually chuckled out loud. He was obviously enjoying this part of the death, despite the pain.

Clay's face opened up and he leaned over to Shali. "It's Hillel. This is Hillel. A number one, big time Jew. He called himself Allal or Hallal, but today he is known as Hillel; the pronunciation changed a bit over time."

Shali furrowed her brow in question. "I really don't know much about this Hillel. What can you give me?"

"Hillel was a famous Jewish figure who lived about the time of Jesus Christ," he whispered in an excited tone. "The Golden Rule is thought to be his, but he phrased it something like, 'What is hateful to you, do not do to your fellow' or something like that. He is known for a whole bunch of other heavily quoted sayings throughout history. There was even some historical speculation that Hillel's soul may have been reincarnated from Moses. Their personalities were similar, as were their purported styles and their fundamental beliefs in peaceful living. They both lived to be one hundred ten or one hundred twenty years old. After we wrap up this life, let's move back in time to see if this is Moses' soul. If this is really Hillel, which I think it is, we've got a great find. Just think of where we could branch off from here. The pod ... think of the soul pod we'd have access to. Oh, wait. We still have to see if this Apollonius' soul."

Shali asked, "So what do you want me to do?"

Clay hesitated for a moment. "Let's not push our luck trying to get directly to Apollonius. If it's him, we can pick it up in the LBL or the Akashic records. If he is going to turn over the cards on the hidden secrets, he'll do it then anyway. Let's finish up this life of Hillel and take him back in time. Try to take him back about three thousand more years. If it is Moses, we should be able to find him in that timeframe. Focus on asking him to visit an important life of that time period. I don't want to get some goat farmer in Spain or a mullet fisherman in Shanghai."

Shali chuckled at Clay's jest while she flipped forward in the script book to start the final round of questions to Iqbal. "What did you learn from this life?" she asked him.

Iqbal took a deep breath. "I had to stop the sacrificing of people. I had to do this. I don't know why, but I had to stop the sacrifices. It was not just religious groups, but they had the most power, so I used them to get societies to stop the sacrifices."

Shali translated for Clay.

"It must be a correction," he said. "This soul was probably bothered by sacrifices he made in a previous life." He signaled for Shali to turn to a specific index script number.

"Did you learn everything you were supposed to learn?"

There was no response, so Clay gave a shot to the Third Eye.

"Did you ever hear of any hidden writings or secret writings, secrets of life, or secrets of the world?"

After a long pause, Iqbal hesitantly responded, "There are no secrets except in what man wants to be secret. Man can know everything if he looks inside."

Shali's frustration showed as Iqbal's soul slipped back into the life of Hillel. "Do you know of a collection of secret documents or scrolls?" she continued. "They were hidden to keep them safe from people who wanted to suppress or destroy them?"

"I know of nothing. It is all there for men to learn. Writings of truth and knowledge have been collected in Alexandria, in the library."

"How do you know these secrets exist in the library in Alexandria?"

"I have been to the library. I also sent rabbis there to learn and bring the knowledge back to Jerusalem. They told me of tremendous knowledge stored there."

"Do you know of any documents that might be referred to as a secret doctrine?"

There was a pause with no answer.

"Have you heard of the seven keys or the seven secrets?"

No answer.

"Do you know the source of Kabbalah?"

Again, he did not respond.

"Do you know anything about stories, laws or writings called the Aggadah, Aggadot, Aggados or Ashkenazi?"

"Yes."

"What do you know about them?"

No response. Shali kept plowing through the script, probing and poking for any knowledge of possible hidden secrets. "Do you know of the ten sefirot and the four worlds within four worlds?" But again he would not provide a response, despite three long shots to the Third Eye.

"Do you know about any of the following: Ma'aseh Bereshit, the Works of Creation; Ma'aseh, the works of the Divine Throne; Sitrei Torah, the hidden aspects of the Torah; Razei Torah, the Torah secrets; or Chochmah Nistara, the Hidden wisdom?"

Iqbal's face grew stern and he snapped back in an aggravated tone, "Not permitted. Only within elders is this permitted to be discussed."

"That was a long time ago, and those men are all gone," Shali retorted abruptly to bring Iqbal back out of the life of Hillel. "You are not living in this body now. You can freely and openly discuss this with no repercussions. Do you understand me?"

There was absolute silence.

"Tell me about these secrets or hidden truths."

No response.

Clay leaned over to Shali. "This is exactly what we ran into in previous regressions. When we get access to a soul who has been exposed to the secrets in a previous life, they suddenly clam up."

Shali acknowledged his disappointment but continued with Iqbal. "Were these secrets written on books or scrolls?"

"Yes, secretly."

"How many copies were made and where were they kept?"

"Alexandria, of course. In a special place in the library. Those in control of others knew this knowledge must be kept secret or they would lose their control. No one was permitted in that part of the library without special permission."

"Did you ever see this part of the library?"

"Yes."

"What did it look like?"

"It was a very large room. Many scrolls and leather-bound papyrus were stored there."

"How many were there, and where did they come from?"

"There are hundreds and hundreds, thousands ... I do not know. They are all very different and came from many different places. I do not know from where."

She translated the last round to Clay. He then handed her a hand-written set of unscripted questions.

"When you came near the end of this life, did you hear of or meet a young man in Galilee, who some said was the son of God? His name would have been Joshua, Lesous, Yeshua, Yahweh or Jesus?

"Yes, I have heard of him."

"What have you heard of him?"

"He was an extremist, a radical, even at his young age. He was radical in behavior, and he was executed in this life for that behavior."

She continued her line of questioning for several more minutes but with little or no response from Iqbal.

Clay leaned closer to Shali. "It's time to move to the next life. Let's go see if he lived the life of Moses."

Shali took Iqbal back to the hall of doors.

Chapter 8

"Walk down the hall to the door to a life about three thousand years ago. Go to a life where you made a significant contribution to human society. In this life, you lived to a very old age: over one hundred years old. Walk to that door now."

Clay shot a micro-pulse to the pads on Iqbal's feet. They saw Iqbal's calves contract slightly.

"I am there."

"Open the door and walk into the room of that life. Go, now."

Clay pressed the button to send a micro-pulse to the pads on Iqbal's shoulders. There was another slight contraction of the neck and shoulders.

"Are you inside now?"

"Yes, I am inside."

"Look around. Tell me if you are indoors or outside. What do you see? Are there buildings, houses, animals?"

"I am inside a building - a big, beautiful building, large, open. Yes, it is a glorious building, beautiful and so ... so rich."

"What are you doing there?"

"I am admiring this place. No, more than admiring; I am proud of the building. Oh my, Allah, Allah, I built this building. I am responsible for such a beautiful place."

"Where is this building? What city?"

"Jerusalem ... no. Yes, Jerusalem."

"Look down at your clothes, your hands and feet. How are you dressed? What do you look like?"

Clay gave him a quick shot of micro-pulse to the Third Eye. Iqbal's head reared backward slightly. His expression quickly changed to show he was pleased with whatever he saw. Clay hoped he might have located the soul of Moses, but he wasn't sure what that expression meant.

"I am dressed in regal clothes. My hands look old."

"What year is it and how old are you?"

There was a slight pause. "It is 950 ... 950, 951 BC. I am forty ... no, forty-nine years old." The corner of Iqbal's mouth curled up in a smile of pleasure.

Shali glanced over to Clay in disappointment. "Clay, this life is a couple hundred years after Moses."

"Sounds like it. Even so, it sounds like we've got an interesting life. Let's dig in."

Shali continued the regression. "Tell me, how do you feel? What do you see?"

"I am very happy, very comforted. My wives ... I have so many wives - a hundred, maybe hundreds. I cannot possibly take my pleasure with all of them. It is a waste to have so many wives. However, I like to have new wives. They are all so beautiful ... so much satisfaction. I can have my way with any of them, whenever I want, and however I want. Oh, so pleasant."

"What else do you see? Look around the building and describe more."

Iqbal hesitated and then inhaled a slow, deep breath through his nose. "The smell of incense is heavy in the air." Iqbal inhaled again as if savoring the sensation. "A large box is in a center area. It is blocked off. There is an open area so no one can get to the box." Again, Iqbal deeply breathed in, filling his lungs with the perceived pungent odor of incense.

"What is in the box?"

"Large stones. It has large flat stones - important stones. I cannot see inside the box, but I know the stones are there. No one is allowed to touch the box. That is what I told them all." Iqbal laughed out loud. "I told them they would die if they touch the box." He laughed again.

"Is it true? Will a person die if they touch the box?"

"No, absolutely not. I just don't want anybody to steal it."

"Is there anything else is in the box?"

"Nothing else. I already took it out - the stick. I took the stick out. It is as important as the stones, but I took it out anyway."

"What kind of a stick? Why did you take it out of the box and what did you do with it?"

"It's a walking stick. I feel that it is mine. I took it to my home, to my palace." Iqbal pushed his head back into the chair, smiled and said, "Whoa, I have a palace."

"What is your name? What do people call you?"

"Sulayman or Sulaimaan. Something like that."

Shali stopped for a moment and translated for Clay. His face flashed first puzzlement, then shock, and then amazement. "Solomon," he popped back in a fast excited tone. "King Solomon. It's Solomon's Temple, on the Temple Mount. The box is the Ark of the Covenant, and the stones must be Moses' tablets with the Ten Commandments. We didn't get Moses but we got his tablets. The stick has to be Aaron's staff. You know the one Charlton Heston used in the movie to turn the water to blood and part the Red Sea?" Clay chuckled and leaned back in his chair, gloating with a look of "how do you beat this?" He rolled his finger in a circle, telling her to keep going.

Shali turned back to Iqbal. "Continue walking through the building and tell me what you see."

Iqbal inhaled again, savoring the incense. Clay pressed the button for a micro-pulse to Iqbal's feet. Iqbal's legs contracted slightly. He hesitated and then responded, "The ceiling is very high. There are many rooms around the temple." His expression suddenly turned to a solemn, almost scornful look. He took a large, deep breath and slowly exhaled.

"What do you see? How do you feel?"

"This room - the room on the end - is for sacrifices. Oh, my God. Allah Akbar, Allah Akbar. They sacrifice people here. My wives. I sacrifice my wives, but usually just the ones from foreign lands. I had them sacrificed for God. I thought it would please God and bring us health and wealth. But I never sacrificed a wife if she believed in my God or if she was from my land. Unless, of course, I no longer liked them. Then I would have them sacrificed, too. All this was in the name of God, in this room and in the name of God. I said it was an offering to God for mercy and goodness, but it was really to clean out my flock of women so I could get new ones."

Iqbal hesitated as his face turned even more scornful. "And this is goodness? I did not have them sacrificed; I had them *killed*. When I grew tired of one or when she made me angry or displeased me, I would have her killed. No one questioned me or stopped me. I was the king, and this was my sacrifice to God."

Iqbal's breath had become short and rapid. Clay looked at the monitors. Iqbal's heart rate and blood pressure increased rapidly.

"You've gotta relieve him," Clay said to Shali. "He's stressing out."

"Anything that you see or feel happened a long time ago," Shali commanded. "Your current life is not responsible for anything you see in this past life. View everything you see as if you are watching a movie at the theater. Do you understand?"

"Yes."

"Step back from the life and watch this life from above."

Clayed watched the monitors until the heart and stress readings dropped back to normal. He looked at Shali and nodded that her instructions had worked.

Shali continued. "Move forward in this life to a time that is very significant to you. Go now."

She looked at Clay and touched a finger to her forehead. Clay pressed the micro-pulse button to stimulate the Third Eye.

"Move forward in this life and tell me what you see now."

"I am in my palace," Iqbal responded immediately. "The big one. She has come to see me, the queen from across the sea, the sea to the west from the land called Sheba. She brought me gifts, but I do not know why. I have so much gold, so much wealth. I like her. She entertains me. She tells me jokes and riddles. She is a challenge to my mind, much more than any of my wives or concubines."

Iqbal slowed and paused for nearly ten seconds. His expression showed sensations of satisfaction and enjoyment.

Shali smiled at his expression and asked, "What do you see, now?"

Iqbal breathed deeply and replied, "She stays with me a fortnight. I wish she would stay longer, but she must return to her land and her people. We have come to know each other, and she is passionate. Yes, oh, a passionate woman. I send everyone away so we can be alone, every day. But, she finally left me. I will never see her again in this life, although the desire is strong in my heart. I was told she carried my son. I wonder ... perhaps he will be a good king - better than his father."

Clay whispered to Shali, "The Queen of Sheba came across the Red Sea to visit King Solomon. Now at least we've confirmed that they had a significant love affair. Speculation was that she had his son after she went back to Africa. At least Solomon, here, seems to think the rumor was true." Clay chuckled. "I wonder if he sent her child support."

Shali ignored his wisecrack and continued the regression for another twenty minutes, uncovering further details about the ancient king's life, and then she began the scripts for probing the end of Solomon's life.

"Move to the end of this life - the last few hours. Describe what you are doing, what you see, and what you feel."

"I was sitting in a chair, like a throne. I was watching my servants or my subjects or slaves. They were building something on the edge of the city, like a pavilion. I was tired, so I leaned back in my chair and I died. This was too fast. I did not expect to die. I felt no pain. I did not think I would die like this. I had more to do ... but this life is over."

"How do you feel about this life? Was it a good life? Did you feel good about yourself?"

"I feel that I was a good person in my heart, but I did bad things. I took money from everybody just so I could have tremendous wealth. I used it mostly for my own purposes, like to build lavish buildings, when I could have used it to help others in need. And I had all of those women killed, and for what? Sacrifice? Humph. God wants no sacrifices."

"What did you learn from this life?"

"I made many wise decisions as a judge, as a ruler. I was fair to people."

They sat quietly to allow Iqbal's soul to linger in the memories of this life. Shali then turned to Clay, translated and asked, "What's the deal with King Solomon?

"He was obviously very disturbed by having used religious sacrifice as the reason to kill a bunch of his wives. When he reincarnated as Hillel hundreds of years later, his soul made a correction. Hillel had to fix what he did wrong as Solomon, so he worked hard to ban human sacrifices, at least among the Jewish sect of that time. By making a correction from a previous life, Iqbal's soul was allowed to move on to new challenges. Otherwise, he would be tested again and again. Most Abrahamic religions say Solomon had as many as a thousand wives. Here he said he had several hundred wives. I wonder how many he killed ... the other eight hundred?"

After a short pause, Shali added, "And so many religious zealots think King Solomon was a good guy? Nah, what a jerk. And he knew it himself, at least after he was dead."

"It's interesting when you find out that even after thousands of years of social maturity, humans aren't much different. You'd think you couldn't really get away with treating women like that in these times, but there was Uday and Kusay Hussein in Baghdad just a few years back."

"Alright, Sherlock, what's next?"

"Solomon lived before the secrets were amassed," Clay answered, "so he wouldn't know of the secrets or who might have wanted them destroyed, so let's skip those scripts. Let's take him back one more time and hunt for Moses, and then we'll bring him out and break for lunch. He'll be ready for a little real life after the past several hours. This afternoon, we'll move to the LBL. If he is not Apollonius, then we'll see if he knows where we can find that soul. This, of course, assumes Apollonius' soul is even living on the planet right now."

Shali turned forward in the script book, glanced at Clay with a devilish grin and said in a lisping Elmer Fudd voice, "Be berwy berwy quiet. We'ur hunting Moses."

Chapter 9

"You are back in the hall of doors," Shali told Iqbal. "Walk to the door for a life that was two hundred years earlier than the life that you just visited as Sulayman - about the year 1,200 to 1,300 BC. In this life, you may have been very famous and very popular among certain people. It may have been a very long life, perhaps one hundred or one hundred twenty years. Go to that door now."

Iqbal's response was almost immediate. "I am outside. We are playing by the river. A girl is with me. She is my older sister. I am twelve years old. Our clothes are very heavy and coarse in texture. They are scratchy - made of wool - but they are warm. The pungent smell of the river is everywhere in the air."

"Where are you located?"

"We are in Goshen, or Gesan … or Kessan, in the far eastern part of Egypt. It is near Avaris, sometimes called Hatwaret. There are different names for the same places. Our tribe is called Levi. It is large, and we are many. We are strong but oppressed."

Iqbal hesitated, obviously absorbing the sights and sounds of this memory.

Shali gave him a few moments to sense the current scene before continuing. "What year is it and how old are you?"

Clay shot a pulse to the Third Eye. Iqbal's head pushed back into the pillow.

"1360… 1380 or 84 – no, 1385 BC. I'm a young boy, about twelve years old."

"What are you doing?"

"We're playing in the river, in the Nile. The water is cool and pleasing; we are having fun. Our mother is nearby, sitting on the shore and watching us. We are having a picnic. It is a celebration that we have every year at the river. There is lots of food, and we are having fun today."

"What is the celebration? Why are you doing this?"

"This is the day that our younger brother went away. He was sent away on the river several years ago."

"Why did he go away? Did he die?"

"No. My mother sent him away so he would not die. The Pharaoh was killing the children, so my mother sent him away to save him. Many mothers did this. However, today we celebrate that he is alive and well."

"What is your name?"

"Harun or Horen … something like that."

Shali smiled a smug look and leaned over to whisper to Clay. "We missed Moses. But, I think we got his brother Aaron. Is that close enough?"

Clay broke out in a huge smile. "Yeah, the next best thing. And remember Solomon's stick in the box? That was Aaron's stick. I guess he missed it, so he took it back as Solomon." He laughed out loud. "Keep going and see if you can validate whether or not this is Aaron."

Shali continued through the standard regression scripts. She drew out the life experiences from this soul that lived the life of Aaron over 3,000 years earlier. She took the soul through Aaron's teenage and young adult life with no particularly special events, although it seemed to be fairly accurate with documented history. She pressed Iqbal, "Move to a later time in this life - a time where you experienced a significant event for yourself or someone else in your life." She paused. "Are you there yet?"

"Yes, I am older. I am about sixty years old, now."

"Where are you and what are you doing?"

"We are still in Egypt. I do not know what is happening. It is very confusing. My heart is pounding so loud I can hardly hear. I am with my brother - the one who went away as a baby. We are in a court or a big room. It is decorated. The smell of sweet, tart perfume is heavy in the air. We are with important people. Oh, Allah Akbar, he is the Pharaoh. It is confusing. I speak for my brother because few people can understand him. He has a voice or speech impediment, so I speak for him. This Pharaoh and my brother are violently arguing, and I am in the middle. My brother is a wise person, but he cannot control his temper. He is acting like a crazy man. Even I can hardly understand what he says."

Iqbal raised his voice and started talking fast and loud, almost yelling, as he relived this intense scene in the life of Aaron. Shali translated for Clay as Iqbal babbled on.

Looking concerned at his stress monitors, Clay said to Shali, "He is stressing out again. You better bring him back out some."

Shali interrupted Iqbal. "Come out of this life and only observe this life from outside. You are not living this life now. This life was a long time ago, and you are only looking back at the life. Do you understand?"

"Yes," he exclaimed, but continued his excited playback. "How can my brother possibly get away with talking to the Pharaoh like this? How can I speak to the Pharaoh in such a tone? If I did not change half the words Moses says, we would have been killed already. We are dealing with a powerful man, this Pharaoh."

Iqbal paused for several seconds and the expression on his face changed dramatically. His tone and manner slowed. "Even so, we also have power. We have taken advantage of events to persuade the Pharaoh that we are powerful. He thinks we caused recent famines and plagues. The whole sea turned orange color. We do not know why, but my brother convinced the Pharaoh that I caused this with my walking stick by casting magic from our God. If the Pharaoh figures this out, we are dead. I saw a snake crawling along the wall, so I threw my stick at it to kill it. The snake was startled and slid into the middle of the room. They think my stick became the snake when I threw it down." He laughed out loud.

Shali explained to Clay what was transpiring. Knowing the historical stories, Clay grinned. Iqbal's soul continued to rattle on about his life as Aaron, so Clay and Shali regrouped in a sidebar.

Clay whispered, "This has got to be one of the many confrontations between the Pharaoh and Moses. It's lucky that Moses and Aaron didn't lose their heads, literally. This sounds like a movie - well, I guess it's already several movies. However, none of them followed this story line." Clay bit his lip for a few seconds while he pondered. "Shali, keep him going for a while. This is a big find, so we've got to milk it. See if you can find out more about Moses. When we get to the LBL, let's ask where we can find Moses' incarnation today. He's probably in the same soul pod."

Shali nodded, "Got it.

"This session is obviously going to take a while, so let's break for lunch and do the LBL after that." Then he added, "Damn you, Iqbal, we need a couple more days of regressions. One day is not enough."

"Hey, you know all of this magical stuff in the old legends and religious accounts? It's really just misinterpretations of facts and coincidences, all turned into stories of magic, supernatural powers and all powerful gods, huh?"

Clay smiled an acknowledgement with a nod of his head. "Yeah. Penn and Teller kind of stuff."

Shali continued with the standard scripts and then, prompted by Clay, she asked, "When your people were released by this Pharaoh, did you walk out of Egypt to a land to the East?"

"Yes."

"How did you cross the sea to the east? Did you or your brother make a prayer to God to part the sea? Did the water separate so you could walk through the sea to the other side?"

"We crossed to the east. I do not understand what you ask about the sea."

"How did you get across the sea without a boat?"

"There were earthquakes, and the sea became very low. Traveling merchants told us we could cross the sea if we went north. We did. We walked across bridges of sand and strips of land until we got to the other side. Several weeks later there were more earthquakes, and the sea came back to normal."

Shali translated for Clay. He smiled and said to Shali, "Urban legends. After two hundred years, George Washington throws a coin across the Potomac River. A thousand years from now, George Washington will have parted the Potomac with his sword and walked across."

Shali gave him a glancing grin and added, "How about the time his brother Moses went off to the mountains to create the Ten Commandments? He was only gone a week, not forty days. And did you catch that Moses wrote the Ten Commandments on papyrus during his trek to the mountains and only carved them on slate stones after he returned?"

"Yeah, no lightning bolts from heaven. So the golden calf of the idol-worship legends was really just a wooden statue with a gold necklace." They quietly laughed together as Iqbal kept talking in the background. Clay added, "Take him to the end of this life and find out how he ends up dying. Every religion has a different spin on Aaron's death."

She nodded and turned back to Iqbal. "Go to the last moments of this life and describe what you see, hear and feel. Go there now."

Clay shot a pulse to the Third Eye. Iqbal's head pushed back in the pillow.

Shali commanded Iqbal, "Tell me what you see."

"I went with my brother, Moses, to the mountains. Ever since we were young, we have loved to walk in the mountains and sleep beneath the stars. We would stare into the heavens and watch shooting stars and clouds dancing in front of the moon. But that night was cold, raining, and we argued about nothing. We found a cave and started a small fire to dry off and warm ourselves. He commented about something stupid that I did many years earlier. And then he told me how stupid I was with the wooden calf. Will he never let it go? I became angry with him. I made fun of his jumbled speech and mimicked his lisping impediment. Hmmffp mumpf ngumph. Why do we argue over nothing? We are so respected by our people, but we constantly fight with each other. I look at my brother, and he is so old. We are both old. This body is so tired. We are over one hundred years old now. We are angry with each other, but we finally stop and try to sleep. I cannot sleep. Hours later, I roll over and see my brother staring at me. I reached my hand to him. He took my hand. I told him I was sorry for the terrible things I said. My brother smiled at me in the last flicker of the fire against the walls of the cave. He apologized to me too. It was good. We are satisfied. I closed my eyes and this body died."

"How did you feel about this life?"

"This was a good life. I am pleased. I helped others and gave others what I could. We gave them freedom. Freedom for people is good."

"What did you learn from this life?"

"I learned much from my brother. He was aggressive but rarely thoughtful. I learned that you must push hard if you are to get what you want. It is important to be assertive. Without my brother, I could not have done that. We freed our people from that Pharaoh. I learned that people must be free from oppression by others and that I must try to break those bonds. I learned that worshiping idols is bad. People may worship beliefs, even Gods, but they should not worship idols and should never make a human into an idol. My brother was so correct in this. His anger was warranted over the wooden calf - it *was* an idol - but I wish he did not hold his anger at me in this life."

Shali questioned Iqbal about any connections to Moses in hopes they could find more leads. They got little, but she knew the LBL might yield more details. Shali walked through the script to bring Iqbal out his hypnotic trance.

"When I count backwards from five to one, you will begin to come back to the present time and regain consciousness. You will not remember anything of the lives or events you visited during our session. Do you understand that you will not remember anything from the last several hours?"

There was no response, so Shali signaled Clay with a head nod. He pressed the button to shoot a long micro-pulse to Iqbal's shoulders. Iqbal's neck and shoulders twisted upward in reaction to the shock. There was no further response, so Shali repeated again, "Do you understand that you will not remember any of this regression to your soul's past?"

Clay shot another pulse to Iqbal's shoulders. His neck and shoulders wrenched again.

"Yes. I understand. I will not remember anything from this session. I will remember nothing."

Clay started rapidly tapping on the Third Eye micro-pulse button. After five seconds, he stopped per the protocol.

"Good. Five. You are now preparing to come out of a deep trance. You feel relaxed and have forgotten everything you experienced or saw in this session. Four. The memory of your past lives is quickly fading and will not come back in this conscious life. You are beginning to waken slightly. Three. You can feel energy returning to your body. You are relaxed and satisfied. You will not remember anything of the last several hours. Two. You are almost awake, now. Your eyes will open soon. The blood is flowing to all parts of your body. You feel totally refreshed and relaxed. You have no memory of the previous lives that you visited today. One. You are fully awake and conscious. You feel relaxed and satisfied. You remember nothing of this session. You may open your eyes at any time. You are now awake. Open your eyes and sit up in the chair."

Shali removed the goggles, cap and headphones. Iqbal opened his eyes and lifted his head up from the back of the lounge chair. Iqbal rolled his head and neck in a big circle to shake out the muscles. Shali gave him a large bottle of water to quench his thirst, which would be strong after more than three hours of intense regression.

Chapter 10

They agreed Iqbal could go home for his lunch and return in two hours. After Iqbal left, Clay closed down their systems and Shali walked to the balcony. She looked down at the security guard posted below their room and waved a hand in gratitude. Then she went back inside and pulled the balcony doors shut behind her. She turned the deadbolt and tugged stiffly to ensure the doors were locked. They finished locking up the regression room and told the guard posted in the hallway they would be back after lunch.

A nearby restaurant tucked in a side street served as their escape from the grueling morning session. The colorful yet heavily worn tablecloths made the already dark restaurant appear even dingier. The pungent smell of curry shrouded the room, which had a low ceiling and only two small windows. The windows were half-blocked by heavy wool curtains, trapping the smells in the room. In near silence, they munched on bread and crackers dipped in thick humus and savored a tasty selection of kabobs. They devoured a Jordanian lunch of lamb cooked in whey and yogurt sauce, served on a bed of Egyptian rice with pine nuts and almonds.

After eating, while quietly sipping on a strong sweet tea laced with cloves and other Eastern spices, Clay said, "We've been working together for almost two years now. It's been good to work with you."

"I'd say 'happy second anniversary,' but the two months that we were involved don't count. We didn't get a damn bit of real work done while we were so busy banging away at each other's bodies. The time that I went back to LA after we broke it off doesn't count either."

Clay laughed, thinking of the three to four months after Shali went home to Los Angeles after their big emotional clash. During her absence Clay immersed himself into his treasure hunting regressions and rapidly went through three other translators.

Clay quickly responded, "Yeah, but we both realized that we had to work together. It was meant to be."

"Professionally, that is. The strict hands-off policy is in full force, you know."

"Of course. Absolutely. I know you have the hots for me but you will just have to be disciplined and stick to the job."

"Yeah … right."

Their eyes connected just for a moment, then both looked away. After a few seconds, Clay looked back. "I know I've been a bit secretive, and I have sensed your frustration with me."

"No shit."

Clay smiled with a blush of embarrassment, "Well, this morning I finally gave you more details on the secrets, even though it wasn't much. I guess if I can't trust you now, then I never can. So I am going to bring you into my little world."

Shali raised her eyebrows in anticipation. "Good. These regressions have really intrigued me, but I need more than you have been willing to give to me. I can't dig in the nooks and crannies in a regression unless I understand more about what is behind it."

"Forgive me, Father, for I have sinned. Here comes the confession. You've been patient with me; so where do I begin?"

"How about you take away my PLR virginity and tell me the source of your regression wisdom? There are more to these protocols than you are giving me." She gave him a sheepish grin to help him break the ice.

"Yeah. It's time for me to show you the ways of the world, young lady."

Clay took a deep breath and looked to the far side of the room while he thought back to how his quest began. He lifted the tea cup to his nose and sniffed the deep aroma of cloves. "I worked at Stanford Research Institute in Menlo Park several years ago. Many years before I joined SRI, back in the 1970s and 80s, the U.S. government was running an eclectic collection of secret black-ops programs. Under the cover of foreign spy projects, U.S. intelligence agencies opened their undocumented checkbooks for PPO's - para-psychology operations. The agencies were looking for any means that could give them an edge on their enemies, perceived or real. CIA spies inside foreign governments during the Cold War had convinced them that both the Russian KGB and the Chinese were doing their own advanced PPO programs, including astral projection, out-of-body experiences, remote viewing, and past-life regression, among others. All of these disciplines, if they can be called that, have had avid followers for millennia. Rather than be left out of the global PPO game, the U.S. intelligence programs followed suit and formalized their own PPO research. The Cold War made it all legit."

Shali's face showed puzzlement and astonishment. She listened intently to Clay's every word.

"The U.S. agencies were not about to let the Russians get the jump on them, so they poured a lot of this black-ops money into PPO research. SRI became the hub of their PPO programs. The government piled mountains of cash in their hoppers as the programs ramped up. Extensive laboratories were built for all PPO disciplines at SRI. Some were secret and others were not so secret. The remote viewing programs were made the most public to distract attention from the deeper, more esoteric PPO's."

"I saw a SciFi Channel program once that talked about remote viewing," Shali interjected. "They interviewed some guys who were at SRI during that time. It was on a ghost show or something. Is this the same thing? The same guys?"

"Yep. The remote viewing programs still have an active, almost cult-like following today. However, on the contrary, the Past Life Regression, or PLR, programs were kept under wraps. Real quiet. They set up PLR work teams across the country and even in a few friendly countries like the UK, Canada and Australia. The PLR program managers were experimenting with regressions wherever willing subjects could be found."

Clay took a sip on the sweet, tartly spiced tea and then continued. "Some programs, such as remote viewing, had less than stellar results but were thought to be more valuable to intelligence than others. Hence they received additional funding and had a favored status for damn near twenty years. Other government security and defense agencies picked up the financial tab for remote viewing and kept it alive longer than other PPO programs well into the nineties. A few of the other programs, such as PLR, proved to be very successful and actually exceeded all expectations. But PLR did not have applicability to immediate military or intelligence needs. Running a PLR protocol on a subject could never track down Osama bin Laden or Saddam Hussein hiding in spider holes or mountain caves. Information from PLR regressions had little value when it came to finding culprits or dealing with them in the present. PLR could not find crashed Russian planes or missing submarines. So you can imagine what happened next."

"What?"

Clay leaned back in his chair and lifted his eyebrows high. He sighed and continued, "During the early 1980s recession, Congress caught wind of these socially unacceptable and politically incorrect PPO programs. How could the CIA and other security agencies spend precious taxpayer dollars on paranormal research and ghost stories? The budget ax came swinging to end the PLR program. Only a few programs, such as the Stargate remote-viewing program, survived. PLR as a government program, despite having surpassed all expectations, was destined for the proverbial cutting-room floor. The entire program was shut down, boxed up, and sent off to the archives at SRI. All researchers were reassigned, released or terminated from employment. There was simply no substantive justification of PLR protocols to the U.S. intelligence community."

"So is this when you came to SRI?"

"A few years later. The programs had been boxed away and nearly forgotten about. I was a senior analyst in the research department at SRI, and I was accustomed to regimented and disciplined research, having spent the previous ten years in U.S. Army intelligence. I was happy doing research for several years at SRI, but after a while it became a bit boring. Fortunately, they assigned me the task of cleaning out the archive storage for old programs.

"My project assignment involved thousands of boxes of terminated or completed research projects from SRI's sixty year history. I had to sort through thousands of defunct and obsolete programs. I was given three junior research analysts and an admin assistant for eighteen months. We were to review each program in the archive, write up a synopsis and make recommendations for disposition. SRI's management reviewed the recommendations and directed disposition of records for each program. "

Shali asked, "So the PLR program papers were all available to you and your team?"

"Sure were. Having a team of analysts and an admin to do the tedious work on the boring projects left me plenty of time to dig into the more interesting ones and read the research papers. We were nine months into the clean-up when I came across the PLR program: one hundred eighty-two boxes of research papers carefully indexed, labeled and categorized. The people running that program had been amazingly organized. What is most surprising is how carefully they documented everything in the midst of what must have been a rapid and emotional program termination. I was amazed at how easy they made it for me to pour through the tons of information. The summaries and indices led me directly to the juicy tidbits I needed to exploit the PLR protocols."

"Exploit? And wasn't all of this proprietary or classified or something? How did you get permission to use it?"

"Because enough time had transpired since the end of the programs at that point, and the documents were declassified as part of my project. The decision was made to digitize and publish the PLR papers through a small group of universities. As soon as we posted the PLR material at the first few universities, there was a big hullabaloo. I figured it was all going to get yanked back, so I got copies of the material I needed for myself, legally. I managed to grab copies of the protocol procedures and a complete copy of the SRD, the Soul Regression Database. That's all I really needed. When SRI revoked the PLR distribution, we pulled it all back, but it had been public domain for a few weeks so I got my copy legally from one of the other universities - not through SRI."

"Sounds like there's a conflict here."

"Yeah. I got into a big legal hassle with the Institute. They backed off and let me keep the copy, but I had to resign. Since I didn't have a job and had time on my hands, I started digging into the protocols and database, looking for ways to make a living."

"Alright. So that's how you got material, but what was really in it?"

"The primary objective of the program was to develop PLR technologies and methodologies to enable consistent collection of information from human souls. This information on the souls was to be stored, cataloged, and correlated for undetermined intelligence purposes. The overall program was divided into two main streams of work. First, developing and refining the regression protocols; and second, building a soul-correlation database through actual regressions."

"You sound like you're giving a college dissertation."

Clay chuckled back. "If you worked with this stuff as intensely as I did, you'd be talking like this too. Anyways, besides the protocols, the PLR program built a sophisticated database system that precisely documented and archived the soul information acquired during their PLR sessions."

"So this is where you got the initial database. I wondered why it was so large and had different regressors names listed. I knew you couldn't have done all of this."

"Exactly. They had designed computer programs to correlate different souls and lives. The archived material included sophisticated FORTRAN computer code and a database of regressions on nine thousand eight hundred human souls. Each had been regressed using various PLR protocols developed by the program. Perhaps twenty-five thousand regression sessions drew out as many as five to ten different human lives for each soul during each session. Some souls only had a few lives, but a few of the more mature souls had as many as a hundred lives. Most souls seemed to have between ten and thirty human incarnations in identified human history."

With raised eyebrows, Shali asked, "Human incarnations? Identified human history? What do you mean by that?"

Clay paused for a moment and slowly rolled his head in a large circle to stretch out his neck. This morning's session had left him a bit tense. Shali waited patiently but anxiously. "Please don't think that we only reincarnate as humans in this world that we live on." Shali sat back in her chair with a blank stare. "We won't go there, yet," he said. "That's a different lunch. After we find the secrets, maybe we can have some fun with that."

"So you are begging off for now."

Clay smiled, "Yes, but not because I am still hiding something. It is going to take a lot longer than this lunch to explain." He paused. "Anyway, the database program and the SRD - the soul-regression database - were stored on eight reels of obsolete magnetic computer tape. I got some Stanford grad students to help me convert everything. In just a couple of weeks, I had the entire SRD loaded and running on a laptop, on a modern database program. This is what we've been using in our work."

Clay stared off at the wall for a moment, reminiscing. "When the government's PLR program finally shut down, they had seventy-eight different protocols. The later, more advanced protocols were combinations of electronic and environmental techniques. Starting at Protocol 75, the process was designed so the subject remembered nothing from the regression session. That's where I focused my work. Not only because I planned to look for hidden secrets and treasures but also because I'd rather not deal with a subject after they've learned what lives they lived before. There would be too many variables out of my control."

"What was in those hundreds of boxes of research?"

"The boxes mostly contained material on how the protocols were developed and refined. I didn't spend much time on that; I got right to the meat of the discipline: how to regress someone and milk them for information about a previous life. The general procedures for all regression protocols are pretty much the same. After some experience, I tweaked the protocols to better meet my needs. In short, you use standard hypnosis techniques to put the subject to a deep trance-like state. Then, just like we've been doing, you guide the subject to their previous lives and to the life between lives. If you get really good at it, you might not only get the soul's guide, you might also get other elders' souls. They know all the good stuff from the past, if you can get them to talk."

"What about the database? And just what exactly is in it, beyond what I've seen?"

Clay responded, "You've probably wondered why we record, transcribe and translate every regression. When I started, I vowed to devote time after each regression to completely transcribe, document and archive the session. I really wanted to capture details of the sessions in case the subject died. We can use that regression data to correlate across different lives and soul pods."

"So what about the correlation stuff?"

"As part of the SRI project, we sorted through thousands of souls, which related to hundreds of thousands of human lives stored in the SRD database. Trying to correlate human incarnations and soul pods was like solving a giant three-dimensional, one-hundred-row Sudoku puzzle: a proverbial gimongous Rubik's cube. But once I really understood what to look for in the database, the task got a lot easier. I bought a commercial database correlation system and built lots of correlation rules to do the heavy work. This would have been nearly impossible for the SRI researchers to do twenty-five years earlier, so extensive soul correlation is somewhat new and untouched ground."

A coy smile slipped across Shali's face. "So, with this fancy correlation engine, are you going to be able to find my soul mate?"

Clay fired back a grin of his own. "I already checked out your soul mate. He's not here now, but will be born when you are seventy-six years old. You'll be a spinster this entire life and will only be able to work with me, professionally. You can leave this soul mate all your money when you die at age ninety-seven. The two of you will have to do a better job of coordinating your next lives if you want to enjoy each other's bodies."

Shali laughed out loud and punched Clay in the shoulder from across the table. "Come on, what did these SRI guys find about soul mates?"

"Well, starting with the hundred fifty-fourth box of archives, I found study papers about linked lives and linked souls. First, they found that many souls like to do certain things, even in their different incarnations. When a soul reincarnates to a new life, they may seek out the same hobbies, professions and even gender-preference they have experienced in previous lives. They did a special study correlating child prodigies."

"So you mean a child prodigy could just be an incarnation of a soul that was good at that specialty in previous lives?"

"Bingo. At the time of the PLR program, they regressed an eight-year-old girl in Scotland. At the age of four, she could sit down at a piano with virtually no guidance and play magnificent complicated pieces of classical music. After several regression sessions, the team determined that her soul was the reincarnate of Amadeus Mozart as well as a half dozen other historically famous musicians before and after him. The study showed there were sixty-four cases of child prodigy regression during the program. The different fields included music, mathematics, science, literature, dance and athletics. Of the five hundred thirty-one past human lives identified in the sixty-four child prodigy regressions, about seventy-five percent of the soul's previous lives also focused on that one particular area the living child prodigy excelled."

Shali said, "OK, what do you think? Madame Curie, Louis Pasteur, Florence Nightingale ... Dr. Gregory House?"

"You've got the idea." Clay smiled at her quip.

"What did you mean by gender preference?"

"Another research paper in the program described a series of regressions on gay men in San Francisco. Their souls had the desire to actually be in the human body of women. This conclusion seemed to smack in the face of claims that gays and lesbians were afflicted by some kind of physiological or hormonal imbalance. It appears that these souls just happened to end up in bodies of a less preferred gender. I did some correlation in the database. The subjects evidently deal with it in the life by migrating towards others in the same situation."

"This one is hard to buy, not even to say it is politically incorrect."

"Hey, I don't make it up. Research is research. In the SRD statistics, it seems that most souls have a preference to live as either a male or female, but it is certainly not a fifty-fifty split. The twenty-three gay men in the database showed more than a ninety-ten split where their soul had reincarnated as a woman. If this soul preferred a female body but ended up in a male body, the study hypothesized that the soul felt locked into a gender that they preferred not to be in. The study speculated that the alternative lifestyle may simply be the soul's way to cope with being in the body of a less-preferred gender."

"If this is so, then why was it never made public?"

"Ah, tut-tut, Shali. This was a government black program. The people working on the project were not allowed to reveal anything about the PLR program. Besides, you have to realize this was nearly thirty years ago and society was not as open as it is today. But anyway, there was a second and even more important discovery that came out from the program: soul pods."

"I've been with you a year and half, we talk about it and leverage it in the regressions. I've read all the books on past-life regression and understand the basic concepts. So finally, yes, after all this time you are going to explain the pods to me?"

"We found in-depth studies on soul pods in the archives. As you know already, in the LBL period, clusters of souls hang around together in that dimension, or whatever it is. These souls often reincarnate in pairs or small clusters. Sometimes they are family members, wives, husbands or good friends in different lives, in different times. But they also cluster by discipline. The archive studies showed that not only do many souls migrate towards the same disciplines in their different lives, they also cycle through lives in the same time periods with other souls who like those same disciplines. It's almost as if these soul-pod buddies follow each other around through time."

"Sort of like the Budweiser 'whassup' guys?"

Clay chuckled. "Yeah. Not quite, but sort of. These souls somehow find each other among the myriad of time, billions of people on earth, and other planets, at any given time."

"You've said it before. What's this about other planets?"

"That's another lunch." Clay raised his eyebrows, shrugged his shoulders and continued. "The correlation showed that linked souls did not always incarnate in the same scenario each time. One of them might be a mentor in one life and yet mentored in the next, or peers in one but deadly adversaries in the next."

"Any good examples to make the point?"

"Yeah. Here's a good one: one pod of three souls contained Dr. Sun Yatsen, founder of post-dynasty China in the early nineteen hundreds. He's like a George Washington to the Chinese; he broke China out of the dynasties. Two of his leading students and protégés were Mao Ze-Dong, Chairman Mao of mainland communist Red China, and Chiang Kai-Shek, leader of the Nationalist Chinese who were forced out to Taiwan by Mao. These two, from the same pod, were arch-enemies most of their lives."

"So who were they before?"

"Back in the eighteen hundreds, this same soul pod incarnated in the United States Civil War period as Abraham Lincoln, General Robert E. Lee and General Ulysses S. Grant."

"No way! Whose soul was who?"

"Sun Yat Sen's was Lincoln. Interesting enough, Sun's core philosophy for China's future was his San-Min doctrine, or the 'Three Principals of the People.' Historically, Sun was enamored with Abraham Lincoln and even publically admitted he took his Chinese San-min principal from Lincoln's Gettysburg Address. Even today, this doctrine is the political foundation of both

Taiwan and mainland China. The San-Min is even the basis of the national anthem of China today - yeah, from Lincoln's Gettysburg Address. It's like he had unfinished business because of his assassination, so he finished it in his next life as Sun, who just happened to be born - or incarnated - in China just a few years after Lincoln's death."

"OK, what about the other two?"

"Well, General Robert E. Lee was Chairman Mao; General Ulysses S. Grant was Chiang Kai-Shek. Lee and Grant were both cadets at West Point and led adversarial roles in one of the worst civil wars of all times. Chiang went to China's military academy and fought with Mao in the same Chinese revolution, and in World War II against Japan. Then Mao became the leader of Communist China while Chiang became leader of the Chinese Nationalist Kuo-Min-Tang party. The two adversaries, who both revered Dr. Sun, led to tearing China into two pieces since World War II. Chiang-Grant stayed on the side of Sun-Lincoln, while Lee-Mao spun off onto the revolutionary side."

"Oh, come on, Clay. This is hard to swallow."

"I'm not done yet. In the preceding fifteen hundred years, at four different times, these same three souls lived clustered incarnations as local village leaders or tribal chiefs. They always fought like hell in some controversial leadership role in a societal conflict. The earliest clustered incarnation by this pod happened two thousand years ago. They were known as the First Triumvirate in the Roman Empire. The Triumvirate consisted of Julius Caesar, Crassus, and Pompey, who came to power in 59 BC when Caesar was first elected as a consul. These three powerful leaders fought together and, at the same time, fought each other for years. Within fifteen years, this conflict led to the assassination of Caesar by the Roman Senate."

Shali chuckled, "'Et tu, Brute?' He put a knife in his chest, huh? Was Brutus in the pod?"

Smiling, Clay responded, "The study didn't say, but I'd speculate he probably was. You never know, unless you can find their incarnation today."

"Did you ever go back and work off the original database regressions?"

"Absolutely. But you've got to figure half of the subjects were over thirty or forty when regressed by the SRI teams. After twenty-plus years, people die or move away without an easy track to follow."

"How'd you ever get this treasure hunting idea?"

"Since SRI was in the middle of Silicon Valley and I was out of work, I thought it would be great to do a venture funded start-up company. Think about it, 'Soul Mate Dot Com ... Come see us, and we'll find your soul mate. No more Internet dating, no office affairs, no bar pickups. We find your soul mate for you. We'll tell you all good and bad things about this person and how to avoid problems. No more divorces. Your perfect mate for life.'."

Shali laughed out loud. "Protocol 95? Did you ever try to look up your soul mate? Or even your pod mates?"

A slow sheepish grin came across Clay's face. "Let's get back to Iqbal. The good stuff comes this afternoon in the LBL. We'll talk more about my treasure hunting, later."

Chapter 11

Back in the regression room, Clay and Shali began the next phase of the regression on Iqbal. Shali worked Iqbal through the preliminary scripts and quickly took him to a deep state of hypnosis.

"Iqbal, you will return to the long hallway of doors. At the end you see a glowing light. Walk toward that glowing light."

Clay pressed the button to the micro-pulse pads on the bottom of Iqbal's feet.

Shali continued, "Move down the hallway. You see that the light is coming from a doorway at the end of the hall. That doorway leads into a very large and beautiful room. Are you at that doorway now?"

"Yes."

"Walk through that doorway now and look around at the many bookshelves - rows and rows of bookshelves. In the center of the room, you see a very long reading table with lamps. This is a library - a very large and very special library, the Library of the Akashic records. Feel the magnificence. Each book is a complete record of every single soul in the universe. The complete history of your soul is in one of those books. Do you see all the books?"

Iqbal responded in a slow, low tone of voice that exuded awe. "Yes, I see it all. This is a beautiful place. So much knowledge, so much experience, so many souls. The shelves go forever in every direction."

"Do you see anyone else in the library?"

"There are several others here. They are dressed in long robes. They are glowing in clouds of deep color: deep blue or red, almost purple, beautiful dark colors. However, their robes are white, I think, although they are shrouded in mists of dark color. I do not understand. They move slowly through the shelves and look at the books. They are so intelligent, so wise."

"Are any of them coming to you, looking at you or waiting for you?"

"Allah Akbar - God is Great. Yes. I know that one. That one is coming to me. She is glad to see me, and I am glad to see her. I know her. I have seen her and been with her many times before. I don't know how I know her, or why; I just know her."

"She is your guide, your teacher and mentor. She helps you with all of your lives. When the body that you live in dies, she comes to help you back to the spirit world. This is so you are not lost or confused when you leave that body. Do you feel OK? Are you comfortable?"

"Yes. I am happy to see her. It is good to be here."

"Tell her you would like to review all the lives you lived before. Ask her if she can show you your book and review your past lives. Ask her now."

Clay pressed a deep long micro-pulse shock to Iqbal's shoulders. His neck and shoulders flinched slightly.

"Have you asked her?" Shali asked.

"Yes. She is taking me to the shelves. I am with her. She is taking out a book and placing it on the table. She opens the book ... the page comes to life. I see everything in this life. I see everything. It all comes alive on these pages. The entire life is like a storybook, like a 3D movie."

"Go to the first life. What do you see in this life?"

"It is a very long time ago. I am ... I am ... I'm not human. I'm some type of... a creature, some kind of an animal. I don't know what I am. I don't like this life. It is boring - not challenging, not exciting."

"Tell your guide you want to move forward in time to maybe three to four thousand years ago. Tell her you only want to see human lives that are relevant to today's world in which you live. Tell her this now. Does she accept this?"

"Yes, she understands. She always understands."

"Ask her if she will talk directly with me."

Shali looked at Clay and nodded while putting a forefinger to her forehead. Clay pressed the button to give a long shock to the Third Eye micro-pulse pad. Iqbal's head pressed back into the pillow.

"No, she does not want to talk with you."

Shali looked at Clay and shook her head.

He whispered, "Let's try again later." The guide was probably the only way to get the real information they wanted, and he knew they would have a better chance at conversing with her after they had spent time reviewing the Akashic records.

Shali then said to Iqbal, "That's fine. Continue reviewing the book. Are you at a life between three to four thousand years ago?"

Iqbal's soul reviewed several insignificant lives in that timeframe. One was a young girl somewhere in Africa, who died of an infection in her leg. Another life was a teenage boy who was bitten by a cobra in India and died a rapid, painful death. Another life was a woman in South East Asia who lived until the ripe old age of fifty-four. Finally, they got to a life of more interest. Iqbal described the details after he turned the page of his Akashic records.

"Yes, such an interesting life. My father was an important man. I was also important. There are many stories about many people in my family. It is in the time of 1700 BC, and I lived in an ancient land - very dry. My father and mother are Ibrihim and Sarai. My name is Yitzak. I have two sons."

"Describe everything you believe is important and relevant in this life."

"Once, my brother Yisma'el and I were very old, and my father was over one hundred years old. My father got so angry with us that he threatened to kill both of us. We were all such old men in these bodies and yet we acted like children. Our father yelled at us that he would kill us if we did not do as he wished."

Laughing out loud, Iqbal continued, "Oh, later, when we came back from the mountain, the stories became fantastic legends. My brother and I played along so we would not hurt my father's feelings. People were saying that God told my father to sacrifice his son." Iqbal belly-laughed even louder. "But the next week, we all forgave each other and made a feast in the village. People said that God changed his mind and told him to kill a goat for the feast instead of sacrificing me or my brother. The stories were amusing to the family."

Shali allowed Iqbal to spew out the history of significant events in this life while she conferred with Clay on the side. "Any idea who this person may have been?"

Clay clicked away on the Internet and said, without looking up, "I think I know who we have here. Let's see. Yes, our buddy

Iqbal here seems to be Isaac. Yitzak is Hebrew for Isaac. I am guessing that his father Ibrihim is probably Abraham. Yes, *the* Abraham, the root of Christianity, Judaism and Islam. He had two sons, Jacob and Esau; and his brother was named Ishmael. Yeah, this has to be Abraham's son. It makes sense to me based on that story about the mountain."

Shali asked, "What do you mean?"

"Supposedly Abraham got a command from God to sacrifice his son."

"And....?"

Still reading from the Internet, Clay said, "The story goes that God told Abraham to sacrifice his son Isaac, but later God changed his mind and told them to sacrifice an animal instead. Remember Solomon and Hillel and the human sacrifices? It wasn't uncommon at that time to just sacrifice a human, even your own child." Clay paused. "If this was really Isaac, then it sounds like Abraham was just a crusty old fart. Being that old and if he was really that nasty, he might have had dementia or Alzheimer's. Although, an angry father is no different than when my dad caught me stealing whiskey from the liquor cabinet as a teenager. He told me he'd kill me if he caught me again." He chuckled. "Hey, maybe exaggerated stories of my dad and me could start a new religion."

Clay sat back in his chair for a moment, glowing in the success for finding another historical hit.

"We can try to validate events tomorrow, after we review the recordings," Shali said. "Yitsak lived way before the secrets were even assembled."

"Agreed. But if this is really Isaac, then we're batting a thousand with this guy. You know, all of these tens of thousands of regressions and ninety-nine point nine percent of the lives are just plain boring people. And now we run across a slew of historically famous people in this one young Palestinian. We've got to dig for other living members of his soul pod. If his soul mates have strings of famous lives, then I'd feel like we were singing in Las Vegas with Frank Sinatra's Rat Pack. I'll bet he's got more famous lives."

"Could be, but don't get your hopes up."

Iqbal chattered on about this life of Isaac for five more minutes before Shali moved him forward in his Akashic record.

Iqbal then revealed two very ordinary lives. One life was a woman in the Olmec civilization of ancient Mexico in 1500 BC. She died of natural causes as an old woman, leaving thirty-seven grandchildren to carry on. The next uneventful life was spent as a fisherman along the Turkish coast. As expected in the timeline, they came to his life as King Solomon.

At the end of the description of King Solomon's life, Shali said to Clay, "The review of the Akashic record validates what we got in the regression earlier this morning, but with a lot less emotion and more objectivity."

"That's why I like to get to the Akashics as quickly as possible."

Shali continued the regression and found three more ordinary, simple lives between 900 and 600 BC: one each in Egypt, the Indonesian islands and Italy.

Ten minutes into Iqbal's description of the next life, Shali was glowing. She turned to Clay and said in smug tone, "We've got ourselves the one and only Pythagoras, here: revered philosopher, mathematician, mystic and scientist. How'd ya like them cookies?"

Looking up from his laptop, Clay said, "You're kidding!" He started clicking away at the keyboard. "Let's see … I've got 480 to 590 BC. Damn, he lived to be ninety years old."

Shali smirked. "Not quite. The official Akashic records here say he died in 478 BC, so that would make him ninety-two."

Clay looked at Shali through the top of his eyes and then back to his screen. "Here, I see that he's known as the father of mathematics."

"Man, if only we could bring this public," Shali said. "Just think of the ramifications. But poor Iqbal here would be eaten alive by the press."

"That is, of course, if anybody believed it. We'd probably be tarred and feathered as heretics, or most likely branded as lunatics. We'd be eaten long before they got to Iqbal."

Chapter 12

They continued the review of the Akashic record for a grueling thirty minutes and three more lives. Shali pulled Clay aside for a quick translation as Iqbal continued describing his lives for the recorder.

Stretching her head back and then rubbing her neck, Shali looked down at her notes and said, "OK, here's what we've got. A couple of uneventful lives in the three hundreds and four hundreds BC: One was a concubine to a low-level warlord in China; the other was a short-lived aboriginal boy on a Southern Philippine island. But I think we may have found who you were looking for. We've got a life in the two hundreds BC named Apollonius, although he said he was from Rhodes, not Tyana. Didn't you say your Apollonius was from Tyana?"

Clay scowled and blew out a sharp puff of air. He looked down at the laptop and furiously clicked away for thirty seconds. "Dammit! We got the wrong Apollonius. Iqbal was Apollonius of Rhodes in the two hundreds BC , not Apollonius of Tyana of the one hundreds AD. We got the wrong one - three hundred years apart."

Shali sat back in her chair, raised her eyebrows and stared at Clay, as if looking for guidance. Iqbal babbled along about the life of Apollonius of Rhodes to the recorder in the background.

Clay continued reading his laptop and then said under his breath, "Why this Apollonius? Why were we led to Iqbal?" A few moments passed and then he exclaimed, "Of course! Of course, I've been looking at this in the wrong way." He glanced up to Shali and said in reserved excitement, "Our Apollonius of Rhodes here was considered one of the keepers of Alexandria's great library. Now I understand why I was led to Iqbal. I have been searching for philosophers, scientists or authors. I should have been focusing on the people who collected and stored the writings of others. There were once great secrets from all over the world stored in the Alexandrian Library about two thousand years ago. However, the entire library was slowly and methodically plundered and destroyed by different groups over several centuries."

Shali rhetorically asked, "What better soul to know of secret writings than the head of the greatest library, huh?"

Clay shot back, "So maybe the key to finding the secrets is in finding the Librarians of Alexandria. We need to focus on the later librarians who were probably involved in stashing the secrets before the library was destroyed. Let's keep going. Maybe Iqbal has more relevant lives later."

Shali continued reviewing the Akashic records with Iqbal for another thirty minutes before stopping to translate for Clay. "Well, there wasn't much more eventful for Apollonius. Then came the next two lives of Hillel and Philostratus, as we expected from this morning's session. Nothing new turned up, there. But the next life was a guy named Iamblichus from Syria in the three hundreds AD. I think I've heard the name." She nodded toward his laptop. "What can you tell me about him?"

Clay perked up with excitement and jumped back into his laptop. "I know about Iamblichus. He was a famous Neo-Platonist philosopher who studied under a guy named Porphyry in Rome. Porphyry, in turn, studied under Plato. They all had a general philosophy of a single connected universe and a possible single world-soul. But they were all at odds with both the Christians and the Jews at that time."

"This must have made for some interesting debates, huh?"

"Oh, I'm sure it did,"

"In the Akashic records, Iqbal's soul described many conflicts they had with religious groups."

Clay looked up from the laptop. "Here, it says that Iamblichus was known for his compendium on Pythagorean philosophy." He chuckled. "Now, who would know more about Pythagorean philosophy than the reincarnated soul of Pythagoras? This soul just didn't want to give up on his opposition to organized religions. Let's keep pushing on. I can tell from the monitors that Iqbal is getting tired."

Shali moved Iqbal's soul to the next life. In just a few minutes, she turned to Clay and said, "It's getting better. His next life was Nestorius around 400 AD. I've heard the name but don't know any details. What have you got there?"

Clicking away, Clay said, "Well, let's see. This Nestorius was the Archbishop of Constantinople in Turkey. He made proclamations that started huge Christian debates over the separate existence of God, Jesus Christ, human bodies and divine souls. Whew."

Shali thought for a few seconds before responding. "That makes senses. His earlier incarnation as Iamblichus saw a merging of individual souls and the divine soul into one. Hence, he must have portrayed God, Christ and all mankind as really just one entity. Our buddy Iqbal's soul has a theme here. But I'm not sure how it plays into these secrets that we're after."

Clay said, "Agreed. This is interesting stuff, but if we don't get moving, we're not going to find these writings. Iqbal only gave us one day."

Shali pushed Iqbal's soul through four more lives before pausing to translate for Clay. "The next two lives in the five hundreds and six hundreds AD seem like normal people in Europe and Africa with pretty obscure lives. But the next life in seven hundreds AD was a guy named Jabir, in Persia. He was into philosophy, science, things like that; seems like he was renowned. Do you know anything about a Jabir or can you try to look him up?"

"I think I know who he is. Give me a second." Clay smiled a dirty grin. "Here he is; I found him on *Wiki*." Clay read for a few seconds then paraphrased what he saw. "OK, Jabir ibn Hayyan was a Persian Arab in the seven hundreds AD. Wow, a prodigy genius. In addition to being known as the father of chemistry, he was a renowned alchemist, astronomer, astrologer, engineer, geologist, philosopher, physicist, pharmacist and physician: a regular wiz-bang guy. Does this sound like the guy you got?"

Shali smiled back and said, "Sure does. He talked about most of those disciplines. At least the history books were spot on. So, Iqbal's soul was the father of mathematics as Pythagoras, and now we see he was known as the father of chemistry in Jabir. I wonder if he's got any more fatherhoods?"

Iqbal continued to describe his past-life experiences to the recorder while Shali and Clay continued conversing in the background.

Still fixated on the laptop screen, Clay said, "*Wiki* says that Jabir was a prolific writer. This guy had some three thousand known writings, many so complex, deep and twisted that the English word "gibberish" is believed to derive from reference to Jabir's writings. He had one book called the *Book of Stones* that supposedly described how to artificially create life, including humans. The text was written in some type of encoded language that could barely be understood, even after years of studying Jabir's gibberish."

"OK, Mr. Encyclopedia, I can tell from the tone of your voice that you have something on your mind. What are you thinking?"

"I remember reading several of the books written by psychologists on past-life regression. Even though I've never run across it in my PLR work, the books said some souls had supposedly practiced the creation of life on obscure planets somewhere else in the universe. I don't know whether to believe it or not. Maybe Jabir's work was an incarnated human's documentation of this phenomenon. I wish we had more time to dig into this Jabir's life. Damn you, Iqbal, we could use a couple more days."

Shali said, "Anything else before I push on?"

Almost ignoring her comment he replied, "I wonder if Jabir had some sort of connection to another dimension or world where he remembered these experiments in the creation of life. If so, it's probably no wonder his writings were all gibberish. This makes me wonder if any of Jabir's writings are part of the collection of secret hidden writings that we're looking for. I wonder if these are the secrets of the universe we are looking for?"

After a few seconds of hesitation Shali said, "I got one more life after Jabir, another Persian named Rhazes. What details can you find?"

Clay turned his attention back to the laptop. "OK, here it is in *Wiki*... The next life of Iqbal's soul was... Muhammad ibn Zakariyā Rāzī, but they called him Rhazes or Rasis. He was another famous Persian jack-of-all-trades around the year 900 AD."

As Iqbal continued rambling, Clay suddenly and excitedly burst out, "Holy Moly, this guy was another hot shot. Although raised and died in Iran, he spent much of his life in medical and academic circles in Baghdad; that's where he kept his main laboratory. Just like Jabir, Rhazes was a renowned alchemist, chemist, physician, philosopher, scholar and musician. As a physician, he was famous for dealing with smallpox. He was attributed with discovering rubbing alcohol, and he authored thousands of books and articles on a wide-ranging set of disciplines. Ha Guess what? He was big in childhood diseases and child medicine: Rhazes is known as the father of pediatrics."

Shali chuckled. "Is Iqbal's soul some kind of a promiscuous intelligent; he has to be the father of all disciplines?"

Clay read on, "It says here he was a believer in the transmutation of metals. He believed you could transform one metal into another. You know, like turn copper into gold. He even wrote two books about transmutation: one was called *al-Asrar* or *The Secrets*, and another was called *Sirr al-Asrar* or *The Secret of Secrets*. Do you suppose…?"

Before he could even ask, Shali cut him off. "Could be. Maybe this guy wrote down a lot of the secrets you have heard people mentioning."

"Yeah. According to the history books, contrary to Jabir, Rhazes was very concise in his writing. Maybe he learned something from his previous life as the jabber-mouth. Maybe that was his soul's correction in this life - to learn how to write intelligible books." Clay chuckled at his own joke.

Shali said, "When Iqbal's soul talked about Rhazes' view toward religions, he wasn't very gracious. Can you see anything about this?"

"It looks like our regression has proved the historians right: *Wiki* says Rhazes pretty much had a disdain for organized religions. He had conflicts with religious leaders, in particular those preaching Islam, even while living in Baghdad."

"I wish we had more time with this guy, but we don't. We'll listen to the tapes later and try to dig out more details."

Chapter 13

Shali continued working Iqbal's soul through the next life. She suddenly looked at Clay and said, "We've got another multi-disciplinarian here. He's another Persian named Avicenna who lived about 1,000 AD. He said he was very experienced as a physicist, philosopher, astronomer, chemist, physician and mathematician. What can you find on him?"

Clicking away on his laptop, Clay replied, "Yeah, he was a Persian, too; but he came from Uzbekistan. The history books say he was also a renowned geologist, logician, paleontologist, poet, psychologist, scientist, soldier, statesman and teacher. Whew." A big grin came across Clay's face. "This guy is a regular Captain America or should I say Captain Persia?" Looking up from his laptop, he added, "OK, Shali, ready for this one? Avicenna is known as the father of the concept of momentum - as in, physics." Clay looked at Iqbal but leaned over to Shali and whispered so only she could hear, "Enough fatherhood, OK, Iqbal?"

Shali quietly laughed. "Promiscuous soul, huh? What else do you have on Avicenna?"

"According to *Wiki*, he was a great pharmacist. Even today, Avicenna's picture is on the diploma of the Pharmaceutical Society of Great Britain. However, I sense that he may have been a bit confused."

"What do you mean confused?"

"He was a devoted Muslim living in the heart of Islam at its crowning peak. Catch this: by the age of ten he had memorized the entire Quran. It seems like he may have found himself at conflict between Islam and science. For the most part, I would say that Islam won the debate. Avicenna became extremely critical of Rhazes, his own former incarnation. He must have been one confused puppy, somehow in conflict with his soul's core philosophies."

"Yeah, but Avicenna was no different than anyone else in any other time who is influenced by the religious, philosophical and cultural environments in which they grow up."

Clay tilted his head to the side and grimaced at Shali before responding, "My Lady, you are getting deep, here." He spun his finger in a circle and said, "Roll on."

She glared at him and then moved the regression session forward. Suddenly, the soul's guide came out in full interaction without prompting from Shali. The change in Iqbal's tone and demeanor was obvious. Clay smiled at Shali and nodded an acknowledgment that the guide had finally exposed itself.

The guide revealed the last publicly known life of Iqbal's soul: "Ezra Pound, 1885; United States, Italy. Writer, poet, political activist…"

Shali immediately translated for Clay, but he was already searching the name. Clay whispered to himself, "Hmm." Not looking up from the screen, he said, "This guy is a mess. How did this soul, who had so many very significant lives over the past four thousand years, end up in a screwed up life like this American, Ezra Pound? I thought lives were supposed to improve over time."

As the guide drawled on in staccato monotone in the background, and Clay continued describing Ezra to Shali, "On one hand, this guy appears to be a popular writer. On the other hand, he's almost a radical nut case: a hyper-liberal. He died only a few decades ago. Pound was politically active in Italy before World War Two and supported both the Fascists and the Nazis. But he was chastised by both sides. Neither side wanted to claim him. He was very negative towards everything. Whoa. After the war, Pound was imprisoned as a traitor by the United States. He was charged and tried as a criminal, but since they couldn't prove it, they just committed him to an insane asylum to get him out of the way."

Shali looked at Clay with a puzzled look. "I'm listening to the guide, and he is saying pretty much the same thing, but from *his* viewpoint. All of this soul's previous lives were so sophisticated and intellectual. How could this be? What went wrong?"

Clay sat back from his laptop and paused for a moment. The soul's guide continued describing the life of Ezra Pound. After a few moments, Clay said, "This Ezra Pound is the same soul as all of these other famous people, and he died in our lifetime. If Pound was the only well-known life of this soul in the last thousand years, could the lasting images of these lives have changed over history? I mean, all the other famous lives were revered and placed on a pedestal. He was the father of half a dozen disciplines and played a role in the foundation of all modern religions. Could history have been distorted by time? What I'm saying is do you think this soul could have been a nut-case in his previous lives, too? And then, after hundreds or thousands of years, history has been rewritten to suit another purpose?"

Shali raised her hand and said, "Shhhh."

The guide continued with terse, pointed sentences. "It was necessary that Ezra Pound's writings be encoded. The world was not prepared to comprehend or utilize the wisdom within. War was dominant, hatred prolific, and society was not stable." Shali quickly translated for Clay.

"Encode?" he whispered back. "It says here that Pound's poetry and prose writings were confusing, almost cryptic. I looked at extracts of some his writings, here. It's like gibberish. Does this have something to do with Jabir from his former life? Hmm?"

Shali waved her hand to shush Clay again.

"The truth was revealed to this soul by the elders. This soul documented knowledge in *The Cantos*. Encoded the knowledge in *The Cantos…*"

Shali quickly looked at Clay and pointed her finger vigorously at his laptop. "What are *The Cantos*? He wrote something called *The Cantos*."

He clicked furiously on the keyboard. After a moment, Clay responded, "*The Cantos* is a series of writings by Ezra Pound. He did these writings over his entire life. There were a bunch of different topics. It looks like he numbered them a bit like Nostradamus' quatrains. Do you figure *The Cantos* are some kind of encoded predictions or prophecies?"

"No. *The Cantos* might be part of the hidden secrets but not the whole thing."

Clay looked puzzled. "You think the secrets could be hidden in plain sight, as in these peoples' writings?"

Shali replied, "I don't know, but on second thought, I wouldn't think so. The previous regressions that led us to Iqbal seemed to say the secrets were physically hidden because someone doesn't what them to be published or available. But *The Cantos* and Jabir's works are certainly published and not hidden at all."

Clay flicked his eyebrows and said, "Maybe this is like *The X-Files*: the truth is out there. Maybe the dark shadowy man with the burning cigarette is the one who wants to suppress the writings and the truth."

Shali glared at Clay with annoyance. "We've got to get going. I can tell Iqbal's stamina is giving out. We've been at this for over eight hours and his body is showing signs of fatigue. Let's push the guide on the writings themselves or locate other living souls that can help us."

Chapter 14

Shali turned to the scripts for the next phase. "I would like to continue to speak directly with the guide, only." Shali signaled and Clay pressed an extra long shock to the Third Eye. Iqbal's head pushed back into the pillow.

In that deep, slow tone of voice, Iqbal responded, "Yes. And what do you wish?"

Clay and Shali glanced at each other with a look of excitement.

Shali said, "We are looking for a collection of writings in the time of this soul's present life. These writings contain great knowledge and wisdom. They are claimed to be secrets. Where are these writings located?"

There was no response.

Shali probed again, "Who has possession of these writings today? Can anyone disclose the location of these writings to us?"

There was still no response, but they both saw a slight wrenching reaction of discomfort in Iqbal's shoulders. Finally, a response came from Iqbal's guide. "The wisdom you seek was once in the great library on the desert coast. The library is no more."

"Yes, we know the Alexandrian library is gone; it was destroyed. Tell me who destroyed it?"

There was no response. Shali put three fingers in the air and made a hard jabbing motion at her forehead. Clay turned up the micro-pulse dial and shocked Iqbal's Third Eye for a long three seconds. Iqbal's head pushed back into the chair, but no response came.

Clay hit it again. Still no response.

Shali rephrased the question, "Has any person or group been trying to destroy these hidden secrets from Alexandria after they were removed from the library? Is anyone still trying to destroy these secrets, today?"

The silence continued. Clay hit the button again. Nothing. Shali looked at Clay and shook her head. She continued with the guide, "Were copies of the secret writings removed from the library of Alexandria before it was destroyed."

Finally, she got a response. "Three copies of this knowledge to which you refer were removed before destruction."

"Who removed them?"

"A group of people took the documents to preserve the words."

"Does this group still exist in the world?"

"Yes."

"What was this group called?"

"Those who desire to preserve the words."

Shali glanced at Clay and whispered, "Smart-assed guide." Then she turned back to Iqbal and asked, "Today, where can we locate those who desire to preserve the words? How do we find the copies today? Where do we find those who protect those documents today?" There was no response.

Shali tried again, "Tell us which souls know the present location of these writings. Where are those souls living in bodies, at this time? Where we can find them?"

A smug look came across Iqbal's face. "You have, in this soul, a librarian. Shouldn't you look for other librarians if you want to find your secrets?"

"Yes. Help us locate the librarians who are living in human bodies at this time."

Iqbal's head, neck and shoulders tightened up. He twisted to the right and then the left, as if looking for something in the air. The guide responded, "The first and last librarians of the great Alexandrian Library are there in your world now."

Clay noted the excitement in Shali and looked at her with anticipation. Shali briefly translated for him and then looked back at Iqbal and said, "Tell us where to find these two librarians."

"One is on the big island to the north, in a village of the castle - the castle in the south, the castle of the holy chalice."

Shali translated for Clay. They looked at each other with puzzlement.

Clay turned back to the laptop and quickly typed in a search for 'holy chalice, castle, island.' Thousands of Internet hits showed up on his laptop screen. He said to Shali. "Big island in the north could be Greenland, Iceland, Newfoundland, Britain or Ireland. I don't know of many big islands north of Russia. Franz-Joseph Land, maybe? You've got to get me closer than this, and dig into this holy chalice."

Shali asked the guide, "What is the name of the castle or village? Or the name of the person living at this time?"

"A castle, no more. Thomas ... Evan ...."

Clay gave Shali a strange look of optimistic exasperation. "From the name, Thomas or Evan, the person is probably Welsh or English. The big island has to be Britain. Wales is on the island. There are probably five hundred castles in Wales, alone, from the Internet search." He clicked at the computer again. "But it looks like only a handful of castles in Wales may have some linkage to the Holy Grail, assuming that is the chalice. But half the people in Wales are named Evans or Thomas. We've got to get more specific details on the person. See if you can find out if they are known by a different name or what they do for a living."

Shali turned to Iqbal, "By what other names is this person called? What does this person do for occupation?

"Tommy is keeper of the castle that is no more."

Shali asked, "How many years has this soul been in this body?"

"Fifty-one years for this life."

Shali smiled and translated for Clay.

"Ask if this Tommy is the first librarian or the last librarian of Alexandria," Clay said. "There could be a four-to six-hundred year window around the existence of the library, and I'd bet the last one would know where the secrets were stashed."

Shali asked Iqbal, "Does the soul in this body live in a place called Wales and what is the name of the castle that is no more?"

They got no response. Shali asked, "Was this soul the first or last librarian of the great Alexandrian Library?"

There was a long pause but no answer.

On Shali's cue, Clay gave a three-second shot of micro-pulse to the Third Eye, but still no response. After a few more hits to the Third Eye, Clay said to Shali, "It isn't worth pissing off the guide or wearing down Iqbal right now. Let's move on to the other librarian."

Shali asked, "You mentioned that a second librarian of Alexandria is living a life at the present time. Who is the person?"

"In the isthmus between the great bodies of land, east of the water that divides the lands."

Shali translated, and Clay pondered for a moment before saying, "The biggest isthmus in the world is Panama between North and South America. The water that divides could be the Panama Canal. If it is to the east of the canal, it could be either the Pacific or the Caribbean side. There isn't much down the Pacific side except some stray villages and a lot of Columbian drug bandits. I'd bet the Caribbean side. Try to get a name of the area or a village or some other geographic description."

Shali asked the guide, "What is the name of the place where this soul now lives?"

The guide responded, "They call it paraiso. Ukuptupu Kuna Yala."

"Clay, did you get those names?"

Clay smiled and quickly jumped to Google Earth on his laptop. "I got it, Shali. I know right where this is. I spent several years in Central America when I was in Army Intelligence. It's gotta be the Kuna Indians around the San Blas Islands on the Caribbean shore. Paraiso meaning paradise in Spanish and it really is a paradise. Try to get the person's name, age, occupation."

Shali turned to Iqbal, "What is the name of the living person for this soul? How old is that body now? Is there anything significant about this person?"

"She is called Sogui and has been seventy-two years in this body. She is a leader of her people. She has been tested with many challenges. She succeeded in the tests and will be rewarded. The end of the challenge is near. Soon to guide others."

Shali translated for Clay, and they looked at each other with big smiles.

Clay commented, "This should be a piece of cake to find her. There's only sixty or seventy thousand Kuna's down there. Having a unique name, fairly precise age and some type of leadership role, we'll find her quickly. However, it may not be easy to convince her to do the regression. The Kuna's are committed to their lifestyle and beliefs. I'm not sure how we'll get an old native Indian to go along with a regression. When we get back, I'll make some connections in Panama to start the wheels rolling. We've gotten as far as we can for now with Iqbal. It is clear the guide is not going to reveal the location of the writings. Let's wrap this up and move on."

Shali tried to start the hypnotic decompression, but it was a too late. While they had been chatting on the side, Iqbal and his guide had also evidently felt the regression was finished. Iqbal had slumped over to the side and was now completely asleep. Clay validated this by scanning his monitoring equipment.

"Shali, we wore this guy out. He's sleeping like a baby. Let's let him rest for half an hour while we start tearing down the equipment. We'll review the tapes tomorrow and get our tickets back to California."

Later, when Iqbal started coming out of his deep sleep, Shali walked him through the decompression script and back to full consciousness. She followed the PLR75 protocol precisely to ensure Iqbal would not remember any details of the regression. They settled up on the agreed fees, and Iqbal left with a nice pocketful of Jordanian dinar. He had absolutely no idea of his own soul's famous lives over the past four thousand years.

As they finished packing, Clay said to Shali, "I wonder if Iqbal, himself, will be another famous person, or just another Akmed Schmuck, Palestinian accountant."

Shali responded, "No doubt the world will see more of this soul, if not from this life, then in a future life. Let's keep our eyes on the Middle Eastern news in about twenty years. You never know."

Chapter 15

Late on the evening of their return to California, Clay called Shali. "Hey, are you settled in?"

"Yeah, why?"

"I'll be right over."

"What?"

"Don't say anything. I'll be there in fifteen minutes. I'll tell you when I get there."

He was at Shali's townhouse in ten minutes. When she came to the door he put his index finger to his lips and said, "Shh." He motioned her to come outside with him to the parking lot.

"Ok, so what's the big secret, Sherlock?"

"Bugs. I found three bugs in my apartment."

"So get some bug spray."

"No, not insect bugs, surveillance bugs. Listening bugs."

Shali's face went blank. She looked back at the door of her townhouse, then back at Clay and pointed a finger at her door with a questioning look.

"I suspect so. I brought my sweeping equipment. Let's go check it out, but don't say anything."

They also found three listening devices in her townhouse. Clay removed and disabled all three devices then put them in a bag with the three from his condo.

The next morning they met for a working lunch of Chinese take-out at Clay's now bug-free condo-turned-office. As the smell of Kung-Pao chicken filled the room, Clay opened the discussion with an air of sensitivity. "How are you feeling?"

Looking concerned, Shali responded, "I'm OK. It's a good thing you are so paranoid."

Smiling, Clay said, "Blame it on my past. Army intelligence makes you like that."

Shali narrowed her eyes to a sharp focus and raised the intensity of her voice. "But I would like to know who in hell planted those things in our places while we were gone. More importantly, what are they after, and what do they want to know about us? I feel violated." She paused, and when she spoke again it was with a lighter tone. "I mean how long have those bugs been planted in my townhouse? Were they listening in on my bedroom the last time I had wild party sex?"

Clay smiled as he threw a punch. "Nah. The perps were probably in elementary school when that happened."

Shali rolled her eyes with annoyance.

Clay sensed her concern and replied in a more comforting and consolatory tone. "They obviously want to know what we are doing, or what we are digging into,"

"It has to be related to our search for the secrets."

"No doubt. We touched a nerve somewhere. Although, we've been pretty quiet about what we are looking for, whatever it is. On the other hand, our regression targets know we are regressing into past lives. Any one of them could have mentioned something to a friend or associate or a priest in confession. The word must have gotten around, and now we've got somebody interested in our doings."

Shali walked over to the window and stared out at the hills in the distance. "I'm concerned. The guy who broke into the hotel in Jordan, he was not just a thief. And now, why plant bugs? Why not just rob our places? There are so many open ends. We know the secrets have been hidden for thousands of years, but by whom and who are they hiding it from? I'm worried, now. There's a connection between the crook in Jordan and these bugs in our places."

"I don't know, madam. Don't fret too much just yet. Although we have to make sure we are careful about what we do with our data and what we say to whom. This morning I checked out the devices with a friend who is still in intelligence. He said the bugs are very current technology - not top government grade, but good stuff. Damn sophisticated."

Turning back to Clay from the window, Shali's tone lightened even more. "Just make sure you bring your bug sweepers everywhere we go. First, we have some guy rifling through our hotel in Jordan, and now somebody is snooping on our homes. Let's go back to work. So, did you get anything else this morning?"

Clay nodded his acknowledgement and paused. "I kept digging for the Welshman named Tommy Evans and found him. I've already got our next target lined up. I searched all the castles in Wales, looking for any possible connection to a holy chalice or grail. Iqbal's soul said the castle was connected to the holy chalice, so I figured it could be a reference to the Holy Grail."

The corner of Shali's mouth turned up mischievously. "But isn't this going to shoot a hole in the *DaVinci Code* theory on a blood offspring of Jesus Christ? I mean, are we back to looking for a wine cup or a human blood line instead of hidden secrets?"

"There are plenty of myths to go around. There were stories that King Arthur had supposedly acquired the Holy Grail, the cup, which had worked its way to Britain from the Middle East. He allegedly hid the chalice in one of his castles in the Wales. Most of these legends connected the Grail to a castle on the West shore of Wales, but Iqbal's guide referred to a castle in the south. The only castle in the South of Wales connected to the grail was Kidwelly castle. However, that connection was only because the British spoof movie *Monty Python and the Holy Grail* was filmed in the ruins of Kidwelly."

"Come on, Clay, there is no way Iqbal's guide would lead us to a place based on some loony-tune British movie."

"Don't sell it short. If the soul that is now Tommy Evans has worked at and around Kidwelly Castle much of his adult life, the Holy Grail has to be a prominent thought on his mind. Those thoughts would carry back with the soul to their guide, wouldn't it? And the guide in Jordan could be one of Tommy's guides. After all, we're not looking for the Holy Grail; we're looking for the soul of the guy associated with that castle, which had some association with the Grail. A spoof movie is an association."

"OK, I get your point, but it is a little hard to accept."

Clay smiled. "Yeah, after a couple of phone calls to Wales this morning, I made contact with our fifty-one-year-old Thomas Evans. He is a town councilor in Kidwelly and works for the Welsh Historic Division. Now get this: Evans is the curator of

Kidwelly Castle." After a bite of fried rice, he continued. "Tommy seems like a jovial guy so it was easy to build rapport. He was open to trying something different like hypnosis, particularly when I offered to pay him for his time. But he openly told me that he thinks I am a wacko."

"If only all regression targets were this easy to find and get a commitment."

"Right on. We lucked out on this one. I told him we'd be there in about a week. Will you be ready?"

Shali nodded, "My bills are paid so I'm ready any time. Tell me when you want to go; I'll book the trip. I should be able to finish transcribing and translating Iqbal's regression before we go. I haven't found anything new in the transcriptions so far this morning."

Chapter 16

Kidwelly, Wales

Shali and Clay landed in Cardiff Airport after a transfer from Heathrow Airport in London. They rented a car, drove an hour to Kidwelly and checked into a bed-and-breakfast style inn with an adjoining room for the regression. Tommy lived in the village of Kidwelly and had made reservations for them. They agreed to meet at the inn's restaurant for a traditional Welsh breakfast the next morning.

They got to the inn's restaurant before Tommy arrived. As they walked into the dining room, both smiled at the high ceilings with heavy wood cornices and finely trimmed doorways. Colorful rounded field stones rose on one wall accenting the large stone fireplace, while a wood fire crackled away warming the room. The slight smoky wood aroma mingled with the kitchen smells of cooked breads, bacon and coffee. As Shali sat down at a table near the window overlooking a brilliant green pasture with cows and sheep, Clay fetched two cups of dark black English coffee.

As he approached the table Shali looked up and nodded a thank you. "Oh, by the way, did you sweep this place for bugs?"

Clay answered in a matter-of-fact tone, "I swept the regression suite. Nothing. But I did not sweep my room. I want them to hear my sex romps with the maid."

Shali glared at Clay until she realized the prank. She instantly recovered and asked, "Oh, the hairy one that looks like a rugby player?"

Clay smiled, knowing he hit a touch of jealousy. Just then, a large, plump-bellied man with thin, disheveled hair and rosy red cheeks walked into the restaurant. He eyed them and waved his hand acknowledging their anticipated meeting. Tommy waltzed across the room, offered his hand to Clay and said, "So, are you my American mutts?" Before Clay could answer, Tommy looked at Shali and reared his head back in surprise. "Well you sure as hell aren't a Yank. What's your name?"

"Shali. Shali Faisal." She blushed slightly at the blunt, straight-forward nature of his introduction.

"Be damned. Are you some kind of Arab? Not Al Qaida, are you?"

With a smile she replied, "No. My family is from Northern India. But I was raised in California."

"Hell. Got that one wrong. But I don't lift a petticoat after pissing."

"What?"

"I don't cry over spilled milk. Are you some kind of a veggie eatin' Indian? 'Cause if you are, you are gonna get hungry here."

Shali smiled and looked at Clay who was enjoying Tommy's jabbing at his colleague. "No, I eat meat. No problem, there."

Tommy plopped down in a chair at the table. "Well that's good, because I told the inn keeper that I wanted a really good, authentic Welsh breakfast. So we're having a big plate of laver cooked in bacon fat. The seaweed is really good this time of year so that is going to be delicious. Then she's got a big steam pot cooking for cockles. We're dipping those clammers in butter and lemon juice. After that there will be plenty of eggs and bacon so you get ready for a real good breakfast. None of this continental European crap." Tommy leaned back in his chair, took a deep breath then stretched out his arms and patted his large belly while smacking his lips.

"I'm looking forward to this breakfast." Clay replied, "Good thing we don't start until tomorrow."

Shali injected, "But when we finish breakfast, we would like to have a little trial run with the hypnosis just to see how you do. Think you can handle it, big guy?"

"I'm ready when you are, my sweetie." He looked up as the innkeeper brought out a large plate of deep green pungent smelling seaweed puree and a pot of steamed cockles. "Ah, and you think those little Orientals are the only ones who know how to eat seaweed? No sir, they've never been to Wales."

The three of them had a long breakfast to get acquainted while joking about classic Welsh dishes. Two hours later, they waddled up to their regression room and spent an hour running Tommy through a set of general hypnosis practice scripts. There were no issues with Tommy's ability to be hypnotized. They agreed to meet early the next morning after a light breakfast. The rest of that first day, Tommy gave them a first-hand tour of the Kidwelly Castle, including highly animated descriptions of the filming of the Holy Grail movie.

Chapter 17

The setup and start of the first day's regression was uneventful. Clay performed the regression while Shali manned the console and recording equipment. Tommy went into a deep trance, through the hall of doors and described many ancient insignificant lives up to Sixteen Hundreds BC. There they found the life of Ismael, son of Abraham and brother Isaac.

"Yeah, my brother Yitzak, he was a limey prick if there ever was one. Always pushing me around, the lame ass. And Dad? Oh shit, the older he got the more his brain went to mush He couldn't keep his dish level. Always hollering at us and even threatened to kill us a basket of times."

Tommy rattled on about his life as Ismael using his strong Welsh slang. Clay smiled and looked across to Shali. "Tommy is definitely in Iqbal's soul pod. They were both Abraham's sons. Listen how he corroborates Iqbal's descriptions of Abraham." She nodded and gave Clay a thumbs-up.

Clay let Tommy play out the life of Ismael and then moved to the next life in Fourteen Hundreds BC. Surprisingly, he described in graphic detail his life as Miriam, the sister of Moses and Aaron. He described how passionately respectful she was of her brothers. But they were surprised when he described his previous life's view toward the wife of Moses.

"Sephora. What a bitch she was. My poor brother Moses was so gullible and manipulated by her. She was a good mother to his kids, but I just hated her. I wish he would have left her back in Egypt. Aaron saw through her, too. There was no Welsh between us, I tell you."

"What do you mean 'no Welsh between us'?"

"We didn't speak. I didn't trust her. I just couldn't stand her."

Clay proceeded with his questioning through the life of Miriam with no significant events.

Clay then moved Tommy through half a dozen inconsequential lives over the next thousand years. In his strong Welsh accent, Tommy then revealed a most interesting life between 367 to 283 BC. As Tommy described this life in graphic detail, Shali pulled Clay aside.

"I'm telling you, we've got a hot one here." Shali pointed at her laptop. "This is the life of Ptolemy Soter. He was one of Alexander the Great's most trusted generals and later became the ruler of Egypt." She grabbed his forearm and leaned toward him. "Clay, this Ptolemy was known as the founder of the Alexandrian Library. I think we've got our key player, here."

Clay's smile grew into a huge grin. "Good stuff. But I think we need the last librarian, not the first. But keep digging and see what you can find about Ptolemy while Tommy's rolling, here. His comedic narration is busting me up."

"Why, hell, I had more whores than I could handle. Yeah, I had to marry this one little bitch, Artakama. Her daddy was some Persian general. Alex was trying to keep peace in Persian so he made me marry her; the twerp. What a spoiled brat, she was. But I had me one really hot lady on the side. Yeah, Thais. She was one fine Greek lass that could suck the paint off a car. I brought her along on our campaigns. We had one hellish big party in the palace in Persepolis one night. We burned the God-damned castle down. I'll bet they saw the flames in Shiraz that night. What a piss. Alexander would have had a big shit about that bonfire, but be damned if he didn't start the fire himself. Thais, she was one hot, manipulative woman. She could make a man skin his own mother. Hell, she pushed Alex into burning down his own new castle. She dared him - told him he didn't have the balls to burn it down. Alex could never pass up a good dare. We had some good times, we did. There were great battles in Afghanistan, India, Syria, Cyprus. Oh, hell, the day we took Jerusalem; wow, what fight. We fought hard and we played hard. Ahh, now those were the days."

Clay and Shali both laughed out loud.

"Why, we kicked big ass like there was no tomorrow. We pillaged every place we went. Now, I always liked books, so I brought back thousands and thousands of books and scrolls to Alexandria." Clay sat up in his chair and glanced at Shali. He turned a serious face as Tommy expounded. "I had trains of wagons taking all kinds of writings back with us. I liked the stories and philosophies of life in those books, but I couldn't read the damn things. All these weird languages. So I brought me back some translators to help me. And, I might add, a few of them slaves were hot little ladies. They would sit and read to me from those scrolls and books, and then I'd have a hot sex romper with 'em." Tommy himself laughed out loud and paused. "But some of those writings were just confusing trash; couldn't make heads nor tails of it. A lot of strange numbers and drawings and weird stuff. Nevertheless, my campaigns with Alexander led me to build a great library with all of them books. At least that was one good thing I did in that life."

Clay looked at his colleague and shook his head. "You're right. We found the first librarian of the Alexandrian Library. Maybe we'll get more details in later lives or in the LBL."

After breaking for a light lunch the three started into the afternoon regression. Tommy described an insignificant life of a Chinese woman in the One Hundreds BC that was followed by a prominent life between 20 BC and 50 AD.

"Good family, you know. Aristocrats, we were. Everybody knew us in Alexandria. We were Jews and damn well connected back to Rome. You had to be connected to Rome or you're at the fords of the river - dead like a sheep. Philo Judeaus, they called me. Oh, and I was a good writer. Wrote a lot of books and they put a lot of them books in the big library up by the coast. I loved the works of Plato, Aristotle, Pythagoras. I wrote about my philosophies, but I got it from these guys." Tommy continued his colorful narrative while Shali pulled Clay aside.

"I'd heard of this Philo guy but never realized his depth of influence. We asked for prominent, and we got it, here."

"Where do you think I should take him?"

"Ask about Iqbal's Hillel. They lived in the same time. I'll bet they ran the same circles. Then see if he knows about JC."

Clay turned back to Tommy who was rattling away about his life as Philo Judeaus. At a slight pause, Clay injected, "Did you know a man named Hillel or Allal? A Jewish man in Jerusalem?"

"Oh, hell, yes. Who didn't? He was a sharp nail, for sure. He was in Jerusalem but I met him once in Alexandria when I was a young man. He came to see the library. After that he sent over rabbi's to the library. I would meet with those rabbis and talk about the problems we had in Alexandria with the Romans and Greeks. Ass-holes they were. They busted our asses all the time."

"Did you know of a man named Jesus Christ or Jesus of Nazareth, perhaps in Jerusalem? He was a Jewish man."

"Yeah. Stupid prick. Got his-self nailed up for shootin' off his mouth too much. I took a different tack. I wrote about our problems. I wrote to the Emperor in Rome several times. I even went to see him, but that Caligula didn't want to hear anything about our problems. The senators were no better. They were pricks, too."

Clay guided Tommy through the rest of Philo's life and then quickly through another insignificant life in the wilderness of Siberia.

Clay started into the next life lasting from 207 to 270 AD. Within minutes Shali nearly jumped out of her chair. With a huge smile she waved at Clay to get his attention and pointed at Tommy.

"We've got Plotinus. Yes, Plotinus."

He smugly smiled in return. "I figured this might be him. We're going to spend some time to dig in, here."

Clay intensely questioned Tommy's soul as Plotinus for more than thirty minutes, probing for any leads to the secrets. They got absolutely nothing and looked at each other with disappointment.

"Ask him about Ammonius," Shali whispered to Clay.

"Do you know a man named Ammonius Saccas?"

"Why, hell yes. Ammonius was a good teacher - a damn good teacher. He was sharp, plus he was a good guy, a real nice man with a good heart, good thoughts. But the poor sap couldn't write for shit. Me and his other students did all his writing, and he let us take credit, the dipshit. We should have signed his name for him and not taken credit. That wasn't right."

"Anyway, he was as queer as a football bat. The guy never married and never wanted to be with women; he liked his fellas, as I recall. What do ya expect? He was a Greek. He tried to get me one time, but I got pissed at him. I told him I'm not into that kinda stuff. No, sir, nope, not me; I like my women. Let me tell you about this time when I was teaching in Rome. You see, I had women students under my study. One wonderful, beautiful lady named Gemina. Oh yeah, she was a charmer and a good looker. I lived in her house for a while, in a back room. Her husband was always off on some Roman Empire kinda bullshit, killing people in some far away land and taking all their money. Well, let me tell you that I had my way with this Gemina, his wife. And with her fine-looking teenage daughter, too. And then there was this other Roman's Legionnaire officer's wife..."

Clay and Shali laughed so hard at Tommy's descriptions, tears streamed down their faces. After finishing the review of Plotinus, they brought Tommy out of the regression through the decompression scripts. After a tiring day of regressions, they all went to a nice dinner in nearby Carmarthen for a fashionable meal of monkfish and lamb.

Chapter 18

The second day of regressions started well as Tommy leapt into a life from 271 to 312 AD.

"My name was Cletus Aurelius. Pretty nice Roman-Greek name, huh? I wanted to be a Roman Legionnaire when I was a boy, but I think I was Greek. No, I can't tell whether I was a Roman or a Greek. Must have been a mutt."

With little prompting Tommy went into thirty minutes of precise detail on this particular life. As he delved into the minutiae of that life, Clay motioned Shali to the side.

"What is Tommy's hang up on this Cletus guy? Did you find anything on him on the 'net?"

"Not a trace. I tried all kinds of combinations on the name but I found nothing that matched the time or places he is describing."

"He's infatuated with this life for some reason, so let's let him run with it a while longer." Clay turned his attention back to Tommy.

"God, my wife was a nagging bitch. Hell, I joined the Legions to get away from her. She can keep her pompous assed family. The Legion sent me to control the Numidians and the Berbers down in North Africa. Those damn barbarians gave us a lot of trouble. But there's a lot of resources down there, loads of grain to send back to the Empire and to feed the army. I controlled a small outpost of Roman soldiers. We were responsible for about ten villages. The boys got a wee bit rowdy at times with the locals, you know, raped a few girls. Well raped a lot of girls and took some extra taxes from the merchants. I should have stopped them, I know it. But what the hell, you can't do everything right? But I was behaved; I just didn't control my soldiers. I was sweet on this one girl in the village where we lived. Her father was one of the elders and I think he liked me. He used to complain about my soldiers. But I didn't listen to him."

Tommy paused for a moment then let out a big sigh. "Anyway, my soldiers and me went for a walk one day to the next village; about eight of us. The rolling hills and golden fields of grain were beautiful." Tommy breathed in deeply through his nose. "Ah, the smell of summer jade was in the air that day. The sky was brilliant blue with lots of white puffy clouds. As we crossed through this small dip in the field, they came running over the hill. Forty or fifty of them came running from behind us, flailing their short swords and spears. We didn't stand a chance. They cut us down like sheep."

"Aw! My back." Tommy's body jerked violently in the chair. He curled to the right side, almost falling over the arm of the chair."

"Tommy, come out of the body!" Clay commanded. "Do not view this scene from inside the body. Only look at this from above the body. You will not feel any pain. Remove yourself..."

"Aw!" Tommy jerked back to the left side of his chair. "He sliced me down the back, that pipsqueak." His head rolled back to the right side, "I'd kick your ass if I could get up."

"Tommy! Listen to me. Remove yourself from the body of Cletus."

"Whoa!" Tommy jerked forward nearly sitting up in his chair. With the goggles, ear phone and shock wires in tow, his head turned down as if looking at his stomach. "They gutted me. The bastards gutted me." The palm of his left hand slid up the side of his stomach as if pushing the intestines back in. He suddenly flopped back in his chair and tilted his head back as if looking at the horizon above his head.

"Tommy, you will not..." but Clay was cut off.

"It's him. Her father and the elders from the other villages. On the hill by the tree line. They're watching. They ordered this and are watching it being carried out. Bastards!"

Tommy suddenly jerked to a complete sitting posture, grabbed his right side and yelled in pain. He began to shake his head and arms to the sides as Clay and Shali stared in near shock. Tommy then reached up and yanked off his goggles and headphones. Tommy looked around the room in a frantic daze shaking his head side to side in disbelief. Tommy had come completely out of his hypnotic trance and was sitting wide awake in the chair, eyes flicking side to side as if replaying the trauma he just experienced.

Shali gave him a glass of water and rubbed his shoulders to help relax him. He sat there motionless. After a comforting pat on Tommy's shoulder she motioned Clay to step aside with her.

"What the hell just happened?"

"I don't know. I've never seen this. He wouldn't let go of that life. You didn't find anything about this guy on the 'net?"

"Not a thing. He really focused on this Cletus, more than any of the prominent people in his past. What do we do now?"

"After he calms down a bit we take him back down. We'll finish his regression and bring him back out through the Protocol 75 decompression. Hopefully, he won't remember. Just make sure we don't mention that life later or he might recall the experience. Tomorrow we'll go for the Akashic records."

She nodded. They re-hypnotized Tommy and continued the regression. In the Four Hundreds AD Tommy's soul revealed the life of Proclus, a famous Greek Neo-Platonist philosopher known for his influence of both Western and Islamic views of that time.

A pleasant surprise came in the next life as Tommy described his life as Dolpopa the Buddha from 1292 to 136 1AD.

"Will you look at the plump little boy? He's got a pot belly like me." Tommy laughed aloud. "I was raised in Nepal but I ran off at seventeen; gotta be a good Buddhist, so I went to Tibet. The temples and teachers were very good, there. I became good at Kalachakra, the wheel of time; there is no start, there is no end." Tommy droned on about his life as Dolpopa.

"Clay, I found him. He's a hot shot Buddhist in Tibet. He actually became a full Buddha. Good stuff, here, but I don't know if he's going to help find the secrets."

"I'll let him play this out and then move him on. He's had a lot of prominent lives just like his soul pod mate, Iqbal."

They continued through another five lives up to his present life as Tommy. None of them were significant or added to their search for the secrets. Clay was particularly assertive with the protocol decompression scripts to ensure Tommy did not remember any of the regression.

That night Clay and Shali met without Tommy in a pub up the street from the inn.

"Except for our little clash with Cletus, so far, so good, huh, Chief? And we haven't even gotten to the LBL yet."

"Yeah. A lot of his lives were historically famous, just as was the case with Iqbal. Correlating Tommy's former lives to the lives of Iqbal's soul, there is definitely a connection between the two. I wouldn't class them to the level of soul mates, but they are certainly in the same soul pod."

Shali smiled. "Tommy's camaraderie has made this regression a pleasure."

Clay chuckled. "Yes, his crude commentary under hypnosis sure cuts the boredom. And when he's not under, he's calling you the West-Asian mutt."

Shali smiled, "At least I'm not the mutt from the rebel colonies, as he calls you."

Chapter 19

The next morning Clay, Shali and Tommy settled into the regression suite to get started on the third session. Clay warmed up the equipment and tested the audio recorder. They were ready to began.

"This is Shali Faisal; it is eight sixteen a.m. in Carmarthen, Wales, on the twenty-ninth of February. This is the third regression session on Thomas Evans, also known as Tommy, subject FK9923-LE3254; suspected soul is ID number TP88-4546. Clay Barton is performing the regression of the subject. I am assisting and will be monitoring and managing the control board. The objective of this session is regression and transition to the LBL phase for interaction with the subject's soul or guide. The subject is very cooperative. Two previous regressions were successful in connecting directly to several lives. Subject understands possible consequences from performing the regression but has shown no signs of adverse impact, nor has he retained any memories of the regressions."

Tommy immediately went into a deep trance. Clay moved into the regression scripts.

"You are now in the hall of doors. See the glowing light at the end of the hallway. That doorway leads to a world where your soul goes between lives: a place between your incarnated lives. Go through that doorway. Are you there yet?"

"I sure am, Chump."

Shali and Clay looked at each other and smiled.

Clay continued, "Go through the door now. You will enter a very large open room that should have many rows of bookshelves, as far as you can see. In the center of the room is a large reading table."

"Bloody hell. Will ya look at that? It's the old library at the University in Aberystwyth. Fantastic! Look at the old bookcases. The ladders go up the side to the high shelves. Look how long those aisles are. They go on forever - gorgeous, dark-wooden bookcases. And the staircases at the end…"

Tommy was so talkative, Clay had to cut him short to keep the regression on track. "Is there anyone else in the library?"

"Holy Mary, mother of Christ, what the hell is that? What kind of shit is this? You never said anything about ghosts, for Christ-sake."

Shali giggled at Tommy's blunt humorous statements, even in a deep hypnotic trance.

Holding back a laugh, Clay clarified for Tommy. "This is not a ghost. This is your guide, the mentor of your soul. It is an older soul who you trust and cherish. This guide helps you in the time between lives and when you are living in person. Do you understand?"

"Squitz. Uh, course I understand. I've known him forever. Can be such a fuddy-duddy at times and gets me goat if I don't do it right. But I have to admit, he is good to me. Helps me improve. You know, if I don't get it right, I get to do it again."

"Ask the guide to review your past lives in the Akashic records from the library."

Tommy paused, then blurted out, "OK, we're goin' to town now."

"Ask the guide if he will speak to us directly about your previous lives."

There was a long pause at this question. Clay waited for a response.

Tommy finally responded in a low, slow crisp voice; he had a very different tone and demeanor. "This soul is a wise one. Many good lives - experienced. Even so, there are more lessons to learn." Tommy's jovial, joking mannerisms were nowhere to be heard.

Clay looked at Shali with a glowing smile and a nod of success. He mimed to her, "We got the guide. The last two days of frolicking with Tommy must have helped."

Clay said, "Please review the lives of this soul starting about four thousand years before the present time. In particular, review lives that made significant contribution to the society in which they lived."

After a moment, the guide spontaneously started to speak. "Yisma'el. 1726 BC, comes to the life. This life was difficult.

Rejection was the challenge, and he did not do well. His brother, Isaac, was jealous and suspicious of him. They fought often. The father, Ibrahim, treated this life with criticism and rejection." Tommy slowly shook his head side to side. "This soul did not do well. Hate and spite filled his mind, despite his outward respect for his father. He will repeat the lesson in a future life. After he left this life, society worshipped him for redemption that he never demonstrated when the life was lived. The people did not see the truth of this life but created images of what was desired to be believed."

Clay leaned over to Shali. "Hey, this pretty much confirms that he is Ishmael, the son of Abraham. The Muslims might be upset with this; Ishmael is one of their prophets." He smiled and then said, "He failed his rejection test and had to take it again in another life - kinda like summer school?"

"Interestingly," she whispered back, "Abraham's family was just as dysfunctional as any family today. They were certainly not the 'Beaver Cleavers,' as the Bible would have you believe. They had all the quirks of any other family anywhere in history."

Clay nodded and then moved the guide forward to the next life.

The guide continued, "Miriam; 1400 BC: sister of a Moses and Aaron. All are notable in future societies. Lessons of rejection, jealousy, and selfishness were corrected from previous lives. Her love for her brother, Moses, was selfless, even as a child. This soul met that challenge but failed the challenge of prejudice. Her brother, Moses, married a woman from Sudan with very black skin. As Miriam, this soul would not accept the brother's wife because of her skin color. She did not make the correction before leaving the body; a correction must be made in a future life."

Shali chuckled and quietly commented to Clay. "You watch. Tommy's soul is going to end up as a black slave in 1840, Charleston, South Carolina."

Clay mimed a laugh and responded, "Yeah, I don't doubt that a bit. He deserved an attitude adjustment."

Tommy's guide continued for ten minutes, reviewing Miriam's tumultuous life experiences with Moses, Aaron and their families.

"Is this cool or what?" Clay whispered to Shali. "There are references to these events in the Bible, Torah and Qur'an, but now we get it firsthand, like a videotape review of a football game. Clay shook his head and added, "Damn, I wish we could bring this public ... but nobody would believe it anyway."

She nodded. "With the guide here, I picture this ghost-like figure in a purple bath robe, sitting at a table with our plump Tommy sipping a beer, eating peanuts and flipping through a giant iPad video book."

"You've read the books. That's sort of how these past-life shrinks describe the LBL. Each page of the Akashic record gives the soul something like a three-dimensional, fast-forward review of one life after another, like a DVR player for your past lives. But this time the guide is adding a lot of critical commentary; a lot more than we've seen in past LBL's."

The guide continued unprompted. "There are many lives for this soul in the next thousand years. These lives are not historically prominent as you asked, but many lessons were learned."

"What is the next life of this soul that had a significant influence on human society?"

"Ptolemy Soter, 367 BC. Some later societies called this life 'the Savior.'"

As the guide described the good and bad side of Tommy's soul as Ptolemy, Clay thought back to Tommy's uncensored description of this same life two days earlier. He glanced across to Shali who looked up with a smile. She was also thinking of earthy frolics with whores, burning down Persepolis and collecting the origins of the Alexandrian Library.

As if on autopilot, the guide continued to the next life.

"Philo Judaeus, 20 BC. Alexandria, Egypt. This soul learned well and demonstrated good correction in this life. This soul learned that the principals of advanced goodness are framed in practice, example and teaching. Those called Christians built the foundation of their philosophy based on his leadership, but this life was not recognized as such. That group chose to worship the icon of a martyr executed before this life of Judaeus was complete."

After hearing that commentary, Shali whispered to Clay, "It seems odd for this guide to make a comment about Jesus Christ - assuming, of course, that's who he meant by the executed martyr."

"Yeah, I also figured JC was probably the martyr," Clay replied. "Let me probe that more." He turned back to Tommy's guide before he could continue. "Tell me more about this martyr.

Did this soul, as Philo, ever meet with this martyr? Did they know each other, or know of each other? Was the martyr known by the name of Jesus?"

There was a pause of nearly five seconds. Shali gave Tommy a three-second micro-pulse shot to the Third Eye, and his head pushed back into the pillow.

However, the guide ignored the question and continued a spiel from the next life in the Akashic records. Clay looked at Shali and shrugged his shoulders.

"Plotinus; 207 AD. Rome. A wise soul in this life. Good intentions. He understood the reality of human life but failed to convey his true ideals and thus created confusion among many groups. These groups then followed divergent paths. The consequences of this failure resulted in disparate organizations who interpreted his teachings in different ways. A correction is to be made in a future life."

Clay's forehead wrinkled with confusion. "This is pretty deep stuff," he said to Shali. "Usually guides describe simple, basic human characteristics such as fairness, kindness, generosity, or jealously. But this guide is a tough one. Remember Tommy's comment when he first saw the guide in the library? He said something like he was a hard-ass?"

Shali replied, "I know what you mean. This guide seems to demand an inordinate level of achievement from those souls under its mentorship."

As the guide droned on about the life of Plotinus, Clay continued his side discussion with Shali. "When I looked up Plotinus on the Internet last night, I was bowled over. Plotinus was Greek but spent much of his adult life in Alexandria, India, Persia and Italy. He made a vast array of metaphysical writings, which evidently heavily influenced Christian, Jewish, Islamic, Gnostic and Pagan religions. He carved himself a notch in history basing his teachings and philosophies on Plato. His concept of 'The One' pressed many religious dogmas to a single God concept."

"But he left a lot of room for debate," Shali interrupted. She pointed at her laptop screen. "It says here that Plotinus was the first philosopher to explicitly push the idea that true human happiness was *independent* of the physical world."

"Understood. So these religions must have picked up on some of his philosophies."

"It also says that he was a student and colleague of Ammonius Saccas for over ten years in Alexandria just like he told us the other day. You always ask about Ammonius at the end of the regressions. What's the connection here?"

"I kept running across Ammonius whenever I get a connection to secret writings. Let's see what the guide says about Ammonius."

Clay interrupted the guide. "Was this soul, as Plotinus, a student of a person called Ammonius Saccus in Alexandria?"

"Yes, this is so."

"Tell us about this Ammonius Saccus. Is this soul living in a person at the present time?"

Clay beckoned Shali for a micro-pulse shot to the Third Eye. However, after three attempts, then waiting, asking and pulsing again, the guide gave no response. Clay leaned to Shali and said, "What a prude."

"Give him a break, Clay. You've got Plotinus and you're asking about Ammonius, a different soul altogether. It's like you are asking the guide to go find another book off the Akashic shelf."

Suddenly, the guide continued to the next life.

Chapter 20

"Proclus. 409 AD, raised in Istanbul, lived in Athens. Correction achieved from shortcomings in previous life as Plotinus. Became prosperous but generously shared the wealth to help others: good correction. Continued to develop and teach truth and realities to others. The soul attempted to change the core philosophies of Christians to correct their path. He failed and they continued down a path of deceit to followers ..."

While the guide continued, Clay looked at Shali, "This guide is awful opinionated. What is this about? Christians deceived their followers?"

"I don't know. He seems harsh ... almost cynical."

"Agreed. If this guide is one of the mentors to this soul pod, they are probably all a bunch of over-achievers. In the tens of thousands of regressions from the SRI studies, I've never seen souls with so many prominent lives. And here we have two in a row, both with dozens of highly successful and famous past lives."

Shali smiled. "I can't wait to see what our next target has to offer, the Kuna Indian in Panama - assuming of course she's in the same pod and has the same guides."

"Yeah. But even with all the pressure from the guides to be super-achievers, we haven't come across one suicide."

Shali smirked and facetiously asked, "Yeah, you mean like all the Asian high schools where there is so much pressure to achieve, the kids kill themselves." Clay nodded.

The guide assertively continued to the next life without any prompting. "Dolpopa Sherab Gyaltsen; 1292 AD; Nepal and Tibet. Known as Dolpa Buddha."

This perked up both Clay and Shali. They stopped their side-chatting and listened to the guide's oratory.

"This soul achieved the highest levels of accomplishment while incarnated in this life. Guides and elders communicated openly with the soul while in the body. This life authored numerous documents that communicated messages and philosophies of life. Truth and knowledge was revealed to this Buddha to teach to others..."

Shali whispered to Clay, "This guide is a non-stop rambler. Must have had influence on Tommy because you can't hardly shut either one of them up. This guy seems like he's like on auto-pilot."

Clay smiled at her comment and then turned to interrupt Tommy's guide: "What did the guides and elders tell this soul as Dolpopa? Did they give special knowledge to this Buddha? Did this knowledge later become known as secrets?"

No response came from the guide, despite several shots of micro-pulse to the Third Eye.

Clay looked to Shali and said, "This is all interesting, but we're not getting ahead. He hasn't turned over any information about any hidden writings. We're up to 1300 AD already and on the first two regression days we did not see any significant lives after this point. I'm going to cut him off and get to the closing scripts on the secrets. Tommy's soul may have been the founding librarian at Alexandria, but he surely wasn't the last one. I think the last librarian is living down in Panama as a Kuna."

Clay walked Tommy through the final scripts, directly asking the guide for information on the actual location of any hidden or lost secrets. They got nothing: no locations, no referrals, no pointers. The session finally wrapped up. Disappointment showed on the two regressors' faces as they tore down the equipment and packed the cases.

On the last night in Wales, all three of them sat together in a pub sipping on pints of lager and lime.

"Well, my little mutts, did you find what you was lookin' for? 'Cause I'll tell you that I sure don't remember shit."

Shali looked at Clay to make the first move. Clay took a slow sip of his lager and lime, savoring the sharp but tangy, sweet taste. He looked up to Tommy with a smile and said, "We didn't find what we were looking for, but we think you lived a lot of very interesting lives. Your soul is somehow connected to our search, but we don't know exactly how, yet. You sure had some interesting lives, though. There was one life as a very prominent Roman-Egyptian scholar who had an uncontrollable libido for women left behind by their Roman Legionnaire husbands. That guy was banging on absolutely every willing woman he could find. You described one mother-daughter *ménage-a-trois* and all kinds of other sexual trysts. I'm telling you, we couldn't stop laughing." Clay went on to describe some more of Tommy's past-life exploits, but with a bit of creative exaggeration.

Tommy belly-laughed throughout Clay's oratory and at one point almost fell out of his chair. Then he said, "I still think your regression stuff is horse shit, but if not, I think you're right about my past sexual conquests. Let me tell you 'bout the time I hooked up with Melanie Jones, up the road, here…"

Clay and Shali laughed as Tommy described his sexual conquests in his present incarnation. Two hours later, after one too many lagers, Clay promised he'd come back some day to perform a special regression using PLR Protocol 73, which unlike the Protocol 75, would allow Tommy to remember everything in his past lives as if he had lived them yesterday.

"Now if you do that, am I going to remember Cletus gettin' killed in that field, again?"

Silence immediately filled the air as Clay and Shali looked at each other with blank stares.

Clay turned back to Tommy, "Are you saying you remember Cletus?"

"Everything including every damned time I stubbed my toe."

"Do you remember any other lives?"

"Nope. Nothin'. But I remember … no, I *felt* every God damned sword slice through my guts that beautiful summer afternoon in the wheat field."

Clay and Shali looked at each other again. Nothing more was said.

Chapter 21

Panama City, Panama

A little over two weeks later at Panama's Tocumen International Airport, Clay and Shali walked outside the terminal to the taxi stand. The heavy smell of tropics filled the air, which was humidity-laden after a late-afternoon rain.

As they loaded their cases of equipment into the back of the large SUV, Clay called out to the driver, "Marriot Hotel, por favor."

The driver acknowledged with "Si," and they drove out the airport exit ramp. Dusk fell as they roared along the parkway and approached the glittering glass towers of downtown Panama City, the Queen of Latin America. Shali slowly gazed over at Clay with the seductive look of a TV wine-commercial. She caught herself and snapped her head forward again, as if determined to keep their agreement not to become involved again.

After freshening up at their hotel, the two met for dinner across the street.

Over their first glass of red wine, Clay said, "Iqbal's guide gave us more than enough leads to easily find this Sogui Iglesias. The problem will be getting her to undergo regression. We have to work our way into her trust. Getting close to a Kuna is not easy for a Panamanian, let alone for an American gringo."

"So how do we break the ice?"

"I'm playing to Kuna history. The Kuna's have always been a fiercely independent people. Five hundred years ago, Spanish conquerors testified to the ferocity of the Kuna's in their reports to the king. The Spaniards were never able to totally conquer them. Then, in 1925, the young Panamanian government was about to militarily crush the Kuna's during a rebellion for independence from Panama, but the Americans parked a fleet of naval warships in the San Blas Islands as a warning to say they must show tolerance to the native Indians. I've heard the Kunas have had a slight endearment to the gringos ever since." Clay chuckled. "Perhaps they saw the '88 American invasion of Panama as a sixty-year-old payback."

Shali looked puzzled. "That's kind of ironic, isn't it? I mean, did not the Americans almost wipe out entire American native Indian population, take away their land and their way of life? So why try to save the Kuna's from the Panamanians?"

"It was probably a gringo guilt trip. Ever since that rebellion, the Kuna's have enjoyed an autonomous relationship with Panama. They have their own government, territory and laws, all of which enabled their society to survive."

"How'd you know so much about them?"

"About ten years ago I served several tours of duty with Army Intelligence in Latin America, chasing drug lords. I worked with several indigenous Central American Indian groups closely related to the Kunas. I looked up some old Indian friends down here and got an introduction to a good contact in Panama, close to the Kunas."

"Is this the woman you've been talking to on the phone the past few weeks?"

"Sure is. She is a psychology professor at the Universidad de Panama and is a Kuna herself. At first, she was apprehensive about our motivation, but she understands our use of regressions. After all, she's a shrink, herself. Nonetheless, I think she was so intrigued that she agreed to help us."

"How did she find Sogui?"

"On our first phone call, the professor knew exactly who we were looking for. Sogui Iglesius was one of the three Sailadummads or Great Sahilas of the Kunas. These three people, plus a secretary general, make up the leadership of the National Kuna Congress. For many years, Sogui was one of the local Sahilas serving in a governor-like role. She was responsible for management of her home island, one of the forty-nine separate Kuna communities. It turns out Sogui was a natural leader, exactly as described by Iqbal's soul guide in Jordan. She had success despite the male-dominated political structure and the terrible physical and mental suffering she has experienced throughout her life."

"I remember Iqbal's guide talking about this soul having great challenges. Did he mean the suffering?"

"For sure," Clay said. "Evidently, Sogui was stricken with congenital scoliosis and extreme physical deformity as a small child, and she has been in constant pain her entire life. The professor told me that the disease twisted her spine hard to one side and stunted her growth. Malaria struck her at a young age and has returned continuously through her life. Twice, she contracted Dengue fever, which complicated the malaria even more. To top it off, she developed rheumatoid arthritis when she was in her late forties. Her entire life has been one giant bodily challenge."

"That sucks. You also said emotional challenges. What was that?"

"She lost both parents in tragic deaths at an early age. In the 1940s, when she was just seven years old, her mother took her into the jungle on the mainland to collect herbs, spices and fruits. Suddenly, Sogui was attacked by a young jaguar. Her mother fought off the jaguar but she was brutally mauled to death in front of Sogui. Sogui survived, but evidently, the traumatic images of that attack give her nightmares, even today."

"Yowsa."

"It gets worse. Just two years later when she was nine years old, her father and uncle disappeared while fishing off the coast of their island. Only broken and chewed-up fragments of their dugout canoe were discovered the next day. Speculation was that a migrating killer whale mistook their canoe for a manatee and, no doubt, feasted on the two unsuspecting fisherman who would have been thrown from the canoe."

Shali shook her head and grimaced. "I can see why Iqbal's guide said Sogui has been so challenged in this life."

"The professor told me that despite her lousy luck in life, her persevering and outgoing personality has driven her to become one of the strongest leaders in her little nation."

"Maybe I should use her as a role model."

Clay smiled at her jest. "Better yet, did you know the Kuna culture is matriarchal? The line of inheritance and family power actually passes down through women. I wonder if that had something to do with helping Sogui rise to societal leadership, even as a woman with severe disabilities." Clay took a sip of wine. "I've read that when a Kuna man marries, he has to move into the mother-in-law's house and work in pseudo-servitude for his new wife's family for a year or more." He sat back and shook his head. "If that's the case, there is *no* way I could be a Kuna man."

Shali gave him an inquisitive look and smiled. "I wonder if I can convert from an India Indian to a Kuna Indian? It's kind of the same, right? We're both Indians."

They laughed as the wine started to take effect.

Shali asked, "So what's up first?"

"We'll be meeting with the professor at the hotel tomorrow just to work out the logistics. Then we fly to San Blas to meet Sogui personally. If all works out, we'll ask Sogui to come back with us and do the regressions in Panama City."

Chapter 22

San Blas Islands, Panama

Clay, Shali and the professor made the short flight from Panama City to the small airfield on the San Blas Island of Ustupu Yantupo. As they walked down the ramp of the plane, the smell of ocean, salt and sea-life permeated the air. A soft, warm moist breeze blew in off the water. They walked from the small terminal building down to the dock where two motorized canoes took them the short distance through the archipelago to the island of Nargana.

They were met at the main dock of Nargana by two of Sogui's great-grand-nephews. The two young, dark-skinned boys with sharp ethnic facial features escorted the three travelers on the short walk to Sogui's house on the far side of the island. As they walked across the island, the musty smell of tropical village life and local cooking permeated the air. Palms leaves rustled in the breeze and the slight rolling of the surf on the beaches all around them was relaxing.

Clay chatted with Shali in English as they trailed along behind the boys. "Are you not just mesmerized by the tropical beauty? It's like paradise lost."

"Absolutely. This is truly a paradise if you can get past the simple living standard."

"The fact that they never allowed this place to be overrun by resort hotels is testimony to the strong will and independence of the Kuna. They managed to maintain their fundamental culture, traditions and simple life despite the lure of fast, easy money. They could have sold off their paradise to the resort chains at any time."

Shali asked, "Did you see the flag at the dock?"

"Yep"

"Is that the Kuna flag with a swastika?"

"Yep."

"I thought the swastika was outlawed just about everywhere. Isn't it politically incorrect?"

"They don't care. They used the swastika long before the Nazi Party. They are the only group in the world that still uses it as their national symbol. A form of the swastika has been the symbol of eternal life to the Hindus and Buddhists for thousands of years, but even they shy away from it today for political correctness."

"But doesn't this piss of the Jews?"

Clay chuckled. "Sorry, but the Kuna's don't care what the Jews think. It's their flag, not the Nazi's. Besides, it's not like it flies over the UN in New York. They are just an autonomous region under Panama."

In a few minutes they arrived at Sogui's hut-like island home, and she met them with open arms at the door. The main room was dark but cool. Light occasionally shimmered through the palm grass that made up the walls, and the aromatic smell of baking lingered in the air. Sogui served them fresh fruit drinks and traditional Kuna snacks. Her hospitality and inviting personality impressed them.

After some Latin-style chit chat to get acquainted, they finally got around to talking about why they were in San Blas. The professor opened the discussion and reviewed what Clay and Shali wanted to do with the regressions. Sogui sat back for a few minutes to absorb what she had heard and what she was being asked. The long pause was accentuated by rustling of the palm leaves above the island home and the lapping of the surf in the background. A waft of a neighbor's cooking drifted through the air. With narrowed eyes, Sogui looked at her two gringo visitors, alternating one to the other. Clay and Shali glanced at each other and knew this was a pivotal moment. Slowly, Sogui focused intently on Clay and spoke in her Kuna-laced Latin Spanish.

"*Senor*, so you will put me to sleep and talk to my soul, and my soul's ancestors." She slowly looked up at the ceiling and then turned her head toward the window. Quickly looking back to Clay, she continued, "Hmmm. Well, I suppose it won't kill me. But you don't want me to remember; your technique means I will not remember anything. If I allow this, will you tell me about my past lives when it is done?"

Clay responded in clear, concise Spanish, although it was laced with a slight gringo accent. "Normally we do not allow someone to remember their regressions. There may be terrible things that happened in a previous life, and it could be difficult for you emotionally. Later, perhaps we could - "

"*Mi Amigo,*" Sogui cut him off abruptly, yet politely. "Look at me. I am an old woman and have had a painful, crippled body for as long as I can remember. And you are telling me that remembering some bad past-life may be difficult for me to tolerate emotionally? Jejeje." She laughed out loud and then, still smiling, lifted a disfigured finger that had been twisted by years of arthritis. "If I see former lives, no matter how good or bad, it can't be more difficult than this life. *Si?*"

Clay politely acknowledged the nature of her supposition. "*Si, Senora.*"

Sogui paused and looked at each of her visitors for several seconds. "If I see that I really had previous lives, then that means there will be future lives, si? If I know that I will get a new body in my next life, don't you think it would feel pretty good to remember the details?"

"*Si, Senora.*"

Sogui paused, looking intensely at Clay. "Is it possible to do this regression where I remember everything?"

Clay looked at Shali then back to Sogui. "*Si, Señora,*" he said hesitantly.

Sogui immediately replied in a rapid, staccato tone, "Well, my young man, I will do it, but only on my conditions. I want to experience it all. I want to remember everything. *Comprende, Amigo?* Do you understand, my friend? You must allow me to remember it all!"

Clay leaned back in his chair and clasped his lips tightly. Shali and the professor stared at Clay, waiting for his response. Clay's expression turned to a smile and then he laughed out loud. "Mi Amiga, my friend, you are so refreshing." Clay paused for a moment and looked at Shali. Their eyes connected, and she nodded agreement.

Clay said, "*Entiendo a mi amiga.* I understand my friend. We will use a technique that will allow you to remember everything. In fact, you will remember much more than you tell us under hypnosis. After the session, even more of your past memory will come to you. But you have to promise me that if you remember something significant after the regressions, you will record it and tell us. We will give you a copy of the recordings of our sessions so you can play it as much as you want. This might help you remember even more. But we do ask you to keep it all secret until we find what we are looking for. Although, if you remember your life as a beautiful hot young woman in Madrid, you don't have to tell us *those* details." He winked at her.

At that, Sogui leaned back as best she could in her distorted body and let out a huge roll of laughter. "On the contrary, my son. If I experienced a good time as a beautiful hot young woman anywhere, I will tell everyone. And I will tell everything!"

All four of them laughed together. The bond was complete. They joined in more afternoon snacks and finished the day with a round of thick, sweet, black Panamanian coffee.

For two days, they stayed in a small lodge on the island and enjoyed the company of Sogui, her family and friends. Then the three of them, including Sogui, took motorized canoes back to the neighboring island airfield and flew the domestic shuttle plane back to Panama City.

Chapter 23

Panama City, Panama

After checking Sogui into her room at the Marriott, they all went to the hotel suite that was set up as the regression lab. To relieve any anticipation for the next day, Sogui agreed to go through a practice hypnosis session, which lasted forty-five minutes.

After coming back to full consciousness, Sogui smiled contently and said, "*Mi Amigo y Amiga*, this hypnosis is like sitting on a Nargana beach watching a beautiful sunset."

Shali smiled with a look of romanticism and asked Sogui, "Do you watch the sunset on the beach every night?"

With glowing smile, Sogui responded, "No, in San Blas, we are hypnotized by the sunset every night."

The next morning, Shali went to Sogui's room and escorted her to the regression suite. Clay helped Sogui settle into the lounge chair and hooked her up to the assortment of regression paraphernalia. As Sogui fidgeted with the pulse pads and goggles, Clay went through the formalities: "Today we are going to use a special procedure that we normally do not use. After the session, you will remember everything you saw and experienced in the regression. Do you understand this?"

"Si, si. I do," she responded and then began to play with her headphones.

"Please follow our instructions closely during the regression. You will be fully cognizant even though you are under hypnosis. At times, we might ask you to remove yourself from your body and only watch what you see like a movie. Please try your best to do this if we ask. OK?"

"Si," Sogui said slowly as she looked inquisitively at the equipment on the table next to her. Then she put the goggles over her eyes and moved her head as if looking around.

With a slight look of impatience, Clay continued, "As we told you in San Blas, we are looking for very important hidden secrets. We do not know where these secrets are located or even what they are exactly. However, we have reason to believe you may know from a past-life, or perhaps your soul guide might know. We suspect these secrets are documents or papers and not gold or jewels or other valuables. If we do not locate them during the regressions, you might see their location in a dream or during meditation in the future. If you do, please, talk to us only about the secrets - no one else. We believe there are people who have been trying to destroy these writings for thousands of years. They may stop at nothing to destroy these writings."

Sogui lifted the goggles from her eyes with an impatient scowl. "Enough foreplay, my son. Do you want me to die before I get to see any action?" She winked at him with a sneaky grin.

Clay smiled, glanced at Shali and put the goggles back on Sogui's eyes. He nodded at Shali to start the recording.

"This is Clay Barton, it is eight twelve a.m. in Panama City, Panama, on the twenty-ninth of March. This is the first in a sequence of past-life regression sessions on Sogui Iglesias, subject RB2837-JK3152; soul ID number DF73-7221. Shali Faisal is operating the control board. The objectives of the session are hypnosis and regression to previous lives. This will later be followed by an attempted transition to the LBL. Pre-hypnotic examination reveals that Sogui should easily adapt to PLR Protocol 73, being used for this regression. The subject will remember the entire regression experience after she comes out of hypnosis. She understands the possible adverse consequences of participating in this regression."

Clay walked Sogui carefully through the PLR 73 scripts. The regression took Sogui to the period starting four thousand years earlier. With excitement they discovered that Sogui's soul was Abraham himself about 1700 BC. Iqbal and Tommy's souls had lived the lives of his two sons, Isaac and Ishmael.

When they finished reviewing the life of Moses, Clay said to Shali, "We sort of anticipated it, but today we hit a good one."

"Agreed. The description of Abraham's life, from his own perspective, was very similar to what we learned in the two earlier regressions. With three versions from the same cluster of biblical characters, the facts seem to be pretty indefensible."

"I'd say so. The gist of many of the stories told by the Abrahamic religions may have happened, but their historical accuracy is far off, based on what we've heard. The Bible, Quran, Torah and Zohar were all obviously embellished to suit each of the religion's needs."

Clay continued the regression of Sogui, while Shali clicked away on the laptop, searching for evidence of the next life. Sogui revealed the life of another famous person from the mid-1600s BC. As Sogui continued describing the life, Shali politely interrupted Clay, "Hey, this Zoroaster was a damn famous Iranian prophet and poet. Try asking her about *The Gathas*. It's a large, ancient collection of cryptic Sanskrit verses he wrote. It's almost unintelligible."

Clay nodded and turned to Sogui. "Tell me, in this life as Zoroaster, did you write a book called *The Gathas*?"

A slight smile of pleasure grew on Sogui's face. "Yes. Poems."

"What were you trying to say in *The Gathas*?"

"The truth of the creation, the sun, the moon and the stars. The creator, the light, the power of one, the universe. All is one."

"Where did you get this knowledge and how did you learn this truth you wanted to bring to others?"

"The Creator."

"Who is the Creator? What and where is the Creator?"

"We are the Creator. We are one."

"Why did you write this truth in poems? In verses? Why not write it in prose or words that were easier for others to understand?"

"I like poems; it sounds better."

Shali gave Clay a quizzical look and then lifted her hands, palms up, and whispered a Homer Simpson-like, "Dohhh."

Clay smiled sheepishly then continued with Sogui. "The words in *The Gathas* sound confusing, like a puzzle. Did you write like this on purpose?"

There was a long pause with no response. He nodded to Shali who shot a long micro-pulse to the Third Eye pulse pad.

No response came after several more prompts and micro-pulse shots.

Clay continued with the uneventful regression of the life and then moved to the peaceful death of Zoroaster at an old age.

While letting Sogui rest and reminisce about that life for a few minutes, Shali said to Clay, "Do you think *The Gathas* are secret encoded messages this soul pod has been writing about for millennia? Like Jabir, and Ezra Pound's *Cantos*? If it is - and assuming we find these writings - how in hell are we going to be able to decode it all?"

"It could be, and to be honest I'm not sure how we'll ever decode any of it."

Shali looked back at the laptop and said, "After Zoro, an entire ancient religion called Zoroastrianism spun off - almost like a cult. It was evidently significant because it was formative for many modern religions. It established the single-god theory and kind of broke people out of worshiping bunches of gods, like the Greeks and Persians who worshiped several gods like Zeus, Athena, Apollo, Neptune and such. Zoro, here, led the change to just one god. But even though it had more initial influence than any other religion, it was nearly wiped out by a big Islamic expansion in Iran. If you don't agree with it, crush it, huh?"

Clay nodded and then moved on to the next life. Another home-run incarnation came with the life of Moses himself around 1300 BC.

Sogui's soul described the details of her life as Moses while Clay whispered to Shali, "Iqbal's soul lived as Aaron, Moses brother; Tommy's soul was Miriam, Moses' sister. More proof that this soul pod reincarnated together."

Shali replied, "Exactly. Sogui reiterated what Tommy's and Iqbal's souls said about Moses and Aaron not parting the Red Sea or turning the ocean to blood. They did not start famines or cause disasters. Moses just took advantage of the opportunity to claim credit for anomalous natural events. The historical rumor mill put the magic into their powers."

Clay turned to Sogui. "Why did you deceive the Pharaoh with these natural events?"

Sogui laughed out loud. "That Pharaoh was so gullible, so naive."

Clay probed further, "As Moses, did you have any prophetic, magical or super powers?"

The soul's reply was rapid, blunt and almost sarcastic: "Are you kidding me?"

Clay and Shali looked at each other and quietly laughed. Shali whispered, "She is using the same direct, spontaneous language as Tommy's soul. His soul must be rubbing off on her."

"Very likely," Clay whispered back. "Think about it: if people hang around together, they often pick up similar mannerisms. It's probably the same with soul mates."

They proceeded to review Sogui's next past life as the Queen of Sheba. It was not surprising that Sogui's soul had incarnated as the Queen of Sheba to be with a soul pod mate in King Solomon. Sogui's detailed description of her passionate sexual liaison with Solomon was not surprising to Clay or Shali considering her current life's experience. Before starting the regression, Sogui had joked she wanted to see hot love affairs of her past lives. Now she would vividly remember every passionate love-making session she had with Solomon - and others. Yet her strong feelings for Solomon persisted through that life. When the Sogui died in that life as the Queen, she said she saw Solomon's eyes in the look of their son as he sat beside her on her death bed.

As they finished the life of the Queen of Sheba, Shali smiled sheepishly at Clay with teary eyes. "What a love story, huh? This would make a good chick-flick. Her past lives are even better than Iqbal's and Tommy's. We'll be disappointed when we end up regressing normal lives again."

"But look at all three of their lives as they live today. They are all plain, ordinary people with no connection between them. Let's keep going and see what's next."

Chapter 24

Clay stretched his arms and rolled his head to stretch his neck. "Move to the door that takes you to the next life of a historically known person. What do you see? Where are you? Are you there, now?"

"Yes. My name is Kong Fudza. I am known as Master Kong. I am a writer, a teacher. No a philosopher. Yes, a teacher and a philosopher, but only for the last years. I have done so many different things in my life. But now I just teach others."

"What year is it?" Clay asked. "How old are you and where are you?"

"It is 460. No, 480 ... 486 BC. I am sixty-five years old. I live in a town in a province in the East. Lu, Lu Qu Fu, east of the mountain. Tai Hang Mountain. It is cold, now. Very cold; but it is beautiful and I am peaceful. It has not been so peaceful in the past."

"Tell me about your past. Return to your younger days."

There was a hesitation, and Shali gave her a shot of micro-pulse to the Third Eye.

"No, my childhood was difficult. My mother was a young girl when I was born and my father was an old man, and they never married. I did not know my father because he died when I was a baby. My mother raised me by herself because she was outcast by the village. We had very little money and life was difficult, but she was a good mother. She died young, though.

"Later in this life, I saw my mother in my son's eyes - and my son gave me a grandson. I am very close to my grandson; we are together all the time. I teach my grandson with my other students. After I am gone, he must continue to teach others what is right and wrong."

Sogui paused and smiled with deep satisfaction. "I once tended cows in the fields, but I did not like that. Then I worked in an office for the local justice. I later became a judge or a magistrate, myself. There was much corruption. I did not like that, either. It was so wrong, so unfair; I could not be a part of that corruption." Sogui continued to expound on this life as Master Kong.

Clay looked over to Shali and quietly commented, "This guy sure is a Chatty-Kathy, huh?"

"Yes, but who the hell is he? Kong Fudza. I'm not finding anything in the files or on the 'net. I need more data points."

"Data points? You techno-weenie."

Shali flushed red and nodded her head toward Sogui, signaling for Clay to keep moving.

Sogui continued describing this life: "My wife was nice when we were young. I loved her very much, but she became a bitch. She nagged me all the time, so I stayed away to do my work. What is her problem, anyway? I love her, but I don't want to be around her; she is just plain nasty. I focus on my studies. I read, study, think and talk to others. I enjoy discussing social and behavioral issues with my students. But sometimes I feel like I am lost, as if I am not in my own body. Sometimes I have difficulty concentrating or focusing, but only sometimes. Other times I feel euphoric, like I am one with the universe and can see to infinity. Most of my life I feel this, but it has increased in my later years in this body."

There was a pause. Clay allowed Sogui time to absorb what her soul saw. He turned to Shali, who was feverishly searching the Internet in an attempt to identify this person.

"Shali, this regression sounds more like what we are used to seeing: a regular person with all of the difficult and confusing problems of life. Sogui's blunt commentary makes this a little entertaining - not as good as Tommy, but interesting nonetheless."

Shali did not even look up. "Yeah, I hear you."

"Find anything at all?"

"Nothing. This Kong guy is obviously Chinese, and that makes it difficult to find connections, even if he was famous. Romanizing Chinese characters often butchers words in translation. Plus Chinese sometimes reverse their names, cut the names short or use nicknames. The pronunciation of a single spoken Chinese character could have a dozen different possible written characters or meanings. To complicate it further, geographic names in China have changed a lot in the last several thousand years."

"Don't worry, Shali. We'll get another shot during the LBL. We can always dig in tonight and see if we can find something. We'll have to wrap up soon anyway. We have to keep our days shorter with Sogui since this has got to be hard on her."

Shali looked up. "You're right. She is remembering everything too, so should we ease off and let her sleep on it?"

"Yeah. Her body is not in the greatest shape. I'll do one more life after Kong and then quit for today. We'll take tomorrow off, head to the mountains and let her rest for a day."

Clay finished reviewing the life of the unknown Chinese guy from east of the mountains. This life ended in a mournful death that followed soon after the death of his son.

Chapter 25

Clay looked over to Shali. She nodded for him to proceed. "Continue down the hall to the door of the next life of a historically prominent person. Enter the door. What do you see? Where are you?"

No response.

"Are you there?"

Shali pressed the button for a micro-pulse shock to the balls of Sogui's feet. Her feet curled up slightly.

"Are you at the door?"

No response.

Shali pressed a shock on the shoulder pads.

Sogui snapped, "No. No. There are two doors. I've went in one but I've already been in that door."

"OK, go to the other door. Open it and go inside. Tell me what you see."

"It is a beautiful house. A big house. Even more. This is a palace. It is huge and beautiful."

"Walk through this palace and tell me what you see. Look at yourself and describe yourself."

"I am a young man. I am a prince, and this all belongs to me. But I am empty, lost. I do not know why I am so confused, so helpless. My wife is in the other side of the palace. She gave me a wonderful son, but I feel affection only on the outside. Inside, there is nothing; I need more."

"Where are you located now?"

"In Nepal, in the West of Nepal. Capi ... lava ... du. Capila ... vasdu. Capilavasdu. It sounds something like that."

Clay leaned over to Shali. "See if you find that on GoogleEarth. Look around Nepal, India and Tibet; the borders have shifted over time. The Indians didn't mess around with their geographical names as much as the Chinese, so it might be easier to find." He turned back Sogui. "What is your name?"

"Sidada ... Gadada ... Sigada ... Gadama. Something like that."

Clay glanced at Shali, but she was furiously clicking away on the laptop, running multiple Internet search engines to figure out who this was and where they had been living.

Clay continued the script while Shali searched and occasionally pressed a micro-pulse shock button on Clay's cue.

"What year is it now and how old are you?"

"It is 500...550...540. Yes, 545 BC. I am a young adult. I think I am nineteen years old."

Shali clicked away on the keyboard and then stopped. Her eyebrows curled inward, her lips narrowed firmly in excitement. She suddenly swung her chair away from the laptop and grabbed the binder with the timeline of the last four thousand years of historically famous people. She furiously flipped through the pages. "Holy crap, Clay. I think this is the Buddha. Yeah, I'm telling you, I think this is Siddhartha Gautama. His father was the king of a small kingdom around Kapialvastu in Nepal before he ran off to India and freaked out on meditation. Could Sogui really be the Buddha?"

A huge smile broke out on Clay's face. "Oh boy. OK, I've got a rough idea of Buddha's story, so I'll play it along. We just might have the pot-belly, himself."

Clay continued the regression for fifteen minutes and took the soul through his many years spent fasting, abstaining and meditating. "Move forward in this life to a time of great peacefulness for your soul. Move to a time when you are always in meditation, deep in thought, deep in peace. Where are you? What year is it? Describe everything around you and what you are doing."

"I am in the south now. India. Platna. No, Gaya. The land is flat, dry, boring. Boring is good for me now, because it is difficult to meditate in a place of wonderful beauty like my father's land. I am fifty-eight years old. Sometimes it is so hot I go into the river to cool down. The rivers are wide and shallow, so I lie in the river. The water is cool from the mountains. I like to lie under the trees to rest and meditate. Many people follow me around wherever I go. They think I have great wisdom and hidden secrets for peacefulness."

"Do you have wisdom or secret knowledge? If you have this wisdom, where did you get it and what did you do with it?"

There was a long pause. Shali shot Sogui with a three second micro-pulse to the Third Eye. Sogui's head turned upward slightly from the stimulus.

"Yes. I was given this knowledge by the elders in my meditation. I am told not to reveal much of the knowledge. The people are not ready. There are lessons to be learned, and they cannot learn their lessons if this knowledge is revealed to the world. They will not know what to do with the knowledge. It will be abused and lessons will not be learned under the best circumstances."

Clay asked, "So what did you do with this knowledge?"

"I write. It is written. For years, I have had two scribes working with me to write it. But what is written cannot be understood by most. The real truth is hidden in the words."

"What is the key to unlocking the truth hidden in the words? Who has this key?"

"The key to the secrets are in the mind. One can only get the key from the elders in the fullest of meditation. You must go to the other side and become one with the universe before the key is revealed."

Clay leaned forward in his chair, "Where did you put these secrets? Where are the writings now?"

"It is all very safe now."

Clay and Shali's heads snapped toward each other. Clay whispered to Shali, "She knows something about the secrets..."

Shali quietly interrupted. "I agree, but there's a problem here. You know the last life we got? The Chinese Fudza guy? It is almost a complete overlap with this life. Buddha-boy here is about ten years older than Fudza, but they both lived to be sixty or seventy. It's nearly a complete overlap. Something is wrong."

Clay looked puzzled for a moment, but then his face grew into a huge smile. "Whoa. Assuming the years are fairly accurate, we may have a dual life here. I've never run across a full dual life. I've had simultaneous incarnations when somebody got Alzheimer's or went into a coma, stuff like that. But never a full-fledged dual life for one soul."

"What the hell are you talking about, Chief? Are you saying that a soul can live two full lives at the same time?"

"Yeah, and maybe more. I read about it but have never seen it. But the soul evidently gets stretched very thin. It takes a lot of energy for a soul to live out a human life. If they live a dual life, the lives supposedly are not up to full speed - you know, circuit-overload. But on the other hand, this Buddha spends most of his life meditating. His soul is up in the hinterland chatting it up with the elders, sucking them dry for the big secrets. In this case, the soul doesn't have to spend that much time dealing with an actual human life; he is just meditating."

Shali's voice rose with excitement: "Hey, remember what King Kong Fudza said? That he often felt lost or wasn't in his own body, or something like that? We can review the recording tomorrow, but it's no wonder he was spaced out. He wasn't getting the soul's full attention."

As Sogui rattled on about her life as the Buddha, Shali's face suddenly turned dead serious. "Clay, Clay, listen: Kong Fudza. KongFudz. Confucius. Could this soul have been Confucius, at the same time that he was Buddha? Wait, let me check the lifespan on Confucius."

Shali grabbed the binder and flipped to Confucius' timeline. "It's a dead ringer!" she exclaimed. "These two were right on top of each other, time-wise. Confucius and Buddha must have been the same soul at the same time. Freak me out, man. *Freak* me out!"

Clay laughed at Shali's out-of-character excitement. "I think you're right. Hey, remember Iqbal's life as Ezra Pound? Pound wrote *The Cantos*. I remember reading there was an entire section about Confucius. These two souls are in the same pod, so it makes sense that one would have an infatuation with the other, and would write about them, albeit fifteen hundred years later. Let's run Sogui through the rest of the Buddha's life and wrap it up for today. She's going to need a day or two just to decompress. This is almost too much to comprehend. She knows something about the secrets, though."

They finished walking through the life of the Buddha and brought Sogui back to consciousness with the seldom-used PLR 73 scripts. After taking off the goggles, headphones and cap, Sogui lay quietly in the chair for a long time. She stared off into blankness, recalling all she had just seen. When she sat up, her thirst was almost unquenchable. Slowly she began to talk just a little about her experience. An hour later, Shali shut down all of the recording equipment and escorted Sogui back to her room. They agreed to meet in the lobby in one hour for dinner.

At dinner, Sogui started to rattle off details that had not come out during the regression session. To ensure they did not miss anything, Shali began recording on her portable voice recorder.

"Mi Amiga, Amigo, my friends, today I was freed from the pain in this life and deprivation of the pleasures of a normal person. These regressions have freed me from pain, physical contortion and social stigma." Sogui breathed in deeply, smiled and slowly exhaled her relief while looking into the distance.

Shali smiled and said, "I noticed that your description of previous life experiences focused on many of the physical bodily pleasures."

Sogui nodded vigorously. "Yes, and I am so upset with my life as Buddha. By choice, I gave up all physical pleasure and I self-inflicted hunger, pain and deprivation on myself. Can you believe that?" She shook her head with disdain. "And I had this beautiful wife. Talk about hot! No sex for the rest of my life? What was I thinking? Just to meditate? Ja! I could have meditated and still had sex with this bonita chica - and what a beautiful chick she was. Stupid me, I go off the desert to meditate for the rest of my life? Ja!"

Clay and Shali looked at each other and laughed out loud. Sogui then flashed back to her life as the Queen of Sheba. "Ohhhh, I was a good looker, you know. So tall, slender, nice boobs and black as the night. Yeah, I was one hot lady. And Solly? Oh yeah, Solly was so good. I'm glad he had all those other wives; they just warmed him up. *Hola Hombre*, hello man, we could heat up his palace to a hot bed of ecstasy."

Fortunately, the three had a private corner in the restaurant. Clay almost fell off his chair laughing as Sogui babbled on about practically every sexual encounter she had experienced in her previous lives.

Chapter 26

After a taking off a day to relax in the cool tropical green mountains west of Panama City, they were back to another day of regression. Much to their surprise and Clay's elation - the first life revealed Ammonius Saccas of 200 AD: teacher and mentor of Tommy's soul's life as Plotinus and the life Clay had been seeking since the beginning of his quest, even though he did not know why. After nearly an hour with Ammonius, Sogui had revealed absolutely nothing of relevance about the secrets.

Clay shifted his focus and asked, "In this life as Ammonius, did you know a person named Plotinus?"

"Yes. Yes, he was a good student: dedicated, focused, older than most students. But he played a holier-than-thou game. Plotinus pretended to be down-to-earth and proper, and everyone thought he was morally righteous. Hypocrisy. Plotinus was such a womanizer. He tried to screw anything he could find, but he was careful not to show it. He campaigned around the world with his philosophical and moral theories intermixed with his private love-making marathons."

There was a short pause and a half-grin slowly grew on Sogui's face.

Clay prompted her. "Please continue."

"Plotinus heard rumors that I preferred men over women. Not so; I could go either way." She laughed out loud. "But he was paranoid about being intimate with a man. One day, I grabbed his ass and whispered love words in his ear. He ran from me like a rabbit in a field of hovering eagles." Sogui laughed again, paused a few seconds then continued in a more serious tone. "Later he moved to Rome. He needed to be around the big players. Alexandria was for intellectuals. We had the library and the museum; we were too studious for him. But Rome - ah, Rome was for philosophers, power mongers, and lovers, of course."

Clay leaned to Shali. "Ammonius seemed to be a bit cynical, yet he is amusing. I've been looking for this guy for almost five years, so I'm going to spend more time on him, even though we haven't found anything significant yet."

Shali nodded.

Later in the regression, as the soul approached the death of Ammonius Saccas, Shali noticed Clay's disappointment in finding nothing significant in this key target of his search. Clay then probed for Ammonius' confused religious positions, which had been documented in the history books. "Your parents were devoted Christians, were they not?"

Sogui chuckled smugly. "Yes, they were in deep."

"Were you a Christian?"

"I left the church," Sogui snapped back immediately. "It was a ruse. They worshiped icons and made this dead fanatical Jew in Jerusalem into an icon, a god. I believe in finding, learning and revealing the truth. That is not the truth. They proclaimed this Jew as the son of the God, but we are all God. We are all one."

Clay's forehead wrinkled. "So how did you feel about the Christian Church?"

"If you speak against them too loud, they will kill you as a heretic - like the Romans, they were."

Clay reared his head at that answer. He glanced at Shali and then continued. "Do you believe that everyone has a soul, and that all souls are connected?"

"Of course I do. Who do you think you are talking to, a ghost?" Sogui laughed out loud.

Shali could not hold back her laughter either. Clay glanced at her as if embarrassed by Sogui's cynical comment and then smiled.

Sogui continued without hesitation: "One soul is a small part of the whole."

While Sogui's soul proselytized, Shali leaned over to Clay, "We can continue this little religious debate with 'sarcasticus' Ammonius, but it is not going to get us where we want to go."

Clay nodded and said with a smirk, "Alright, I'll cut off the philosophical chatter and get Ammonius to die for us."

After the life-ending dialog, Clay let Sogui rest for a few minutes. He said to Shali, "Did you notice we're getting some big gaps in time? Hundreds of years are missing. We haven't been that selective on prominent or famous people so we should be getting most every life."

"Yeah, I wondered about that. Maybe these lives were so intense that the soul needed time to recuperate – charge the batteries, so to speak."

"But I feel like we're missing something, here."

"Maybe there were simple, less-complex lives in those gaps. When we get to the LBL phase, we can always poke it again."

Chapter 27

Clay prompted Sogui, "Move to the next prominent life that you lived. Open the door. Walk through, and look around. What do you see? Where are you? Are you there yet?"

"Yes. Yes, I am there. I am a woman now. Oh, I am a beautiful woman with long silky hair and fresh golden skin. But I am committed to my work. It is a man's world now, so I am out of place. I have offended many because I am a woman and I assert myself. I am in Egypt. Alexandria. This is such a beautiful city. I have traveled much, but to me, Alexandria is home and has the most beauty, the most character, the most culture."

"What year is it? How old are you? What is your name?"

"It is now 400. 405. Yes, 405 AD. I am forty-five years old and well respected. I feel good about this life. I have accomplished much, but I have much more to do. My name is Hipaja. My father was Theon. He was famous both in Alexandria and throughout the entire Empire. He was a great mathematician - a true scholar - and he knew medicine and architecture. He was very wise and intelligent and was known as the 'man of the museum' - the great Alexandria Museum. He also worked very closely with the library."

Hearing this, Clay and Shali looked up intently at each other. They both leaned forward in their chairs with a sense of excitement. Shali turned to her laptop and began clicking away.

Clay said, "Tell me more about the Alexandrian Library."

Sogui's face shone with pleasure. "The library was beautiful and so full of knowledge. The writings were in every language from all over the world; so much knowledge and truth!" Then her face grew scornful. "But there were people, people who wanted to destroy the library. We had to protect the knowledge before it was destroyed. Daddy was sure they would destroy the most sacred knowledge in the library."

"Tell me more about your father. What was he like? What did he do with the library?"

"Daddy was my mentor, my teacher. When I was young, he sent me to the great cities of the Empire to study and bring back knowledge. Rome, Athens, Florence, Constantinople. I studied, learned and debated with great philosophers in all these cities. I owe him gratitude for his kindness, his wisdom and his devotion to knowledge and truth."

Clay perked up and his eyes widened. He now realized precisely who they had in Sogui's regression. He whispered to Shali, "This has to be Hypatia. There should be a lot written about her. I even think there were some old movies about her. See what details you can get and find out whether she did anything with the contents from the library. Maybe she was the one who stashed the writings!"

Shali madly clicked away on the laptop. "I'm ahead of you; I've got her already. Damn hot, Clay. *Wiki* says she was believed to be the last librarian of the Alexandrian Library. Even the famous Carl Sagan was convinced Hypatia was the last Alexandrian librarian before its demise. This has to be why Iqbal's guide pointed us to Sogui. Why the hell didn't we figure this out before?"

Clay turned back to Sogui. "What do you do in this life of Hipaja? Do you work in the library?"

"I have been the director of the Platonist School of Alexandria for five years now. The school teaches philosophers and educators the knowledge of Plato, Aristotle, Plotinus, and Ptolemy. We believe in and encourage open debate and the discussion of different philosophies. My students come from all corners of the Empire. They are from famous and wealthy families. In our school, we want truth to be revealed."

Clay probed Sogui harder. "Tell me more about the library. How are you involved with it?"

There was a long pause, and a two-second micro-pulse shock that did not get a response.

Clay prompted again. "Be aware that you are not actually living this life; this life was lived many, many years ago and you are only viewing it. No one and no *thing* can harm you in any way. Did you try to save the contents of the library?"

Shali shot Sogui a three-second pulse to the Third Eye.

"Yes," Sogui responded immediately. "I was the head of the secret council to save the knowledge. We were a small group of men and women - all wealthy, all powerful. We all had the same desire, the same objective." Sogui's voice became higher in pitch and volume. "But I made enemies over the years. I must be more careful. These people are powerful and stand to lose if the truth comes out."

Clay asked, "Who are they?"

"Right now, there are two men in particular, who have grown to despise me. The first is Cyril, in Alexandria, who just became bishop. He is a Greek and an influential Orthodox, and he has become powerful even at his young age. I do not agree with his ideals or with his religious fanaticism, and I have personally told him this many times. We have debated and argued and now he is angry and full of hatred for me.

"Also, there is Socrates Scholasticus from Constantinople. He was a follower of the teachings of Ammonius Saccas. However, he has distorted Ammonius' ideas. I *know* he distorts Ammonius, and I have told him so. He is another Greek Christian, and a hypocrite. There are others too - religious zealots who are not open to other ideas or thoughts; they will not allow other beliefs. They have only their selfish desire to retain power over their people. But I must be careful. At least until we arrange safe passage for the writings from the library."

Clay moved to the front of his chair and said, "You talked about a secret council for the library. Who is on this council? What has the council done?"

"There are several of us, but we represent many more. We want to preserve the thousands of years' worth of writings that have been collected. There is so much knowledge, so many documents. It will take a lifetime, maybe more, to read, analyze and understand the words in the documents. There are so many languages, so many thoughts, and so much wisdom. But now, we must move it all to a safe place where future scholars and philosophers can recover the knowledge and begin again."

Sogui began to talk about details of her life as Hypatia, some of which were revealing but others that were confusing. Shali asked Clay, "She seems to be jumping back and forth between past and present tense. What is all of this flipping back and forth?"

"I don't know. We haven't seen much of this behavior before."

"It sounds like they haven't moved the secrets yet, and according to history she doesn't have much longer to live in this life. We have a better chance finding the location of the secrets in the LBL, so we should move on," Shali said. "I suspect only the guide can tell us where to find the writings."

Clay turned back to Sogui. "Go, now, to the last moments of this life. Tell me what you see and what you experience at the end of this life."

Sogui said in a matter-of-fact tone, "I am on my way home from the school; it is late. We had a council meeting tonight to discuss the first move of the documents from the library, and now I am on the back of my chariot. It is a cool and clear evening with beautiful and crisp air. The smell of kitchen fire is in the air tonight. Someone is baking bread." She took a deep, slow breath and smiled. "My driver is always so careful. It is a nice ride home tonight. We turn the corner of the street to my house. What is this? Who are all these people? Why are they outside of my house?" Sogui's voice suddenly rises to a higher pitch and volume. "Wait! They see me and are coming this way with their torches, running and yelling. They hide their faces in shrouds and robes. They are coming at me. My driver is trying to turn the chariot. Please, hurry! Turn! Go quickly. They are running at us. Go quickly."

Sogui began to wrench her head from side to side as the regression was obviously putting her under stress. She continued yelling in an increasingly terrified voice, begging her chariot driver to get away from the fast approaching mob.

"Oh my God, Clay!" Shali shouted over Sogui's cries. She quickly looked up from the laptop. "Clay, they are going to kill her. A mob butchered her alive. She is in first person and reliving this. You need to bring her up! Get her out of there."

"Yeah, I know, but we've never had a problem. She'll be alright. There's been a debate about Hypatia's death for a thousand years. Every movie and book made about her gives it a different twist. Let's get the real scoop."

Clay focused on his target. "Sogui! You will not be hurt by what you see. This is not happening now. It happened thousands of years ago. You will not be harmed in any way. Come out of the body and only look at the body from above."

"Stop! No!" Sogui screamed. "They are pulling me off the chariot. They are hitting me! Beating me! Why are they doing this? Why? No, stop. Please stop! They are beating me with sticks and whips. Ten, twelve of them. It hurts so much. I can hear my bones breaking. Please, stop. Now they are stripping me, tearing off my clothes, tying ropes to my arms and legs. Please, no. They are dragging me down the street to the courtyard and yelling terrible things. Ahh, stretching me out with ropes, pulling me, stretching. Who are you and why are you doing this?"

"Sogui, listen to me," Clay shouted loudly. "Remove yourself from the body. Remove yourself from the body, now. Only look down on the body as if this is a movie. Get out of the body, *now*."

Shali yelled, "Bring her out. Get her out."

Sogui's screams echoed through the hotel suite: "Ahhh! No, it's you! I know you. And you. You are the monks, the monks. Please stop. Why are you doing this to me? No! What is that? Stop. No. Oyster shells, broken oyster shells scraping the skin off of my body. The pain!"

She continued screaming as Clay shook her in an attempt to break her out of the hypnotic trance. "Sogui, you will awaken now! Wake up. Leave that body and come back to the present. Come back to here and now. Sogui! Sogui!" He shook her with near violence.

Sogui screamed again. "Scraping skin off my body. Raw, bloody. My flesh. I see the bones. Cannot stop it, only pain. No! No, stop. Not fire. There is wood and fire, torches on fire. No, please just kill me. Please kill me. Stop dragging me on fire. I am not dead. I will not die. Let me die, please. The fire. Stop. The pain. Die. Please die."

Clay physically lifted Sogui up in his arms. "Sogui, wake up!" He propped her up to full sitting position and pulled off the headphones, goggles and cap. As soon as he pulled the pulse pad from her forehead, Shali threw a glass of water on Sogui's face and slapped her cheeks. She stopped screaming, and with Clay holding her upright, she finally opened her eyes and glanced around the room with a dazed look of absolute terror. She looked as if she was about to scream, but nothing came out.

She slowly shook her head side to side, as if still trying to wake up from the nightmare. Sweat soaked her body. In a few minutes, her body began to tremble and shake from the withdrawal of adrenaline.

"For Christ's sake, Clay," Shali yelled in a near panic. "Her heart rate hit over one hundred eighty beats per minute. This is entirely too fast for a frail, old woman."

Clay nodded and held a glass of water to Sogui's mouth. She sipped the cool water to quench her parched throat.

Shali wiped Sogui's face, neck and arms with a wet cloth to calm her. It took several minutes after coming out of the hypnosis before Sogui had recovered enough to be cognizant of the surroundings. She looked Shali directly in the eyes and then at Clay. In a colloquial Kuna-accented Spanish she blasted out loud, "Wow. What a ride. Those bastards! I'd kick their asses if I could. Damn it, Clay, you said it wouldn't hurt."

At that, Clay and Shali looked at each other with relief.

"Sogui, I am so sorry," Clay said in a conciliatory tone. "It should not have hurt. We've never had this happen. You went inside your previous life and relived the experience. This is why we don't normally allow people to remember their regressions. When we control everything in hypnosis, we try to keep you away from bad events, but your subconscious pushed itself inside that life and would not respond to us. You obviously felt everything that your soul felt that night. It should not happen when we get to the next phase: the life between your past lives. One thing we do know is that your soul is definitely connected to what we are looking for, but we need to be more careful."

"I understand," she said, "but this hurt. I felt every cut, every scrape, and every burn. And yet right now, I feel so alive. I feel rich. I am energized." She looked at the ceiling, paused and then said, "Let's keep going."

"No, no, no," Shali fired back. "We're stopping for today. You need to recuperate. This was harder on you than you think."

"OK, but you are looking for what we had in the library, aren't you? She knew – Hypatia knew. *I* knew. You want those documents. You want that knowledge, don't you? That's what you are looking for."

Clay glanced at Shali with a sheepish grin as if he had been caught with his hand in the cookie jar. He looked back to Sogui and responded, "Si, Si, yes, of course. We don't know exactly what we are after, but it is probably what your soul was trying to move out of Alexandria before the monks killed her."

"Oh, mi Amigo, I want to help you. When you find it, I have to see it all, in this life, in this body. I must see it. Will you do that? I have a job to finish, you know. Well, Hypatia has a job to finish, and I am going to help her."

"I promise," Clay responded. "If we find it, I will personally see to it that you can see, touch and feel every document again, in this life. But we are going to skip the individual life regressions from here. It is too risky. If we continue this way, we won't know what we are going to run into. Your soul evidently wants to relive the past despite how painful it was. We will try to deal directly with your guide from now on. Is tomorrow OK, or do you need another day to rest?"

"Tomorrow is fine. But did you know that I was a virgin? I mean, Hypatia was a virgin. I was a gorgeous, beautiful, voluptuous, fifty-five-year-old virgin. What the hell was wrong with me? Look at this body of mine, now. It's torn, tattered and twisted, but I'm not even close to being a virgin. Hell, I'll get up from this chair and take you on right now. Bring it on, my young boy. Can you handle me?"

Clay and Shali broke out in rolling laughter at Sogui's raw sense of humor. They closed up the regression suite and migrated to the hotel lobby for afternoon Sangria. Despite her current difficult life, Sogui was completely alive and vibrant with energy.

On their second pitcher of Sangria, they told Sogui about their regressions with her soul-mates Tommy and Iqbal, and they explained Iqbal's former life as King Solomon.

"Hola! When I was the Queen of Sheba and this Iqbal was my Solly, we had the hottest sex-filled summer Jerusalem has ever seen. Tell Iqbal I'm ready to do it again. Some day in this life, maybe you can bring my two soul mates to the beach in San Blas. I'd like to show them paradise."

The three of them joked and laughed through dinner. Later, when Clay and Shali met alone in the regression suite to review what had happened before they retired for the night, Shali revealed her concern. "This incident with Hypatia was simply too close to the edge for comfort."

"I know. I've seldom used Protocol 73, so I'm not sure what went wrong."

"Like you told Sogui, let's restrict the dialogue to the guide or an elder from here on and not get in direct contact with the soul, especially when we get to Hypatia's life."

Chapter 28

The next morning, they started the regression at eight a.m. sharp. Sogui immediately dropped into a deep trance. The guide came forward, and Clay moved directly to the LBL phase. He walked the guide through a review of each life identified in the earlier regressions.

In late morning, Shali pulled Clay aside and asked, "Have you noticed how different this guide is compared to the two previous guides?"

"I sure did. Sogui's guide is softer in composure and less rigid, although she is still another hard-ass."

"It seems that each guide has a unique personality."

"But if you think about it, guides are just advanced souls. Every soul is different, just as living people are all different. This particular guide was much more objective and less opinionated than the others."

Shali said, "Well, the Akashic records affirmed everything we heard from Sogui's soul before the incident with Hypatia. But this guide was awfully opinionated about, and almost spiteful toward, organized religions. There was certainly no holding back on criticizing them."

Clay nodded. "All of the guides in this soul pod seem to be somewhat critical of religions."

Shali said, "Agreed. We better roll though the rest of her lives and get to down to asking about our treasures."

Clay led the guide through many past lives that had not been previously revealed before the Hypatia incident. The first life revealed for Sogui's soul was Al-Farabi, a renowned Arabian scholar in Baghdad in 900s AD. Al-Farabi had been heavily influenced by Aristotle, Plato, Porphyry, Ptolemy, most of whom were lives of the other souls in the pod. The next life was Solomon ibn Gabirol, a Spanish medieval scholar in 1,000 AD. Gabirol was suspected of having rewritten parts of the Bible's Old Testament but was murdered by an Islamic follower of Mohammad. Next was Henry More, a 1600s Platonist in Cambridge, England. More was a prolific writer of philosophical positions against idolatry. Then Sogui's described the life of Thomas Paine in 1700s England and United States. Paine had authored a written piece called *Common Sense*, which stimulated the American Revolution against England. Paine was also the author of many other documents that helped lead to the French Revolution. He also authored *The Age of Reason*, which advocated Deism, rejected notions of supernatural Gods and threw serious doubt in the face of religious beliefs, even in those days.

They finally reviewed a final life in the late 1800s, after which they paused the regression to regroup and let Sogui's mind rest.

Clay said to Shali, "I just cannot believe that three souls from one pod could have had so many lives that contributed so significantly to human society. But this last one is intriguing to me."

"I know. I'm reading here that Helen P. Blavatsky was the Russian-American founder of Theosophy and the Theosophical Society. Blavatsky was the author of a book called *The Secret Doctrine, the Synthesis of Science, Religion and Philosophy*? It's supposed to be a large multi-volume reconciliation of ancient Eastern knowledge and modern science." Continuing to look at her laptop screen she continued, "She claimed that she got knowledge from Indian mahatmas who retained the secret knowledge from the Ancients. She also claimed she was the one 'chosen' to reveal the knowledge to mankind. Ironically enough, Blavatsky's writings were sometimes said to have been a foundation for Hitler's Nazi Germany."

"Yes, I know. I'm well versed on her. But the rumors about Hitler were later proven to be politically motivated fabrications. There were organizations trying to discredit both the Theosophical society and her reputation. In her writings, she often referred to Aryans, but I think it was fundamentally different than Hitler's Aryan race. Her ideas totally were taken out of context."

"Then what's this secret knowledge of Blavatsky's from the Ancients?"

"I've been trying to figure that out for a couple of years. I tried reading her books, but to me they are almost incomprehensible. I guess if you really studied her material, you might catch on after a while, but it never came to me."

Shali gave Clay a slight smile. "You mean it's like gibberish?"

He looked at her intently. "Yeah, just like Iqbal's writings from his previous lives as Jabir and Ezra Pound."

"I still think we're missing lives in Sogui, though. There is a five-hundred-year gap between Buddha and Ammonius, and then again after Hypatia. But I think we've got what we need for now. It's punch-line time. We need to get to probe her about the location of the secret writings."

"OK, I'll wrap it up. Keep your fingers crossed." Clay turned his attention to Sogui. "There are large collections of secret written documents that are hidden and protected. Does this soul know where those secret writings are hidden?"

"Yes."

Clay and Shali's eyes popped wide open and their heads turned toward one another. An optimistic look of success came across both of their faces.

Clay leaned forward and asked, "Where are these writings physically located at the present time, and how do we locate those who are currently hiding the secrets?"

The guide hesitated. Shali gave a long shot of micro-pulse to the Third Eye.

Sogui responded, "In the mountains is the location of the hidden truths written by many, beneath the peak of Sipri, near the place called Tingri, by those who call themselves Drukpa."

Clay jerked his head toward Shali. "Did you get that? Quick, see what you can find on any of these words or places."

Shali furiously clicked away at the keyboard while Clay continued to probe the guide for more leads. Shali was still staring at her laptop when she quietly interrupted Clay in a low, slow voice. "I'm not sure of the spelling, exactly, but it looks like this place is probably in the Himalaya's. In Tibet, I would say. Yes, here is a Mount Tsipri, and just off to the south is a small village named Tingri. It's close to Mount Everest. Now, the other word, Drukpa, if I've got the spelling right. Let's see..."

Clay waited for her as she read from the screen.

"There are references to a Drukpa Kargyü Buddhist sect based in Tibet. I'd venture a guess that we're going to find some kind of a Buddhist temple out in those mountains. The bad part is that this is in the heart of Tibet. We're going to have problems with the Chinese government. Tibet has been in on-again-off-again lock-down status for years."

"If our secrets are hidden in Tibet, we've been talking with the Buddha himself," Clay said. "Remember Tommy; his soul lived as Dolpopo, another full Buddha living in that same area. I'll bet there is a connection."

Shali took a deep breath and then exhaled. "I'd say so. I think we've got what we need for now, and I'm a little concerned for Sogui. We've worked her over for three long days. This is stressful for her, especially considering what happened when we ran across Hypatia."

Clay sat back in his chair and said, "You're right. Unless you have other ideas, let's bring her out. There is a trip to Tibet to plan."

Clay brought Sogui out of the trance and they debriefed her for an hour. Their work in Panama was finished for now. They locked up the regression suite, freshened up and met in the lobby for dinner. Sogui promised to honor her agreement not to reveal the names or details of her previous lives. It was their little secret for the time being. Clay was mostly concerned about her revealing the location of the hidden secrets before he could locate and recover them himself. They agreed that after recovering the writings, they would work with Sogui to publish a documentary on the lives she had lived before. In return, she agreed to keep recording any more details from her past lives as she remembered them.

That night they went out for seafood and invited the professor from the university to join them for dinner. Sogui knew a great little hole-in-the-wall by the waterfront that served fabulous traditional shrimp ceviche, Panamanian Sancocho soup and broiled corvina fish.

After sharing several bottles of red wine, Sogui cut loose with her stories again, just as she had at the steakhouse a few nights earlier. Before the evening ended, the professor was nearly rolling on the floor with laughter due to Sogui's non-stop recollection of sexual exploits, each told in provocative, sensuous detail.

Part II – Quest of the Present

Chapter 29

Lhasa, Tibet

The Chinese Embassy in San Francisco granted Clay and Shali sixty-day visas to visit Tibet as photo journalists. Several weeks later, they landed in Tibet's capital. On the long ride to downtown Lhasa, the occasional scent of burning coal sifted through the air in the back seat of their taxi.

After freshening up, they met for an early dinner. The smell of stale carpet permeated the air of the hotel lobby. They walked down a hallway lined with intricately carved wooden wall hangings certainly made by earlier generations of Tibetan craftsmen. At the hotel restaurant they took their seats and ordered from the rather limited menu.

Still waiting for their meals, Shali broke the silence. "A few days before we left, I met with some monks at a Silicon Valley Buddhist temple to get inside scoop on the Drukpa's," Shali said. "It seems they are typically a passive, non-radical sect that makes no trouble for the Chinese occupiers. Because they are so low key, the Chinese don't bother them. From what they could tell me, there may be some monasteries in the mountains and valleys in that remote area. But they did not have any specific locations or details. We're going to have to research further from here in Lhasa, if we can. There are some Drukpa temples here. Hopefully we can get some leads."

"OK. A monastery is probably a good place to stash secrets if you want to keep them away from the prying eyes of the Chinese government, or from any of the other foreign governments that controlled Tibet in the past."

Their dinner finally arrived. After a few minutes, Shali broke the silence again, "Did you realize that Milarepa lived somewhere out West around Mount Tsipri about nine hundred years ago? I'm a little surprised that one of our three friends wasn't Milarepa in a past-life. We had Buddha, Confucius and Dolpopa; it would have been nice to get Milarepa, too."

"Agree. I remember reading that Buddhists still make pilgrimages to the caves where Milarepa meditated. Those caves are sort of like what Mecca is to the Muslims, or what Jerusalem is to the Christians and Jews."

"Did you know he was a big-time Yogi who ultimately reached full Buddha-hood, even though there some questionable stunts he pulled earlier in his life."

"Sure did. I'm up on him." As the second beer kicked in, Clay got playful. "I'll bet you that given a little time we would find that Milarepa has the same soul as the Dali Lama himself."

Shali acknowledged Clay's quip with a nod and a grin. "Hey, while we're out here, maybe we could head over to Nepal or India…"

They looked at each other intensely, simultaneously thinking about seeking a past life regression on the Dalai Lama. Clay interrupted, "No. Come on. We've got too much to do, plus we didn't bring our regression gear."

Looking sheepish, Shali nodded. "Back to business, big guy. I figure we do some sightseeing over the next few days and see if we can find a taxi driver we can trust. We need a driver who will take us out west, stick with us and keep his mouth shut."

Clay nodded. "If the Chinese government knew what we were searching for, we would be detained and deported before we knew what hit us."

"But I think we have a good front. All the camera equipment and photo bags definitely make us look like freelance writer-photographers for *National Geographic*."

Clay pushed the food around his plate with chopsticks. "Kind of a mundane meal, here, huh? Egg drop soup, steamed dumplings and fried noodles."

Shali chuckled. "What do you expect, Jose? Burritos, tamales and tacos?"

Within an hour, they were feeling the effects of the jetlag, so they retired to their rooms and collapsed in bed.

The next morning they met in the lobby with their cameras and backpacks. Somehow the lobby seemed a bit more cheerful and did not smell as grungy as it had the night before. They walked out the front of the hotel and hired a taxi to drive them around Lhasa for the morning. Shali easily conversed with the driver in her fluent Mandarin Chinese. However, neither Clay nor Shali were comfortable with the driver, so after the first temple they switched to another taxi. Shali was not comfortable with the second driver either. She felt his Chinese dialect was simply too good. They picked up a third driver and kept him for the rest of the day.

That evening, they walked down the street from the hotel to a small restaurant for dinner. This one was quainter, brighter and more bustling than the one at the hotel. There were many more people dining there, and the smells from the kitchen were more aromatic too. Their dinner conversation was mostly about the sight-seeing of the day and the other patrons of the restaurant.

While sipping on a harsh-tasting tea after dinner, Shali said, "I feel better about this last driver. He's got deep, native Tibetan roots. Plus I like his demeanor and flexibility. Over the years, the Chinese have moved a lot of settlers-come-infiltrators into the major Tibetan cities and towns, but he is definitely native; not a settler."

Clay replied in a cynical tone, "I guess the Chinese are no different than Israel injecting Jews into the West Bank. Sort of like a dog and fire hydrant - ya gotta mark your turf."

Shali glanced at Clay out of the corner of her eyes, acknowledging his tone. "Sort of? The Chinese influx has been a definitive and concerted effort to drag the Tibetans into Chinese society; they planted the Chinese inside to try to curb dissention. But the embedded colonists will rat out their Tibetan hosts in a second. I didn't sense this driver's harshness toward the Chinese, but he certainly has no love lost."

"Alright. If you're comfortable, let's keep this driver for the next several days to hit the local tourist traps around Lhasa. If he works out, maybe we can try to hire him for the month to go out west."

"I already asked if he would be willing to stay with us when we head out to the boon docks. He agreed and saw it as a change of pace from the big city."

"Did you get a price?"

Shali smiled. "Yeah, I negotiated a really low rate. It may seem cheap to us, but he probably feels like he won a lottery from a pair of Western suckers. It's a perfect match - win-win.."

Clay's tone became more serious. "Before we left California, I spent a good deal of time studying Google and the Yahoo satellite maps of western Tibet, along with a bunch of other Internet sites and articles dealing with that area. The terrain is really rough and barren out there, but I downloaded satellite maps onto my laptop and installed a GPS module so we can know where we're at all the time. We'll have an eye-in-the-sky on geography while we're out there looking for our secret treasures."

She smiled at his quip but then turned serious. "Have you picked up any traces of anybody tapping or following us? I'm still concerned about what happened at the hotel in Jordan not to mention the bugs planted in our place back home."

Clay shook his head. "Nope. Nothing."

"It still bothers me what that Jordanian crook was yelling before he jumped out the window. There is more to our suitors than you think."

"Yeah, but I was very secretive when I made our travel arrangements. Anyway, whoever they were, maybe they have just given up now."

"No way," Shali snapped back. "I don't believe it. They might not know what we've been up to, but I don't believe they've given up for one minute. Clay, if they know we are out here and if they have a few connections, we could end up as goners. Done, *finito*.. Their Chinese connections could make us disappear in Tibet and no one would find a trace."

Clay hesitated and bit his lip in thought. He nodded acknowledgement to her comment.

In a more cheerful, upbeat tone, Shali said, "Let's call it a day. We've got photo journaling to do tomorrow for National Geographic." She winked at him.

Clay reared his head back. "Is that wink for the cover story or is that an invitation?"

Shali stood up from the table and smiled seductively. "Don't you wish, big boy." She put her hands in a square shape before her face, miming taking a photo, and said, "Click. Let's meet at seven-thirty for breakfast." She grinned at having stirred her partner's libido.

Chapter 30

On the third day of touring, they visited the famous Potala Palace. This beautiful, white historic structure was perched on the hill in the center of the valley.

At dinner that night, Clay said, "It's beautiful, huh? A lot of Dalai Lama's and Buddha's have hung out here the past six hundred years."

"That's for sure. As a veritable fortress, it must have been a challenge to ancient invading neighbors. I read that it has recently been a focal point for some of the riots and civil revolts against the Chinese occupation."

Clay shifted his tone. "Speaking of invaders, do you feel a bit odd? Like, are you getting any odd stares from the Chinese authorities and locals?"

"Not the way you are. I could probably pass for a Nepalese or maybe a light-skinned Northern Indian - maybe even a Tibetan. The stares I get seem to beg the question of why I am hanging out with this big-nosed, white barbarian. That's what the Chinese call you guys." She laughed again. "But I don't think it is just the locals. Everywhere we've been in Lhasa, the uniformed Chinese overseers seem to be conspicuously staged at every other street corner. Plus I'll bet there is at least one covert undercover agent for every Chinese in a uniform."

After a several minute pause in the discussion, Clay said, "I thought it went pretty good with this again driver, today. You think?"

"Agreed," Shali replied. "I like him. He doesn't ask too many questions, and I sense he can keep his mouth shut. He helped us find those Drukpa's without wondering why."

"Good. So what's on for tomorrow?"

In an upbeat tone, Shali said, "We're up for a visit to a temple where we can meet some of our Drukpas. From the temple in

California, I've got the name of a specific monk to look for. Maybe he can help us."

The next morning the three of them went to a particularly mundane looking temple. The driver located and introduced them to the Drukpa monk they were looking for. The monk excused the driver, and he and Shali began speaking in Mandarin. Clay quietly watched the low-volume, polite dialogue that seemed laced with intense body language. Finally, the monk politely bowed to them both and smiled. He pulled a cell phone out of his robe and moved about thirty feet away to make a call.

Looking puzzled, Clay looked at Shali and asked, "What is going on, here?"

"I don't exactly know, but we're on to something."

"What's happened so far?"

"He spent several years of his earlier monk-hood in the Mount Tsipri area, where we want to go treasure hunting. He is definitely not Chinese so I took a chance and told him we were looking for secrets held by the Drukpa's."

Surprised at her boldness, Clay said, "Isn't that pushing our luck a bit?"

"Hey, we can't just drive out into the Himalaya's and start asking for hidden secrets. We've got to make our own leads. So I did."

They moved over to a bench closer to the monk and sat down. As the monk continued to chatter away, the two of them pretended to engage in idle discussion.

"Look at him, over there," Shali said. "He's been on that phone for quite a while. He's talking in a slurred Tibetan slang, so I can't understand it, although I could tell from the first few minutes of the call that he was reminiscing with an old friend. But he's become very serious and lowered his voice now. I can't make out much, but it seems the other guy is asking a lot of questions."

"Any idea what it's about?"

Shali's eyes showed her uncertainty. "It has something to do with us, because he keeps glancing at us, but I just can't tell."

The monk closed the cell phone and walked toward them. As he approached he spoke to Shali in clear, crisp Mandarin Chinese, but obviously in a serious tone.

She conversed with the monk at length, and then he escorted them back to the taxi where the driver was patiently waiting. The monk spoke with the driver in a local Tibetan dialect for another ten minutes. From his hand motions, it was clear even to Clay he was giving the driver specific directions.

He then exchanged contact information with both Shali and the driver. Before they left, they all placed their hands together in front of their chest in prayer fashion and bowed their heads with closed eyes: a classic Buddhist farewell.

As they drove away, Clay glanced back and saw the monk contemplatively watching them depart. He had a sorrowful, sad look on his face, as if some ill fate had come to pass. Just before they passed out of sight, the monk took out his cell phone out again and appeared to be making another call.

"Shali, you're killing me, here. What the hell is going on?"

Shali gave a huge sigh of relief before responding. "Clay, we're on the way. This monk has set us up to visit a colleague of his, close to Mount Tsipri. He said his associate would introduce us to other Drukpas, if necessary, to get our story for our 'photo shoot,' of course. He gave the driver specific directions and contact numbers in case there were any problems. The driver thinks we're just going to interview with the Drukpa's. We leave in the morning. The temple is almost two days drive to the southwest, so they're expecting us the day after tomorrow."

Clay asked in a concerned tone, "Do you think we're being set up?"

"No. Both the monk and the driver are native Tibetans. We need to trust someone or we're never going to find our hidden secrets."

Early the next morning, the adventurers packed their bags into a small minivan and headed off across the Tibetan countryside. After a seemingly long morning of bumping up and down curvy mountain roads and being stopped at many Chinese checkpoints, they stopped for lunch at a roadside café. An hour later they were back on the road where within thirty minutes they were stopped at yet another checkpoint.

Late that afternoon, as they drove into at larger city called Shigatze, Clay said to Shali, "These checkpoints are starting to suck. At every point we have our papers scrutinized like a bad day in the immigration office. And the last one, those Chinese soldiers damn near stripped the van looking for contraband."

Shali chuckled. "Yeah. I was getting ready for the rubber-glove treatment. Look here on the streets. There are guys in uniforms on almost every other corner. I'm getting a bit claustrophobic. Imagine how the Tibetans feel."

The driver pulled up in front of an old hotel. Shali looked at Clay and said, "I let the driver pick the hotel. I hope that was a wise move."

They checked in for the night and went to their rooms to freshen up.

Chapter 31

Shigatze, Tibet

At dinner that night in the dark, dank dining room of their dingy little hotel, Clay broke the ice. "Did you know this town was founded in the Fourteen Hundreds by the first Dalai Lama? It carries quite a bit of significance to Tibetans and for sure the Buddhists." He took a sip of his beer and breathed in the raw aromatic smells rolling out of the kitchen. "But at this point, to me, this is just a dumpy little Tibetan town."

Ignoring his geography lesson Shali said, "Clay, I'm getting some weird feelings here."

"You are *not* alone. You first."

"I'm really uncomfortable with the Chinese. I feel like they are all over us. If we do find the secrets and the Chinese find out, they are going to take them away."

"And we are going to *go* away. Yeah, that's bothering me, too. I feel like I can't even go to the bathroom without some soldier or security goon looking in the hole when I'm done. It's stifling. What about the driver? Do you think he was planted to watch us? Can we trust him to keep quiet?"

"I really don't think he is one of them, Clay. He is not a fan of the Chinese. I don't think he would rat us out. On the other hand, if he could capitalize on it …"

"We've got to be careful. If we get close to finding the secrets, we absolutely cannot let him know anything. What about the monk in Lhasa? Didn't that seem too easy to you?"

Shali clamped her lips tight, paused and said, "Yes, something bothered him about us - more than he bothered me anyway. Yet he still made the connection out here. It's like he was expecting us, but at the same time he was not happy to see us. It's almost as if he was leading us on. Yeah, it was just too easy."

Looking concerned, Clay said, "Yeah, I expected to be roaming all over the countryside, bumping up and down looking for Buddhist temples with hidden treasures but getting nowhere. I did not expect to be pointed to a specific place and given a gold-plated invitation."

"But, Clay, this does not mean that we are being led to the secrets. They could be setting us up for a rip off."

Clay pulled his head back. "Are you kidding me? The guy is a monk. Why would he set us up for a rip off?"

Shali laughed out loud. "Come on; business is business. A Buddhist monk will rip you off faster than a Jewish rabbi or a Southern Baptist crusader. You have to watch them all the time. Just remember that we don't have much money, OK?" She winked at Clay. "Remember, we are poor, hungry, freelance writers and photographers just trying to squeak out a living. All we want is to take some pictures and get a story about the Drukpa's."

"Alright. I'll chill out. You know, this beer is not too bad?"

Shali nodded. "At least it'll kill our senses so we can't smell the sulfur in our rooms. Did you smell those blocks of coal used for heating our rooms?"

"How can you not smell them?"

Shali shook her head. "Next time, we arrange our own hotel and don't depend on a driver to find us a place to stay. There are some nice hotels here. At least then, we might get normal heat."

Clay replied, "One more beer before we retire to our quaint little rooms with a smoldering block of coal?"

Chapter 32

The next morning the trio headed out after a simple breakfast of hot soy milk, fried breads and boiled eggs. The second day of traveling was even more difficult than the first. The roads were rougher, steeper, more winding and obviously less maintained. Many of the village roads were clogged with farmers and their herds of cows, all trekking to the fields. The strong musky odor of manure penetrated deep, and the smell of burning farmyard trash drifted across the roadways along the way. The driver pressed on. After pondering over the directions from the monk in Lhasa, late in the day they turned off onto a small dirt lane that took them through a long desolate valley and then up a steep ravine.

Near Mount Tsipri, Tibet

Finally, they arrived at a monastery that blended into the rugged mountainside. An older monk came out of the main door into the courtyard at the entrance; they were obviously expected.

The monk invited the three travelers into the main foyer to sit and enjoy a cup of hot tea and sweet almond biscuits. Two younger monks took their bags and scurried off up a set of stairs. The driver was asked to accompany another monk who took him off to some unknown place.

Shali engaged the elder monk in staccato crisp Mandarin Chinese, and Clay patiently waited for her sporadic translations along the path of the conversation.

"Miss Faisal, is it?

"Yes. Please call me Shali."

"Fine, Shali. What is it that you seek?"

"We are here to take photos and interview Drukpa's for a magazine article for National Geographic. More importantly, we are also seeking other information."

The monk nodded his head. "You have come in search of something in particular, I hear."

Shali smiled. "We are in search of ancient writings from long ago - perhaps as old as two thousand years or older. These have been referred to as secrets or treasures by people from long ago. The writings may have come from the great library in Alexandria, Egypt. Many ancient people have even said these writings may contain the secrets of the universe."

The older monk facetiously chuckled before responding. "Well, well, secrets of the universe? Isn't this a bit of fantasy, perhaps something from a Hollywood movie? I mean, what could be the secrets of the universe possibly be?"

"We do not know. We have been told that they exist, but we do not know what is in the writings."

"Why do you come to Tibet in search of these ... these secrets?"

"We were told that the Buddhists in this part of Tibet, specifically the Drukpa Kargyüs, should be able to help us find the writings."

"And who, might I ask, told you that we could help you?"

Shali had known this question was coming, but she still wasn't sure how to answer in Mandarin. She took a deep breath before she continued. "We use special techniques to hypnotize people and take them to the previous lives that their souls have lived. They sometimes tell us of things they knew in their previous lives - things that are no longer known. During these past-life regressions, we speak to elder souls who act as guides for the souls. Sometimes they also tell us about these hidden things. In this case, an elder soul told us the Drukpa's could help us locate the writings we seek."

Even though Clay did not understand Mandarin, he saw the clearly surprised expression on the monk's face.

The monk continued questioning Shali but in a slower, less confident tone. "And, may I ask, could you please describe this soul or person who told you that we could help you?"

"The person whose soul told us about you is a native Indian in Central America. Her soul, in her past lives, has been many very prominent people."

The monk now showed constrained stress; his body language was giving him away. "And just who were some of these previous lives?"

Shali reached into her bag and pulled out a folder containing the information of the three key regression subjects. She explained the succession of lives they had identified in Sogui, and her description had an obvious impact on the monk. When she concluded, he remained silent, closed his eyes and took a long, deep, slow breath. Then he exhaled slowly. Finally he opened his eyes, smiled and looked first at Shali and then at Clay. "Mr. Barton and Miss Shali," he said in clear, crisp English with a slight British Accent. "You have had a long journey; you must be tired and hungry. We will talk more tomorrow. I invite you to your rooms to refresh yourselves with a warm bath, perhaps. We will then have a meal together, if you please. Shall we meet here at, say, seven-thirty?"

Clay stuttered and stammered from shock at hearing the English. "Of course. It will be our pleasure, for sure. Seven-thirty. Yes. Fine. Thank you. *Uh, Xie Xie, Ni.*"

Clay's effort at Mandarin elicited a smile from the old monk.

At dinner, the conversation was much lighter and, fortunately for Clay, in English. However, they did not discuss the writings or regressions. The dinner talk focused on the Drukpa sect and their flavor of Buddhism. After several glasses of a deep, red wine, the monk engaged them in lively dialogue about Hinduism and the Abrahamic religions. After another glass of wine, he rolled into an emotional damnation of the Chinese occupation and colonization of Tibet. Soon the three said their goodnights and retired for the evening.

After a hearty breakfast of hot yak milk, chunky rice congee and fried breads, the three met in the monastery's library. This time, two other monks joined them. The discussion lasted all day but this time it was almost entirely in Mandarin. Shali provided Clay with periodic translations of the discussions and occasionally solicited his responses to questions.

One of the two new monks did most of the talking. The other one was busy taking notes and referring to documents bound in an old leather folio. The discussions almost seemed to be a test. They would ask questions, and then rephrase the questions in a slightly different context and ask them again. Several times during the day, the two monks excused themselves and went to another room down the hall while another young monk politely served Clay and Shali with hot tea and sweet sesame-paste buns. Despite the closed door, it was obvious from the voices echoing through the hall that the monks were in intense discussion about what they were hearing. Unfortunately, they spoke in a sharp dialect of which Shali had little comprehension.

Late that afternoon, the interrogation suddenly concluded. The two monks politely excused themselves and left. They got into the back of a car waiting outside and were whisked off down the dirt lane, away from the monastery.

Clay and Shali freshened up in their rooms and later met the first monk for a more elaborate meal.

As they sat down to dinner, Shali opened the conversation in English: "May I ask what the next steps may be?"

The older monk smiled, tilted his head slightly and said, "Yes, of course. We need more time to discuss among ourselves how we might assist in accommodating your request for more information. This will take time, and you must meet more people. You are no longer in need of your driver from Lhasa, so we will send him home."

Clay responded, "Oh, but we need to pay him - "

"That will not be necessary," the monk responded, cutting Clay off politely but tersely. "We are taking care of this. The driver confirmed that you are photographers and writers for a magazine. Did you ever discuss these secrets with the driver, or talk about them while you were in his presence?"

Shali sensed urgency and responded before Clay had a chance to absorb the question. "No. Never. We only asked questions of a geographical and cultural nature - things that might be relevant for our photography and magazine articles. We asked him about the Drukpa sect while we were in Lhasa, but we just said that we had heard the Drukpa have no problems with the Chinese and did not want any problems. There was never any discussion of the secrets or the writings. We did not know him and could not trust him, so we were very careful."

The monk smiled. "I see," he said in a lighter tone. "I just ask, because sometimes our people understand a lot more English than you might believe. We watch a lot of American television and movies, you know."

Clay added, "But we're sure he could not speak English."

The old monk nodded. "Yes, of course. Anyway, we will accommodate your transportation needs from this point. For much of the next week, you will fulfill your role as photographers. One of our monks will take you on a wonderful travel tour of the region and you will see many beautiful sites and be very visible to the Chinese authorities - as the photographers that you are, of course."

As dinner progressed, the discussion lightened up as they discussed the sightseeing they would do over the coming days.

Chapter 33

The next morning, Clay and Shali met in the library after breakfast. Peering out the small front window, Clay saw their driver, escorted by a monk, walking to his waiting minivan. He nudged Shali to look out the window.

The monk pulled his hand out of his robe and handed a large roll of Chinese Yuan to the driver. The driver smiled and fanned his thumb through the wad of money. The two politely bowed a farewell, and then the driver got in his van and drove off down the dusty lane.

Even though they were alone, Shali whispered, "We're onto something, but we have got to be careful. I'm uncomfortable about the whole situation."

"Me, too," Clay said in a low voice. "I think we're still being tested."

Shali looked directly into Clay's eyes. "I sense there are others who are higher and more authoritative than the monks we've seen so far."

Clay saw a young monk wearing street clothes enter the library and then walk in their direction. He turned to Shali and said, "OK, Madam Photographer, I'll bet this is our tour guide. Get your camera and let's go."

To Clay's relief, their new guide spoke a little broken English. He took them outside to a rugged well-used Toyota SUV. The three of them spent the next three days touring areas within a day's driving distance of the monastery. The tour included a great deal of time navigating up and down the valleys which were populated with trail heads to the base camps of Mount Everest. The villages seemed to be alive with Western hikers and bicyclers, most likely who had come across from Nepal. The Himalayas had an amazing beauty even though the topography was rough and barren.

On their way back to the monastery at the end of the third day, Shali nudged Clay and boasted, "I'd say we played our photographer roles pretty well."

Clay responded, "And if we don't find what we are looking for, we can publish a great photo journal about life in remote Himalayan Tibet."

Shali said, "We're supposed to get a reprieve tomorrow. Evidently we have more meetings at the monastery."

As they pulled up to the monastery, Clay said, "Hurrah. I'm soaking in a tub tonight before dinner."

Shali only smiled at her partner's demeanor.

The next morning after breakfast, they were met by the English-speaking monk. After a casual exchange about their tour, he took them to the library. There they were met by two older gentlemen in heavily worn business suits. They spoke Mandarin to Shali, but she could not place their strange accents. That day consisted of nearly six hours of intense interrogation interrupted only one hour for lunch. Clay and Shali met for tea before dinner in a back courtyard.

"What's your take on today?" Shali asked.

"We're being tested hard. You remember when I took a bio break? When I walked down that back hall I walked past a door to some room and there was a slight crack in the door. I saw five or six people watching you on a monitor. There are hidden cameras in that library. They weren't monks but they are studying our every move. I couldn't tell you until I got you out here."

Shali sat in silence. The serious look on her face was only interrupted by her occasional sip of tea. She finally said, "We don't know what we have gotten ourselves into, but there's no way we can back out of this, now." Nothing was said the rest of the evening.

The discussions the next day were a near repeat of the first day but with a different middle-aged woman and man, dressed in business suits. That session was over by noon.

At lunch Clay said to Shali, "Today's questions were more focused and seemed to go into more detail. I sensed yesterday was fact finding. I would say that today was the real test."

Shali nodded agreement, "It seems like it to me."

"Do you know what's up this afternoon?"

"We are to go back to the library and wait. He said it could be a while and asked us to be patient."

When they finished eating, Shali and Clay were taken back to the library. They entertained themselves with their laptops for almost three hours. Finally, Shali got up and walked around the room to stretch.

She noticed a regional Chinese newspaper on a reading table in the corner, inadvertently left behind by one of the visiting businessmen. She flipped through the paper but stopped abruptly when she saw the headline on page six.

Shali exclaimed, "Oh my God, Clay - the driver!"

"What?"

Shali's voice cracked as she translated the Chinese: "A Lhasa taxi driver was killed in a car crash two days ago on the Friendship Highway going east toward Shigatze." She hesitated. "The brakes failed on the van he was driving, and it plunged down the side of the mountain into a river. He was killed instantly." She began to tremble. "The authorities are still investigating ..."

At that moment, the English-speaking monk walked into the library from the hallway. The monk saw her near-panicked expression and asked, "Are you alright? Is there a problem?"

Shali stammered out a response. "Uh, no, uh. Well, maybe. I ... I don't know. I saw this article in the newspaper. I think this might have been our taxi driver. The picture of the van looked like the one he was driving. Do you know if this was him?"

"How tragic. Please let me see." The monk took the newspaper from Shali and quickly read the article. "Ms. Faisal, there are many vans and taxis that drive along that road every day. As you know, our mountain roads can be very dangerous. Unfortunately, this type of accident happens more than we like to see. If it was your driver, then I suggest you are very lucky it did not happen on his way here, while you were with him."

Shali said, "But I feel badly if it was him. We hired him to bring us out here."

"Please, you should not feel guilty. He may not have been so innocent. He knew much more of your quest than you realize. During the two days he was here, his questions to our staff were clearly focused on your search for secret documents."

Clay and Shali abruptly looked at each with expression of surprised guilt compounded by fear that the mishap may not have been so accidental.

"Could we have been so careless to have talked in front of him?" Clay asked Shali.

Shali replied in a staccato tone: "I'm pretty sure we didn't. I don't remember doing so. We tried to be careful."

"Our rooms," Clay said. "They could have bugged our rooms - or the restaurants."

"Who would have done this?"

"I don't know. But Jordan, our condos. It could be whoever has been trying to find out what we are doing."

The monk sat quietly observing their expressions and dialog. They stood looking at each other until the monk finally broke the silence. "There are obviously other people looking for your same secrets. We should be more careful. But for now, my friends ..." The monk smiled, shifted his shoulders and demeanor, "you will have one more day of touring. The following day you will move to a new location."

Shali asked, "Is it far from here?"

The monk gave them a courtesy smile. "It will be a bit of a journey. But for tomorrow, you must start very early in the morning. Your breakfast will be at five a.m. I will allow you to dine alone tonight; I have to make preparations for your journey."

He smiled again, bowed and left the room.

They were then escorted to their rooms to relax before dinner. Dinner that night was uneventful and extremely quiet.

"He took the paper with him," Shali said. "It was tightly rolled in his hand and he left with it. I just can't shake the thought of the driver."

"Shali, it probably was not even our driver. And like he said, if it was, it was just an unfortunate accident."

"No, I just don't feel that way. I'm afraid that if we make a wrong move, we'll suffer a similar fate. We are dealing with something beyond our control here. The Chinese just lock you up; but our driver was silenced - maybe rightfully so, but nonetheless he was taken out of the picture."

Clay's face became stern. "I hope you're wrong. Either way, I'm not sure what we're into here, either."

Not another word was said the rest of the night; they ate together in silence.

Chapter 34

After an early morning breakfast, they met their young tour guide monk and drove off down the road in the SUV. Hours later, without stopping for photo opportunities, they drove through Tingri once again, but this time they turned west up the Friendship Highway, which led to the Peace Bridge river crossing from Tibet to Nepal. As their SUV wove up and down the steep, narrow mountain roads on the way to the border, Shali wondered if the brakes would fail or if they would meet a fate similar to the driver from Lhasa.

At the border crossing, the guide took their passports and went into the Chinese border control office. Sitting in the SUV, they strained to see through the window of the small office. They could see a low-key dialogue between the guide and the officers. The guide was then escorted to the supervisor's office and the door was closed behind him. Several minutes later, the guide returned to the SUV. Without saying a word, he pulled the SUV into the line of cars and trucks already waiting to cross the bridge into Nepal.

Once across the bridge in Nepal, the guide showed their passports to the immigration officer, who stamped their passports and waived them on. In the Nepalese border town of Kodari, the driver pulled over in front of what appeared to be a prominent main-street location. The guide asked Clay and Shali to get out of the SUV. When they did, they were introduced to a dark-complexioned Nepalese man who, oddly enough, was standing behind another SUV with a set of luggage on the ground beside him. The Tibetan tour guide asked Clay and Shali to stand next to the Tibetan man beside the luggage. The guide positioned Clay and Shali in such a way that the Tibetan license plate would be visible between them in the photograph and the main street of Kodari would clearly be in the backdrop.

Smiling for the photo, Clay whispered to Shali, "This is being staged. Do you have any idea why the hell we are in Nepal?"

"No idea whatsoever, Sherlock. I should have used more deodorant this morning. I'm sweating like a horse after the Kentucky Derby."

Clay cranked his head to look at her. "You're telling me."

"There's not a thing we can do right now except play along. Our fate is in their hands. But I tell you, Clay, if we make it out of here alive, you owe me a huge bonus and giant pay raise." She nervously giggled under her breath to cover the stress.

Clay chuckled and said, "Deal. I'm giving myself a raise, too; and two more weeks of paid vacation."

The guide snapped several more pictures, and then the three climbed back into the Toyota and drove back down to the Peace Bridge crossing to China. At the Chinese immigration point, the driver went into the supervisor's office with their passports. Within minutes he returned, and they were on the long trip back to the monastery.

Ten minutes after leaving the bridge, Shali calmly asked the guide, in English, to explain why they crossed to Nepal to have a photo taken in Kodari.

"Ms. Faisal, picachur is for case to show you go Nepal from this place. You leave China, you know? We have picachur you leave Tibet to Kodari in Nepal."

Clay and Shali looked quizzically at each other after his response in broken English. There was total silence on the long bumpy ride back to the monastery.

The next morning, they were met by the English-speaking monk. "Ms. Faisal and Mr. Barton, I ask that you please be patient for a few more days. We must make travel arrangements, and this will take some time."

Clay politely questioned, "Can you please tell us where we will be going or what we will be doing?"

"Just a few more days, please. You will learn more after you leave our monastery. It will be safer there."

They spent two more days sequestered in the monastery. Shali occupied herself by transcribing past recordings of regression sessions. Clay kept himself busy by working with the SRD database or playing solitaire and video games on his laptop.

On the afternoon of the second day, they were asked to pack their bags and prepare to leave the monastery after dinner.

. Finally, at about nine p.m., the familiar face of their young tour guide showed up. He politely bowed and, without a word, loaded their bags into the back of the SUV. He motioned for Clay and Shali to climb into the back seat. The English-speaking monk rode shotgun in the front seat. Not a single word was exchanged by anyone.

In the pitch-dark night, they slowly drove down the dirt lane to the entrance of the mountain ravine. This time they followed a second SUV with four unknown occupants. On the main road, they turned to the west. The night travelers wove through valleys and across dark, curvy mountain roads.

In the back seat, Clay turned on his laptop and connected the external GPS antenna. He tracked their route on the satellite map as they traveled through Tingri towards their destination high up the back trails of Mount Tsipri. The monk riding shotgun occasionally glanced back at Clay, but his facial expression showed patience for Clay's tinkering. At one point, the monk glanced at Shali and smiled at Clay's preoccupation with the GPS and the maps.

Shali smiled back and whispered in Chinese, "*Ta shr yi ge* techno-weenie. He is what he is. I can't change him."

They laughed together at Clay's expense.

Chapter 35

Drukpa Kargyü Monastery, Tibet

The last twenty minutes of driving was on a rough, winding trail up the side of a ravine in the pitch dark of the moonless night. They finally pulled up in front of a plain, stone-block building. Only dim lights shone through the small windows on either side of the main door. According to Clay's GPS, it appeared they were nearly half way up the south side of Mount Tsipri.

Inside the building, they were quickly escorted through winding hallways to the back of what was obviously yet another monastery. They were then taken to a large storage room. Their robe clad guide leaned down, grabbed a hidden handle and lifted half of the wooden floor on a set of hinges that creaked and groaned as if fighting the opening. They descended a wide set of stairs into an underground world below. The hallway walls had obviously been carved out of solid stone as evidenced by chisel marks on the rock walls. The cave was dark and dank, but lit by a closely mounted row of muted lights running down the right side of the hallway. On the upper left side of the hall they could hear the rush of air flowing through some type of ducting. Clay and Shali were then taken to separate individual sleeping rooms deeper inside the cave. Their sleeping quarters were much more comfortable with white plastered walls and warm, dry, conditioned air. Even the room amenities were considerably better than they expected, being in the back end of a crude underground cave. The rugs on the floor were warm, of high quality and colorful in the well-lit rooms. The separate bathrooms were also very comfortable with a large, clean bath and hot water. Seeming so ironic, the night stand even had an iPod docking station.

Gathering outside of Clay's room, one of the monks who had escorted them said in heavily accented English, "Please make self comfort for many weeks. Please not to leave building except go courtyard. If hear bells ring three, must to immediately go your room here. This is warning if authorities come this place. They must not find you in this place."

Clay nodded acknowledgment and then commented to Shali, "The Drukpas certainly thought out the details of this little mountain fortress."

"Yes, but they've had a few thousand years to refine it."

The English-speaking monk who rode with them to the monastery walked in with two young monks who were carrying their bags.

Clay asked, "Sir, we are assuming that somewhere in the cave is the hiding location of the writings?"

"Patience, my friends. In the morning you will be shown more. You have had a long day; it is time to rest. Everything you need is in your room. We will wake you in seven hours. Please rest now."

There were no arguments from the weary travelers.

The next morning after a hearty breakfast in the monastery dining room, Clay and Shali were taken back down into the cave and far down the tunnels to a dead-end piled with trash bags and discarded items. One of the monks leaned down at the edge of the trash heap and brushed away the dirt and rocks. He pulled a lever, and the floor lifted up the trash heap. Underneath was another set of hidden stairs that led into a huge darkened room further below.

As they entered, the dank, stale air of the cave gave way to fresh, obviously climate-controlled conditions. The humidity and temperature was significantly different compared to the cave above it. The escort reached over to the wall and flipped a switch. Muted lights flickered on down another long, deep cave. Before them stood hundreds of wooden shelves neatly stacked with what appeared to be thousands of old scrolls and leather-bound books, all neatly covered with white linen cloths.

Clay looked at Shali and said in a slow, quiet voice, "I assume this is what I have been looking for these past five years."

In awe while staring at the shelves, she responded in a whisper, "Looks that way, Gonzo."

The old monk smiled at the shell-shocked stares on their faces. "My friends, there will be much time to learn about this all of this. But for now, please, join me for tea upstairs. The dining room has a wonderful view."

Clay and Shali stood quietly as if ignoring their host. After a few minutes of silence, they politely followed him out of the cave, glancing back to capture a parting image of what they had just seen.

As they sipped their tea to discuss the next steps, Shali and Clay were mesmerized by the view of Mount Everest just fifty miles to the south.

Clay looked at the monk and said, "I must say, the Drukpa's know where to put their monasteries for the best views."

He smiled at Clay. "It seems not many people want to live here, so we might as well take advantage of it." His eyes grew laser like, he breathed in a deep breath and then exhaled with slow intensity. He then said in a serious and decisive tone, "My friends, it is our decision that you will become the new custodians of the writings. These documents have been in our possession for thousands of years. However, we are already making arrangements to transport these treasures to America. We assume this is where you would want to take them. America is probably the safest location in the world right now. We have found a place there where we believe they will be safe until you decide what you are going to do."

Clay and Shali looked at each other in absolute surprise.

"Custodians?" asked Clay.

Before they could gain their composure, the old monk continued: "Accepting these writings comes with great responsibility. After we move the writings to the new location under your control, you must ensure the protection and safety of both the documents and the knowledge contained within. There is great truth in these writings, and we believe it is time to bring that truth to our human society."

Clay now had the look of sheer shock. He looked at Shali and said, "Be careful what you ask for, for you might just get it. I'm not sure I want this new job." He then turned to the monk and responded in the nervous, machine-gun interrogation style he had learned to use in Army Intelligence: "I am not sure what these responsibilities are. I do not even know what is in the writings. How will I know what to do? Who do I work with? If I find out what is in the writings, and if I actually understand it or agree with it, what am I expected to do with it? What do you mean by custodian, anyway? How will I know what my responsibilities are for protecting it? And who do I protect it from? And - "

The monk, sat back in his chair, laughed out loud and cut off Clay's rambling. "My friend. You are the chosen one. You will know what to do when the time comes. We will provide assistance for your work ahead, so please relax and absorb your new responsibilities, one step at a time."

The monk then explained logistics of living in the monastery for the coming weeks. He also provided each of them with Internet-ready satellite phones that could be used for phone calls or for connecting their laptop computers to the Internet. After lunch they spent the rest of the day catching up on email and current events after the past few weeks on the road.

They had a good night's rest in their bedroom-cave suites, and in the morning after breakfast, the monk bid them farewell and left the monastery.

From that point on, nearly every day, Clay and Shali met with three old monks who were the current, primary custodians of the writings. They found themselves extremely busy with high level orientations on the history of the writings. Unfortunately for Clay, all the discussions were in Mandarin Chinese, which had to be tediously translated by Shali. But they were assured they would get more substantive details after the secret writings were moved out of Tibet.

A week later, Clay and Shali were still confused about their roles even amidst the flurry of activity around the secrets hidden under the monastery. At dinner with Shali that night Clay reflected on their situation. "I really don't know what the hell I've gotten us into, here."

"You're telling me, Dr. Strangelove."

"Discounting all of this custodian-stuff with God-only-knows what kind of responsibilities we've taken on, I'm just about yak'd out. Yak milk, yak jerky, yak steak, yak kabob – oh, and the goat stew. Plus I don't want to end up living like a monk in cave somewhere guarding all of these secrets. But mostly, right now, I really just want a cheese burger."

"Don't complain so much. Despite the isolation out here, they *did* give us a satellite phones. That's better than the last monastery. We've got the Internet so you know when *'you've got mail!'* You're connected, man, so what's the problem?"

"No, I'm not complaining about that. Yes, with the phones we've gotten a lot of prep work done, even being locked up in this cave. But I really don't know what's going on. What are we going to do with all these documents? I'm just a bit overwhelmed."

In a comforting yet somewhat facetious voice, Shali said, "Let's just break it down into bite-sized things to do. We need to get these docs safely transported out of here, and then get them digitized, transcribed, translated, interpreted and communicated without being locked up in a loony bin. It's simple - just one step at a time."

Clay narrowed his eyes with skepticism, tilted his head to the side and said, "I don't know if you are being nice or patronizing to me, but it isn't working, either way." He smiled and then continued in a serious tone: "Shali, I am really concerned."

She reached over and firmly grabbed his arm. "Don't take all of the burden on yourself. We'll do fine. We've just got a lot of work to do, but we'll be OK. Trust me."

Clay smiled and nodded in gratitude.

Chapter 36

A few weeks later, Clay and Shali were eating breakfast in the center courtyard, admiring the view of Mount Everest and reflecting on the long days of preparation they had put in. A waft of burning coal sulfur filled the air as they sipped on cups of hot spiced tea in the cold mountain air. They watched a young monk walking a herd of yak down the road to their mountain feeding spot for the day.

Having watched a half dozen monks meticulously wrapping and packing the scrolls and books into large, gray casket-looking cases, they chatted about the process.

"They must have spent years preparing for this moment in time." Shali said. "There are one hundred seventy-eight of those cases. I counted them twice."

"Did you get a chance to look at the manifest they are using?"

"Yep. Damn detailed. Every document has a very specific place in a specific case."

"What's the deal with the colors and the numbers?"

"They said they will try to separate the yellows from the reds, if possible. I think there is some duplication between the documents or something. If we lose all of the yellows, then the reds still have much of the secrets."

Clay nodded. "Even though the cases are fiberglass, they don't have that deep, pungent resin smell, so they are definitely not new. I'd guess they are at least ten years old. These people have been preparing for this day for a long time.

"It is obvious that they don't trust the Chinese. So how do they plan to get all one hundred seventy-eight cases *and* us out of here without getting caught?"

"Have you been able to find out how and when we are getting out of here?"

"Yes. This afternoon, they told me the first stop is Nepal. Kathmandu to be exact. The trick is getting over there. I don't have any idea how they can move this much stuff inconspicuously without the Chinese finding out, but they assured me they are working on it. One thing is clear, though: this group - whoever they are, *whatever* they are - is very organized."

"Have you asked them about the organization?"

Shali pressed her lips together before replying. "Yeah, I've asked them, but I haven't gotten squat. They talk in circles and avoid answering me directly. It's like they are talking gibberish."

She caught her pun relating to Jabir. Both of them paused and looked at each other. Slowly they both smiled at each other and chuckled.

Clay then asked, pointedly, "So, when do we get out of here?"

"They tell me it could still be another week or so."

He shook his head side to side. "Let's hope it's not much longer or I might start to speak gibberish. I probably should have taken up studying Mandarin while we were locked up out here. All of you yakking away in Chinese is like gibberish."

Nearly a week later, they met for breakfast in the courtyard. Shali breathed in deeply and exhaled slowly and deliberately. In a matter-of-fact tone, she said to Clay, "It's show time. This morning they told me we are leaving tonight. We are to pack all of our bags today and be ready to go after dark."

Clay's eyes lit up and he excitedly shot back, "I'll be ready to go in five minutes." Shali smiled. "But why all the secrecy? Why wait until the day we leave before they tell us?"

"They are not very clear on that, but I gather they have been waiting for the proverbial stars to align. I don't know what is going on, but it sounds like the logistics has been giving them problems."

They spent the day preparing to leave and watching the final logistical activities for moving the cases. After dinner their bags were moved up to the main entrance. An hour later, they stood out front and anxiously watched a row of truck headlights slowly dance their way up the road to the monastery at a snail's pace. The slow grinding of transmissions could be heard echoing in the hills as the trucks shifted gears up and down to squirm up the trail.

Clay asked Shali, "Do you figure this is our ride out of here or a posse of Chinese soldiers?"

She smiled at his quip. "I would sure hope it's our ride. If it were the Chinese, our monk buddies would be shoving us and the cases back down into the caves."

They stood quietly watching the bouncing lights for another ten minutes. Four canvas-covered trucks finally pulled up inside the monastery drive in front of neatly stacked piles of the gray cases sorted by color, code and number. The trucks turned back to the front of the monastery as their engines revved up. The trucks spewed sulfur-laden, hazy blue diesel exhaust into the courtyard as they jockeyed for position in front of the piles. Nearly simultaneously, the drivers turned off the engines. The loud roar instantly turned to near dead silence. The smoky blue air slowly drifted off down the valley. Like an army of ants, every monk in the monastery began loading cases into the back end of the trucks.

Standing on the sidelines, Clay and Shali watched the three custodians supervise the operation and check off the cases as they were loaded into the trucks. The red numbered cases went into the first two trucks and the yellow cases went into the last two trucks.

Shali leaned over to Clay and said, "A lot of thought went into the logistics of this move. It's almost as if this is a routine. Imagine what the plan would have looked like a thousand years ago, had it been necessary to relocate the treasures back then."

Clay chuckled. "Yeah. Probably a couple hundred pack mules would have been standing in that courtyard instead of just four trucks."

The two of them traded more jokes as they walked around the back of the trucks to get a closer look. Each truck had jerry cans of diesel fuel tied down along the right side. On the left side were jugs of water and boxes of food.

Clay and Shali noticed the three custodian monks had gathered near the monastery's entrance and were obviously discussing the progress of the loading. One of the monks motioned for Shali to join them. Clay continued watching the trucks being loaded for ten minutes until Shali returned.

"Clay, here's the scoop. We're going to be driving to some remote airfield where everything will be loaded onto two cargo planes. Then we fly to Kathmandu."

Clay looked puzzled. "I don't understand. We're not that far from Nepal. It would seem easier to just drive there."

"I know what you mean, but they told me there was too much chance of being intercepted by the Chinese Army."

"So does that mean they were not successful in paying off the Chinese officials along the border?"

Shali grinned politely at Clay's facetiousness.

The loading of the trucks continued through the night. Before morning broke, Clay and Shali were separated and escorted to ride in different trucks. The custodian monks climbed into the cabs of different trucks as well.

Shali leaned out of her truck and yelled to Clay, "Hey, race you to the bottom." He waved her off.

One by one the trucks fired up their engines and barked out huge bellows of black smoke. The silence of the early morning was broken by the belching trucks with grinding, whining gears. The drivers slowly pulled their trucks out of the monastery's courtyard. Over the next thirty minutes, the convoy made the slow bumpy trip down the steep mountain trail in the darkness of the early morning. Slight glints of morning sun just began to peak out from behind the mountains as they reached the bottom of the mountain.

As the parade reached the valley floor, they were joined by several heavily armored SUV's. Clay, Shali and the three Tibetan custodians were taken out of the trucks and escorted to the three waiting SUV's. While waiting for the drivers to finish a five-minute break, Shali and Clay moved to the side of their SUV.

Clay said to Shali, "These vehicles have so much firepower, the Army Rangers still patrolling Afghanistan in Hummers would be envious. These are like rolling fortresses."

Shali's tone was serious and concerned: "Yeah, but that won't help much if we drive off a cliff into a river."

Surprised at her reaction, Clay replied in a soft voice, "It's still bothering you about the driver, isn't it?"

She looked at him in the glow of the headlights that still lit up the Tibetan daybreak. "And what do you expect? After we have served our purpose, are we too disposable?"

Clay reached over and stroked her arm. "I understand. It's going to be OK. Hey, they are ready to go. Let's get in."

Two of the SUV's pulled out in front of the four trucks and one pulled in behind. After reaching the main road, the convoy turned right to the northeast.

Clay said to Shali, "I expected to drive back to Tingri in the direction of Mount Everest. I remember seeing a Chinese military camp in Tingri, so I figured there must be an airfield close by. See if you can get anything out of our driver or the other guy riding shotgun."

Shali had a cordial but brief discussion in Mandarin with the driver and the heavily armed security guard riding shotgun in the front seat.

"Shali, what did they say?" Clay asked.

"They politely asked me to sit back and relax because the ride could be as long as eight hours."

"Wow. At this rate, I figure we'll probably be driving one hundred fifty to two hundred miles or more." Clay opened his laptop and viewed the screen for a moment. "Following the GPS, here and the direction we are going ... two hundred miles out...." His mumbles trailed off.

"I worry about you, sometimes." Shali smiled as she shook her head and looked out the window.

After several minutes, Clay finally finished his sentence. "Look here. There is an extremely long airfield tucked in a valley between these surrounding mountains. The airstrip has to be at least three miles long - long enough to land a Space Shuttle! There appears to be a military camp on the south side. It looks unoccupied, but who knows how old this satellite photo is."

Looking across at the laptop, Shali responded, "I see. And it's just east of Shigatze, where we stopped overnight with the driver from Lhasa..." A frown slipped across her face, eyebrows furrowed.

Clay said, "I remember seeing that airstrip as we approached Shigatze. What the hell could the Chinese use this monster airstrip in the Tibetan boon docks for?"

"I don't know - maybe heavy transport planes for tanks and troops to suppress these troublesome Tibetans?"

"Hey, ask our friends if we're going to this airfield."

Shali leaned forward and casually asked them in Chinese, "*Wo men dau XiGaZe feijijang ma?*"

Their reaction showed astonishment at how these foreigners could possibly know where they were going. After regaining their composure, the two Tibetans in the front seat looked at each other and then glanced back at Shali. The passenger riding shotgun looked directly at Shali, slowly tapped his fingers on his AK-47 and then gave a single nod in answer to her question. Then he turned back to face the windshield and made no other gesture or verbal response.

Shali looked at Clay and said, "Shigatze airfield. That's the destination."

"It seems a long way in the opposite direction from our safe haven in Kathmandu, but I guess we are just cargo at this point. Don't argue, huh?"

The convoy continued bumping and weaving along the valley road for another four hours. They rumbled through many small villages, each with its own tattered temples. As they drove through each village, the smell of coal sulphur filled the vehicles and then dissipated as soon as they reached the open countryside again.

In a barren stretch of road tucked between several surrounding mountains, the convoy came to an abrupt stop on the roadside. The drivers got out to stretch and motioned for their human cargo to get out. The drivers took out the jerry cans of fuel and filled the tanks of the trucks and SUV's. The sharp smell of diesel fuel filled the air.

Standing along the side of the road, watching the activity, Clay said to Shali, "It seems odd they are carrying their own fuel. We passed several gas stations in the larger villages along the way."

"Evidently it's less conspicuous to refuel their trucks out here in isolation, away from prying eyes."

Some of the men pulled boxes of food out of the trucks and opened them up. They passed wrapped up packets of dried yak meat around.

"Hey, Shali, when we get back do you think we can find big bags of this yak jerky at Costco or Sam's Club?"

She smiled at his quip.

Large aluminum cans of now lukewarm boiled vegetables were opened up. The salty bland soup was poured into bowls for the hungry drivers, guards and passengers. Tall aluminum thermos-bottles of warm, sweet yak milk were also opened. The milk was poured into tin cups and handed out. Most of the men and guards began passing around pungent spice-laced cigarettes, and then, seemingly one by one, the men all relieved themselves of bodily fluids along the side of the road, with no modesty for Shali.

In less than thirty minutes, the vehicles were reloaded and the convoy was back on the road. In another three hours, they were driving through Shigatze.

Shali nudged Clay to look at the small hotel where they had stayed on the inbound trip well over a month ago. With eyes narrowed, he smiled slightly, as if seeing a familiar old friend. He rolled down the window to smell the air. "There's the burning blocks of coal again. Such memories, huh?"

The convoy barreled through the main street of Shigatze almost without slowing. Dogs scurried out of the street to avoid being run over.

"Did you notice the total absence of any military or police so far?" Clay asked Shali. "I don't understand. This time, there were virtually no uniforms anywhere - and not a single checkpoint. No soldiers; no police."

"Someone obviously got to the authorities. I'll bet it cost a bundle to bribe that many bureaucrats and Army officers."

Chapter 37

Shigatze Airfield, Tibet

Eventually, the convoy pulled up near the mysteriously long runway in the middle of Tibet. Two nondescript, four-engine military style cargo planes sat quietly on the tarmac. With the orchestration of a well-rehearsed Broadway play, two trucks pulled up to the side cargo-doors of each plane. Clay, Shali and the three custodian monks were dropped off next to one of the planes, along with a contingent of four security guards who had been riding in the trucks. The SUV's then drove off to surrounding positions, each about one hundred meters from the planes.

The cases were quickly offloaded from the trucks, inventoried and reloaded into the cargo planes. The yellow labeled boxes went into one plane and the red labeled boxes into the other. The cases were then carefully and tightly strapped down with heavy cargo netting. The entire transfer was orchestrated as if it had been rehearsed many times.

The five travelers remained chatting beside one plane as the logistics were executed. Just as the loading was finalized, they heard a loud ruckus coming from the side of the airfield near a cluster of buildings. Suddenly, three Chinese military Humvee type vehicles burst out from the side of the buildings toward the planes, kicking up a trail of dust.

The escort guards positioned in the SUV's immediately jumped to action in their own high-powered machines. Tires squealed on the airfield tarmac.

Looking concerned, Clay said to Shali, "Looks like somebody didn't get the word."

Squinting into the dusk of the setting sun, Shali said, "You're telling me? This is not looking good, Chief."

The top panels of the three Tibetan SUV's popped open and guards wielding machine guns emerged. The six heavily armed tactical vehicles screamed together as if caught in a vortex. The Tibetans burst out with blazing machine fire, pelting the Chinese Humvees with bullet spray. The Humvees skidded as they scattered in different directions, each attempting to evade the Tibetan onslaught. Their own machine gunners suddenly emerged from their top gun ports and returned blasts of machine-gun spray.

To the bystanders beside the planes, this seemed like a slow-motion death dance of six fire-belching vehicles, all intertwined in a skidding dance of destruction.

Clay and Shali were jerked out of their mesmerized state when the security guards grabbed them. Shali was shoved into the nearest plane with two of the monks while Clay was rushed off with one of the monks to the other plane. In all of the excitement, neither of them had heard the yelling around them or the rapid wind-up and growing whine of the planes' engines. Even before the cargo doors were closed and latched, the planes' engines began to scream as the pilots pushed the throttles full forward.

The guards pushed their passengers into the cargo seats on the sides of the planes and secured their seat belts before running to their own seats. The planes twisted about on the airfield in an attempt to escape the gun battle still blasting away outside.

Chapter 38

In the dusk light, the two gray cargo planes roared down the runway, one tucked closely behind the other. They lifted off the runaway and headed east toward Lhasa in a shallow climb before veering sharply to the right and slipping between two mountain peaks. Neither Clay nor Shali had any idea what route they were taking to their destination in Kathmandu. Strapped onto the canvas cargo benches in their separate planes, they could see nothing but the mountain peaks that flashed by the tiny windows.

Suddenly, without warning, Shali's plane banked hard to the left, and then to the right. She got a quick glimpse of Clay's plane peeling off in the opposite direction; they were taking two different routes to Kathmandu. Nevertheless, they were both relieved to have escaped the firefight taking place at that long airfield outside of Shigatze.

Strapped into the violently shaking cargo seat and numb from thirty-six hours of non-stop activity, Clay drifted into a daydream about being an American Airborne paratrooper. His fantasy flashed him to June 1944, on the way to the battlefields behind the Normandy beaches. Bouncing around a noise-racked cargo plane, Clay anxiously waited for the green jump-light when he, his Tibetan monk buddy and two armed guards would jump out of the plane into a hail of German gunfire over Northern France. But an extra hard pitch to the left snapped Clay out of his daydream and back to reality.

The plane jerked violently back and forth, dodging in and out of mountains, obviously flying low to evade Chinese radar. Clay noticed the Tibetan custodian sitting next to him was wide-eyed and obviously concerned, and yet he was staring at the near ninety coffin-like boxes strapped in the center of their plane. His concern was not about his own safety; he was clearly worried about the boxes strapped under the netting.

The two of them sat across from the watchful eyes of security guards toting AK-47's, but everyone remained tightly strapped in their seats to prevent being thrown into the ceiling or walls of the plane. Through the small hatch windows in the side of the plane, Clay saw the sides of mountains flash by on both sides. The wingtips dipped and bobbed as the plane wove through the valleys. Sometimes the wings appeared to just miss the jagged snow-covered slices of mountains. Clay found it more amusing and comforting to sit back and enjoy the carnival ride rather than think of plowing into the side of a mountain. He wondered how Shali was doing in the trailing cargo plane - or at least, he thought it was trailing his plane.

When looking at the satellite map earlier that afternoon, Clay had calculated that Nepal airspace was barely one hundred miles from the Shigatze airfield. At an estimated two hundred miles per hour, he figured they should be over Nepal thirty minutes after takeoff. But they had only been in the air for twenty-five minutes and were probably flying slower because of the evasive maneuvers.

Suddenly fifteen or twenty very loud *whooshing* sounds came from the sides and rear of his plane. The plane jacked over to the right almost ninety degrees, as if standing on a wing tip. The plane pulled several G's in the ensuing hard pull to the right. The two passengers and two guards were thrown around in their strapped seats like rag dolls. Clay saw the ninety cases of ancient documents straining against the tightly strapped cargo netting.

Seconds after the whooshing sounds, there was a loud explosion outside the plane. Pieces of shrapnel pierced the side of the plane's fuselage, and Clay saw a huge fireball out of the windows on the left side. His first thought was they had hit a mountain, but then he realized they would have been cremated instantly; the explosion had to be an air-to-air missile fired from a Chinese jet fighter. The whooshing sound must have been anti-missile chaff or flares shot from the back of the cargo plane to defend against the missiles.

Whomp. The cargo plane veered hard to the left, pitching the passengers to the opposite direction in their chairs. *Whoosh whoosh whoosh* - there more flares and chaff, and then another explosion on the right side of the plane. With a sudden jolt of adrenaline, an insane number of crazy questions rushed through

Clay's mind in seconds: Would his life insurance company pay the policy to his nieces and nephews if he was blown out of the sky by a Chinese jet fighter? Had he paid his last insurance premium? How many canisters of chaff and flares does this Goddamned airplane carry? How many missiles are on a friggin' Chinese jet fighter? How far back is that fighter? How many mountains are between us? How many mountains *can* the pilot put between us and that fighter... or fighters? How many fighters are really back there, anyway? How the hell far are we from Nepal airspace, for Christ's sake? Does the pilot have a healthy heart? Where the hell is Shali's plane and did they shoot her down? Just what the hell am I doing here? Did my mother raise a fool or what?

As fast as the explosive action began, it suddenly stopped. The plane settled into level flight and the engines slowed to a steady drone. The cargo plane started a slow climb to a higher altitude. The word "Nepal?" went through Clay's mind.

The rattled and shaken passengers looked at each other in disbelief and relief. The three normally bronze-skinned Asian guards were as white as albinos.

A few minutes later, the door to the cockpit opened slowly and the Asian-looking pilot confidently emerged and took a few steps into the cargo area. Clay could see the co-pilot casually flipping switches and adjusting gauges in the cockpit.

The pilot yawned, reached his arms high into the air and slowly stretched his arms to the left and then to the right. He looked directly at the still shaking passengers, smiled a huge grin and gave them all a double thumbs-up before turning to the left, opening the door to the toilet and vomiting his guts into the stainless-steel toilet bowl.

As the pilot was bending over the toilet, Clay noticed the crotch of the pilot's pants was soaked in urine. He pointed and laughed out loud from relief. His three fellow travelers also burst into a nervous laughter. Even knowing his words could not be heard or understood, Clay yelled out, "I feel better than I have in months. I'm ready to go home."

As the pilot emerged, Clay waved at him to get his attention and then made an inquisitive hand motion about the status of the second plane. The pilot smiled and flashed a circular OK with his thumb and forefinger. Clay sat back in his jump seat and smiled with relief, knowing that Shali's plane had also made it safely out of Chinese airspace.

About ninety minutes later, Clay noticed the drone of the engines slowly drop from a roar to a whine. Total darkness had set in and twinkling lights could now be seen through the small port holes in the side of the plane. They had dropped significantly in altitude, and he could tell they were getting fairly close to the ground.

Clay nudged the monk sitting next to him, pointed at the port hole and asked in a near shout, "Kathmandu?"

The old monk smiled and nodded his head.

Within minutes they felt the bump as they hit the tarmac and then heard the bouncing squeal of the plane's tires. The loud roar of reverse thrusters slowed the cargo plane to a crawl. The plane made a quick left turn off from the runway onto a taxiway. Clay prayed Shali's plane was close behind, and he strained to look out the port holes from his seat.

The plane lumbered along for what seemed a long time. The heavily armed security guards became obviously anxious at this point, unbuckled their belts, picked up their AK-47's and moved to the side doors.

Getting antsy to get up himself, Clay talked to himself in a low voice, "Please remain seated until the aircraft comes to a complete stop. Be careful when opening the overhead bins. Thank you for flying Drukpa Airlines."

The two guards looked at Clay in a confused scowl and then looked at the monk. There was a casual exchange of dialogue that Clay could only imagine was about his self-conversation.

The plane slowly pulled up to a hangar at the far end of the airfield and came to a stop. The crew chief came back from the cockpit, opened the side cargo door and flipped down the steps. The guards jumped out of the door and posted themselves on either side of the plane.

A neatly groomed, well-dressed Asian man climbed the steps to the cargo plane and walked over to the Tibetan monk. They bowed and shook hands, and then began a hearty verbal exchange as obviously long-time friends.

Chapter 39

Kathmandu, Nepal

The Asian man then turned to Clay and introduced himself in crisp, clear English. "Mr. Barton, my name is Mr. Yongten. Welcome to Kathmandu. I will escort you and our treasures to the United States on this journey. We will be briefing you on all the details of these arrangements shortly."

Looking astonished, Clay replied, "Thank God. I am so glad to speak to someone who knows what's going on - and in English, no less. I have so much to ask you."

"Good, we will have much time to talk. But now we must move to another plane."

Yongten politely motioned for Clay to follow and moved back to the door. He paused to inspect the shrapnel holes splattered across the mid-section of the plane and then turned back to Clay with a smile. "I heard you had a little excitement on your way out of Tibet." He shrugged his shoulders. "Murphy's Law, huh?" He then laughed and continued down the stairs.

As Clay descended the stairs, he saw Shali's plane sitting beside theirs, its engines just shutting down. The other plane's cargo door opened and the stairs flipped down, and Shali bounced down the steps with her two Tibetan custodians in tow, all three gaily conversing in Mandarin.

When Shali saw Clay, she ran up to him and hugged him, totally to his surprise. She quietly whispered in his ear, "We heard you nearly got shot down by a Chinese fighter. Are you OK?"

Clay hugged her back, taking advantage of the moment. "No big deal, just a lot of shaking."

Shali then grabbed his arm and turned him around. She pointed at the side of the fuselage of his plane where he saw the huge burn mark and hole-splattered aircraft skin. His mouth dropped open. After staring quietly for several seconds, he mouthed, "Holy shit."

Shali shook his arm and pulled him away from the plane to follow Yongten and the three monks. She said, "Our flight was uneventful; we took a slightly different route out of Tibet."

"What the hell happened at the airfield, with that firefight?" he asked her excitedly. "We didn't see a damn soldier or policeman the whole way, and then three Hummers come out, blazing away when we are ready to go."

"We talked with Yongten on the way back," Shali said. "Whoever they were, they were not the police or military, or at least not under control of the local authorities anyway. Our friends are not sure who these people were. Now, about the fighter: apparently the pilot disobeyed orders and went rogue. They figure somebody must have paid him a huge bribe to disobey his orders to stay on the ground."

Clay looked at Shali with intense concern. "Do you think these are the same people who screwed with us in Jordan and back in California?"

"No doubt in my mind, but they are getting a lot more aggressive. Come on, let's catch up with the rest. We'll have more time to talk later."

They emerged from behind the plane and gazed up as they approached the shiny gray 747 DHS cargo plane that towered over them.

Clay said, "Being the largest air transport company in the world, DHS finally adds some legitimacy to getting these coffins moved half way around the world."

"Yeah, imagine how much this cost."

"There hasn't been a quibble on costs, so far."

They caught up with the entourage and ascended the long portable staircase to the front side-door on the huge 747. The group continued up a second internal staircase to the upper-level lounge in the bulbous head of the giant 747.

Clay said, "Wow, it looks like a sports arena in here."

Shali replied, "It won't once they get those cases in here."

Entering the passenger area, Clay commented, "This is decked out pretty nice for a cargo plane."

Shali counted under her breath. "Fourteen first-class sleeper chairs plus a kitchen and dining area. Real nice."

"I see everyone seems to be staking out their seat."

They scurried over to grab two adjoining seats, and then Clay walked back to a window to view the cargo planes that had brought them out of Tibet. There was bustling activity around them as workers offloaded the gray cases and stacked them neatly on the tarmac. A short accountant-looking guy with a clipboard appeared to be making an inventory.

They felt a jolting thump as the side cargo-doors of the 747 were opened. Clay walked back down the stairs to observe the loading activity. The cases were being fed up a long portable conveyor belt into the belly of the flying beast where they were being carefully stacked four high in numerical order: yellow numbers in front, red in the rear. Each row of cases was then securely strapped down and large cargo nets were thrown over them and securely tied to hooks on the floor.

While the loading continued, Yongten gathered the five passengers in the upstairs dining area. Sitting at the table next to him was an attractive, well-dressed Asian woman in her mid-thirties. Clay couldn't tell if she was Nepalese, Tibetan, Chinese or Indian; perhaps she was a mix. Sitting beside her were five plastic book-boxes.

Yongten then started his briefings in English: "Please let me introduce Pema Lingpa. She will ensure all of the paperwork is in order for both the people and the materials we are transporting to New York. We have all of the necessary papers to prove that the scrolls and books belong to us. No government, institution or individual can claim ownership. Nepal customs and immigration will come to the plane soon and clear us for departure. We have all of your passports and documentation prepared. There is no need for you to say anything.

"After we depart, we will refuel in Hong Kong before proceeding directly to Stewart International Airport, north of New York City. We have processed all the necessary documentation for this also. Your U.S. visas are already in the passports; you only need to sign the forms. When we arrive, U.S. Customs will inspect our cargo and clear us. After processing through U.S. Immigration, we will transport the cases to a secure storage location. We will tell you more on the way to New York."

Clay and Shali stared at each other with a look of relief and anticipation.

"Mr. Yongten," Clay said urgently, "we have a lot of questions. Who or what is the organization that has protected these writings for all these thousands of years? Who has been providing the funds to move them? And who approved the custodians to reveal the writings to me? Why am I now to become the custodian?"

Shali reached over and grabbed Clay's arm as if to say, "slow down."

Clay paused, acknowledged her and bit his lip. He then looked at Mr. Yongten with pleading eyes and said, "Please accept my apology. I am a bit anxious right now."

Yongten glanced at Pema, who politely responded to Clay: "Mr. Barton, let us just say there are people who care about the future of our society. We do not wish to be recognized, awarded or thanked for what we do. We only want the truth to be revealed when the time is right. We believe that it is close to the time to reveal the truth, according to an ancient prophecy. However, we do not discuss who we are or what we do, as there are others who are against us and who wish to stop our plans. There will be more time to talk later, when we get to New York. But right now we must prepare for the local authorities."

Twenty minutes later, three uniformed men were escorted up to the dining area in the 747. They sat at the table with Pema and reviewed many different documents from the five book-boxes next to her. They also reviewed the passenger and flight crew passports and a large pile of official-looking customs documents. Then came a flurry of stamping and signing. Any document that wasn't glued to the table got a stamp.

Afterwards, they all stood, politely bowed and shook hands. Pema escorted the officers down the stairs to the tarmac below. From the port windows, Clay noticed the two cargo planes that brought them in had already taxied away out of sight.

He watched the flight crew in the cockpit going through the pre-flight checklist. When the engines started to wind up, the sole flight attendant asked him to be seated for takeoff. He settled next to Shali again, and in moments the behemoth cargo plane was rolling down the runway of Kathmandu's Tribhuvan International Airport. Next stop, Hong Kong.

Chapter 40

After the plane took off and was in level flight, the attendant served an evening meal to the passengers. The five travelers who had started in a Himalayan cave a day and a half earlier ravaged the pre-prepared meal. After dinner, night caps were offered, as well as a selection of sleeping pills, melatonin and herbal teas. Pema suggested everyone try to sleep until they reached Hong Kong, which was where she would start briefings.

Clay had a shot of cognac and took several melatonin tablets. Shali quietly sipped on a Bailey's. The three Tibetan custodians coddled a pot of a strange-smelling tea. The flight attendant turned the lights down as they all nestled into their sleeper chairs and bundled up in warm wool blankets. Before strapping in for the night, the three custodians knelt beside their chairs and performed a bowing prayer ritual.

Clay leaned across the aisle and said to Shali, "Do you still think these guys are pure Buddhists or some other religious sect hiding behind Buddhism? Or are they not a sect at all and just some people doing the job they've been trained to do?"

"I figured the three amigos were probably raised as Buddhists," Shali replied. "But I'm guessing that the secrets in the writings have nothing to do with Buddhism itself. There may be nothing in conflict between Buddhism and the knowledge in those cases downstairs. Of course, we don't really know what is in these writings, so who knows if it is the real truth, anyway? We're taking these guys' word that there really are some kind of secrets in there."

Clay paused for a moment. "If these writings were just another Torah, Bible, Koran or Zohar, I might agree with you. But their existence and location was only revealed to us through the regressions. The information that led us here was not contaminated by religion or human prejudice. I suspect the knowledge is not a religious thing but is maybe a merging of science and spirituality. Some kind of philosophy mixed with practical science."

Shali twisted her mouth as if admitting her lack of knowledge. "Could be. We'll see what we learn after we start work translating and interpreting the writings."

Clay leaned closer. "But these documents were written by people with human prejudice and weakness. The writers were influenced by what happened at home the previous night or in the market last week, or because of the low-pressure front sailing through - or or maybe even by what a religious leader told them the week before."

They both sat back in their chairs and quietly sipped on their nightcaps. After a few minutes, Clay leaned back over again and asked in a slow, inquisitive voice, "We were told that the three monks, here, will help us interpret the writings. But just suppose there is yet another copy of these hidden writings, but in Europe, the Middle East or Asia. Would the interpretations by those custodians be influenced by their own local cultures or religions? I mean should we substantively depend on interpretations from these three monks in wooly bathrobes? And does this mean that we too will be making our own interpretations of the writings, based on our backgrounds?"

Shali hesitated. "That is all very possible. I know you suspect there may be another copy of the writings, but we don't really have any proof. Clay, for now let's just worry about our copy in the cases downstairs. You are over-stimulated and over-tired. So lay back and get some rest."

She looked at Clay with tired eyes, her lips tightened, head tilted sideways, and then slightly shrugged, as if to say, "Wait and see what happens."

The three robed monks finished meditating and took their seats. All were asleep and snoring ensemble within minutes.

After tossing and turning for a long while, Clay wondered if the custodians' approach of meditating was better than his cognac.

The night flight was short and the stop in Hong Kong was brief. The pilots were rotated, the plane was topped up with fuel and back in the air on the way up the coast of China. After takeoff, Clay and Shali took a quick shower and cleaned up in the small bathroom behind the kitchen area. They all had a quick breakfast and prepared for a day of lessons during flight.

Throughout the ocean crossing, Clay and Shali were briefed by Yongten and Pema on the history of the writings and about Clay's responsibility as the new custodian. The discussions included a background on the three current custodians and their predecessors. They were also told of the many lives sacrificed to maintain the secrecy of the documents and very high level expectations of their new tasks as custodians.

In a break from the briefings, Clay pulled Shali off to the side and said, "Isn't there some way we could get the secrets without all this burden of custodianship? The earlier regressions did not reveal anything about this responsibility. Maybe we can find some philanthropic society to take on the burden of custodianship."

Shali smiled at Clay. "Maybe we should just start our own secret organization, too. How about we set up a Yahoo Group or an Internet blog? The Secret Society of Hidden Himalayan Secrets of the Universe?"

Clay smiled at her wisecrack and shook his head.

Shali then said in a more serious tone, "I think we can do that as soon as we digitally scan, store and makes lots of backup copies. At that point we should be able to turn it over to somebody else to manage the logistics; maybe a university, a museum, the Smithsonian. After we capture the secret knowledge, we're the custodians. We should be able to control the destiny of the physical documents."

Clay looked up at the ceiling of the plane and slowly responded, "Yeah, I suppose.

After several more hours of briefings, a snooze was in store for the travelers as they flew across the Bering Straits to Alaska and across Canada's great Northwest. As the plane approached the Northeastern U.S. border, the flight attendant woke the travelers for a home-style American breakfast of scrambled eggs, sausage, toast and fresh fruit. This was a real welcome for Clay and Shali, who had left California more than a month earlier.

Chapter 41

Stewart International Airport, New York

As morning broke, the plane landed at Stewart International Airport, sixty miles north of New York City. The 747 cargo plane rolled down the taxiway to the DHS cargo hangars at the far end of the field. Within an hour, they were all in the International processing area. Pema had every document in its precise place in the five book boxes, and judging by the scrutiny of the customs officials, it looked as if she needed every single document. Shali and Clay answered the immigration and customs officer's questions precisely as they had been coached earlier. Yongten spoke on behalf of the three Tibetan custodians.

By the time they cleared U.S. Customs and Immigration, the one hundred seventy-eight gray cases of ancient scrolls and books had been neatly stacked by color and number in the center of a large hangar. The DHS cargo-handling crew unloaded the plane under the watchful eye of customs agents. As a group, they all walked to the warehouse where the customs agents carefully broke the seal on a random selection of cases. The contents were exactly as depicted on the manifest and customs declarations forms.

They were then cleared by customs to take the ancient writings to their next stop. Pema placed new seals on the cases that had been opened by customs officials. Yongten returned to the office with the agents to finalize the paperwork. The five passengers watched curiously as the cases were loaded into two Mayflower moving vans, again separated by red and yellow colors. Each truck was then sealed before Pema placed her own padlocks on the trucks' rear and side doors. In contrast to the Tibetan trip, this U.S. convoy had a small but very comfortable bus for the passengers. Everyone had their own row to stretch out and nap on the way to the next destination. This trip had only two

SUV's, but each with two armed guards. Both of the two moving vans also had an armed guard riding shotgun for the driver.

The convoy pulled out of airport and followed the signs to the New York State Thruway. As they approached the entrance ramp, Clay saw a sign for the Beacon Bridge that crossed the wide Hudson River.

Clay looked over to Shali and said, "I know Pema was telling you more about this place we're going to. What's the story?"

"The new cave is in an old iron-ore mine near Livingston," Shali replied, "about one hundred twenty-five miles north of New York City. Yes, another cave. The mine was closed and abandoned in the early Nineteen Hundreds when the ore was depleted. In the 1930s, it was converted to a mushroom farm. Then, after World War II, the Copper Canyon Atomic Storage Company was formed and converted it into a records storage vault for Wall Street and New York City banks. The mine was cleaned out, outfitted with storage rooms, vaults and other environmental controls. It's been used for storage of paper records and computer backup tapes ever since. It is perfect as a temporary home for our writings. Plus the Copper Canyon company can digitize, encrypt and archive it all for us if we want."

"Slick. It's got to be better than the Tibetan caves."

"Pema arranged for the writings to be secured in a separate climate-controlled concrete vault within the mine. When our new, secure research facilities are ready, we'll move the writings down to Washington D.C. That's when the real work will begin."

"But before then, we have to focus on preparing our announcement of the writings and the best methods to do the work," Clay said.

"Pema told me they will help us with an approach to translate and interpret the writings. Our three Buddhist custodians will be very important to this work. Without them, analysis of the writings would be like interpreting an alien encyclopedia from outer space."

Clay smiled and nodded.

The convoy rounded the on-ramp to the New York Thruway and headed north. An hour later, it took the exit east across the Rip Van Winkle Bridge. Still in a mind-numbing daze from the trip, Clay felt he could sleep for years, just like good old Rip. He looked forward to sleeping in a contemporary setting after spending a month in a Himalayan cave.

Chapter 42

Thirty minutes later, the convoy pulled up to the main gate and guard house outside of the Copper Canyon mine. After signing in, the bus and two trucks moved forward to the administrative building. The SUV's and their armed guards remained stationed by the main gate while the bus and trucks pulled ahead to the main office.

Pema and Yongten went inside with Clay. From her familiarity with the staff and surroundings, it was clear Pema had personally visited the site in the past few weeks.

The convoy was directed down the long sloping ramp into the cave entrance. A short distance inside the cave, the trucks pulled up next to a large steel-vaulted door, which was already open and waiting for them. Almost before the trucks stopped rolling, Pema was out and checking the seals on the truck doors. She cut the first set of seals and unlocked the side doors. A small crew of movers immediately began offloading the gray cases and carrying them into the vaulted room. The armed guards from the trucks stood alert and holding shotguns.

Pema orchestrated the movement and inventory of the cases. The cases were neatly stacked in the vault, once again by color and number. The rest of the team quietly stood aside in the large storage room while Pema worked her magic with the movers.

Clay leaned over and whispered to Shali, "Hey. Look at our three Tibetan friends huddled together in their wool robes. They have the look of a mother watching her baby being swaddled in the nursery. I'd say they like the new cave home."

A grin came across Shali's face. "Yes. I'd bet that for most of their adult lives they feared the Chinese would one day find the writings in the Tibetan caves. They knew if that happened, the Chinese would probably take all the writings to Beijing to be scrutinized and ridiculed as ancient lunacy. They are old enough to have witnessed the wanton destruction during the Peoples' Revolution in the sixties. So many ancient artifacts were destroyed in that debacle. And then they certainly experienced the Chinese occupation of the Tibet."

Clay replied, "Had the Chinese known about these writings during the Revolution, they would not have survived and probably wouldn't have survived the next Chinese revolution."

"Yeah, the monks can be more confident that their treasures will be safe, here."

Once the cases were neatly stacked in their new home, the truck engines roared to life in the hollow cave chamber. The trucks left the cave to crawl their way back up the ramp to the entrance.

As a group, the travelers and two of the movers entered the vault and walked down the row of yellow-labeled cases until they reached number twenty-seven. At Pema's direction two movers carefully lifted the case off of the stack and set it on the floor to the side of the room. Pema then checked her list against the seal number of the seal on the latch of the case: it was a match. Shali and Clay looked at each other with continued wonderment at the meticulous accountability exercised by Pema. The seal was cut and the case was unlatched. The lid was carefully lifted open. Inside were neat stacks of individually wrapped and cushioned leather-bound manuscripts.

After rechecking her list, Pema motioned to one of the custodians. He moved forward and carefully withdrew four different manuscripts from the case. He examined the binding labels on each of the four books one by one and opened the cover of each to review the first several pages, confirming they had removed the desired books. As he scanned the contents, he grinned with obvious contentment and satisfaction. His lips whispered out words in an unknown dialect.

Clay glanced at the open book, leaned over to Shali and tapped her forearm. "All of these scribbles … Hebrew, Arabic, Aramaic? What are these written in?"

"This one looks like an ancient Sanskrit."

Overhearing the discussion, Yongten smiled and affirmed her response. "Correct. These are written in Sanskrit, but you will find that the thousands of artifacts are written in a dozen different languages. It makes the job more challenging, but also more rewarding, of course."

"We have not been allowed to look closely at any of the writings so far," Clay said. "We have learned very little about the source and origination of the writings."

"Only safety precautions, Mr. Barton," Yongten answered. "We felt it necessary to get you and the writings out of Tibet to complete safety before we got you too ingrained in the writings. If the Chinese had discovered you, the more you knew the more dangerous it would be for both yourselves and our secrets."

Clay said, "I just wish we'd had an opportunity to examine them in the Himalayan cave."

Yongten replied, "We understand; please be patient just a little longer."

Clay's eyebrows furrowed in query. "But if it was that dangerous, why not bring photo equipment, computers, and scanners to the Tibetan cave? You could have digitally photographed, scanned, cataloged and indexed every page of every document and scroll. At least you could have captured the knowledge."

"Yes, that was considered, but the risk of tipping off the Chinese was too great."

"But if anything had happened to these treasures on the way out of Tibet, the loss …"

Yongten's face turned to a near scowl. "Believe me, Mr. Barton, we understand."

The four books removed from the transport case were passed to the other two custodians, who packed them in a specially padded aluminum suitcase. Smiles of contentment and satisfaction shone on their faces. The large gray case was carefully resealed and placed back in its assigned position in the stack. The group then moved down the row to a case marked with a red number forty-six. They repeated the same process and extracted three additional carefully selected manuscripts. Afterward, this case was also resealed and put back into its place.

Pema then placed a new seal on the shiny aluminum suitcase containing the seven books just extracted. She motioned for the tired and weary entourage to proceed back to the bus, and as they walked she waited by the vault, watching as it was closed with a loud bang. The echo of the steel doors resounded throughout the giant cave. The Copper Canyon staff escorted the group onto the bus while the vault was locked and sealed.

From the expression on her face, it was obvious Pema was relieved. The treasure of knowledge locked up in these cases was now safe from the Chinese government and from any other group who had interest in the writings, whether benevolent or malicious. Pema released the trucks, SUV's and security guards. The rest of the entourage moved back onto the bus.

As the bus pulled away, Clay pointed at the silver case being coddled by one of the monks and asked Pema, "What is in these seven books that you pulled out?"

"Those books will help us with pre-indexing the other writings. It will help you prioritize the sequence of digitizing and documenting the languages used for the original texts, as well as with translation and creating databases."

Clay acknowledged with a nod and a smile and leaned back in his chair as the bus pulled out of the Copper Canyon parking lot and began its seven-hour journey to Washington D.C., their next stop.

The aluminum case containing the seven leather-bound volumes was then carefully strapped into a seat across from Yongten and Pema. Clay could hear the two of them talking quietly in a foreign tongue, but couldn't tell whether it was Chinese, Tibetan or Nepalese. Even though language proved a barrier, their body language came through loud and clear. They were obviously relieved and comforted by the knowledge the treasures were finally secure and protected after thousands of years.

Clay glanced at Shali and mimed a question with his lips: "What are they saying?"

"Idle chit chat," she whispered back with a little smile.

Early that evening, the bus arrived at their hotel in Arlington, Virginia. Their rooms had a scenic view across the Key Bridge and Potomac River, toward Georgetown. The weary travelers settled into their rooms after the long journey from the Himalayas.

Chapter 43

Arlington, Virginia

The entire team met for breakfast at the hotel the next morning. Everyone was considerably more relaxed than the previous days, but were ready to begin working on next steps. Pema had rented a small meeting room in the hotel. As they made their way to the work room after breakfast, Clay said to Shali, "Until we get these documents copied, the most important thing is to ensure the writings are secure."

Shali gave him an intense look. "I absolutely agree. I just can't help contrasting these writings to the Dead Sea scrolls. Those scrolls had simply been stuffed into clay pots and then left, forgotten, in little mountain caves for thousands of years. On the other hand, I'm amazed at how much care and protection our writings have had during that same time."

"I've had the same thoughts, but I don't buy into the whole evil plot thing by some sinister group trying to destroy the documents. It sounds like an Austin Powers movie. I understand the issue with the current communist Chinese government, but they've only been in control of China for sixty or so years. Who, or what, could possibly see such a huge threat from simple words in old documents for thousands of years? On top of that, why would they feel that this knowledge should not have been revealed until now? Of course besides some ancient oracle stories."

"I don't know. We just have to trust them. They've kept the documents safe this long; who are we to argue?"

Once settled in the work room, Yongten kicked off the morning's session with Pema, Clay and Shali. The three Tibetan custodians were not needed at this point, and so were allowed to visit local sites in Washington during the day.

Yongten started, "Pema has documented the story that you must use whenever discussing the writings. If you vary from the story and reveal the truth about the real location in Tsipri, many people will suffer severe consequences."

"What type of consequences?" asked Clay.

"The gravest. If the Chinese authorities believe the cave and monastery were hiding the treasures, they will detain the Drukpas and everyone associated with them. The Drukpas will certainly be tortured and imprisoned; they could even be executed as traitors to the State. The government will claim ownership of all of the documents, and send their people to take the writings back. If this is so, you will not be safe. They will fight you in your courts and use your personal lives against you. They will use your family to blackmail you. There are already enough challenges without making the Chinese angry, so please do not stray from the story."

"Several times, you have talked about a threat greater than the Chinese," Clay said. "If not Chinese, then who else might give us problems? What do these other people want and what will they attempt to do?"

Yongten's replied sternly, "There may be many organizations that do not want the world to know the truth that is in the writings. Some may go to any length to stop you. Most organized religions will try to discredit you, because revealing the truth will threaten their power base; it always has, and it always will. There are also philosophical groups, academicians, scientists and engineers who have reason to want to stop you, but they probably won't kill you - unless they are just crazy. But you must be wary of the deeply religious groups. Don't worry too much about Hindus, Buddhists or others like the Kabbalahists. They will not see conflict with the writings. Plus they don't care much about others, as long as they can practice their own beliefs. They are more passive."

Shali asked, "OK, but what are they afraid of? What is the real truth, anyway? What are we going to find in these writings?"

"You will find out soon enough. Your three new friends in 'bathrobes,' as you say, have a lot to teach you in the coming months - or should I say, years. You will not easily understand the knowledge for many years, so please be patient. You will be confused at first, but it will come to you in time. You have to learn the code to the truth."

Clay piped in, "But what *is* this knowledge? And what is this code?"

"The knowledge is what will make it easy for us to live our lives as humans. This knowledge had to be hidden, encoded. However, the code is not simply a translation of alphabets or words. It must be internalized."

Shali asked, "So how did all of these ancient authors get this knowledge?"

Yongten paused, looked at the ceiling and then slowly said, "You do this regression to get your information, yes? You found our treasures by connecting to souls and tapping their knowledge, correct?"

"Yes," Shali said, "but what does that have to do with the truth in the writings?"

"Everything, my friends; everything. Do souls talk to you from between their lives on this earth?"

Clay and Shali looked at each other, confused.

"If you mean from between lives," Clay said, "yes ... but not freely. It takes a lot of coaxing. If we push too hard, they shut down, and we lose contact."

Yongten slowly expounded, "So in your regressions, it is like you need to develop a working relationship with souls on the other side. The Ancients who wrote these documents did something very similar through meditation. After they developed their skills, the knowledge was revealed to them." Yongten glanced at Pema with a small smirk then looked back at Clay. "If you have not received any of this same knowledge in your regressions, then perhaps you have not asked the right questions. Patience, my friend; it will come to you."

Clay and Shali's expressions clearly showed their confusion, but they let it drop. The four of them continued to discuss the logistics of translating the writings. Later that morning, Clay cornered Shali during a break.

"So just what do you think Yongten is saying? That we might get the knowledge in regressions if we asked the right questions?"

Shali turned and looked out the window across the Potomac River. She hesitated for a few moments before responding, "Well, think about it. You exploited the regression protocols for the purpose of locating physical objects in the present world. Your regressions focused on finding those treasures, and you found them. And you did this by asking the right questions."

"So..."

He paused and there was a silence between them. Shali looked deep into Clay's eyes and lifted her eyebrows high as if saying, "Hello, Clay, wake up."

"Could I be that naive to think I could not get the same knowledge directly from our regression subjects? Get the answers from the source? Is that what Yongten was getting at?"

"Maybe you should be targeting the subjects in the LBL state with an entirely different line of questions."

Clay moved close to Shali and said in an intense but quiet voice, "I don't think they'll give it to us directly. Look at how difficult it is to get souls to focus on discussing the physical lives they experienced. The elders just seem to want to focus on the experiences of the souls under their tutorship and on developing those souls."

Shali shot back, "I understand. But only with the right questions is it possible to get the older souls to spill the beans on the knowledge."

They both looked at each other in contemplation but didn't say a word.

Chapter 44

That afternoon, Pema reiterated details of the story that was to be used: "To cover the history of the treasures, we have created a verifiable trail of documentation that shows the scrolls and books have been in a private collection outside Kathmandu for over five hundred years. For fifteen hundred years before that, the writings were hidden in secret locations associated with Buddhist monasteries and Hindu temples across the region. For the past five hundred years, a private yet wealthy family in Nepal kept the writings stored in a cave on their secluded estate near the Indian border. Tibet, China and India are purposely excluded to avoid any political problems with them. Even with the political problems in Nepal, we have more control there than in these other countries."

Clay interrupted, "What about our three Tibetan friends?"

"You must say that they were hired by the family to preserve, translate and interpret the writings and are part of a Buddhist sect used for many centuries to care for and pass down the ancient languages in the writings. Compensation for their custodianship was paid to the Buddhist sect for temples, monasteries and other expenses. It all looks legitimate, and our associates will verify the authenticity of our claims."

"Isn't this going to look strange?" Clay asked. "I mean, if the documents are not directly related to Buddhism why would these monks be involved?"

"The Buddhists were simply hired to work for them. They were paid for their time." Pema paused to let him think, then she said, "To outsiders, this would be no different than the Swiss Guards hired to protect the Vatican in Rome. You can use that as an analogy if you are asked."

"Yes, but won't the Chinese know about our three custodians from Tibet. Won't they be in danger?"

"They will only use their Nepalese names, not Tibetan or Chinese names. The Tibetans and Chinese won't know them by those names. For all practical purposes, their old names will no longer exist for them. When the publicity comes out in Tibet, if any of the local Tibetans or Chinese figure it out, we will ensure their discretion. Besides, they know if they tell the authorities, they may be imprisoned for not coming forward earlier."

Shali's face grew stern. "What do you mean 'ensure their discretion'?"

Clay and Shali looked at each other, thinking of the incident with the Tibetan driver.

Pema sensed her concern but chose to divert her. "Shali, we have to be very careful not to allow any association with the temple in Tsipri. The consequences would be disastrous."

Clay injected, "So, we claim to have found the writings in Nepal. How did we get there? Someone can easily see that we went into Lhasa and spent over a month in Tibet."

Pema responded, "No, you did not. Have you looked at your passports since we gave them back? You left Tibet across the Peace Bridge one week after arriving. There are photos of you in Kodari, where you picked up your new driver. You then spent a month in Nepal at the custodian-family's private compound near the Indian border, where you worked with your three new friends. Oh, and the flight from Tibet where you had a chance meeting with a Chinese MIG? That never happened. The Chinese will never admit it, either, seeing that their pilot went rogue and took a bribe from someone. The Chinese have already executed him."

For the rest of the day, Pema continued to review details of the manufactured story. She explained every document that had been crafted to build the plausible cover story.

Pema summarized at the end of the day. "All of the documentation is complete and accurate. Please stick to the story. Someday, perhaps to respond to publicity, you may have to actually go to the caves at the family compound in Nepal, and *60 Minutes* or some other TV program would be happy to join you for the story. If you go there, you will be treated as if you are family."

Clay finally loosened up and smiled. "Pema, you ought to be in Hollywood; you're too creative."

Pema smiled and nodded. "Now, what is *your* story for how you found out about these treasures?"

Clay said, "We should tell the truth about the regressions, I guess."

Shali's eyes got big and her head swung quickly toward Pema, as if anticipating a sharp, adverse response.

"My dear Clay, people will not believe you," Pema said. "They will think you are crazy. You will have more difficulty convincing people that you are *not* insane than you will have convincing them our treasures contain the truth about our world. They will say that you talk to ghosts who told you about ancient secrets of the universe. Then you would have two mountains to climb at the same time. Climbing one will be very difficult; might two not be impossible?"

Clay thought about what she said for a moment. "Yes, I hear you. Alright, we'll stay away from regressions and work on making up a story."

"But you don't know what the truth is, yet," Pema said, narrowing her eyes as she played devil's advocate. "What if the truth is something that you don't understand - or worse, something you don't believe? What if you believe it is all just a myth or a lie?"

Dead silence. No words were necessary. They all knew Clay had to come up with an answer to that question.

"Later, Pema," Clay said. "Shali and I need to talk more about that, first. I've been so busy pursuing the writings that I haven't really thought about it. On the other hand, I didn't really expect to end up a custodian for a hundred seventy-eight giant caskets with thousands of secret writings. I never expected to be on a cargo plane escaping hostile Chinese territory either. And we can't even tell anyone about it, or some group of crazies might try to stop us from bringing the secrets to the world."

Pema and Yongten chuckled at Clay's expense. Then Pema said, "We know the burden is heavy. We are here to help you."

"I guess I should have played less solitaire in Tsipri and thought about this more. But on the other hand, you never told us everything while we were there."

Pema looked at Yongten and smiled before turning back to Clay. "Had we told you all of this in Tsipri, would you have agreed to your new responsibilities?"

"Hell no. No way."

The room fell dead in silence. Pema's smile grew ear to ear and she slowly nodded her head, "My friend, destiny was set thousands of years ago. You cannot change destiny."

Chapter 45

After a good night's rest, they started again the next day. Clay kicked off the morning discussion. "So, after we connected, why did you rush to get the writings out of Tibet so quickly? Why not try to digitize the writings there first."

Yongten responded, "It was becoming too dangerous. Somebody knew you were there and they knew what you were looking for. The moment the Chinese would have found out about the writings, all of Tibet would have been locked down. The Chinese would have had a lot more than a rogue MIG on your plane's tail last week; and they wouldn't have stopped at the border."

Shali asked, "The cover story involves private caves in Nepal. Why didn't you just take the writings there at some time in the past?"

Pema answered, "If the current regime in Nepal found out about the writings, they would have proclaimed the documents a national treasure and confiscated it all. Everything would have been destroyed, whether by neglect, improper handling or lack of security. One of our adversaries would have ensured destruction. The Tibetan caves were more isolated than those in Nepal, so it was decided to leave the writings there."

"So your only alternative was to get it all to the U.S.?"

"Or some other safe place. The prophecy said you would come, and you did, so it was best to put trust in following you. Your country is safe and ensures rights to personal property. It was felt you would take proper care and work hard to bring the truth to the people. This was the prophesy."

Clay leaned forward and, in anxious tone, asked, "OK, what about the prophecy? Who, how, where, when? What was in the prophecy that we don't already know about?"

Yongten looked intensely at Pema and then glanced at Shali before answering. "Dear Mr. Barton, you will learn the details of the prophecy in due time. Your three new colleagues are fully aware of the details. The prophecy is in the writings, and your team can translate it in due course. Until the time you can read it yourself, our Tibetan friends will brief you on what you need to know. Please understand, though, as with any prophecy, sometimes it is cryptic; we do not exactly know what is described until after an event has occurred."

"So... you're still not going to tell us." Clay smiled. "Let's have a cup of tea and then please tell us, Mr. Yongten and my dear Pema, what you do for our world? You know, your occupation?"

"I am a businessman," Yongten said. "Import and export, you might say."

Pema added, "And I work for Mr. Yongten. I arrange import and export of products. I simply expedite processes to make the business work smoother."

Clay asked, "And so what is your interest in these writings? Is your interest personal or has someone or some other group hired you to do this?" There was a quiet pause with no response, so Clay clarified. "What I really mean to ask is, who else is behind this? What is the organization involved in protecting these writings? Who were all those people at the first Drukpa monastery who questioned us? Is this some secret organization like the Knights-Templar, Opus Dei, the Illuminati or the Freemasons?"

Yongten grinned and chuckled. "Your mind is telling you that this is an adventure and spy movie with secret clubs."

Clay smiled back. "No, no. I really just want to know who is pulling the strings behind the scenes."

"Let us say that these are people who are very interested in protecting and revealing the knowledge of our treasures and ensuring the prophecy is fulfilled."

Clay blasted away again: "But are you organized just for this purpose or for other reasons, like a brotherhood? Are you an organization just to protect this knowledge, or are you part of a larger entity? Are others trying to destroy you, like you say they are trying to destroy the treasures? Are you all in Nepal, China, India, Rio de Janero, or elsewhere? How do you know who knows what and who you can trust?"

Yongten smiled and replied in a quiet, slow tone, "The organization is very old - as old as the writings. We are very private but widespread. It is not a fan club or hobby group. No one joins; no one leaves. Believe it or not, you are now part of this organization. When you learn and know the truth, you will truly become one with us, and then you will understand why we are the way we are."

Clay asked, "When do I get to find out more about the organization?"

Yongten smiled again. "In due time. Think of it as a movie with you as one of the stars. Simply follow the script and do not try to be the director or the producer; play your part, at least for now. A good movie requires a lot of players, all doing their individual part. You will learn more over time, but right now it is important for you to focus on your challenges."

Pema smiled and added to Yongten's analogy, "Clay, as the Wizard of Oz said to Dorothy, do not look behind the curtain. You will learn soon enough. So, now let's talk about how you plan to explain your regressions to the public."

Clay raised his hand. "Wait. First, what about the cost for all of this? Where does the money come from and what do the people who are funding this expect in return?"

With a hint of annoyance in his voice, Yongten said, "Let me ask you a question: Who gave the money to you to find our treasures in Tibet? What you have done so far has certainly not been cheap. Did your funders expect a return on that investment?"

Clay paused, took a deep breath, looked across to Shali and exhaled through his lips with a fluttering sound. Looking back, he responded, "I used my personal funds. I did not expect a financial return; I only wanted to find the truth of these hidden secrets and bring it out for the benefit of our society, and yet we don't even know what this knowledge is yet."

The four of them sat quietly for several seconds, looking at each other in silent understanding.

"Well, you've got me again," Clay said. "So I guess I already understand more about the motivation of this organization."

Smiling, Yongten replied, "My new good friend, if one can see the big picture, money has no value; truth is the highest return. But let's get back to work. Unfortunately, I will be leaving in a few days to tend to business. Pema will stay longer to help you. We have a lot of planning to do before I leave."

Chapter 46

A few days later, Yongten left for Asia. Clay, Shali and Pema spent the next several days meeting in the workroom, debating about the organizations with which they wished to align.

"Ladies, you know the position. Our sponsor must be a large philanthropic or academic organization. No government, religious, philosophical, social or cultural society should be trusted with any significant, direct involvement in the effort."

Shali said, "We all agree, Clay. The potential for misdirected or special interest influence is too great. Any influence by Christian, Jewish, Islamic or any other Abrahamic-derived religious sects may make it impossible to bring out the truth. The Christian and Jewish domination of U.S. and European governments means we should have no affiliation with or financial dependence on government funding or support sources. There's no need to even mention the Middle-Eastern or Asian governments."

"Yongten and I agree about the governments," Pema said. "Since there is an historical hang-up on freedom of speech in the U.S., we should be safe from government interference here, as long as we are not directly affiliated with them. If you base your operation in a fairly liberal American university, you will have access to skills, knowledge and academics to bring out and present the hidden truth in the words."

"Shali and I began the culling process when we were in Tibet," Clay said. "The reason we wanted to base in Washington, D.C., is because we narrowed the decision to a few universities and they are in this area of the U.S. Our preferred sponsor is Georgetown University here in Washington. In my discussions with them, I piqued their interest, but we still have a lot of sales work to do."

Shali added. "Georgetown University has a broad environment balanced in religious, philosophical, foreign language and psychological programs. I agree this would probably be a good choice. But this is a huge obligation they would have to take on. They are going to want to see that it will be successful and that we are not chasing some phantom."

An intense look came over Clay's face. "Our success is dependent on whether the truths are believable and verifiable. Shali and I still don't even know what the secrets are yet. How can we tell the world that we know these secrets are real and not - as you said - because we talked to ghosts?" Clay smiled at his own joke.

Shali piped in, "I agree, but I am convinced this will take many years of translations, interpretations and debates, so we need a sponsoring organization who will stick with this through years of ups and downs. How do we know Georgetown will stay the course?"

A coy look came over Pema's face. "Perhaps I can help with that. I have already had contact with associates at the university. We have an appointment with the chancellor tomorrow morning, and the Board of Trustees will hear our proposal next week. They have tentatively agreed to provide us with facilities and access to faculty and graduate programs for support. If we convince them to be the sponsor, we could have working agreements signed within two weeks."

A deafening silence fell over the work room. Clay and Shali looked at each other, stunned.

Chapter 47

Georgetown University, Washington DC

Within just a few weeks, the agreements were signed. In the terms, with support and backing of anonymous donors, Georgetown agreed to pay all capital and operating expenses for the endeavor for the next five years, including a substantive stipend for Shali and Clay's time and effort. Within a week of signing the agreements, Georgetown University provided them with a large workroom in the philosophical studies department.

On the first day in their new workroom, Clay commented, "It's a bit musty, and the decor is dated. Quite typical for an old university."

Shali replied, "But the dehumidifiers have helped considerably already. We just need to get some climate control in here. Either way, this is certainly better than working out of a cave in Tibet."

Clay nodded, "Agree. But the storage vault downstairs is really going to need work, particularly from a security standpoint."

Pema added, "Humidity and temperature control systems are to be installed in the vault to ensure long-term preservation of the scrolls and books. This must be completed before we move the writings down from Copper Canyon, but they still have to do more plumbing and drainage work. They are already starting work on new vault doors and security systems." She reached over the table and grabbed Clay's forearm. "Clay, you and I have intensely debated the pros and cons of where and when to perform the digitization of the writings. Now is the time to settle this. I believe it is critical to get all the writings digitized as soon as possible before we move them down from Copper Canyon. If anything happens to the writings before the content is digitally captured on computer, the information will be lost forever. Our three custodians would be the only source of knowledge, but there is no way they could remember everything written by the Ancients."

Clay looked at Pema. "I understand but I think it will be much better to move the writings down here to D.C. first. Let's get it set up here so we can have it all done quicker and safer. We will have more and better resources to work with. We could use specialty companies and even grad students to get it done quickly."

"We have to be realistic," Pema responded tartly. "It could easily take four to six months to digitize all of the writings, even with skilled professionals working on it. There is a lot of work to do if it is to be done correctly the first time. As the writings are digitized, we could move them down here in batches."

Shali interjected, "Pema's got a point. The documents are too fragile and delicate to do it fast or to scan them over and over. We only want to digitize each page once and then capture the image in several different media formats, just in case. It could easily take six months to do this."

Pema added, "And the longer it takes, the longer the writings are exposed and at risk of being damaged or destroyed. I still suggest we digitize them in New York. Copper Canyon can do all the digitization for us. They can then encrypt it, archive it ... the whole bit. We can delay the fanfare and events until after we have it all captured digitally."

"That's not possible or practical," Clay responded. "There are just too much logistics to be able to scan it at Copper Canyon. Politically, we have to do it at the university with their teams."

Pema continued her plea: "Then we could get a work space in Livingston or some other town near the cave and have our university teams do it there. We could take out a few cases at a time; digitize the documents, and then take those back for more cases. It is just too much risk to move them all here first."

"But Pema, we are not in Chinese-dominated Tibet now. We are in one of the largest metropolitan areas of the U.S. Terrorist activity has been in check for several years, and a modest amount of security should be enough to protect the writings."

Shali remained a bystander, quietly watching the ping-pong debate between her colleagues.

Pema's expression showed her anxiety, but her tone of voice dropped to conciliation, "Sorry, Clay. Perhaps I am challenging my past lack of action. I should have smuggled some computers, cameras and scanners into Tibet. The custodians could have easily learned how to use this simple technology to digitize the writings. I could even have smuggled in a few specialists to do the work. The digitization could have been completed already. Then the physical documents would simply be a formality and would pose no risk them."

Recognizing her sense of guilt, Clay countered her argument. "But doing that would have exposed the writings to discovery by the Chinese. If they had found the writings, there would be nothing left to show. No, you were right; it was not worth the risk after these thousands of years."

Shali finally added to the debate: "But the writings are in America now. We're going to get this done, Pema. We should be OK with doing the work down here, as long as we take extra precautions."

Pema looked up from the table, conceding. "Alright, I'll get off of the soap box. We'll do the digitizing in Georgetown after relocation from the caves in New York. We'll work out the timing and details so everything is ready to move once the university's storage vault and work area is completed. The Georgetown facilities manager told me to expect completion within four weeks."

Trying to lighten the conversation, Clay concluded, "And that is near lightning speed for any university."

Chapter 48

Clay kicked off the next morning's session in the work room by asking Pema for answers to his unanswered questions. "Were our three Tibetan friends the only custodians at the temple in Mt. Tsipri?"

"They were the only active ones. There were others in training who were preparing to take their place, and there are older ones who have retired to a simpler life after many long years at the monastery."

Shali asked, "What kind of training did they experience before becoming custodians?"

"The selection process was by invitation only. It was many years before they were even told about the existence of writings, and then it took many more years before they were fully prepared to assume their duties. In fact, their training was never really complete. But once they came to the monastery, they become stronger and more fluent, and they gained better understanding of the knowledge."

"What do you mean by fluent?" Shali asked.

"Fluent in the languages of the writings and the literary codes the Ancients used in their writing." Pema saw the curious expression on Clay and Shali's faces, so she continued, "The oldest scrolls are Babylonian cuneiform, but there are some Egyptian and other hieroglyphs. These older forms are anywhere from three to five thousand years old. Many writings are copies of original clay tablets, palm leaves and wooden slabs. The originals disintegrated many centuries ago, of course." Pema paused, then continued. "Some of the scrolls and books were written in ancient Greek and some in Aramaic. However, the largest portion is in classical Sanskrit, the Indo-Aryan form of the language. Some were written during the Bronze Age and into the Iron Age. Interestingly enough, many were written during the Axial Age from about 200 BC to 800 BC. Some of the newer, larger leather-bound books you see are translations and interpretations made between seven hundred and one thousand years ago. These were also written in Sanskrit. Sanskrit has a good structure for explaining complex technical and philosophical concepts."

Clay smiled and glanced at Shali. "Pema is on a roll; let her run."

They both listened quietly while Pema spewed out hours of background information about the writings.

At lunch, Shali commented, "You sound like a university professor in ancient history."

Pema's smile showed appreciation. "Thank you, but it is really not my field. I just felt I needed a deep understanding if I was to be part of what we are doing."

They attempted to find out details of Pema's personal life, but with limited success.

After lunch Pema pulled their attention back to the language of the writings. "Many of the prominent Ancients, who understood the truth and were willing to talk about it, conversed verbally in Sanskrit, regardless of whether it was their first language or not. However, substantive written Sanskrit is only about three thousand years old and was often times transliterated by sound into written phonetic alphabets of other languages. Before that, it was primarily a spoken language used mostly by intellectuals and societal leaders."

"But it nearly became an extinct language, like Latin," Clay interjected, "despite being a root source of so many other languages. I know that back in the late eighteenth century it became popular to transliterate Sanskrit into written Romanized languages, which enabled wider Western populations to study and comprehend ancient Sanskrit texts. But still, it was almost lost."

Pema nodded and looked down at the metal suitcase sitting on the table. It held the seven volumes that had been extracted from the writings stored in Copper Canyon. Since their arrival in Washington, she had kept the case locked in the hotel's vault, but today she brought it with her. "These books are somewhat of an index to the writings; a summary of the contents, so to speak. But there are so many things we still do not understand about the source of the writings. Before you came to us," she said in a slow, contemplating tone, "we considered having the custodians begin transliteration of the writings into Romanized Sanskrit. There are computer translation programs available that can do a general translation of Sanskrit into other languages. Because many of the writings have no identified authors, we wanted to correlate the writings and identify individual writers and eventually understand the sources of the knowledge. We also wanted to know if some documents were perhaps copied from other documents. Even with what we understand, we still do not know where they could possibly have gotten the kind of advanced technological knowledge that is in the writings."

Clay and Shali looked at each other inquisitively, then Clay turned back to Pema. "Advanced technology? What do you mean by that?"

"The content of the writings; the knowledge. Some of the content is about technology more advanced than we have today. But we'll get to that later."

Turning to Shali, Clay said, "This is going to be bigger than we thought."

"Agreed."

As if ignoring Pema, Clay leaned toward Shali, "We have to build out that database Pema talked about and build an interface to our SRD soul database."

Shali nodded. "I see the connection. If we can correlate the data between the two databases, I'll bet the souls of our recent regression subjects are somehow connected to the originators of the writings. I'll bet the souls are linked somehow. If we can find souls living today that were original authors of the writings, we could regress them. As Yongten said, if we ask the right questions, we could get direct access to the real knowledge in the writings, without having to sort out and decode these thousands of documents."

"Plus, we might be able to get even more knowledge. Imagine asking Jabir's soul to describe his *Book of Stones* on how to artificially create life; or Zoroaster's *The Gathas*."

Shali fired back, "Or Ezra Pound's *The Cantos*. What the hell was he thinking, anyway?" They chuckled at their joint excitement.

Pema smiled and sat quietly, absorbing the side conversation before commenting, "I think you understand."

The three closed up for the day and had a quiet dinner together. After dinner, they retired to the hotel lounge for an evening cocktail.

Clay asked, "Pema, where are our three little robed Yoda's anyway? We've hardly seen them since we arrived in Washington?"

Pema answered, "Please understand they have spent much of their adult lives isolated in the Tsipri caves, studying the writings, discussing and absorbing the content, preparing for this moment in time. This, of course, is in addition to the mundane routine maintenance tasks required to care for the documents. They have also been accustomed to having a great deal of time to meditate." Pema took a sip of her Amaretto. She nodded her head and the corner of her mouth lifted in a slight smile. "And now, without the writings, when they are not meditating, they play day-long marathons of Mah-Jong. Ai-yaaa; they are so addicted." She laughed quietly.

Chapter 49

After breakfast the next morning, they again met in the university work room. But this morning Clay brought a small black leather case. He opened the case and removed several small electronic bug sniffing instruments. The other two watched intensely as Clay started sweeping the entire room for electronic surveillance bugs.

Even knowing what he was doing, Pema could not hold back, "Is there some reason why you are doing this?"

"I found a bug in my room last night when I got back to the hotel. I will come sweep your rooms this afternoon. I think we need to get out of this hotel. Maybe we should move into apartments where we can get more security."

Pema's face turned nearly white from her naturally golden color. Her wide-eyed stare became so intense her right eye began to twitch, and her breathing deep and pronounced. "They know we are here."

Clay continued his sweeping but replied, "I know. It was only a matter of time before they found us."

Looking at Pema, Shali asked, "Who are they anyway?"

"We really don't know. There may be more than one group. For a thousand years, our strategy has always been to stay low and hide. There have been debates in our organization for centuries to become aggressive, seek them out and destroy them. It would have become a small war. But cooler heads prevailed."

Clay finished the sweep and put his instruments back in the case. "We're clean, for now." There was a pause until he continued. "I suspect they now know where the writings are located. But the more publicity and exposure we get, the harder it will be to stop us. I think as soon as we get this all in the open, they will have to back away or risk getting exposed."

In a hopeful voice, Pema said, "Clay, I certainly hope you are right. It is time to bring out the secrets, so we cannot stop. We cannot totally hide from them anymore. There is a thousand year trail of blood following our writings; it is time to end it." She looked at both of them, clearly committed. "Let's get started. Where are we at?"

Clay started the questioning, "OK. Earlier, you mentioned that the Axial Age was a period of time that was a large source of this knowledge. Can you give us more details on how it fits with the writings?"

"So have you heard of Karl Jaspers or Martin Heidegger?"

Clay shrugged his shoulders, implying his knowledge was limited.

"They were German philosophers of the early Nineteen Hundreds through until after World War II. Jaspers coined the term Axial Age: the period from 200 to 800 BC, when many of our secret treasures were written. He wrote a book called the *Origin and Goal of History*. His book defined this period of time as the great source of revolutionary thinking: the period that led to all modern religions and philosophies. You should read his book."

"It is going on my reading list, now."

Pema continued, "We believe Jaspers was correct. He touted the greatness of Greek philosophers like Socrates, Homer, Archimedes, Parmenides, Heraclites, and Thucydides. In that period, he also revered the Chinese Lao-Tsu and Confucius, and the Hebrews Elijah, Isaiah and Jeremiah, and the Iranian, Zoroaster. And this is not to mention the great Hindu philosophers or even Siddhartha Gautama, the Buddha."

Clay and Shali glanced at each other, each looking like the cat that ate the parakeet. They had difficulty holding back the revelation they had spoken to the souls of many of the people Pema had just named.

Pema picked up their knowing glances and hesitated for several seconds before continuing. "It is ironic that Jaspers' Axial terminology, from the German word '*Achse*,' formed the basis for the name 'the Axis Powers' during Hitler's reign in the last century. It is also a bit strange that despite Jasper's Jewish wife and his criticism of the treatment of Jews, they both managed to survive the Holocaust, living quietly in Heidelberg through the war. But one might see that Jaspers was incorrect on one of his postulates. He believed there was virtually no interaction between these great philosophers and the societies of what is now Europe, the Middle East, India and China. He felt there was little exchange of ideas between the cultures, but I believe he was wrong. Many truths identified in the writings were the same across all the distant geographical cultures, regardless of the source. That was one thing I want to prove in the writings: that these people were somehow all interconnected."

Clay injected, "I think we understand what you are saying. Just in our quest for the writings, we have seen there are many connections across the cultures; but maybe we have seen it on a different level."

Pema's eyebrows curled inward. "By different level, do you mean through your regressions?"

"Yes. If we could validate a connection of the writings through our regressions or vice versa, we might be able to substantiate the authors and sources of the knowledge. This may help us convince people that the knowledge in the writings has a truthful foundation."

Shali piped in abruptly, "Don't count on it. There will be a huge number of skeptics, first on the writings but more importantly on your past-life regressions. Most of the religions were derived during this Axial Age and have had two thousand years to ingrain their prejudices into the cultures they control. Even the Buddhists and Hindus might repel anything we bring out. Organized religions of any form probably won't permit their followers' to accept what is in the writings." She looked at Pema with raised eyebrows. "Whatever that is."

Pema lifted her eyebrows in return, surprised at Shali's abrupt yet astute observation, and her pointed nudge for more details on the knowledge. "I agree with you on this point, Shali. And yes, we'll get to the knowledge soon." She then smiled to acknowledge Shali's impatience.

"Let's go back to our history lesson," Clay said.

Pema started again. "Jasper's associate, Heidegger, another German philosopher in the early Nineteen Hundreds, was quite a different story. It is hard to tell if Jasper and Heidegger were on the same or opposite sides. He wrote a book called *Sein und Zeit*. In English it is called *Being and Time*. I assume you have not read this book either?"

Clay slowly responded as he glanced at Shali. "Guilty. But I'll *Wiki* it tonight."

"You what?"

"*Wiki*. Wikipedia. You know, the Internet encyclopedia? You can find out anything about anything on the *Wiki*. It may not always be true, but at least it's a good start."

Pema smiled and went back to her lecture. "The book is difficult to read. It may put you to sleep, but it will give you a sense of what you will be in for with these writings. However, there are several differences. Heidegger never finished the project he described in this book. We believe the Ancients did finish their projects, so to speak. I suspect Heidegger never would have gotten his answers, or at least not the real answers. He was too constrained by the European environment - well, the German environment, at that time. Plus, he never got into the technology aspects that many of our writings go into. Later, being affiliated with Hitler's Nazi Party, he could never achieve his truths in any form."

Shali and Clay gave each other confused looks.

Clay asked, "What do you mean by projects and technology? I thought we were talking philosophical or religious things with these guys."

Pema hesitated, realizing she was moving too fast. "These secrets are not just about philosophical outlooks on life and reality."

"Clay and I have seen the words *'being'* and *'time'* used quite often in the regressions. What is the significance of these words? And why are you bringing in these contemporary German philosophers? The writings in Copper Canyon were made thousands of years ago."

Pema paused in thought and looked intently at Clay and Shali. "Let me give you more of a philosophy history lesson and then maybe it will come together. I need to set your context or you will have difficulty bringing out the truth from these ancient writings."

"Please continue," Clay said. "I'm confused, and it's driving me nuts."

Shali glanced at Pema and they exchanged smiles at Clay's expense.

"Philosophically, the Sixteen Hundreds and Seventeen Hundreds became known as the Age of Reason, and the Eighteen Hundreds and Nineteen Hundreds became known as the Age of

Enlightenment. Some people have referred to this latter period as the second Axial Age. It is not unlike the first Axial Age two thousand years ago. Think of all the tremendous technological advances made in the Eighteen Hundreds and Nineteen Hundreds: the second Axial Age. The first Axial age also had its technology advances."

Shali queried, "Are we still in this second Axial Age?"

Pema clasped her hands together and placed them over her lips. She leaned her elbows on the table, slowly lifted her head from her hands and replied, "I have no doubt, what with the booming technological advances in the Twenty-first Century and the tumultuous churning of religions."

Clay saw Pema's eyes drift off for a moment, not realizing her mind was again reflecting on prophesies of the Ancient Oracles.

Pema shook out of her trance and continued. "If we have entered a new period, beyond the second Axial Age, so to speak, I hope it will be a step forward, not backward. I hope it is a time that takes our realization of truth to a new level: a maturity of our human society. But only hindsight will tell. I expect it will be hundreds of years before we know what kind of period we are in today."

Clay slowly shook his head, confused.. "I guess I don't get it. If we have been in a second Axial Age for several hundred years, then why has there been no more cultural, social or peaceful progress than what we have today? This world has been a social mess for the last couple hundred years, and no one has even come close to deriving, documenting or communicating anything close to the truth, whatever that is. So why has the world not progressed further, despite all the advances in technology?"

Pema gave him a cynical grin and replied in a snappy, confident tone, "The religions and religion-like philosophies of the world came about as a result of the first Axial Age, when most of our treasured writings were created. These groups created their own selfish beliefs from the words of those who had discovered and documented the truth during the first Axial Age. Look at Christianity, Islam and Judaism - all came from the same words of Abraham, and yet they are all filled with hatred, suspicion and non-acceptance of each other. Their individual beliefs could not be farther apart, despite being essentially the same. How do you get such power-hungry organizations to accept a new view of truth that may be contrary to some of their fundamental beliefs? That is going to be your biggest challenge: getting them to accept any real truth."

Shali asked, "Is it just the religions we are going to have trouble with?"

"No, it's not just them or even today's society. Look at the ancient leaders of Kabbalah who created the foundation of the Abrahamic religions. This was before the organized religions, and even they had to encrypt their words in the text of the Zohar for fear of persecution. There are even terrorist groups hiding behind sects of Hinduism that could challenge you. Even many Buddhists, although benign in nature, have a strict view of the world and they may reject your attempts to reveal the knowledge in these writings. Remember, the truths had to be buried in caves at the end of the first Axial Age just to survive. With over two thousand years of incubation of their own version of the truth, today's belief systems will make it difficult to bring out the real truth. Your challenges will be huge. Perhaps insurmountable."

There was a lull as all three contemplated the intense discussion. Clay slowly picked his next words. "But today, isn't the world more flexible? I mean, doesn't the open nature of technology and the Internet give us the chance to get the messages across? Can't we bypass the religious, cultural or philosophical roadblocks?"

"Yes, that is possible, but people are not so gullible that they will accept everything they see on YouTube. People must have validation if they are to turn away from beliefs they have followed since the first Axial Age. That's thousands of years of brainwashing to overcome."

Shali asked, "But can't technology help overcome this?"

"On the contrary, all of this technology and rapid information actually distracts people from self-realization. Even the pure technology in the writings have a foundation in self-realization. People cannot accept the truth as it is conveyed to them without personal validation. They can only do that if they have ample personal time, motivation and tools. If Buddha or Confucius had been hooked on Tetris, do you think they ever could have come to the great realizations that they did? No way! They had to reach a state of self-realization in order to see the truth inside their souls.

Everyone carries the truth inside, but they have to access it, and that can't be done with technology."

There was a long pause as Clay looked at Shali with a mischievous grin. "Or," he said, "could it be accessed inside through technology? Like our PLR technology?"

Pema hesitated, looking intensely at Clay and then at Shali, perhaps sensing the question was rhetorical. She took a deep breath and exhaled slowly. "Time for lunch," she said quietly.

Chapter 50

Clay started the afternoon session, "You said Sanskrit was an Indo-Aryan language. I've read what that means technically - like a noble language and such - but you also made the connection to the German philosophers, Jasper and Heidegger." Clay paused and then continued in a more deliberate tone: "You know the evil connotation the word Aryan carries because of the Nazis. Is there also a connection to the writings? And if so, what is it?"

Pema slowly scratched her chin. She clicked her tongue, contemplating her next words. She looked at Shali, who was now wide-eyed and waiting for a response. Shali understood what Clay was doing to Pema and thought he was bit conniving for doing it.

Pema said, "That term, Aryan, was used all through the second Axial Age, mostly by the Europeans in the Eighteen Hundreds and on through World War II. It became distorted in meaning by the Germans and by the Nazis in particular. It was taken completely out of context and horrendously misused during Hitler's reign of terror. The Nazis supposedly - and I say *supposedly* - leveraged the written works of Helen Blavatsky to build their case for Jewish extermination."

Clay quickly glanced at Shali, who knew exactly what he was thinking.

Pema caught the glance and hesitated but then continued. "Blavatsky talked about Aryans in her writings, but it was certainly not her central focus. She founded the Theosophical Society out of New York, not Nazi Germany; besides, I think she might have died even before Hitler was born. The Theosophical Society is an interesting organization and still exists today. Blavatsky's best known written work is called *The Secret Doctrine*. However, it seems to be encoded with cryptic analogies and is very difficult to understand. Are you familiar with her?"

Clay and Shali again looked at each other, thinking of their last regression with Sogui in Panama where they conversed with the soul of Blavatsky. Clay took a deep breath and let the air out slowly before answering Pema. "Yes, we know her. I agree: her books are not exactly easy reading. I believe she was not well understood and that many people misread her writings and did not understand her positions or beliefs. After she died in India, there were even efforts to totally discredit her postmortem. From what we - "

Pema cut him off. "Clay, you said you know *her*. What do you mean by that? Did you regress her?"

Clay glanced at Shali, as if she might get him out of a touchy situation.

Shali spoke up, "Well, technically, we did not regress her. She died a hundred years ago."

"But, you found her incarnation, didn't you? You regressed that next incarnation?" Pema queried in rapid fire. "Am I right? You found Blavatsky, and you talked to her soul?"

Shali glanced back to Clay as if to pass the baton back to him. The two of them looked like kids who had just been caught stealing apples from a neighbor's tree.

"Yes and no," he responded. "We did find her next incarnation and got lots of information from her soul ... or his soul, or whatever sex a soul is." Clay was almost stuttering.

Pema's voice rose in excitement. "That's how you got to us, isn't it? Her soul is connected back to the first Axial Age, or some previous custodian, or maybe even one of the authors or protectorates, yes?"

Clay took an obvious big, slow breath. He tapped his fingers on the table, revealing his evasiveness and attempt to stall. "Yes, we now suspect that Blavatsky's soul was likely an author of some of the writings in the caves, probably from the First Axial Age over two thousand years ago. But we won't know until we are able to correlate our database with the one you were planning to build from the writings - the database we now need to build."

Pema's eyes sharpened. "What other lives did this soul live? And who or what soul led you to us? Was it the same soul?"

Clay responded with more confidence. "Your first question is answered in our SRD database in detail. Someday we'll sit with you and go through it. Yes, her soul got us to you, but we're not sure which life was the key to finding you. We suspect one of the more recent lives knew where it was hidden in Tibet - perhaps the one before Blavatsky. We focused on her prominent lives and did dig into all of her previous lives. Fortunately, the soul's guide opened up to us. We didn't have to dig it out of regressions to individual lives. But since we got the location from the guiding soul and not the soul itself, it could have been another soul in the pod who knew how to find you. We found several very prominent souls connected in one pod. Many of their incarnations were quite notable people."

Pema shot another targeted question, "What lives, Clay? What other lives did you find in this soul?"

Clay looked up in the air as if remembering the names. "You already mentioned many of them." Clay took a deep breath and looked directly at Pema. "Abraham, Zoroaster, Moses, the Queen of Sheba, Confucius, Buddha, Plato, Ammonius, Hypatia...." Clay let the last name trail off.

Pema sat back in her chair. Her eyes were glazed and her mouth opened slightly.

Seeing the shock, Clay said, "Don't worry, we've got time to fill you in before you leave for Asia."

Pema stammered, "I mean, did you... how did you...?"

Clay smiled. "They've got some great stories to tell along with their pod mates. These three souls were a lot of fun."

Chapter 51

The next morning, they started again. Pema took the lead. "I must leave in a few days, but we have a lot of ground to cover. I plan to come back to Washington after your grand opening, but before the real work begins on the transliteration and translation. In the mean time, you will learn a great deal from our three friends."

"Well, Professor," Clay said humbly, "let's get started."

"You've been bugging me about what is in the writings, so it is time I gave you some high-level concepts of the content. But I am not going to give you a lot of detail. You will have to learn that yourself. It cannot be taught; it must be learned, and that could take years."

Slight frowns grew on both Clay and Shali's faces. Pema had expected that reaction, so she kept going without acknowledgement. "First, you will find there is a specific viewpoint or philosophy of life in the physical world as we know it. This physical world is such a very tiny piece of the real world; the one percent, as those in Kabbalah say. You will also learn about the world of our souls between our earthly lives - the source of all energy in the universe - or the Kabb'rs' ninety-nine percent … their *'light'*. But I suspect you already know about this ninety-nine percent through your regressions. Actually you may know more about this than I do. When you have your chats with souls on the other side using your secret protocols, you have more insight into this than could ever be taught. I think you've got this one nailed."

Shali and Clay looked at each other and nodded.

Pema continued, "Our custodians know much more than I do on this first topic. It will be interesting to see how their knowledge correlates to what you have grown to know with your regressions. You use your protocols to talk with souls and their guides; they use deep meditation to do the same thing." Pema smiled with the corner of her mouth as she threw a tease at Clay. "But our friends don't cheat using CIA spy machines."

Pema hesitated for a moment, and then her face grew stern again. "Next topic: time. Wouldn't you like to know about time? What it is? What it is not? Do you want proof of what it really is? After studying the writings with our three friends, you will begin to understand. After that is science. Much of the knowledge in these writings focuses on the reality and mathematics of energy, but not exactly as we know it. The knowledge you will learn is how energy relates to the universe. Would it not be a good thing if all energy was free for the taking?"

Clay jumped in before she could continue: "Are you saying there is information on how to get free energy in these writings? Like those zero-point energy theories of tapping unlimited free energy? Tesla-like stuff? But most of our scientists say it can't be done; nothing is free."

"I don't really understand it," Pema coyly responded, "but the information is there. When we bring the documents down here to be digitized, you will see for yourself. Some of the books contain extensive schematics, tables, diagrams and mathematical equations."

Clay sat forward with an excited look again. He launched into his machine-gun interrogation mode, "OK, I believe you when you say the books have this information, but I don't get it. I mean, where did these ancient people get this from? They didn't have laboratories, did they? At least, there is no substantive evidence they did. How can they jump ahead of modern technology when foundational aspects of energy technology didn't even exist until thousands of years later? How do our custodians really know what these science writings are and what they mean? And by the way, how the hell are we going to get this information from our three Tibetan friends after you leave."

Pema laughed out loud. "Patience again, my friend." She leaned forward and quietly whispered to them, "Our three robed Yoda's, as you call them, they're like little mad scientists. They hold PhD's in science and physics from MIT, Paris, and Dusseldorf; plus they are all fluent in English. But please don't tell anyone. Shh!"

Shali and Clay sat back in disbelief. Their jaws fell wide open.

Clay asked, "How could we have so completely misjudged their capabilities? How or why have we been so deceived?"

Pema smiled. "You never asked them if they spoke English. Had you asked them a question in English, I'm sure they would have responded. When Shali spoke to them in Mandarin, they naturally only responded in Mandarin."

Clay looked at Shali, "Well, I guess we can't assume anything."

Before they could react further, Pema continued with her story. "You asked how we know the secrets are real? Every once in a while, our little mad scientists built prototypes in the caves, just to test the theories in the writings. Then they would destroy their prototypes, for safety reasons. Sometimes it was quite comedic. They would have little contests. A bit like the old TV shows where little robots would try to chop each other apart. They would invite some of us to the monastery, and we would sit in a circle of chairs in the cave and watch the games. One time they were testing the anti-gravity secrets. We smuggled in some remote-control model ships, cars and boats for the test. They had these models flying around the room, running on nothing but some crystals, magnets, wires and the like. No batteries, no motors. These demonstrations simply validated why we had to continue to shelter the treasures." Pema started to giggle. "There was one time when…"

"Pema," Clay cut her off abruptly, not necessarily seeing the humor in the robot games. "How could you know of this and *not* bring this technology to the world? The world would do anything for free energy. And anti-gravity? What's this about, anyway? Why not give this knowledge to the world?"

Pema took a conciliatory tone: "Well, first, the Ancients forbid it. The prophecies were clear on when and how this truth should be revealed. We had to trust them. Secondly, the world was not ready for this knowledge. I'm still not sure it is, but I can't challenge the prophets. They have been accurate so far." Her face slowly turned to a seemingly remorseful frown, but she caught herself and snapped out of that mood.

"Come on, give us more than that. Why would the world not be ready for this kind of knowledge or technology? Look at the oil shortages and the demand for more energy. Wouldn't this help the world settle down and help us all live together peacefully? We wouldn't have to selfishly compete for resources."

Pema tilted her head at Clay. "We have to be realistic. If everything was essentially free, do you think this would change anything fundamentally? Greed will still be here; greed for money, political power, religious power. The story line would be different, but the plot would be the same."

The three of them sat quietly, looking at each other. Pema finally broke the silence. "Let's go back to the Nazis again. It seems you understand much of their history, but let me refresh your memory. I'm going to give you some facts, and then you sort it out. You must remember the Nazis historical infatuation with Tibet, Nepal and Sanskrit. They made several expeditionary quests throughout Asia in the nineteen thirties and nineteen forties in search for the Holy Grail or other ancient treasures. They were supposedly looking for the Fountain of Youth, the occult and the truth of life. It was not exactly like the Indiana Jones movies, but yes, the Germans really were all over the Himalayas and Tibet. What do you think they were looking for? Be honest with yourself, now. You may soon learn that the Sanskrit word for *"svastika"* means "good to be." That was what the Germans called the Nazi emblem. Add that to the fact that the Nazi Swastika is very similar to the Hindu symbol for "health, prosperity – and rebirth.""

Clay glanced at Shali, "And the Kuna flag."

Pema asked, "What?"

"Sorry. Never mind; I'm just thinking out loud. Go ahead. Please continue."

Pema went on: "You probably know of Karl Haushofer? He was Hitler's mentor. Rudolph Hess was a student of Haushofer and introduced them. Haushofer was a renowned German general in World War I and later became the director of the Institute of Geopolitics in Munich. This institute became the foundation for Hitler's Third Reich. After Hitler rose to power, Haushofer convinced him to create a government bureau called the Ahnenerbe, or the Study for Ancestral Heritage. Yes, the Aryan heritage. Hitler then made the Ahnenerbe an official SS protection squad and appointed the head of the Sanskrit Department of Ludwig-Maximilians University as the director. He then created the Tibet Institute, which expanded their expeditions deep into Nepal and Tibet in the early nineteen forties. Supposedly they were searching for ancient underground cities." Pema's voice turned facetious at this point. "Yeah, right."

She hesitated for a moment. Her voice was almost trembling as she continued. "They got very close. They knew what was there and they were searching for it. But fortunately they never found the caves in Tsipri. The Nechung Oracles in Lhasa, at that time, warned of these Germans. The writings would have to have been destroyed if the Nazis had found the cave. If they *had* found the writings, the world would be a very different place now. We would all be speaking German, I'm sure."

There was absolute silence.

"Even though the writings were safe in the caves, as a precaution, our people in Tibet made copies of many parts of the writings and had them strategically scattered around the region. The Nazis found some of these copies and tried to make use of what they found. They got close to our writings, but the war ended before they could leverage what they had discovered. Their research was confiscated by the American and Russian governments after the War. Who knows what they did with it. Well, after the war our people collected up the copies that had not been discovered and destroyed them."

Shali pointedly asked for clarification. "So you are saying that the Nazis were after the same writings we now have?"

Pema grinned in relief. "Fortunately, my friends, the Nazis did not have your PLR protocols; D-Day came before they could find anything."

"You keep dropping these bombs," Shali said with a bit of a smirk. "What's next? You've got more big ones for us, huh?"

"Oh, yeah, many more."

Chapter 52

Pema took a deep breath and said, "Alright, next is medical. There is advanced medical knowledge in the writings that dwarfs anything currently known in Western or Eastern medicines. To me it is more important than the information about the technological advances. These fragile bodies in which we live can be healed much more rapidly than we could comprehend, and life can be extremely prolonged. The knowledge contained in the writings shows the many ways to do this. You could say it just makes life fairer and easier. I mean, why should a young person have to suffer with juvenile diabetes, or a middle-aged person with leukemia, or an older person with Alzheimer's? These can all be dealt with very easily. That knowledge is sitting in Copper Canyon, right now."

Clay gave Shali a confused look and then asked Pema, "How do you know it's true?"

She replied in a matter-of-fact tone, "At age twenty-seven, I was diagnosed with highly malignant uterine cancer. I had maybe six months to live. Needless to say, I am many years older, now, and I am cancer free - no surgery, no chemo, no radiation. Cured in just a few days."

Her two listeners stared at her blankly for a moment, then Clay scowled. "If you and your organization have had this medical knowledge for thousands of years, why the hell haven't you brought this to society? What's the purpose in letting people suffer for thousands of years?"

Pema started to speak, but Clay continued in a terse, cynical tone, "And how did our mad scientists validate this truth? Float deformed babies in the air and cure them in-flight?"

Shali reached across the table and grabbed Clay's forearm. She squeezed with a sense of comfort yet firmness, telling him to get a hold of himself. Clay looked down at the table, embarrassed by his loss of control.

He looked at Shali gratefully. He then looked at Pema. "I am so sorry for speaking to you like that. I didn't mean…"

"No need to apologize to me," Pema interrupted him politely and smiled with empathy. "When I learned this, I physically came across the table, grabbed the man who told me, and shook him. But now I understand. When you understand the reality of being, the reality of life, then you too will know why we continue to keep the truth hidden in caves. It is not just prophesies that tell us what to do."

Shali asked, "Can you at least help us understand the fundamental reasons for holding back these secrets?"

Pema leaned back in her chair and looked up at the ceiling for a few silent moments. Finally she responded, "Through your past-life regressions, you understand the fundamental process of being. Souls reincarnate again and again to learn and grow - to mature. You even told me that if a soul does not learn its lesson in one life, then it will be challenged again by a similar challenge in a subsequent life, perhaps even more intensely."

"Yes, that's right."

"The physical world, the one percent, is really just a school for the soul. The soul itself is the other ninety-nine percent, is it not? If you have a school but there is no learning, then what is its value? In our real world, how do children grow and develop if their school provides no learning. If we take away all of the pain, the suffering, the sickness, and the challenges of life from the physical body, how is the soul to learn?"

Silence filled the room. Shali looked at Clay, then back to Pema. "I think we understand. But if this is so, why should we do anything with the writings at all? Why bother? Why struggle to preserve this knowledge, let alone bring it out to the world now?"

"My friends, the prophecies of the ancient Oracles say it is time for the next phase of this world. You are a part of bringing out the truth. It is time."

Clay asked, "Besides the prophecies, why do you think it is time?"

Pema hesitated again, looked across the room, and then she squinted her eyes at Clay. "We don't exactly know. We are hoping you can help us figure that out."

Chapter 53

After a light lunch where they talked about anything but their work, they convened in the workroom. Pema said, "Let's get back to work. There are several more areas we have not talked about; the big ones."

Clay and Shali looked at each other as if caught off guard. But with a bounce in her voice, Shali quipped, "Just how much bigger could this get than free energy, anti-gravity and perfect health?"

"Time... Destiny ... Cycles of our human periods on earth," Pema said.

"Whoa. Slow down. One at a time."

There was a pause and hard stares between Shali and Clay as they sorted out what she had just said.

Pema continued before they could react. "Time is an illusion, my friends. We see time as one line, one string, continuous and unstoppable." She raised her eyebrows and tilted her head to one side. "Except, of course, on TV, where you can jump in a machine or leap through a void, star gate or time warp, then suddenly pop up in a different century. No, that is not possible. These physical bodies cannot travel though time. But as for the soul, the spirit, that's a different story. You've certainly read all of those regression books about Michael Newton, Brian Weiss and the other psychologists who created a near cult following due to their past-life regressions? I'm sure you know their clinical studies say they can do future-life progressions too. Tell me you haven't done a few *progressions* along with your regressions?" Pema grinned. "Maybe you've tried for a few lotto jackpots?"

Clay nodded with a smirk. "Alright, I think we understand the time topic. We'll get the details from our three mahjong-addicted doctors, in English this time. But what's this destiny thing? And cycles?"

Pema's demeanor became almost somber. "I haven't said much about the destiny aspect of the secrets. You'll have to wait until you dig in to get the grimy details. I just know that's what the Oracles predicted thousands of years ago, and many of those prophecies have come to pass. On the prophecies that our predecessors followed, the Oracles were very accurate in calendar time, scale and detail. Their predictions make Nostradamus and Edgar Cayce look like tricksters in a circus sideshow. If the fact that someone can so accurately predict the future is not destiny, then I don't know what is. Destiny is somehow related to time. If someone can move forward in time to accurately see what is coming, then is destiny not set for us?"

Shali saw that Pema was struggling, but she pushed her anyway. "This destiny thing, and your prophecies, it all relates to the cycles, doesn't it? You don't want to talk about it because of the cycles. Does this cycle have something to do with the existence of humans on this earth? Is this human cycle ending?"

Pema was really struggling now. Her face flushed in emotional pain, and her eyes were almost tearing up. "I don't know. I just don't know. The prophecy ends soon after this period we are in now, but this could be because we are giving you control of the secrets. In the writings, there are descriptions of five great human cycles. We may be nearing the end of the fourth cycle, if the timing is correct. But it is unclear to us."

Shali quietly asked, "Are you talking about human extinction? Like an apocalypse?"

Pema simply shrugged her shoulders.

"Was the last cycle the period of Atlantis?" Clay queried. "There was always talk about some kind of crystal power source in Atlantis, like free energy. Is that how our three Yoda's figured out how to fly their little crystal powered cars in the cave?"

Pema chuckled and slowly said, "I really don't know. I'm sure you'll learn in the near future. There is so much for you to learn; it may or may not be in the writings. This has always been difficult for me to think about, so I never spent much time on it." She smiled. "Hey, I'm not a monk, and I didn't live in a cave for half of my life, so I don't have all the details. But those three Yodas do."

Shali asked, "So if this cycle is ending, why would the prophecies say we are to release these secret truths to the world?

Why would we suddenly make everybody healthy, and make all energy free, and get technology that could solve hunger, disease and pain in the world?"

Pema said, "Some of us have this theory. I read the past life regression books. They say that if a person has a very difficult or traumatic life, then the soul has a more difficult recovery period in the in-between lives period. Suppose that all on this earth was much easier, more peaceful and healthy, as it was in the supposed time of Atlantis. Then, if the entire living world comes to end in a very short time period, most of the souls should be at peace. Because, it may be a long time before souls reincarnate on this earth, the souls can rest without bad experiences from recent life problems. Then when the fifth human period starts, the souls can again start living lives to learn. But this is just our theory."

Shali saw the barely hidden pain showing in Pema's face, so she diverted the conversation. "I think we understand. We'll work with our PhD buddies on this. But can you help us understand where and how these ancient writers got the knowledge? They had none of the technology we have today, and yet they acquired the knowledge. How did they do it, and where did they get it from?"

Pema relaxed a bit and regained her composure. "If you look back in history, the first Axial Age was a tremendous period of human advancement. Some of the greatest alchemists, mathematicians, and scientists of all time thrived in that period. They did not need all of our modern tools to understand the fundamentals of their world. They *thought* about it, reached into their deepest subconscious knowledge and wrote it down. And, yes, Clay, to partially answer your earlier question, there were certainly previous cycles of advanced human existence, like Atlantis, and they were supposedly more advanced than we are after our tens of thousands of years of development. By reaching deep into their souls through meditation, these ancient writers could pull out knowledge from living lives in the earlier cycles. The information is there, they just had to pull it out. The knowledge was gained through deep thought and meditation."

"As in self-regression ..." Clay commented, almost as if talking to himself.

Pema broke the ensuing silence. "Take a contemporary scientist like Einstein for example. How did he really know about relativity? Could he actually see sub-atomic particles? No. Could he really see an 'e' and an 'mc' squared? No. And where did Einstein ever get that time-space continuum thing? It's similar with our Ancients of the first Axial age, although there are subtle differences."

Shali interrupted her. "Are you putting Einstein at a level equal to - or perhaps below - these ancient mathematicians and alchemists?"

Pema grinned. "I have to tell you that my PhD dissertation in nuclear physics was on Einstein."

Shali and Clay winced at another new surprise from their colleague.

Pema moved back into lecture mode: "Einstein has been my idol, my hero, since I was a small girl. This is partially how I ended up where I am. Let me explain a few things about Einstein and why the Ancients were not as handicapped as our contemporary scientists. Einstein once said, '*Die Natur verbirgt ihr Geheimnis durch die Erhabenheit ihres Wesens, aber nicht durch List.*' This basically means that 'Nature' hides her secrets because of her essential loftiness. But to help you understand the context of his scientific window, he wrote, 'Science without religion is lame.' I have to rhetorically ask, could not Einstein's potential in science have been constrained by his religion? Was not Rhazes' potential limited by Islam? Since the end of the First Axial Age, the core religions have permeated nearly all societies. Could their religions have limited all those souls during our Second Axial Age?"

One could have cut the air with a knife, but Pema was not done. "Let me give you a few more quotes from Mr. Einstein: 'Theosophy and Spiritualism is for me no more than a symptom of weakness and confusion. Since our inner experiences consist of reproductions and combinations of sensory impressions, the concept of a soul without a body seems to me to be empty and devoid of meaning.'"

Pema started to chuckle, "Yes, my friends, Albert Einstein was referring to Blavatsky's Theosophical Society. He never believed a soul could have meaning without a body. With all of your regressions and protocols, do you have that same belief? Do you believe reality is about the human body, or is reality about the soul? Einstein was clearly limited in this Axial age by his culturally driven beliefs. Hey, he was my doctoral thesis and I now believe he never reached the full potential in this life compared to what he could have reached over two thousand years earlier. They did not have as many artificial bounds on their beliefs."

Clay drew in a huge breath and then slowly exhaled.

"One more Einstein quote and I'll let this rest," Pema said. "In 1950, he responded to a young student at Rutgers University who had written a letter to him. This student was despondent and saw no purpose to life; nor could he see any help from religion. Einstein's return letter to the student pretty much gave his view on the capabilities and achievements of the Ancients during the Axial Age. Einstein said something like, 'It is undeniable that the enlightened Greeks and the old Oriental sages had achieved a higher level in this all-important field than what is alive in our schools and universities.' Shortly after I published my dissertation on Einstein, I came into association with the organization that has been preserving these secrets for you, today. That last quote of Einstein's is why I am here. The Ancients knew so much more than our scientists have been able to learn on our own through physical science. That knowledge is now locked up in our cave at Copper Canyon."

After a several more days of intense preparation work, it was time for Pema to leave. Early the next morning, Pema was packed and ready for her journey back to Asia. The three of them met in the lobby of the hotel to say their goodbyes.

"My good friends, I promise to return after the opening events. I will then assist with the digitizing and help with translation and interpretation. I know things will get very crazy for you between now and the formal opening. But if you can, please try to spend time with our robed Yodas." She smiled. "They have fundamental knowledge you will find invaluable in serving your new role as the custodians."

Chapter 54

The next few weeks were insanely busy for Clay and Shali. Shali worked on construction logistics for the workroom and storage vault at the university. Clay concentrated on work with the university public relations department, pre-announcements, press releases and engagement of university sponsors. They worked together to plan for the opening night. Unfortunately, the three monks could not contribute much at this stage, so they continued to enjoy their time meditating, reading and debating politics. When the monks went off for a weekend mahjong marathon with some new friends, Clay and Shali agreed to take off one Saturday night and relax at a restaurant in Georgetown.

"Damn, Shali, this has gone too fast to suit me. We haven't spent nearly enough time with our three friends, especially since they now speak English to me," Clay said with a laugh.

"I know. There's never enough time."

"The university bureaucracy has been really difficult to work with. Every professor, trustee, dignitary, historian or philosopher associated with Georgetown seems to want to weigh in on everything we do."

"We can't be swayed off course by any group or individual, good intentions or not. We're going to dig the truth out these writings and get it out to the people."

Clay reached into his pocket and took out a pack of Tums. A motherly scowl came over Shali's face. "You've been going through a bottle of those antacids every week; stress induced, no doubt."

He smiled with a wince. "No, I have a calcium deficiency, so I'm building up my bones." He munched down several of the tablets, then continued with a stern look and serious tone: "We've got a balancing act here, you know? All this outside influence by special-interest groups plus having the press poking around is hard to juggle. We can't cut them off or alienate them, or they could turn on us. Remember the regressions with Blavatsky's soul, and the dozens of other lives who told us about false information that were put out from groups with adversarial motivations? We can't let them do that. We have to just stick to the truth of whatever we find."

"We anticipated these problems. We should have brought on a PR firm to take the heat off us. I expected pressure from the organized religions, but they've been the least of our problems. I certainly never expected this much interest this early from all these other groups."

"I know. Leveraging the university's PR department just isn't enough. We've got to get a PR firm to help."

"I agree, but maybe after the opening night. It's too close to change right now." Shali added, "We've got to make sure we have the storyline straight on the content. We've been pretty elusive about the technological secrets like energy, gravity and medicine. We only know what Pema has conveyed to us and it is all built on trusting her. Even with the little bit we are leaking, these topics are creating a lot more interest and controversy, any way you shake it. So we better stay clear of the technology until we know more."

"I'm ahead of you. At the opening, I'll talk about it in very loose terms, but we've got to keep it high level and admit we don't know the details. The storyline is that we won't know for several years until we can sort through and validate things described in the writings."

Shali said, "Although, as soon as we understand enough about the technology, we have to patent every possible shape and form of it, and quickly. No individual or group must be allowed to gain financially or politically from these secrets. As noble as it seems, this technology is for the benefit of humankind, not a few greedy entities. If you are OK, I'll line up a few intellectual property law firms to help us with that."

Clay nodded his head. "OK."

"How's your new apartment?"

"Fine. That's a nice complex in Arlington. It's convenient to Georgetown and more secure than a hotel room. How's our three buddies doing in their apartment?"

"Good," Shali said. "They've each got their own room, plus a big living room to play mahjong and meditate. They made friends in Chinatown, Arlington and Alexandria. Their friends are now coming over to join them in night-long marathons. How do you think our five grad students are doing with the project so far?"

"So far, so good. I had them order fifty custom-made glass display cases for the writings. The cases are museum quality - sturdy with shatterproof glass and UV film."

"Is fifty going to be enough?"

"It should be; they're big. But if not, the local supplier can fill the orders pretty fast."

"How many cases should we display at the opening?"

"I figured we'd put three or four cases out on stage - just enough to whet the appetite. We can keep the rest locked up in the storage vault."

"There's a lot of demand for opening night, you know."

Nodding his head, Clay said, "Yeah, this is spreading like wildfire. The Internet blogs seem to have a cult following, already. What did you find out about moving our opening night to the Kennedy Center?"

"I tried like hell to get it, but it just isn't going to happen. It would be at least three to four months before we could get it for just the one night. We're going to have to use the main ballroom in Georgetown's conference center."

"Can we really pull this off by stretching the opening over three consecutive nights?" Clay asked. "Won't it be anti-climactic for the second two nights?"

"We should be OK. It will be smaller crowds, which should be easier to manage - a little more personal Q&A. But the time slot is locked in. We cannot slip it."

"Then we just have to keep on schedule - no slack time. Did the moving vans confirm today?"

Shali replied, "Sure did. They're ready to bring the cases down from Copper Canyon but it is only four days before the opening event. We'll get the writings tagged and into the storage vault within two days. We've got fifteen archeology students lined up to work with us. Our grad students will oversee them with guidance from the three monks. The tags and labels are being made up from the inventory sheets. We know exactly where it all goes in the display cases. The three amigos have been really helpful with this. As of this morning, construction on the storage vault and work room is right on schedule."

Chapter 55

Over the next week, all the arrangements for the opening events in the Georgetown Conference Center were finalized. Five days before the grand opening, Clay made the trip north to Copper Canyon with three grad students and two of the monks to inventory, load and return with the hundreds of cases of ancient writings. At Copper Canyon early the next morning, six laborers from a moving company carefully loaded the one hundred seventy-eight gray coffins into two moving vans and tied them down. The grad students and monks carefully checked each seal and case number: red numbers went into the first van; yellow into the second. The two SUV's with armed guards watched diligently from a close distance, ready for the trip back to Washington.

The entire exercise was uneventful, and by noon, the convoy was on its way to Washington. When they were only three hours out of Washington, Clay's cell phone rang.

"Clay, it's Shali. We've got a problem down here."

"What's up?"

"There was an accident in the storage vault. Strangely, a main water pipe broke, and the entire vault is flooded with six inches of water. There is no way we can put the writings there."

"Crap! How long is it going to take to fix the pipe and dry out the room?"

"Plumbers are working on the water main, but it will take at least a week to dry it out enough to store the writings in there."

Clay put his jaw in his hand and bit his lower lip as the trucks rolled down the highway. "Opening night is in three days. We can't wait. What about the warehouse where the fifty new display cases are staged? Can we use that temporarily?"

"Nope. I checked it out already. It's not big enough and there is absolutely no security. There seems to be plenty of room at the university's conference center though. There is enough space in the side meeting rooms to store the cases. If we hire a security detail we should be OK."

"What if we moved the new glass cases over from the warehouse and put all the writings on display for the opening nights."

Shali's forehead wrinkled as she contemplated. "I'm concerned about the safety of the writings; they seem too exposed. But if we are going to have the security guards anyway, it might make more of an impact to show the whole lot at once."

Clay nodded, as if Shali could see him over the cell phone. "Alright, let's plan on it. It's an extra step, but we've got a lot of help now."

"Understood. I've already checked with several security companies. They can have half a dozen armed guards at the conference center before you get here."

"Great. We are on the I-95 and will be there about seven p.m."

"Bring the trucks to the conference center loading dock when you get here. We'll be waiting."

When the vans arrived, six armed guards were already waiting at the conference center loading dock. Rather than off-load the trucks that night, the guards positioned themselves around the two moving van trucks, in addition to the armed guards that escorted them down from New York.

Early the next morning, twenty students, the three monks and six laborers were standing by, ready to go. Half of them moved the large gray transport cases off of the trucks and into two large rooms in the conference center. The other half moved the fifty new display cases onto the auditorium stage that had been set up in the grand ballroom. By noon, the student teams were carefully opening the cases and loading writings into their assigned shelves in the display cases.

Alongside the monks, Clay herded the students like a sheep dog. He constantly barked out orders to the students. "Hey, hey ... whoaaaa. Take it easy, Rough Rider. These things are thousands of years old. Be gentle, please."

Shali smiled and let out a loud "baa," as if sheep were being herded.

The students mimicked in unison with resounding, "baa... baa... baa... baa." Spirits were high, despite the setback with the flooded storage vault.

The trucks and movers were gone shortly after a lunch of pizza and sub sandwiches. At the end of the first day, with half of the writings securely locked in their new glass display cases, the teams went home for the night while a crew of armed security guards remained posted around the ballroom and entrance ways to the conference center.

Clay and Shali drove over to a little Spanish cafe in downtown Georgetown for a quiet dinner. Clay placed his elbows on the table and put his chin in his hands. He let out a long sigh of relief and said to his partner, "We'll easily finish this up tomorrow. You are almost as good as Pema. Your orchestration has been so efficient and organized."

Her eyes lit up and she smiled. "Why, thank you. But you don't show me the hot eyes that you have for Pema."

A huge grin grew across Clay's face. He tilted his head to one side and said, "Is that jealousy, I hear? And for the record, I am not hot for Pema. Well, maybe for her body, but I have no interest in any relationship-thing with her."

Shali responded, "Just checking. You won't have time for any serious social relationships for the next several years anyway, Mr. New Custodian. Your relationship is sitting in those glass cases on that stage back there. If I can't have time for a relationship, you can't either."

Clay smiled. "Alright. That's a deal."

"How are you coming with your speech?"

Clay breathed deeply. "Making progress. I'll be ready, as long as I get in some rehearsal time tomorrow."

Her face grew more serious. "I'm still uneasy about displaying all the writings at once."

"Me too. But not as much as I was a few days ago. I guess the guards and guns make me feel better."

They spent the evening reviewing their journey to this point and nursing an icy pitcher of Sangria.

Feeling no pain, Shali said, "How about a toast to Sogui."

Clay said, "OK, here's a German 'prost' to our Kuna Indian with the swastika flag who got us this far."

"Yeah, plus a Chinese 'Gan Bei' - bottoms up, for our three custodian predecessors."

Chapter 56

Clay felt exonerated as he was rushed through the parking-garage passageway beneath the Georgetown Conference Center. The narrow tunnel had the distinct musty smell of concrete, damp from years of being buried below the earth near the Potomac River. He was intent on keeping up with their escort, who was rapidly walking toward the far end of the long passageway where the audience anxiously awaited the start of his speech.

Clay glanced back at Shali, shook his head and smiled as he motioned with his hand for her to hurry along. "Come on, let's go. We don't want to be late to our own show."

Shali mumbled aggravations as she stumbled along behind. "I'm coming, I'm coming, and we won't be late. Besides, if they can wait a couple of thousand years, they can wait a couple more minutes. I'm not used to high heels; they're killing me."

They emerged from the tunnel and walked down the hallway to the backstage area behind the podium. Their escort linked them up with the three custodians, who were decked out in their finest bright orange robes.

Shali took a quick peek through the side of the curtain and gasped at the packed house. She glanced toward the stage behind the curtains, where the rows of large glass display cases waited with their hidden secrets. The cases were surrounded by four armed guards who were gazing at the rows of sealed glass cases with obvious curiosity. Two other guards were stationed in the hallways leading back stage.

While waiting those last few moments, Shali said to Clay in nervous anticipation, "I looked through the attendance roster. This place is packed with dignitaries, senior clerics and intellectuals from all over the world. They obviously all want to hear your speech."

"Nah, they don't care about me," he responded, fidgeting. "They just want to see the writings up close. And they know there was a lot of demand for these seats, even though the evenings were invitation only, so they must feel a little special."

"It's like a menagerie of every possible contemporary religion, philosophical cult and discipline. Perhaps they believe the secrets will substantiate their beliefs or cast out their adversaries'."

"I suspect most will see this discovery as little more than another set of ancient writings, like the Dead Sea scrolls - nothing more, nothing less. They'll probably just expect to get a clearer picture of the philosophers and alchemists who lived thousands of years ago. Little do they know what may be revealed over the coming months and years."

Shali turned her head toward Clay. "That is, of course, if it all turns out to be true."

He looked back, raised his eyebrows and nodded acknowledgment.

They looked at the display cases behind the curtain. All of the writings were carefully organized in the cases. Each item was tagged, labeled and neatly shelved. The old scrolls, rolled around rather ornately carved wooden shafts, were tied shut with burgundy-colored, woolen ribbon. The large, thick books bound in brown leather looked majestic.

Shali looked at Clay who appeared half mesmerized. "Are you OK?"

"What? Oh, yeah, I'm OK; just reviewing the speech in my mind. I've been rehearsing it for several days, but I've been mentally preparing for tonight for five years. I just didn't expect my search for these secrets to reach such a crescendo of attention … or to call for an event of this magnitude. I would have been happy with a few interviews on the evening network magazines or the morning shows. I'm just amazed at how much interest has been generated in the short time since we announced the discovery. All these years of hard work and millions of dollars of my own money is about to pay off - not financially, of course, but I never expected financial compensation. I simply wanted to find the truth in the supposed secrets." He chuckled. "Whatever that is."

"Don't fret too much, though. You're not giving any details of what's in the writings; just a high level concept of what we *think* they contain. You've got the story line nailed down for how and where we found the writings. "

Clay added as if he was rehearsing, "Yes, plus I will describe the process by which the translation, interpretation and publication will be performed. I have to make it clear that it could be many years before we can reveal any substantive details on what was recorded by the Ancients. I will talk in general terms about the major categories of the secrets and what we surmise they might reveal."

Shali smiled at him, rubbed his cheek as if for good luck and said, "You're ready."

Looking at her watch and peeking out of the curtain, Shali looked at Clay, straightened the lapel on his jacket and said, "Alright, it's time. You're on."

Chapter 57

Clay stepped out from behind the curtain. He briskly walked to the podium at center-right stage to a large, courteous round of applause. As the applause subsided, Clay cleared his throat and took a sip of water.

"Ladies and gentlemen, I want to thank you all for coming tonight. I appreciate your kindness and patience in waiting for these last few thousand years."

Thunderous laughter broke out in the audience.

"My name is Clay Barton, and I have been looking for these ancient secrets for many years. After a great deal of research and a few strokes of luck, we managed to locate these hidden writings. It took us quite a while, but fortunately we managed to convince those who have been protecting them for these thousands of years to work with us in bringing the secrets to humankind."

Clay had loosened up and become more comfortable with the audience.

"We used some very special techniques to identify and verify the existence of these secret writings. I will not be talking about specific details of the content of these writings because we do not have a lot of those details, yet. That will all come out in future announcements and releases as our work progresses. And believe me, there is a lot of hard work ahead of us. Besides, long lectures can be boring and I do not want you to fall asleep on me."

The audience laughed aloud and several people clapped.

"Tonight, I want you to know that we got very lucky. *Very* lucky. In fact, the day we found the writings, my colleague, Shali Faisal, told me I needed to buy a lottery ticket. And believe me, it was very difficult to find a Mega Millions Powerball lottery ticket in Kathmandu on a Saturday night."

Laughter broke out in the audience again.

"And now, ladies and gentlemen, please allow me to introduce my partner in arms, Shali Faisal, without whom these writings would still be locked up in a cave in Nepal."

A resounding round of applause broke out as Shali stepped out from side stage. She nodded a thank you to Clay, bowed courteously to the crowd, and then took a seat in a chair next to the podium.

"Please allow me to give you a little background on our search," Clay said. "I'm sure you want to know how and why we so persistently pursued the writings. We only found these writings after we had conducted a great number of interviews with prominent archivists and historians. We also leveraged a great deal of research already done by others. Finally, there were other, shall we say, *private*, organizations that believed as strongly as we did that it was time to find and bring out the content of these treasures. So we certainly cannot take all of the credit."

As he spoke, Clay thought of how they had correlated their interviews of historians to their regressions and others' research to the SRI secret government SRD soul database. But this crowd did not need to know that and would not believe if it they did. Yongten and Pema's nameless organization was the private organization, but there was no need to tell the audience any details about that either. If he were to reveal that information it would only raise questions, stir doubt and detract from the gala nature of the event.

As if he were a campfire story teller, Clay told elaborate ad-lib stories of the search, leaving out parts such as the scuffle in Jordan, the shoot-out at Shigatze, or the Chinese Mig jet chase through the Himalayas. He simply described how they believed the writings had been created, collected and stored for millennia by many different groups.

"My colleagues, we believe the original source of this collection may have been the great Library of Alexandria in Egypt. You've heard historians tell us that all of those ancient secrets were destroyed during religious crusades, or by the earthquakes, fires and floods. You've watched the History Channel, right?"

Loud laughter rolled across the auditorium.

"Well, it appears that it may not have all been destroyed. What you will see tonight has been hidden away for the past several thousand years. We all have to thank great historians such as Ptolemy and Hypatia for collecting and protecting these works, but we must also give credit to the original authors of these writings who, before Alexandria, prepared these documents in all corners of the known world of that time. It is not as if wizards created stupendous fantasies from the ether or some hither world. These writings were created by men and women, scientists and philosophers, who connected with some source of knowledge beyond what most humans can comprehend. This knowledge is no different than what has been written or discovered by Einstein, Edison, or Ben Franklin; or for that matter by Michio Kaku on the Science Channel or Neil deGrasse Tyson from Nova."

The audience laughed again.

"As many of you know, the great library of Alexandria was plundered and methodically destroyed over a period of five hundred years by many different factions. When it became apparent what was happening, a group felt it was essential to preserve and protect the most prolific knowledge that had been collected in a special section of the library. That group included academicians, historians, philosophers and scientists - people no different to many of you here today."

Clay played back the complete storyline he had been given by Pema and Yongten. He described the private, but wealthy Nepalese family who had hidden the treasures in a cave on their palatial mountain estate for dozens of generations. The silence and interest showed the audience was awed by the story. He went into detail about the three Nepalese custodians, just as Pema had coached him, and then briefly described the process of how the writings had been moved to Copper Canyon and then down to the Georgetown stage just days earlier. Clay then moved on to describe the next steps.

"Ladies and gentlemen, we have a tremendous amount of work ahead of us. We have assembled a team to take on the arduous tasks of digitization and transliteration to Roman alphabets, as well as translation and interpretation, followed by indexing, cataloging and correlation. Whew. No surprise here; there is a lot of work to do. Please expect to wait many years before substantive information can be fully released, although we will do our best to publish high-level preliminary information within the next few months. We know you are all anxious, but rest assured the real truth and knowledge will be made freely available to all mankind as soon as possible. You will all get your chance to make your own interpretations, but please be patient with the process."

Next, Clay walked through carefully worded statements on what they believed would be found in the secret writings. He used extra caution with the energy and medical technology secrets. Over an hour later and to a still attentive audience, Clay wrapped up his oratory.

"And now, ladies and gentlemen, I introduce you to the three Buddhist monks from Nepal who devoted nearly their entire lives to studying, preserving and protecting these documents. They are the last of probably five hundred custodians who have been taking care of these secrets over the past two thousand years. Even though I have worked closely with them for many months, I will not even attempt to pronounce their full names; I only know their nicknames - and they are not Moe, Larry and Curly."

The crowd laughed at Clay's comedic flavoring.

"First, please allow me the pleasure of introducing to you to Dhamma."

The first monk stepped out from back stage in his brilliant orange robe. The audience began a loud round of applause. He bowed in gratitude to Clay and then to the audience before he took a seat next to Shali.

"Amrit." Clay raised his arm horizontally in a welcome gesture.

The second monk stepped out, bowed politely and took a seat next to the first monk. The applause increased in volume.

"And last but not least, Bikas."

The applause reached a crescendo as the third monk bowed to Clay, Shali, and his fellow monks and then to the audience. The audience stood in ovation, and the applause continued for nearly a minute.

As soon as the audience was seated and the applause had subsided, Clay continued. "My distinguished guests, scholars and clergy, I now present to you the collection of the Secret Writings of the Ancients, which, as I have described, has been so carefully preserved for thousands of years, most recently in a cave outside of Kathmandu."

The deep purple curtains quickly slid open to reveal the fifty large glass display cases. Four of the security guards were diligently posted offstage, just behind the curtains. There was a collective gasp from the audience, and they stood in ovation.

After the audience settled in and sat down, Clay said, "This concludes our presentation for tonight. We would now like to take your questions for the next thirty minutes. Then we will offer you the opportunity to file up to the stage, meet our three custodian friends and get a closer look at the secret treasures - the hidden truths - from the great Alexandrian Library. As we progress with our work and begin dissemination of the knowledge, we look forward to intense debates and discussions on the content of the writings." He smiled. "And believe me, I am sure everyone will have their own interpretation of the truth when you all eventually have access to everything in digital form. And now, if you have questions, the microphones are coming down the aisles."

The next thirty minutes was a non-stop barrage of every shape and flavor of question. Shali and the three custodians also gave many answers to add diversity of opinion to the Q&A.

Finally, Clay concluded, "We thank you for being patient these last two thousand years."

Laughter broke out in the audience.

"Now I invite you to form a line on the right side of the stage and to come up to take a closer look at the ancient scrolls and books. This may take a while, so please be patient. We will stay as long as you like tonight. And please, no flashes. You may take photos, but turn your flashes off. Also, please come and meet our Nepalese friends, who played a huge part - along with their predecessors - to bring this to you tonight. As the *X-Files* television show says, 'the truth is out there.' We will try to find it and share it for a better world. We thank you."

Chapter 58

As the applause died down, many reporters quickly moved to the rear of the hall with netbooks to file their stories. Several lines quickly formed in each aisle. The lines went past Shali, Clay and their three custodian colleagues and then split down the two aisles between the glass cases. Large rope barriers kept the on-lookers three feet away from the displays. In the front cases, some of the scrolls had been rolled open and several books had been opened to interesting pages with medical drawings, scientific formulas and technology diagrams. The drawings and sketches on some of the writings made the information enticing to the now gawking lines of people. Clay and Shali overheard comments such as "Exactly what *are* those?" and, "It looks like my college engineering book."

It was nearly midnight when the last of the invited guests left the convention center. The six security guards took their positions for the night. The next shift of security guards was scheduled to replace them at seven a.m. in the morning.

Clay looked at Shali tiredly and said in a hoarse voice, "Our three friends said they want to stay longer to do last-minute checkups on the documents and ensure everything is locked down tight for the night. Their escort has already left for the parking garage to move the car to the front of the conference center. Are you ready to quit for tonight?"

Shali politely covered her yawn. "You bet. It's been a couple of long days. Let's get our escort and get back to Arlington. Stop by my apartment for a nightcap."

The three of them walked down the back-stage stairs and into the long concrete tunnel leading to the parking garage. The escort talked non-stop with complimentary chatter about the evening's event, expressing honor and pride to be part of their project team.

Just as they approached the center of the long concrete tunnel, a thunderous roar shook the ceiling and walls around them. Chips and chunks of concrete sprayed from the ceiling and from the side of the tunnel facing the ballroom. The hail of concrete fragments spattered the three unsuspecting victims and knocked them against the far wall. They were all knocked out cold. It was a blessing they were not conscious to feel the ensuing blast of near thermoplastic heated gas that rushed through the tunnel from the stairwell to the ballroom.

Chapter 59

Georgetown Medical Center

Clay only remembered regaining consciousness in the hospital bed at Georgetown University's Medical Center. Fortunately, the medical center was located in the building next to the conference center, and there had been only minor damage from the massive explosion that had shelled out the core of the conference center.

Shali wasn't as lucky because she remembered almost everything after the initial blast and shock wave. She remembered the ebony darkness of the tunnel and the silence - almost complete except for the loud ringing in her ears. She remembered the smell of crushed concrete and dust, and the strange chemical fumes that saturated the air.

The experience had seemed surreal to Shali as she lay in indistinguishable rubble, not knowing whether she was dead or alive and with little recollection of where she was, when it was, or who she was with. All she was aware of was the stabbing, cutting pain she felt all over her battered body. She knew she was hurt, but she had no idea how badly. The ringing in her ears vibrated her skull.

She slowly recalled that she had walked into the tunnel with Clay and the escort, and she ascertained there must have been an explosion. What else could it possibly be? She had no idea of Clay's whereabouts or his condition. Shali had faded in and out of consciousness until she was finally sedated at the hospital later that night.

Shali and Clay woke late the next morning in hospital rooms that were just two doors apart. Neither was in a life-threatening condition at that point, but both were bruised and battered. Georgetown police detectives and FBI agents were standing by to question them about the explosion, but hospital security and the

Georgetown police kept the press far away from both of them. The previous night's incident was being considered an act of terrorism, and so the FBI took the lead on the investigation.

Clay woke to find a tall stranger standing over him. "Mr. Barton, I'm a special agent with the FBI. We need to ask you some questions about last night. Can you speak to me now?"

Clay hesitated, stretched his head side to side to try to clear the stabbing pain in his neck. "Yeah. I think so."

"Do you remember anything about what happened?"

After a few seconds, he finally responded: "We were in the tunnel. It went dark, and here I am." His mind flashed pulses of denial in between the pangs of pain. Clay suddenly became the interrogator. "Wait. What about Shali? Shali Faisal? Is she OK? And the kid? What about the three monks upstairs? Oh, God, the writings. What happened? Are the writings OK? Were they damaged? Was this intentional or some kind of freak accident? I can't believe anybody would do this intentionally."

That agent held up his hands. "Hold on, hold on. Not so fast. I'll answer your questions, but I need you to answer mine. First, Ms. Faisal is fine. Like you, she is pretty banged up, but nothing really serious. Her room is down the hall. We'll get you over to see her a little later. The young man in the tunnel with you has some broken bones, but he will heal. He's young and strong so he will be fine. As for the people upstairs in the main room, they did not fare so well. By writings, if you mean books in the glass cases - or what used to be cases, they were completely destroyed. We don't know exactly how this explosion took place yet, but it was complete and thorough destruction. There was no particular focal point of the detonation. It's as if the cases themselves blew up. In a typical bomb, there would be larger pieces of material blown around, and maybe one giant hole in the floor. But this was widespread and complete destruction."

Clay looked over toward the window. "OK, I get it. It's all gone." He leaned back in the bed, tipped his head back and looked at the ceiling. "What about the people? The monks? The guards?"

"Well, that's what we need to ask you. We're not finding much. Some pieces ... well, parts ..."

Clay closed his eyes as tears formed.

The agent continued in hopes of pushing past the sensitivity of the loss. "Do you remember how many people were upstairs in the conference hall, where the stage was?"

Clay opened his eyes and continued looking at the ceiling. "You can't tell how many bodies there are?" Tears streamed down his cheeks.

The agent stood quietly beside the bed. After a long silence, Clay regained his composure, although his eyes remained focused on the ceiling.

"There were three Buddhist monks from Nepal, all wearing bright orange robes. When we left to walk down the tunnel, they were working around the cases: fifty glass cases filled with old scrolls and books, all thousands of years old. There were two security guards with the monks on stage, and two more in the lobby or in the front of the conference center. Two other guards were somewhere backstage ... maybe by the side or rear doors. I don't think anyone else was around. There might have been some janitors in other parts of the conference center, but I did not see them. Oh, there may have been a grad student waiting in a car out front. We had just left the stage and were walking down the tunnel to the garage when it blew. We couldn't have been but a minute away. Maybe two minutes at most."

Clay paused and then dropped his head and eyes to meet the agent's eyes. "What's the real story? Just how bad is it really?"

"There is nothing left of your books or cases, period. We have not been able to identify how many bodies were in the main area of the stage. That whole area was completely destroyed. Fortunately, the ensuing fire was not large and was quickly put out by the fire department. The two guards out front are going to be OK, but they got banged up pretty good. The two guards in the back area didn't make it. The Bureau's best explosive specialists are in the center working on forensics now. This bombing is being classed as an international act of terrorism. It is on the top of our list - on everyone's list."

"Please, you have to find out who did this. You have no idea of what they have destroyed here. Our world will never get to use the wisdom hidden in those documents."

"We'll do our best. Do you have any idea who may have done this? Is there some group or organization that could have wanted to do this?"

"Somebody has been following us for months trying to find out what we were doing. We have found electronic bugs in our rooms and thieves stealing our material." He began to drift off but suddenly snapped back and re-engaged. But the expression on his face made it clear that the pain from his injuries was distracting him. "No, I don't know who it could have been, but I know some people who may know. That is, of course, if I can get them to talk about it."

"Can you give me their names? How can I contact them?"

"They went back to Asia recently. They are very private; it may be difficult to find them. I wouldn't doubt that they are also on the hit list of whoever did this." Clay paused for a moment and looked across the room as if looking out to sea. "But I'm not even sure they would know. They told us the writings were in danger and have always been in danger. They told us there were people who have wanted to destroy these treasures for thousands of years." He took a deep breath, but he grimaced in pain. Then his eyes focused, as if he had just seen a ship across that distant sea. "She knew it was going to happen," he said in a slower more definitive tone. "She didn't know when or how or who, but she *knew*. The prophecy. Pema knew this was going to happen."

"Who are you talking about?"

Clay put his hands up to his face and rubbed his palms up across his eyes to his forehead. He jerked his head to the side, feeling the burning in his face from the bruises and cuts. He jerked in pain. "She couldn't tell us that she knew."

"Who is she? What is her name? And why do you think she knew?"

"Whenever she talked about the prophecy, she got a sour face; she would turn away."

Clay snapped his head back to the agent. "Oh, I'm sorry, I'm not thinking clearly. Pema is her name. Pema Lingpa. She's in Nepal. I'll give you her contact information if my phone still works." Clay fished around his clothes that were folded on the table stand next to the bed. He found his phone and gave the agent the contact information for both Pema and Yongten. Then his expression changed again as he focused, trying to concentrate despite the pain and anguish - a skill that was the product of his years of military training. "That's why she was so adamant that we digitize the writings at Copper Canyon. She wanted to get the words and drawings captured before anything happened. How could I be so stupid and selfish?"

The FBI agent looked confused. "What are these prophecies?"

"They are ancient predictions made by these oracles several thousand years ago. Oh God, the books are at the apartment - in a case at the apartment. We were in a hurry and forgot to bring them tonight, thank God. Seven books. Only seven books remain from all of those writings. One contained the prophecies, but she said the prophecies end soon. Maybe last night was the end of them."

"Can we get these books?"

"Yes, but it won't do you much good. They're written in ancient Sanskrit, an old, almost extinct language. We haven't spent much time on them."

"OK, let's go back to who might have done this instead of concentrating on old fortune tellers," the agent said impatiently. "Have you got any ideas at all? Any starting points for us?"

"Well, from what Pema told us, any religious group could want to do it. The writings potentially threatened all the established religions."

"How could they be threatened?"

"By undermining their power and authority. Maybe it was the church ... the Christians or Catholics ... or maybe Muslims or Jews?"

"Are you saying this could be an organized religious group and not just fringe religious fanatics?"

"The group Pema and Yongten belonged to had been hiding these writings from somebody for thousands of years. Fringe fanatics don't last for thousands of years. Plus, I don't think it was some little rogue group. I can't see it threatening them. For Christ's sake, it could have been the Chinese."

The agent's frustration with the interview and Clay's inability to closely focus was starting to show. "Now, why would it be the Chinese? Do you mean the government, or some Chinese organization, like a mafia?"

"Oh, no. Not just the Chinese." Clay suddenly reflected on the adverse consequences of making a connection back to Tibet and realized he had to shift any focus away from China. "I meant it could have been any government that wanted the secrets hidden in the writings. But now that I think about it, if someone had wanted the information, they wouldn't have destroyed it, at least not until after we had made copies of everything. They would have stolen the writings, not destroyed them."

"Let's go back to these people in Nepal. Do you think they could help us with who did this?"

"Well, maybe. I don't think they would know who it was, but maybe they could get you some leads."

The FBI agent knew he wouldn't get much more right then. "That's enough for now. I know your mind and body are still in shock from last night. Let's give it a rest and try again tomorrow. We've got a lot of work to do at the conference center. But one last question: do you recognize this writing?" He pulled out a photograph and showed it to Clay. It was a picture of some graffiti on a wall:

أك بر ا لله

"It's Arabic. Allah Akbar, or God is Great," Clay said. He looked up at the agent. "Why do you ask?"

"We found this written on the wall in the front lobby of the center. It was written shortly *after* the blast."

Clay paused in thought for a few moments. "It's too obvious. It's got to be a diversion."

"That's what we thought. But let's see if anyone steps up to claim credit. Get some rest, and I'll see you tomorrow. And call me if you remember more or if you want to talk."

Chapter 60

As soon as the FBI agent left, Clay set out to find Shali. One of the four police officers standing in the hallway helped him hobble over to her room. He saw that she was asleep, but when he reached over and stroked the back of her hand, she slowly lifted her blackened eyelids and glanced through the slits in her puffy eyes. Her smile showed that she was pleased to see him.

Without opening her eyes any further, she said, "They destroyed it, didn't they? Whoever they are, whatever they are, they destroyed it. They didn't even know what the writings would say, but they felt threatened enough to do this. For Christ's sake, *we* didn't even know what the writings would say, so how could they possibly know?"

Clay smiled through his pain. "Yes, but just rest for now. You need to rest. I just came down to see that you were alright."

"Two years of my life. Five years of your life, Clay. Gone. Everything we searched for, everything we found … it's all gone, in seconds. Gone. Thousands of years of history: gone. Our three friends: gone. The innocent guards: gone."

Her despair was his inspiration. Clay gently clasped both of her nicked-up hands in his hands. "Shh, shh, shh. Hey, look, I'm the one that should be talking like that, not you. It was my idea to go find the damn things. I'm the one who said we should display it all at one time. I'm the one who didn't listen to Pema when she said we should digitize the writings in Copper Canyon. If we would have had Copper Canyon do everything for us, we would be just fine; but now it's all gone. I'm the dumb one. You're supposed to be encouraging me to go on and find the other set of writings, you know."

They painfully smiled at each other's attempts to comfort one another.

"Don't patronize me, guy. We got lucky in finding this set. Besides, we found no evidence that another set even exists."

"True, but there's time to talk about this later. Go back to sleep and get some rest."

Chapter 61

Clay and Shali continued to recuperate over the next week. As the bruises on their bodies yellowed, their spirits got more upbeat, despite their remorse for the loss of the treasures and of their three Buddhist colleagues. Nothing turned up during the FBI's intense investigation except confusing and misdirected leads. They had determined the bomb was made of a special grade of Italian-manufactured plastic explosives called T4. Two obvious but dead-end leads took them on probes of the American Petroleum Institute and the American Medical Association. But overall at that point the investigation found no substantive leads in the case.

On the first day out of the hospital Clay headed to the FBI to get an update on the investigation. Shali went back to her apartment to call Pema for the first time since the bombing.

"Pema? It's Shali."

"Oh, it's so good to hear your voice. We are just happy that you are both safe after that terrible night."

"Our three friends…"

"Don't worry. We have taken care of everything. The Nepalese embassy has collected their remains and personal belongings. The logistics are all finished."

"And the writings?"

"Shali, I know that you and Clay are feeling guilty. Please, do not feel that way; it was not your fault. First, I should have had it all digitized in Tibet, despite the risk. But more importantly, this was destined to happen. It did not matter what we did; it was going to happen."

"The prophecy?"

"Yes."

Shali asked, "So what now?"

"The writings are gone, so put that behind you. Just get better and heal yourself. But more importantly, you and Clay must be careful. You are in the public eye now, and whoever did this may not stop with the writings. They do not know how much you know, and you may still pose a threat to them."

"Did the authorities contact you?"

"Yes. The American FBI called us. We met with Interpol agents in Kathmandu, and they told us everything that happened. Unfortunately, there wasn't much we could tell them that could help the investigation."

"Do you think radical Muslims did this?"

"Because of the Arabic graffiti? No. Someone did that to divert attention. Islamic extremists don't really have that ax to grind."

"Did they tell you about the bomb material from Italy?"

"Yes. They said it was plastic explosives called T4. The Interpol told us that in the late ninety-nineties, by international treaty, Italy agreed to destroy its national stockpile of land mines. A military factory north of Rome had the government contract to destroy thousands of tons of Italian anti-personnel mines, but someone obviously stole some of the explosives before it was destroyed."

"Do you think the Vatican could be behind it?"

"They would not be that foolhardy to use explosives that came from Italy. Besides they could get explosives from anywhere, or, for that matter, they could make their own untraceable explosives. No, we believe the Italian explosives may have just been an attempt to point the finger at the Catholic Church."

"But why the diversions? Why not just leave it a mystery about who planted the bombs?"

"Shali, we wish there were answers. Whoever they are, whatever they are, they have been doing this for a millennium. They just finally succeeded. But either way, it is too late. What is done is done. We knew this would happen, eventually. It is time to move on."

"OK, but we are going to continue our search. "

"I understand. Let's stay in touch. Maybe we can help you at some point." Before they hung up, Pema added, "Oh, and please tell Clay that he must ask the right questions."

Shali met Clay for dinner that night in Arlington. She summarized her conversation with Pema and then turned the discussion to the investigation. "Did you learn anything from your meeting with the FBI, today?"

Clay said, "There is still no evidence to connect any group or person to this insane destruction. The whole site is clean."

"How do they think the explosives were planted?"

"They have a theory. When the grad students were putting the writings into the new glass cases, some of them noticed fresh window putty in the edges around the display glass; it was probably the plastic explosives, and every case could have been lined with it. The FBI suspects it was planted while the cases were stored in the warehouse over those few weeks. There was very little security there. If the theory is correct, it is understandable why there was total destruction of the scrolls and books without complete destruction of the building itself. They found no substantive evidence of the detonation device - just a few suspicious bits and pieces. The explosion was probably triggered by a cell phone call."

"Did they come up with anything regarding the Arabic writing?"

"Nothing. The press jumped on it and stirred up a hornet's nest. You've read the papers."

The two of them looked at each other without a word. In just the short time since the bombing, there was a revival of anti-Arab, anti-Muslim fervor across the U.S. Paranoia was boiling over with 9/11 anti-Islamic sentiment. It was as if everyone on the street was on a witch hunt for Muslims and Arabs. Right wing groups called for expansion of military operations back into Afghanistan and to forcefully move troops into northern Pakistan, whether welcomed or not. Since the bombing was in the U.S. capital, the U.S. Senate called for new Congressional hearings on terrorist activities. Political editorials in India claimed the ancient writings were historical Indian artifacts targeted for destruction by a radical Pakistani government. Anti-Pakistani sentiments bubbled over in India. That entire region became a political powder-keg in hardly a week's time.

Shali finally replied, "But there is no proof that Arab terrorists did this." She gestured with open palms, "So what's next for us?"

Clay hesitated. "There is nothing left to do in Washington, so let's take the next few weeks off to recuperate. I think I'll visit some family, and then I'm going to Maui to chill out on the beach for a week. Let's keep in touch, and I'll meet you back in Silicon Valley in a couple of weeks. You're welcome to join me on the beach."

"I think I'll spend that extra week with my family. I've been away quite a while, and after almost getting blown to pieces, I might appreciate them more." A slight curve of her lip showed a smile beneath her bruised cheeks. "Besides, if I came over to Hawaii, you wouldn't be able to control yourself; you know what happens, then."

"Me, control myself? Hmph. You're the one with the problem holding up our bargain."

Part III – Forging into the Future

Chapter 62

Palo Alto, California

After two weeks of recuperation, Clay and Shali returned to their homes in Silicon Valley, south of San Francisco. Because they had booked their flights to get into San Francisco Airport at the same time, they linked up and shared a taxi back to Silicon Valley. Clay was dropped off first at his large double condo in Palo Alto, near the downtown train station, and Shali continued on to her townhouse, a few miles away in downtown Mountain View.

Clay opened the door to his condo, and saw something he had hoped never to see. He checked the adjoining condo he used as the office to run his business. The same. Still in shock, he called Shali.

"Hello, Clay? I figured you would be calling."

"Well, did you get a surprise, too?"

"Let me guess: everything in your place has been turned upside down or has gone missing? Every drawer dumped out?"

"Yup. You, too. Who the hell are these people? Everything I had that looked like it might have any kind of information is gone. They even took the PLR books off my shelf." Clay, recovering from the shock, tried to lighten the mood. "Hey, and I had autographed PLR books by Brian Weiss, Michael Newton and Tom Silver. Now, how am I going to replace those?"

They nervously laughed together, covering the pain caused by their personal lives being violated by some faceless, nameless organization.

Clay continued, "They took all of my computers and backups. It's a good thing it's all encrypted."

"It is also good that almost everything was on the computers and not on paper. Your paranoid, spooky Army intelligence experience paid off this time."

Clay smiled. "Fortunately, it's all worthless to them without our computer token chips and our secret pass codes. Since everything is backed up on-line, we just need to get some new computers, and then we'll be up and running in a few days."

"No rush. We've got our laptop databases for the time being."

"Shali, we have to call the local cops, but we should get in touch with our FBI contact first. This has got to be the same people who planted that bomb. I'll call the agent now and get back to you in little bit. You should go check into a hotel. Don't touch anything until the FBI or police have done their magic."

A week later, they both had their houses put back together and had new sophisticated security alarms installed. Shali met at Clay's office condo to plan their next steps.

Shali said, "It looks like the local authorities and the FBI did a thorough job of investigating the break-ins, but again they didn't find a single trace of evidence. Nothing."

Clay nodded. "These people are pros for sure. Clearly, somebody wanted to know what we have been doing and how we are doing it. From now on, we need to be extra cautious about everything."

"The security sweeps you ordered for both of our places also turned up nothing. The guy said they will come back twice a week for the next couple of months."

Clay pointed at several dots on his ceilings and walls. "The security company did a good job on the hidden cameras. We can monitor the video on my smartphone via the Internet. Pretty cool."

In a positive tone, Shali said, "Well, now that all the databases are synchronized and backed up, and our bruises and cuts are healed, I think we're about ready to go back to work. So where do we go from here?"

"I've been thinking about it. We've got a few options; each has its pros and cons."

"So shoot."

"First, we could try to pull the secrets that were hidden in the writings straight out of regression subjects. As both Pema and Yongten told us, if we ask the right questions from the right souls, we might get the knowledge directly from the source. Before we found the writings, we didn't know what we were looking for, but at least now we've got an idea of the topics and categories. If we can dig out the secrets during regressions, we can package it on our own and skip the whole Sanskrit and sheepskin-thing."

Shali reared her head back and pulled her arms as if she were reining in a horse. "Whoa, Tonto. We've got to be a bit practical. There were thousands of writings destroyed in Washington, written over perhaps more than a thousand year period by hundreds if not a thousand authors, each of whom spent dozens of years - if not their whole lives - gathering the knowledge they documented as their little piece of this huge base of knowledge. How many decades or centuries will it take the two of us to replicate that, Clay?" She raised her eyebrows and smiled to show that she knew she was being hard on him. "To pour a little salt on that wound: two things. First, few people are going to buy the validity of regressions or the PLR protocols as a means of verifying this knowledge. Second, there is no telling whether we could even get our subjects' souls or guides to turn their cards over and give us the secrets. You know what happens every time we start digging into details. The souls and their guides hold back; they are always cautious about what they tell us. If they suspect we have ulterior motives, they clam up. You know they're all interconnected. What if they put the word out on the proverbial soul street and make us incognito? We'd get shut down."

The fifteen-second pause seemed to last fifteen minutes. Shali knew she had hit a sore spot.

Clay got up and asked, "Tea?"

"Sure, that would be nice."

Chapter 63

Clay came back with two cups of tea. He sat down and took a sip from his cup. He took a deep breath and exhaled slowly.

Shali leaned over and rubbed his forearm. She broke the silence, "What's the next option, Cowboy?

"You are too practical, my lady." He perked up and moved on. "Our second option is to start with the last three souls that led us to the writings in Tibet. We dig out the data just like before and look for another set of the writings, if another set exists. These three souls were in the same pod. There may be other souls in that pod who are incarnated today. Maybe some of them could help us find another set."

Shali nodded. "OK, I hear you. Got more options?"

"Yeah. We could ask Pema and Yongten to set us up with any previous custodians who are still living. If we regress them, maybe we will find they were custodians in a previous life too, perhaps for the other set of writings. Maybe we can find the other set of writings through them."

"And?"

"Or we could take a more direct approach. We could just talk with the old custodians and document as much as possible about the knowledge they can recall. If we pick out the high points, we could replicate the writings' most important aspects. That shouldn't be thousands of books worth of information. You know how writers are - even the ancient ones. There's a lot of fluff in those writings that don't add much value and are just examples of an author's literary freedom. A writer might take a hundred or a thousand pages to say what could be said in ten. We only want the plot right now. Once we get the foundation, we can supplement it with regression details from our last three targets in Jordan, Scotland and Panama."

"Alright. That's an option. Any others?" she asked.

"I'd like to regress both Yongten and Pema, or maybe some of those others we saw at the first Tibetan monastery. Some past-life experiences must have compelled them to do what they did for those writings. I'm sure we could find something in their regressions. Maybe a combination of all of these approaches is what we need. We won't know until we start digging in."

"Several things come to my mind. First, Yongten's secret mystery club appears to be very well connected internationally. Why wouldn't they already know where the second or third set is located? Why wouldn't they just tell us so we can bring it forth?"

Clay tilted his head and looked intently at Shali. "Hey, come on. We just got all of their ancient books blown to smithereens. They've been hiding this stuff for thousands of years, and in less than two months we managed to get it completely wiped out."

"Yeah, you're probably right. Even if they knew where a set was located, I can't see them helping us find it. But more importantly, there is no evidence of another set of writings existing - it's only been alluded to in our regressions. I don't give us much chance of finding it through Yongten's and Pema's organization. We'll probably have better luck on our own."

Clay's voice shifted to a slow, remorseful tone. "How could we have been so careless?"

Shali chided, "It is *not* our fault. Look at the prophecies Pema kept talking about. We don't know what is in the prophecies, yet, but Pema seemed to know about the bombing before it happened. We need to translate the seven surviving books and find out what is in the prophecies. I especially want to know whether it ends with the bombing or continues a little longer. Plus I would like to find out how we play in this prophecy game."

Clay nodded. "That should be a priority."

"Good. I'll start work on translating the seven remaining books. I can't read the Sanskrit fluently, so I'll need help. Leave that to me though. You can start reviewing the transcripts and tapes of the regressions of our three pigs in a soul pod."

Counter to Shali's perky attitude, Clay frowned. "There's one thing that's been on my mind about the prophecy. Were we supposed to die in that bombing? And if not, what is our role now? Do we just fade away or is there still a part for us?"

Shali put her fingers on her lips in contemplation. "I have the same questions, but my biggest concern right now is who bombed

Georgetown. They'll do it again, so we have to figure out how do deal with them. It's interesting that they blew it up when so few bystanders were there. They were targeting the writings, and perhaps the three monks who knew everything that was in them. But they kept the collateral damage to a minimum. Would a hard-core terrorist group be so careful? I think not. Terrorists would blast away for maximum effect, but these people had some scruples. Although I think they intended to get us, too. My other question is, will they come for you and me again, beyond a simple break-in of our condos? Are we a threat to them, particularly if we continue? Unless these bad guys are dealt with, they're going to blow up any set of writings we might find."

Clay said, "Total agreement."

"This is particularly so since the press has been all over us the past month. They started working on me after they realized they couldn't crack your shell. I saw that *60 Minutes* clip about the bombing in Georgetown. They cynically called it 'Kathmandu's Secrets of the Universe.' You made me laugh when the cameras pinned you against your car in the grocery store parking lot. I loved your comment about pretending to be Indiana Jones looking for the magic ruby cabbage in the vegetable section. You're precious."

They both laughed.

"Unfortunately, they made us look like zealots or cultist quacks," she continued. "Now that they know about the regressions, they're just painting weirdo pictures of us as 'ghost talkers.' I'd guess it is only a matter of time before a couple of our past regression subjects come out in the open and get us really blasted."

Clay looked at Shali with conciliation. "I'm not sure they will. We used Protocol 75 on all of them except Sogui. None of them should remember anything about the regressions. They may not even recognize us if they saw us on TV. But first the press has to find them. That's why it is all the more important to keep our data and systems locked down. Some young, weasel-like roving reporter would do anything to crack us wide open. They won't care what it takes."

Shali said with a teasing tone, "You know, we're going to end up on the road doing regressions, regardless of the path we take."

Clay smiled back at her. "For sure. But that's the fun part. Hey, there's a Giants baseball game tonight. Are you up for taking the train to the city?"

"Only if you buy me a big hot dog."

Clay nodded. "Deal. So, are you breaking your vegan shroud tonight?"

"Hey, if the beer and the dogs are free and it's a good game, I'll lower myself to barbarian meat-eating habits. But I want the fat, juicy polish sausage, not a cheap beef dog. And deli mustard, with extra relish, and kraut on the side."

Chapter 64

The next morning after the San Francisco Giants took a whopping defeat by San Diego, Clay jumped straight into work at his office condo. At her townhouse, Shali went to work on arranging translation of the seven surviving books.

Clay started by reviewing the series of regressions on the three souls that had led them to the writings. He loaded up the SRD database and retrieved the incarnation summary for the three target subjects. He remembered their soul registration numbers by heart:

SE49-5433 Iqbal Al-Suhari
TP88-4546 Tommy Evans
DF73-7221   Sogui Iglesias

Two days later, they had lunch in downtown Palo Alto to catch up on progress.

Clay opened the discussion. "I retraced our footsteps over the past year in hopes of picking up some clue that we missed. I was hoping we could get enough data points to connect the dots. I started on Iqbal's regression by reading the English transcripts from the encrypted database, but I've found nothing more than what we had before. I'll spend the next several days working on Tommy's files.

"I suspect you won't find anything new in Tommy's file, either," Shali replied, "but there was something different about Sogui's soul."

"Yeah, her guide clammed up several times. The guide got us to the writings, but there's more there than meets the eye - Third Eye, that is." The corner of Clay's mouth turned up in a smile at his own little pun. "So, did you make any progress on getting a Sanskrit guru to translate the books?"

"I narrowed it to a couple of college professors from India who claimed they can do the job. I also found a multi-lingual translator from Nepal down in LA." She hesitated and then said in a reserved voice, "Clay, somebody has been digging around and asking Sanskrit translators about us and looking for people who can translate Sanskrit. This Nepalese lady told me she was contacted by someone who offered a lot of money to get a copy of anything she translated for us. I went back and asked the other two if they had also been contacted. Neither one would own up to it, but I could tell they had also been approached."

Clay just sat there with a blank stare.

Shali continued, "I called the FBI agent this morning and told him. He said they would check it out and let us know if they get any leads. However, he feels positive that the same group that blew up the writings is trying to find out what we are doing."

Clay nodded, still thinking over her words.

"I did a rough translation of the Sanskrit on an extract from the one of the books," Shali said. "I gave the extract to the translator, just to test of her skills. After I get her version back, I'll check for accuracy and clarity. If I can get her cracking on the books, it will take a couple of weeks to get the translations done, by her estimates. I'll want to translate the prophecy, first. It is a small book, so we could get that back in a few days."

"Sounds like a plan, but can we trust her?"

"I think so. She asked if these were part of the writings that were destroyed in Georgetown. She seemed to be truly appalled. Plus she openly told me about the strangers inquiring about our work."

"OK, let's go back to work."

A few days later they met at Clay's office to catch up on progress again.

"I got nothing new out of reviewing Tommy's recordings," he said. "But I feel we may get a lead if we regressed him again. Tommy's life as Dolpopo the Buddha seems key to me. When we regressed him before, we didn't know that the writings were hidden in Tibet. Tibet was a hangout for Dolpopo. It's too much of a coincidence. His soul might know about one of the other sets."

Shali shook her head in disagreement. "I don't know. Whoever was hiding the writings would not want any connection between the hiding locations. It's a bit like Al-Qaeda's technique of keeping terrorist cells independent of one another. None of the 9/11 World Trade Center bombers knew each other. I don't know if his soul would be aware of the other writings just because he knew about our first set." Turning more conciliatory, she added, "But it's worth a try."

Clay said, "I hear you, but even if Tommy's soul doesn't know, maybe his guide does. Let me finish reviewing Sogui's recordings this week and then we can decide what to do next. Are you making progress?"

"Yeah, I hired the lady translator in LA. She finished the prophecies and a couple of the other books. The oracles who made these predictions lived in Claros, Turkey. This was just north of Ephesus, where Jesus Christ's mother Mary lived out her life after his crucifixion. Claros was a hot bed of oracles and psychics as far back as 500 BC. In fact, even Alexander the Great used to have his fortune told in Claros. Supposedly the Claros oracles told Alexander where to build the great city of Alexandria. Maybe there is some connection to the library of Alexandria. Anyways, the prophecies were written in a poetic style of stanzas. The translations were not as cryptic as I expected. They contained poetic filler to make the prediction fit the flowing style. On the other hand, there could be more prophetic secrets hidden in the filler. I just can't tell at this point."

Clay asked, "What time frame were the prophecies written in?"

"From the style, the translator thought it was written about 100 to 200 BC. It's a little spooky, but the predictions described your appearance at the Drukpa Monastery in Tibet with a fair amount of accuracy. It is no wonder the custodians felt it was time to relinquish control of the writings to us. The auditorium and bombing were also described in enough detail to be scary, including the fate of the three custodians during the explosion."

Looking a bit stunned, Clay asked, "They knew they were going to die, didn't they? They knew their destiny."

Shali's face turned serious, showing she was obviously disturbed. "They not only knew they would die, they knew we would *not* die; they had to get us out of the auditorium that night."

"What are you saying?"

Shali's voice dropped low. "They purposely stayed behind that night. Remember they told us to leave and go back to the hotel while they finished up? They were simply enabling the prophecy to be fulfilled. The prophecy ended abruptly at that point. We were not to die that night. Listen to the last stanza:

'And hence on the night of first announce,
To world of men who doubt and deny,
From flame and fire, burn the skins of truth,
And the three who protect, shall perish from earth.
The ones who came from land afar,
To bring the truth to all who shall hear,
Have no proof from which to speak,
But continue the quest for truth to teach.'"

Silence permeated the room as a tear slid down Clay's cheek. Shali had trouble seeing Clay through her own tear-filled eyes. Neither understood why, or how, they were destined to continue the search and bring out the truth.

Shali finally broke the silence. "Do you think there are other prophecies that take us to the next step?"

Clay said, "There probably are, but we don't have them. I'd like to find them, though, because if we can't control destiny, I'd at least like to have some idea of what is going to happen next."

Clay walked over to a small liquor cabinet in the back of the office and pulled out two crystal snifters and a bottle of cognac. He poured a small amount into each glass and passed one to Shali.

He lifted his glass in the air. "To our three friends: may we have their courage to continue the quest, and may we be as strong as they were to look destiny in the eye."

Chapter 65

Early the next week they met at the office again. Clay leaned back in his chair, interlaced his fingers behind his head, and exhaled slowly. "After going through the recordings and transcripts of all three regressions, I think we've got two options. First, we should get back to Tommy in Wales. I'd like to target his life as Dolpopo. I still think there's a chance that he, or the soul, was aware of our writings hidden under the Drukpa Monastery. He might even have been one of the earlier custodians, or his soul might have been a more recent custodian of one of the other set of writings."

Shali said, "I'm up for it. What's the other?"

"We go back to see Sogui in Panama. We got the location of the first set of writings from the guide, not the soul. Seeing how this pod is intertwined, maybe another soul the guide mentors is aware of another set of writings. Besides, I've still got the feeling that Sogui's soul and the guide were purposely holding back."

Shali reared her head back. "Holding back? Holy cow, Clay, she gave us the location without us even having to pry it out. That's holding back?" She smiled with raised eyebrows to show she was playing devil's advocate.

"That's not what I mean. We know there were a couple of four- or five-hundred-year stints that didn't reveal any incarnations. Does that sound normal for a soul that is used to being so prominent in society - to just take off to the beach and relax for half a millennium at a time?"

Shali shrugged her shoulders. "Yeah, yeah, but she did live a couple of tough lives where her soul may have needed time to recuperate. The life as Hypatia still bothers me. We damn near killed Sogui. Clay, I agree we need to regress Sogui again, but we have to stay away from Hypatia's life. It was just too traumatic for her."

"Agreed. I suggest we go see Tommy first and then head down to Panama."

Shali smiled. "Let's do it. I could use some of that golden Welsh lager with a big squirt of lime juice. I'll call Tommy and Sogui as soon as we wrap up today. I'll be ready as soon as you are. "

"What about the last of the books? Did you find anything?"

"Yes and no. I didn't find much more in the prophecies. It just stops, like the Mayan Calendar. There's no end of the world in 2012 or anything like that, but the prophecy just ends at the destruction of the writings."

"What about the other books?" he asked.

"We finished all the translations, but at this point I'm not sure there's much to work with. It looks like most of the books were written only about one thousand years ago, as far as I can tell. The books are mostly summaries of the collection that was blown up with our three friends in D.C. The content simply explains what Yongten and Pema told us about the secrets."

"Does it give any leads about the secrets that we could use in future regressions - you know, to help us ask the right questions?"

"Just that the seven secrets were categorized by discipline: medical and the body, energy generation, magnetics and gravity, elemental transformation, life and soul transitions, and time and destiny."

Clay counted on his fingers and looked at her inquisitively. "That's only six."

"There was another category but I couldn't figure out what the hell it was - some weird stuff. I'm speculating the authors used some cryptic writing technique. There was reference to what I believe was the Akashic records. I know this much, though: There are no real details of the secrets in these seven books. Some have diagrams that appear to be schematics or design drawings of physical devices or mechanical things, but probably nothing that could be used to prove anything or develop any type of prototype."

Their conversation was interrupted by a knock on the door.

Clay answered the door and was greeted by a neighbor from across the hall. "Clay, I'm really sorry, but I just backed into your car in the parking lot. Can you come down and check it out? I'll pay for the damages."

Suddenly there was a thunderous explosion outside the condo that nearly knocked them off their feet, followed by the ear-piercing sound of shattering glass. After gaining their composure they all rushed to the balcony of Clay's condo and looked down to the parking lot at the side of the building. Car alarms were blaring as smoke billowed out of the heaped chassis of metal that used to be Clay's car and the other cars parked around it.

Clay and Shali looked at each other with a dumb-founded gaze filled with paranoia. That explosion had been meant for Clay, if not for both of them.

Chapter 66

A week after the car bombing, with advice and consult from the FBI, Clay and Shali decided to go underground. The police and FBI investigation had discovered that when the neighbor's car bumped Clay's fender, the bomb's timer had been triggered. Forensics found more of the same Italian T-4 plastic explosive that had been used in the Georgetown explosion. However, no more evidence or leads were found. All that Clay and Shali knew now was that this organization was motivated to stop them permanently.

Analysts from the FBI's witness protection program guided them in how to assume different identities and evade the unknown organization that was targeting them. Until the logistics could be arranged, for the next week heavily armed FBI agents and local police provided twenty-four-hour surveillance for Clay and Shali.

Several days later, while packing up Clay's office condo, Shali's cell phone rang.

"Hello?" She heard the momentary clicking of the connection from a long distance international call.

A quiet and subdued, yet familiar, voice choked out a greeting. "Shali?"

"Yes. Pema? Is that you, Pema?"

"Yes, Shali. Are you OK? Is Clay OK?"

"We're both fine. So you heard about the car bomb?"

Pema exclaimed, "What car bomb? A bomb?"

"Yes, someone tried to kill us with a car bomb. But we're OK. No one was in the car when it exploded. The FBI believes it was the same people who blew up the writings. It was the same plastic explosive from Italy."

Out of character, Pema almost screamed, "Oh, no! You must go away and hide. They will not stop until they kill you!"

Clay, seeing the expression on Shali's face and only hearing her side of the conversation, gave her a puzzled look.

Shali asked, "But how did you know to call us?"

A cry burst out on the far end of phone, loud enough for Clay to hear five feet away.

"Oh, Shali," Pema sobbed into the phone. "They killed him; they put a bomb in our house and they killed him and everyone else. The explosion was so large. Everything and everybody is dead. I had gone into the wine cellar to get a special bottle of wine, in the cave below the house, when the bomb exploded. I wasn't hurt, but I was trapped for two days. They killed my daddy; he is gone."

Shali's face showed utter shock and Clay could see her pulse beating in the arteries in her neck, but he was still totally confused as to what was going on.

"Pema, why would someone kill your father and everyone else? Why would they blow up your house?"

"They killed him because we said we had the writings. They killed my daddy and my family and tried to kill me, too."

"Pema, was Yongten your father? Is your family the one that supposedly had the writings for all those years? Was your house our cover story in Kathmandu?"

Shali could hear Pema sobbing, completely out of character for her professional style.

"Yes, yes, yes. Shali, you have to get away before they kill you. Go away and hide. I have to hide, also. We must all hide. They will not stop until they destroy us - the same as it has been for a thousand years."

Shali had tears rolling down her cheeks now. Clay simply stared at the phone trembling in Shali's hand.

"Pema, we are going into hiding. The FBI is helping us. You have to get away. Can you do that? Is there anything we can do to help you?"

"No, no. You just go hide for now. You are destined to go on. You must not die, do you hear me? You are destined to continue. You cannot let them kill you. Do not worry about me. I have help from our associates. They will care for me. Go now, please." The sobbing continued on the far end of the phone.

Shali choked back the tears and whimpered, "We will. You take care of yourself. Wait, how do we get in touch with you?"

The sobbing continued, and then there was a click as Pema hung up the phone.

Shali slowly lowered the cell phone from her ear and snapped it shut, and stared at her trembling hand.

Silence permeated the room for several minutes until Clay said, "Yongten's dead, isn't he?"

Shali nodded, tears streaming down her face. "Yes. They almost got Pema, too. She was just lucky."

Clay's anger came out. "Damn it. We should have called them after the car bomb."

After a few seconds, Shali said, "Yes, but don't lay another guilt trip on yourself. We have been underestimating these jerks from the beginning, whoever they are. They are getting aggressive now. We've got to get the hell out of sight."

Clay snapped back, "Yeah, but we need to find out who they are."

"There's time for that later. First, we have a job to do. If they find out about Tommy and Sogui, they will probably silence them too."

Chapter 67

The next day Clay and Shali secretly packed their lives into a large non-descript semi-trailer truck and rode off into the night. Regardless of who or what this organization was, they intended to continue their work in underground modus operandi. New cell phones were arranged under alias names, and corporate credit cards were opened under an anonymous Swiss corporation. Their Silicon Valley homes were closed up and moth-balled. They leased side-by-side inconspicuous condos in San Diego, which became their home and office for the time being. They just hoped that whoever was trying to stop them would not be able to trace them to San Diego.

Two weeks after the move, they were completely set up and back to work.

Shali said, "The translator finalized the seven surviving books. There's nothing new, although many of the translations came out like gobbledy-goop. It has to be the coding to disguise whatever they were writing. I'll bet our three Tibetan buddies could have translated right through the code by rote. They could probably think or dialogue in the code. Remember Ezra Pound's poetry that we found when regressing Iqbal? Or Jabir's gibberish? I looked up copies of their writings: it's the same cryptic garbage. Either these people were all horrible writers, or they figured out how to encode their secrets in the text. It's the same with Kabbalah's Zohar. Its encoded secrets are supposedly embedded inside of ancient Aramaic, probably the same kind of code. We will have to learn to think in this code before we can really understand the translation of the writings."

Clay added, "It doesn't sound like these books are going to get us very far. I'm confident if we find another set of writings, we're going to find custodians that can help translate and interpret the text for us."

"With Yongten now gone and Pema going underground, their secret group of good guys are not going to be able to help us much."

"Yeah, so let's just get on with the search."

They traveled back to Kidwelly, Wales, to run another regression on Tommy. After the regression session, they met for a lager at the pub next to the hotel.

Clay said, "Well, as I suspected, Dolpopa was indeed part of the organization that controlled the hidden writings in Tibet. He was fully aware of the hiding location in the Tsipri caves, but neither the soul nor the guide gave us any of that during earlier regressions."

Shali replied, "But I'd say we know a lot more now and asked better questions."

Clay paused. "But neither the soul nor the guide 'fessed up to knowing anything about another set of hidden writings, despite my constant probes."

"I think we're dead-ended on Tommy. It's time to head back to Panama."

Clay nodded. "What's the scoop on Sogui?"

"I've arranged to meet her again. Unfortunately, she had a relapse of malaria and has not been doing well. She agreed to do the regression but we have to go to her home in San Blas. She just can't make the flight to Panama City."

"Should we just wait a few weeks?"

"She doesn't want to wait. She would like us to go there now. She said she has a few more tapes she recorded while remembering details of her previous lives. That's in addition to the twenty-one tapes she already sent us."

Clay's face grew a huge grin. "I read the transcripts. She picked up fantastic details. I've been thinking we should use Protocol 73 more often."

"Yes, but only under very controlled conditions." Shali's face turned serious and her voice dropped low. "Do you think they know about Sogui? Could they possibly target her?"

Clay sat back in his chair, eyes turning to peer out the window as if searching for something. "I don't know. I don't think so, but all the more reason to get down there as fast as possible."

Chapter 68

San Blas Islands, Panama

The smell of ocean and outboard motor fumes seemed more prominent on this boat trip. Clay and Shali's boat wove through the lagoons between the small island airport to Sogui's island home on Nargana.

Midway, Clay yelled to Shali over the roar of the engine, "Good thing we got this bigger boat."

Shali yelled back, "Yeah, but even at that we're getting salt spray. But the spray won't hurt our equipment through these shipping cases. If those canoes had tipped over last time, I don't think the equipment would have survived."

Clay lifted his sunglasses and looked intently out toward the open water of the Caribbean. He squinted, pointed and asked Shali. "What's that boat? It's moving like hell toward us."

Shali spun around in her seat to see. After staring several seconds she replied, "It's a cigarette boat, and it's moving fast. I can hear the engines screaming even this far away." She turned to the dark-skinned Kuna driving the boat. His hand was resting on his hand-held radio. He, too, was intently watching the oncoming race boat. She asked him in Spanish, "What's that?"

He looked back with a huge smile and replied, "Oh, just drug runners from Columbia. No big deal; we see them all the time. I already called it in."

As he said that, two military-style dinghy patrol boats came screaming across the lagoon from the large island they had just passed. They were heading in their direction.

Shali yelled back to the driver, "And what's that."

The driver yelled his reply to the big-eyed passengers. "Hola! The good guys. We're going to have a show. This should be a good one; it's two to one."

As their boat bounced along the waves, they watched the three other boats rapidly converge on their position.

Shali tapped Clay's leg and yelled over the engine's roar, "Look!" She pointed at the two rapidly approaching navy gray patrol boats. The boats sported both a Panamanian and the Kuna flag on the back with the black swastika angrily flapping in the wind. Mounted on the front of each boat was a .50 caliber machine gun, each with a sailor desperately hanging on so not to be thrown out of the boat.

The racing boats continued converging directly on them, with the drug runners taking the edge and closing in fast. Clay and Shali's boat now seemed to sputter along compared to the speeds of the three converging speed boats. All three on board began to grow concerned and fidgeted as they bounced around on the seats.

Shali yelled to the driver, "Why do they keep coming at us?"

The driver yelled back, "This is not right. Not good; not good. They usually stay away. You better get down in the bottom of the boat."

At that moment, as the cigarette boat came within range, two men popped out of the top and leaned over the windshield with hand held machine guns.

"Son of a bitch!" Clay yelled in near panic. "Shali, it's not drug runners, it's the assholes who have been trying to kill us. They're coming for us. Get down!" Clay leapt across the boat seat, grabbed Shali and dragged her to the bottom of the boat beneath him.

They saw bullet splashes tracing toward them and heard pings as the bullets pierced holes all along the side of their boat. A fraction of a second later came the delayed rattatat of the guns firing. The driver jerked the boat hard to the left and then right to take any evasive maneuvers possible. Seconds later more bursts and bullets sprayed around their boat, but this time the bullets hit the boat at the waterline. Salty water began to spray through holes along the bottom edge of the boat. Shali could taste the brine of the spray and licked it off of her lips.

Then came loud firing thunks from the two .50 caliber machine guns mounted on the swastika flag bearing patrol boats. In the next instant, the assaulters blasted past the front of their boat, sending a huge plume of salt-water washing across all three of them. They could see the two gunmen spinning their machine guns over the top and side of the boat as they passed, still sporadically shooting at them. Water spouts jumped up all around them from the bullets that missed the target.

Seconds later the two patrol boats shot past them with roaring engines, blasting guns and waving flags. One patrol boat screamed past them just in front of their boat. Another cascade of water washed over Clay and Shali.

As the second patrol boat approached along the rear, Clay and Shali's driver stuck his right arm in the air and began stomping his feet on the bottom of the boat. He screamed out something in the native Kuna language and made exaggerated motions with his right arm. That patrol boat flew across their wake just behind the driver. Salt spray again cascaded over the boat, which was now wildly bouncing around from the wakes of the three passing speed boats. As that patrol boat continued away in pursuit of the assaulters, the driver of the patrol boat briefly looked back, then mimicked the waving, stomping and screaming.

Now sprawled on his hands and knees in the bottom of the boat, Clay yelled to Shali, "An old Kuna war dance. I sure as hell hope it works."

They both stuck their heads slightly up to see what was going on. The cigarette boat and the two Kuna patrol boats were now locked in a wave-jumping, circular death dance, guns blasting away from all three boats. In the close setting, the cigarette boat was no match for cross-firing .50 calibers. Both gunmen took bullet hits from the patrol boat and fell into the boat's cockpit - no longer firing back. Pieces of shattered fiberglass and windshield flew off of the assailant's boat as it careened back out toward the open sea under pursuit. However, the patrol boats could not keep up with the open-water speed of its souped-up engines, even in its shot up condition.

The two patrol boats quickly gave up the pursuit and turned back to check on Clay, Shali and the driver. Fortunately, none of them - or their regression equipment - had been hit or damaged. The patrol boats escorted them to the dock on Nargana.

Chapter 69

They settled into the Nargana guest house after shaking out the adrenaline high of the afternoon's shoot out. Sitting on the beach at sunset, Clay said to Shali in a low monotone voice, "They found us ... and her."

"I know."

They were thinking of their arrival at the dock when the island's Sahila told them they have never seen an attack like this. The drug runners occasionally threaten villagers and leaders, but never blindly attacked. But they knew the attack had nothing to do with drugs.

After a few moments Clay added, "But we should be alright for now. They put on more security here and increased patrol security around the islands. The problem may be when we leave."

"Who the hell are these people anyway? Is there anybody they can't buy?"

Clay slowly shook his head and stared at the sunset. Not another word was said that evening.

Mid day the next day they went to Sogui's house. She was feeling much better and said she was ready for the regression again. After an hour of typical Latin socialization, the three of them sat on her patio sharing the beautiful view looking out across the Caribbean.

Sogui said to her two visitors, "I saw the news about the bombing in Washington. I am so sorry. I have to say, I know more than anyone in the world what was destroyed that night. For the last six months since we were last together, I have remembered so much from these lives. I remembered the scrolls and books, and I remembered the secrets. I wanted so badly to see these writings again."

Shali reached over and gently touched Sogui's arm. "Perhaps we can find another copy of the writings for you."

"That would be nice, mi Amiga. When I sit on the beach at night and meditate as the stars shine above, the words and meaning become clearer in my mind. Plus I know now that I have lived so many lives - and I hope many more to come."

They talked for another hour then had a quiet, early dinner brought in by Sogui's family. During dessert, Sogui asked, "So I heard you had a little excitement coming to Nargana from the airport. Are you OK?"

Shali glanced at Clay before answering. "Yes, we did have trouble. The Sahila told us that this was unusual so we think they may have been trying to kill us. Perhaps they were paid by the same people who planted the bomb in Washington."

Sogui smiled and nodded her head. "No doubt. Someone has been poking around here for several weeks trying to find out about you. However, our community is small and protective, so they did not get much from our people. We knew something was up. That's why our two patrol boats were waiting and so close to you."

Clay added, "They probably paid off someone. That would be easy to do. But we're more worried about you. If they knew what you know, they will be going after you."

"Don't worry; they don't know about me yet. Besides we have our Nazi PT Boats. Isn't that what you call our Coastal Security Force?" She laughed out loud at the surprised expression on her friends' faces.

Flushed with embarrassment and smiling, Clay said, "OK, we won't worry about the bad guys getting to you. But we are worried about regressing you. Are you sure you are well enough?"

"Absolutely."

Shali said, "You should get some rest then. Clay and I will come back early tomorrow to start the regression. But maybe tonight we'll try some of your Nargana beach meditation."

She leaned to Shali and whispered, "If I had my Solomon, here, we would be on the beach … but not meditating. You should try it." She winked at Shali.

Shali whispered back, "I have tried it," and then nodded her head toward Clay. "But we have a busy day tomorrow and need rest; so not tonight."

The two of them giggled like high-school girls.

As Clay and Shali walked along the beach on the way to their bungalow, Clay said, "Sogui realizes the precariousness of her situation. She is still pretty weak, you know. If we regress her before she is fully recovered from this bout of malaria, it could cause her condition to worsen."

"Yes, and she knows that if she has another regression run-in like she did with Hypatia, she might not survive this time."

"But if she dies before she is fully regressed, the truth may never be known - at least, not to us. We will lose our big chance. And remember, if she *does* see the secrets in this regression, she will need time to help us understand the meaning and translation of those secrets."

"Then we'll have to coax it out quickly but gently. She has not been able find another set of writings in her beach-side meditation recordings. If she is still doing well after digging for another set of writings, maybe we can try asking for some of the secrets directly - you know, ask the right questions."

"Agreed. Although, she seems convinced that her soul or guide can help us find another set of the writings."

Shali grabbed Clay's arm, "I would still like to use Protocol 75, just to be conservative and avoid a flashback. Don't let her remember these regressions, Clay."

"I know what you're saying, but she really wants to remember. That was her sole condition. Plus look at all of the details she has recalled in the past months after the first regressions. We could never get that level of detail with Protocol 75."

"I understand. But we have to stay focused on the guide and avoid Hypatia's life altogether."

"We'll pull the plug on the regression if there is any danger whatsoever. It's good that you arranged for the island nurse to be on standby at the island's medical clinic, just in case."

"Let's just hope we won't need her."

Chapter 70

The next morning after breakfast, Shali and Clay chatted while sitting on the patio outside their bungalow. Clay took a sip of his sweet, rich, black Panamanian coffee. "Just listen to the ocean swooshing on the beach. So relaxing."

Shali pulled her head back and covered her mouth to hold in a belch. "You mean in between the fried plantain and corn meal cakes?"

Clay looked at her and chuckled. "Come on, you were nursed on curry. This is nothing for you."

"Then it must be the chorizo sausage."

Clay sipped his coffee again. "You ready to go?"

"Yeah, but I insist on doing the regression. You're too aggressive at times, and you might not pull the plug quick enough if we run into problems with Hypatia again."

"Alright, you take the lead."

They both walked up the street to Sogui's house and after a hearty morning welcome at the door, they went into the house and set up for the session. Clay started the recording equipment and tested it to ensure it was working properly. He then set up the Wi-Fi connection for the laptop and connected to the Internet. Sogui was already sitting in her favorite lounge chair and fidgeting with the headphones and goggles. Shali chatted with Sogui as she hooked up all of the regression gadgetry.

Shali said to Clay, "It seems a bit weird to have this high-tech regression lab set up in a grass hut on a tropical island."

"It certainly is more enjoyable than most places we go." He looked over to Sogui who lifted the goggles and nodded to him. "Sogui is anxious and ready to go. Let's get started."

The beginning of the session went exceedingly smoothly. Sogui immediately fell into a deep trance, and the guide came forward with little coaxing. Within ten minutes, Shali was talking directly with the guide concerning the hidden secrets.

"You previously gave us the location of a large collection of hidden writings in Tibet. Do you know that these writings were destroyed?"

"Pity."

Shali narrowed her eyes at the curt response but continued, "Do you know who planted the bombs that destroyed those writings?"

"Those who are threatened by the truth."

"Who are these people who are threatened by the truth?"

"Those who do not wish for the truth to be known. If it was not them who destroyed the writings, it would be another."

Shali glanced at Clay. He curled his lips and shook his head with a look of confusion.

"We are searching for another set of secret writings that are also hidden, like the first set. Can you tell us where a set is located and who is hiding it?"

"Which set?"

Clay and Shali glanced at each other again with puzzled looks. Clay repeated the guide's question in a mime to Shali, "Which set?"

Shali shrugged her shoulders, looked back to Sogui said to the guide, "Each set. Who has each set?"

"One is kept by those who do not want the truth to be known. The other is kept by those who are afraid to let the truth be known."

Shali rolled her eyes and shook her head but continued her questioning on the location of any other sets of hidden writings. The cryptic dialogue with the guide continued for nearly thirty minutes. Shali and Clay could not get anything definitive out of the guide; it was as if they were playing charades.

Shali leaned over to Clay and whispered, "From all of this back and forth, it sounds like there may be two sets. She used the same terminology of '*those* who do not want the truth known' for the group that is trying to kill us and for one of the groups that has a copy of the secrets. But she doesn't seem to want to reveal any more than that."

Clay whispered back, "Keep probing. The answer may be hidden in all this back-and-forth chatter. We'll transcribe the tapes later and see if we can sort out what the guide is saying. See if she knows our three friends who died in Washington."

Shali nodded then asked the guide, "You know of the bombing in Washington that destroyed the first copy of the hidden secrets. There were three people who died in that explosion. They were Buddhist monks who were the custodians and keepers of the secrets. Do you know these three people?"

A smile grew across Sogui's face. "Yes."

"Do you know them well?"

"It is good to see them. They are funny." Sogui's smile then grew cheek to cheek.

Shali and Clay looked at each other as if humored.

"Can we talk to their souls?"

Sogui's face immediately grew serious, almost scowling. The guide snapped back abruptly, "No. Resting."

Shali looked at Clay and shrugged her shoulders with a grin. She whispered, "I tried, but, evidently they are doing well." She continued her questioning, "Are there lives that this soul lived that you have not told us about before?"

There was a very long pause and still no response. Clay hit Sogui with a three-second micro-pulse burst to the Third Eye. Sogui's head pressed back into the pillow and then curved hard to the right, as if trying to escape or evade the external stimulus. Still no answer.

Shali pressed Sogui for a response again: "There was a life or lives for this soul between 400 and 800 AD. Please describe those lives." No response.

Shali asked the question again. "Tell me about the lives between 400 and 800 AD, now."

Clay shot a five second micro-pulse to the Third Eye. Sogui's body drew back into the chair as the pulse of energy surged to her forehead.

"Stop that! Irritating!"

Shali and Clay sat back in their chairs, looking at each other in surprise. She mimed to Clay, "Enough pulsing, OK?"

Chapter 71

To their surprise, after a few moments, Sogui's guide continued without prompting: "601 AD. Arabia. I was on the Arabian Peninsula. I was a follower of Nestorius, and I studied the Jesus Christ that the Christians followed. For many years I studied his teachings. But they distorted what Jesus intended, so I followed a different path. I made a new way."

Clay leaned over to Shali and whispered excitedly, "Keep digging. I'll see who was living about that time. And watch it; she flashed back into first person from the guide and is back inside the life. We knew she was hiding some lives."

Shali continued with Sogui: "Was the person in this life famous or prominent in society?"

"Not at this time."

"How old is this person in 601 AD, and what did he or she do?"

"I am thirty years old now. I am a merchant. I have been married for six years, and I am happy. My wife is good to me - and good for me." There was short pause, and then suddenly Sogui continued in a very different tone of voice; the voice of the guide. "He became famous later in this life ... and much more famous *after* this life."

Shali and Clay looked at each other with mutual stares of excitement mixed with confusion. They leaned over to each other for a whispered conversation.

Shali asked, "What is this flipping in and out of first person, again? We were talking with the guide going through the Akashic records, then she jumped back into first person ... reliving the life ... then back to the guide?"

"I've never seen this. It looks like we've got both her soul and the guide conversing with us, almost as if they are competing for air-time. The soul was talking about the life but the guide just flipped in two cents of commentary." Clay grinned. "This soul must have one hell of an ego, huh?"

"Well, look at all the famous lives she has lived. I'm going to try to focus on the guide and stay away from the soul?"

"Agreed. If you can't keep the guide engaged, try to pull the soul into the LBL - perhaps into the library but not in the life. Those were violent years in that region, and we don't know what is going to happen. They could end up in a battle or a raid and get chopped up like Hypatia. And we know what happened when Sogui slipped back into Hypatia's life."

Shali nodded. "They have been hiding this life from us. Any idea why she might have wanted to hide a life?"

"I don't know, but she definitely held back. Maybe she is willing to talk now because we are using Protocol 73. On the other hand, Sogui spent the last six months pre-conditioning both her soul and the guide through meditation. Maybe they are comfortable enough to let it all hang out. Keep her talking, and let's try to find out who this person was. There is another big gap earlier in her timeline and I want to check that out, too."

Shali acknowledged and turned back to Sogui. "What is the name of the soul in this life?"

"They called me Al-Amin ... Abdullah. Childhood was difficult. Everyone around me kept dying. My father died before I was born, so my mother sent me away to live in the desert with the Bedouins until I was three. She brought me back, but then she died when I was six. I never really knew her. I was passed from one family member to another. I lived with my grandfather, but he died a few years later. My uncle Abu took me into his house, but I was never really part of their family. I was like a stray dog from the street. But they were family, and at least they gave me a home. I am grateful for that. When I was twenty-five, I met Khadijah, and I finally had my true family. She was fifteen years older than me, but she loved me and I loved her. She cared for me, nurtured me. She taught me so many things. She was like the mother I never had."

Shali glanced at Clay and whispered, "Oedipus complex? Was this wife filling the role of a mother figure because of his troubled childhood?"

"You could be right. But it sounds like they were closely bonded souls."

Shali turned to Sogui and continued: "Move to the place where you are between lives, and then look back at your experience in this life. Do not go into the life - only view the life after it was finished. Look at it from that special time between lives. Do you understand?

"Yes."

"Did you and your wife, Khadijah, have children?"

"Yes, we had six children. She was a good mother and a good wife. But she died later."

Shali probed, "When did she die and how?"

"When I was forty-nine years old, she died. She became ill and left me. It was to be expected, but I was very sad."

"What did you do after she died?"

"I meditated. I went to my special places in the mountains and I meditated."

"What did you learn from your mediation?"

"I began to see reality through my meditation. For ten years before she died, I would meditate in the caves. But when she left me, I would go to the caves to be alone and think and meditate. Images and visions would come to me."

"What kind of images? Describe your mediations and what you saw."

Sogui continued to describe the meditations for almost fifteen minutes, with Clay guiding Shali to ask a series of strange questions relating to traveling through time and space.

Afterwards, Clay motioned Shali into a short quiet discussion off to the side.

Chapter 72

Clay leaned forward in excitement. "Two things. You are not going to believe either one."

"Try me, Cowboy."

"First, this person was not meditating. He was remote-viewing."

"What?" Shali exclaimed in confusion.

"Remember how I found the PLR protocols? I told you about the SRI's Para-Psychology Operations, PPO, and the CIA black-ops intelligence programs? There was a program for remote viewing called Stargate."

"Come on, Clay, let's not get into TV shows, here."

"No, no - not the TV series. There were several intelligence-funded PPO initiatives from the nineteen seventies through the mid-nineties, and one was called Stargate. This was way before the movie and TV shows, but that is probably where they got the name. When I was cleaning out the SRI files, I read through the documentation stored in the archives about remote-viewing. This person in Sogui's past life was not meditating; he was remote viewing. There are a bunch of famous remote-viewing weenies in that program that came from SRI. They would be proud of Sogui's life back in the Sixteen Hundreds. Our soul's life, here, was remote viewing into the future. I'm convinced. His meditating techniques were very similar to what remote viewers use, even today. But this is probably the same thing that the oracles and prophets did when they got visions of the future. Guys like Nostradamus, Edgar Cayce - "

"Yeah, yeah," Shali cut him off. "I'm with you so far. So our friend here was ahead of her - or *his* - time. He could see into the future and was prophet. What's the other thing?"

"Get ready. I couldn't find this Al-Amin on the 'net, but I'm sure I found his wife. I tried several different spellings, and it all comes back to one person: Khadijah was the wife of Mohammad - Islam's Mohammad."

Shali snapped, "What?"

"Yeah. Starting at about age forty, Mohammad supposedly began getting visions from God, who guided him to structure Islam. But he wasn't necessarily talking to God; he was remote viewing the future. Think about it; it's like a self-fulfilling prophecy. If you have a vision of a massive battle to conquer Mecca and Medina, you are going to put together an invasion to conquer Mecca and Medina. He found the water in the desert because he saw the water in the future. He built reality into what he saw in the vision, because he believed God told him to do it."

Shali's face showed absolute shock; her eyes were half-glazed and her mouth was slightly open.

Clay continued, "Tonight, *Wiki* the word 'prophecy.' All of the religions and philosophies of the world talk about prophecies, including Mohammad and Islam. These prophecies come from dreams, visions, meditation, talks with God. But I'm convinced that they are all just a form of remote viewing into the future. Or maybe it's some form of future-life progression, like past-life regression. Remember, if the secrets are true, time is just an illusion - Einstein-style. I am willing to bet the Oracles who predicted the destruction of our writings in Washington, simply remote viewed or future-life progressed themselves to see the future destruction of the writings. Remember, one of the categories of hidden secrets had to do with time and destiny. Pema talked about that Nazi, Heidegger, who wrote the cryptic book *Being and Time*." Clay looked away and whispered to himself, "Damn, I should have read that book." He shook his head and then looked back at Shali. "I'll bet there's something good coded in Heidegger's book."

Shali was still sitting with a glazed-over look. Here she was, conversing with the soul of Mohammad. She couldn't talk, couldn't continue.

Sogui lay quietly in her chair with a smile of pure satisfaction.

Clay shook Shali's arm to snap her out of her thoughts. "Shali … Shali, probe her for confirmation on her identity."

Shali shook her head side to side, as if waking up from a trance. She took a deep breath and slowly exhaled.

Chapter 73

Shali continued the regression of Sogui: "In this life in the Six Hundreds, where your wife was named Khadijah, were you also known by the name of Mohammed?"

"Yes."

"Did you build on a new way of life called Islam?"

"Yes."

Shali glanced back to Clay, who now had a beaming smile on his face. He pumped his right forearm hard to the rear while miming the word, "Yes."

Shali looked back at Sogui and asked, "After the death of Khadijah, and after you meditated, what did you do in this life?"

A smile broke onto Sogui's face. Her sexually driven Latin personality suddenly poked into the regression, "Hola, Mama-cita, I got more wives, of course. I got myself twelve more wives before I died. Not bad for fifty years old, huh? They were much comfort to me, and so much pleasure indeed. I got all the sex from these wives that I could ever want. Oh, what a life."

Clay and Shali glanced at each other with smiles of relief.

Sogui suddenly returned to the more serious demeanor of the soul: "Eleven wives, but none of them gave me the feelings of my love for Khadijah, not until my last wife Maria. But she was a Christian, and it was not permitted for her to be my wife. However, I secretly married her, anyway. We could tell no one that she was my wife, but we truly loved each other, more than all the others together; and we were happy to be together again."

"What do you mean 'again'?"

"We have lived together in many lives. We enjoy living our lives together. We are together for all time."

Clay leaned over to Shali with a big smirk and whispered, "Now, this is what I call soul mates."

Shali nodded acknowledgement but stayed focused on Sogui's regression. "Tell me more about Maria. What was her full name?"

"Maria Qupthiya; they called her Maria the Copt."

Shali looked up to Clay and pointed at his laptop. He nodded and whispered, "I'm ahead of you. I've got her already. Keep digging; it's good stuff."

Sogui's soul continued, "My Maria was a Coptic Christian from Alexandria. She was given to me as a gift from the ruler of Egypt, Muqawqis. Some time before, I had sent a letter to the rulers of all nations, inviting them to join me in the gift of Islam. As a gift in return for my invitation, Muqawqis sent me a beautiful horse and two young maidens. The girls were sisters from a prominent family in Alexandria. But when I met Maria, my beautiful new slave girl, I immediately felt our connection to the past. We were finally together again. I gave the horse and her sister to my good friend, and I secretly made Maria my wife. However, the other wives knew about her and were jealous of my feelings for her. They despised her because of my love and because she was a Christian."

Shali asked, "But could she not come to join Islam?"

"She was Coptic, and her father raised her as a strong Christian. She would never be a Muslim, so I had to accept her as a Christian if I wanted to be with her. I could not tell anyone that I had made her my wife. Maria strongly believed in the Prophet Jesus and would not fail her devotion to him. I do not fault her; Jesus was a great prophet. I worshiped him for many years before I saw the reality of the Christian worship for this prophet. But oddly, my Maria despised the Roman Christians, the Greek Christians, and the Egyptian Christians. She believed they had distorted what Jesus taught. She felt they were selfish and could not hold their empires without changing the truth of Jesus. I know this is so. Maria was as committed to me as she was committed to the life of Jesus."

Shali paused and looked at Clay inquisitively, and then turned back to Sogui. "Please continue."

"Maria gave me a child, Ibrihim. Not one of the other eleven wives could give me a child - except , of course, Khadijah, who gave me six children. But some of these other wives tried to kill our Ibrihim when he was two years old. He survived, but I told everyone that Ibrihim had died. I had to protect them, so I secretly moved Maria and Ibrihim to a house outside of Medina. I gave her two eunuchs, four soldiers and a servant girl to care for them and protect them. They were loyal, and I told no one where they lived."

Sogui smiled with a look of satisfaction and happiness. Shali looked at Clay who scowled in confusion at the laptop. Suddenly the corner of his mouth curled up. He commented quietly to Shali, "That tricky bastard. Historical accounts say that Ibrihim died as an infant and that Mohammad died shortly thereafter. Maria supposedly died shortly after that. Someone probably killed her, and maybe the boy too."

Shali responded, "Nobody killed them. It was a ruse ... to protect them."

Sogui's voice dropped to a lower tone as she continued without being prompted: "Maria lived secretly in her house with her son Ibrihim. Al-Amin died a year later. One year after that, Maria secretly took young Ibrihim to Alexandria to be with her family. In Arabia, everyone was told that Maria and Ibrihim had also died." There was a short pause and then Sogui continued in yet a different tone of voice: "No one could know that Mary and I had a child together. No one could know the last time; no could know this time. Ibrihim lived long in Alexandria and produced many generations of Coptic Christians in Egypt; to today."

Shali shook her head as if clearing her ears. "You called her *Mary* instead of Maria. Why? And what do you mean when you said no one could know last time? When was the last time? Do you mean in a previous life?"

There was no response from Sogui. Clay looked at Shali with as much of a puzzled look as Shali was giving him.

Shali asked again, "Why did you call her Mary? When was the last time you could not tell anyone about your child with Mary?"

No response.

Shali looked at Clay, put three fingers in the air, and then touched her forefinger to her forehead. Clay shot a three-second micro-pulse shock to the Third Eye.

Sogui's head pushed back into the pillow, as if trying to get away from the stimulus. Sogui slowly started to talk in the guide's lower, definitive tone: "When they were together before, in another life, she was Mary; she likes that name. They could not tell anyone that they were married. They could not tell anyone that they had a child. They had to hide Mary and the child. They would be killed if the others knew. They killed her husband, and they would also kill Mary and the child."

Chapter 74

Clay pulled Shali off to the side to chat. "Shali, we'll get back to this other Mary in a bit, but I suspect this Maria may be a missing link to our secrets. Maria came from a prominent family in Alexandria, and we now know that she went back to Alexandria after Mohammad's death. If she was a strong-willed person like Hypatia, she may have become involved with the organization that has been hiding the secret writings. She lived a couple hundred years after Hypatia."

"I see what you mean. Where do you think I should take this?"

"First, try to get the location of the hidden writings from the guide again. Then try to find the location of the person who might be living with Maria's soul today, if she is living right now."

"Will do." Shali turned back Sogui. "Do you know where another set of writings containing the great knowledge is located now?"

"Yes."

"Where are these writings?"

The response from the guide was abrupt and terse. "This I have told you already."

Clay and Shali looked at each other with mutual astonishment. Neither one remembered any description of a location of hidden writings. Clay made a circular motion with his hand for Shali to try again.

"Tell me again where they are located."

The guide's response was even more terse: "Have already told you."

Clay leaned close to Shali and whispered, "What a bitchy guide. Let's move on. Maybe we can try again later. If she said she told us, then she probably did. We'll get if from the tapes. Let's try for Maria's current incarnation, and then go dig in for more details on her and her husband in a previous life. These two are definitely soul mates."

Shali turned back to Sogui. "This Maria, who was the wife of Mohammad... or Al-Amin; is she living a life at the present time?"

"Yes."

"Where can we find this soul today? What is the name of the person, and where do they live?"

"I have told this to you already."

Again, Shali and Clay look at each other with stupefied stares.

Clay fired a quip to Shali, "What the hell. Did I sleep through part of this session or what?"

Sogui lay quietly with a big smirk on her face. Clay glared at her and stuck his tongue out at her.

Shali almost laughed out loud at Clay's frustration and then asked him, "When was the other gap in her timeline?"

Clay responded, "Give me a few seconds." He clicked through his laptop files, looking for the gap in this soul's time line. Finally, he turned back to Shali and said, "The last life we got from Sogui's soul, before the other gap, was the dual incarnation of Buddha and Confucius. They both died before 475 BC. The next life we got was ... Ammonius Saccas, born about 175 AD. OK, try 450 BC to 150 AD as the target period. We found no lives for this soul during that time. I'll bet that is when this soul was married to the Mary, Maria's earlier incarnation."

Shali turned to Sogui. "The soul of this body lived a life, or lives, between 450 BC and 150 AD. One life during that period was a man. He was prominent in society and was married to a woman named Mary. Was there a life for this soul at that time?"

"Yes."

"Describe the life."

Mimicking Shali's supposition, Sogui's guide replied "This life was prominent in society and he was married to a woman named Mary."

Clay shook his head and mumbled three enunciated words: "Smart-assed guide." He whispered to Shali, "She needs to go back to guide-school." Out of spite, Clay pressed the button to send a short micro-pulse shot to the Third Eye.

Sogui's head pressed back in the chair, and the guide shouted, "Stop!"

Clay reared back as if he had just been slapped for pinching a woman's buttocks.

Shali gave him a look of impatience, as a mother would to a misbehaving twelve-year-old boy. She said to Sogui, "During what years did this life live?"

"From 2 BC … to … 36 AD."

Absolute silence fell over the room.

Chapter 75

Clay and Shali looked at each other with disbelief.

"H-holy Christ, Shali," Clay stuttered. "I mean, really ... Holy Christ! It's Jesus Christ, for Christ's sake. But wait, I don't get this. Mary was a virgin, and she was his mother, not his wife. Is this another Oedipus-complex like his later incarnation with Kadijah?"

"No, no, it's not his mother Mary; it's got to be Mary Magdalene, the supposed prostitute he used to hang out with. Come on, Clay, you know: *DaVinci Code* and the holy-grail stuff. She was his wife, not his whore."

"So Mary Magdalene really was his wife, and they had a kid. Whoa, what a paradigm shift. Jesus and Mary had to hide both their marriage and their child, just like their dual incarnations six hundred years later as Mohammad and Maria." Clay chuckled. "It's like the movie *Groundhog Day*, huh; keep living it again and again?"

"Clay, cut the jokes, please," Shali snapped. "We're at a touchy point, here."

They sat in silence, looking intensely at each other and wondering what to do next.

Clay spoke first: "Nobody is going to believe this; not in the least. This almost pales the secret writings that we are after. Even listening to the taped session recordings, nobody is going to believe us."

"I know what you mean. So, where do we go from here, Jose?"

Clay breathed out a long exhalation of air. "First, validate the identity just to make sure it really is Jesus. If it is, get her to talk about real life events of Jesus. There are a lot of myths and legends in the Christian Bible; it would be good to validate or refute some of them. Sogui must be getting tired, so we need to plow through this last regression and then stop for today. We'll let her rest tomorrow while we review the tapes to see if we can decipher the location of the writings. If we can't figure it out, on the next round we'll try again to get the guide to give us more details."

Shali smiled. "Can you imagine all the details Sogui is going to remember about her lives as Jesus and Mohammad over the next six months? I can't wait for that. I think I am going to spend some time in San Blas for the next few months. This is gonna be good."

Shali continued the regression protocol scripts with the guide of Jesus' soul. The guide's descriptions confirmed many of the embellished historical events in the Bible but with blunt twists of reality. For forty minutes, they reviewed the life of Jesus from a boy to a grown man. Both Shali and Clay noticed that the regression continued to toggle between the soul reliving the life and the guide.

Closing in on the end of the session for the day and wishing to avoid the crucifixion, Shali commanded, "You will move past the death of this life. You will *not* experience the death of this life; you will not view this death. Is that clear?"

"Yes."

"Tell me about the wife and child of Jesus."

The guide replied in a serious, monotone voice, "They were married in secret because this life was threatened by many. They produced a female child, who was secluded with family in a far section of the city. The wife, Mary, lived with the family and child; the husband secretly visited as much as possible. After the death of this Jesus, the child was raised by the mother's sister, Martha, who became known as her mother and who raised her in the family castle on the shores of Galilee. Mary's brother, Lazarus, became a powerful military leader and ensured that both Mary, the daughter and Martha were safe from danger. The souls of the mother and father continued to protect and guide the child, and her children, and their children."

Clay whispered to Shali, "It sounds like they became guardian angels to the family blood lines on earth at least for a couple of generations."

"This must be why there was such a big gap in time after Jesus' life. The soul was busy being a guide to generations of descendants."

Suddenly, Sogui screamed and slammed her head back into the chair. "Ahh. They're beating me! The thorns ... ahh, the pain ... cutting my head! They are pushing it into my head ... I cannot see! Blood in my eyes ... it burns! Stop, please stop!"

"Shali, get her the hell out of there!" Clay yelled over the screams. "We lost the guide. Sogui's soul is back in the life. She's reliving the life, and they're going to crucify him. Get her out. Wake her up ... bring her out, now."

Shali jumped up from her chair and started shaking Sogui. Sogui was jerking back and forth in the chair, still screaming with agony. "Sogui, you will come out of this life, now! Get out of the life and go to a peaceful place. Sogui, you will now wake up and come back to this present life. You will leave the life of Jesus now. Leave it now, and wake up to the present. On the count of three, you will wake up. Three ... two ... one. Wake up, now!"

"Aahh! The Romans ... they are nailing my hand to the beam!" She began screaming again, and her left arm jerked out straight and with each scream. Her hand, crippled from twenty years of rheumatoid arthritis, slammed hard against the table next to the regression chair repeatedly and became contorted and deformed - almost unrecognizable. Each scream for each pound of the spike through her hand caused her entire body to convulse in blood-curdling pain. Her body violently jerked to the right, and the screams of pain as she felt her right hand being nailed echoed through the island house and across half of the island.

Shali pulled the headset and goggles off Sogui's head. Together, she and Clay pulled Sogui up and forward in her chair. Clay threw water on her face, and Shali slapped her cheeks and forearms. But they could not wake her up, and by this point Sogui was drooling, as if in a drunken stupor - the stupor of unbearable pain that came from reliving a Roman crucifixion of two thousand years earlier. Her already contorted legs convulsed uncontrollably as the spikes were pounded through her feet.

"Ahh! Ahh ... ahh ..."

The screams from her hoarse and strained vocal chords became guttural. Sogui's eyes rolled back in her head.

By then half a dozen people had run into the room, including the nurse from the island medical center. They gathered around Sogui.

Sogui reared back and blared out in a loud, deep painful voice. "Father Joseph ... care for my child, for she shall be without father.... Father, forgive me, for I know not what I do ... Why did I do this?"

Sogui's body became limp, and she slumped down in the chair. Her eyelids opened, but her eyes only stared dully and her head drooped to the side. She breathed in a last deep breath and sighed out a long low moan with a slight smile of relief and contentment on her otherwise blank face.

Chapter 76

Realizing the dire situation, the nurse aggressively pushed Clay aside and immediately began CPR: pump, two, three, four, five, six - breath, breath; pump, two, three, four, five, six - breath , breath. No luck. She checked Sogui's pulse: nothing. The nurse opened Sogui's shirt front and flipped open the case of a portable defibrillator. She pressed the *on* and *charge* buttons and lubricated the shock paddles. There was a long *beep*.

"*Soporte Claro!* Stand Clear!"

Whomp!

Nothing.

"Claro!"

Whomp!

The nurse continued CPR and then reached into the medical case, rapidly loaded a syringe, and injected a needle of adrenaline directly to Sogui's heart. She followed this with another hit from the defibrillator: still nothing. She continued CPR for another ten minutes, but to no avail. By now, nearly forty Kuna's were standing outside of Sogui's house. Shali was crying uncontrollably in Clay's arms, and Clay's eyes were swollen with the burden of more guilt.

The nurse stepped back from Sogui's now calm and outstretched body. She took a clean sheet from the nearby cabinet and carefully spread it over Sogui's body, and then she looked up at the quiet, mournful crowd gathered at the door. "*Ella puede ahora reclinarse*. She can now rest. Her life has been difficult; it is now time for our Sogui to move forward. She now goes to the Mother Kuna God and to the Father Kuna God to continue the cosmic cycle."

The regional medical officer came to Nargana by boat that night to confirm the death of Sogui. The village Sahila, the island elders, and Sogui's family made all the arrangements for her passing ceremony, burial and memorials. At the insistence of the

Sahila and the island elders, Clay and Shali stayed on the island for five more days.

On their last day on the island, they met the Sahila for afternoon coffee. Regretfully, Clay said, "Senor, I cannot express how badly we feel about Sogui's passing. We feel that we are responsible for the stress that caused Sogui to pass."

The Sahila smiled, shook his head, and waved his hand in non-acceptance. "This is not your fault. Please understand that we have all seen the difficult life Sogui has lived. I was ten years old when she was born. I saw her entire life of pain from diseases and misfortunes. She seldom experienced the simple pleasures of other people." He paused to take a sip of his coffee. "When our Sogui came back from Panama City six months ago, she was so happy. We all watched her spend the sunsets on the beach, contemplating, meditating. She talked to the Mother and Father God, and they revealed things to her that we do not understand. But we all know she saw more happiness in the last six months than she did in her entire life. She was free of pain in her mind. She was at peace. No, you did not cause this death; you gave her new life. You were the reason for this happiness. And for that, Sogui and all Kuna thank you."

Clay and Shali blushed with astonishment and gratitude for being relieved of the emotional burden of Sogui's death. They nodded acknowledgment with smiles and nods.

The Sahila closed by saying, "You are most welcome on our island anytime. You are welcome to stay with my family." He grinned and added, "But of course, it would be appreciated if you would PLR 73 me. I believe that is what Sogui called it? I would like to reach my happiness before I am too old to do so in this life."

Clay and Shali looked at each other and smiled. Shali replied, "When we come back to visit, we will certainly do that for you. It is the least we could do to thank your people for this kindness and understanding."

The next day, they packed all of the regression equipment and took motorized canoes back to the airfield on Ustupo Yantupo island for the short flight to Panama City.

Chapter 77

Panama City, Panama

Clay and Shali met for dinner that night at a restaurant on Calle 50 in the city. Clay lifted a glass of deep red Chilean wine and said, "In celebration of the end of one soul's life on this earth; may she reflect and return again soon. *Salud*."

"Cheers, Sogui, until we meet again."

After several minutes of silence, Clay said, "So we're going to stay in town for a few days to review the tapes from Sogui's regression session?"

"Yeah. We can transcribe the recordings into English after we get back to our hideaway in San Diego. But I want to review the original Spanish recordings before we leave. The guide said the location of the secrets had been revealed earlier in the session. I would like to get those details before we leave."

Clay nodded. "In the morning, let's set up the equipment to playback and duplicate the recordings. I'd like to make another copy since we can never regress Sogui, again."

"Do you think the location of the writings might be encoded like the writings themselves, or do you think we just missed the clues altogether?"

Clay scratched his head. "It's possible it is encoded. If it is encoded in words, maybe we can get enough information from the other seven books to decipher it."

"Remember, the guide said that the soul of Mary Magdalene and Maria the Copt is living a life *today*. He said that was revealed, also."

Clay excitedly said, "Yeah. We have to try and find her incarnation." He paused, took a drink of his wine. "You know, her guide was a real pain, but maybe that's part of their job as a guide. They want the souls to figure out their own path, so they make it like a game. If a guide provides all of the answers, a soul can't learn. Souls can only learn while living a life."

"Yes, but if the prophecy said we are to reveal the secrets now, then much of the pain of life goes away."

After a brief pause, Clay's look turned to inquisitiveness. "Does that mean the end of the world is coming, at least as we know it? Is that why it is time to reveal these secrets at last?"

Shali picked up on the facetious nature of his comment and smiled. "It can't come to an end, now, Mr. Dudley. The secrets were blown up in Washington."

Clay smiled. "Maybe we should stop looking for the secrets. Then the giant meteor might miss the earth."

They laughed together, finished dessert and retired to the hotel.

The next morning they met and set up the regression equipment in their suite.

Clay commented, "This is weird. Just days ago we were sitting on a tropical paradise island, talking with the soul of Mohammad and Jesus, the idols of Islam and Christianity, while sitting under the only flag in the world with a swastika, the symbol for the extermination of the Jews."

"… the writings hidden by the Buddhists and me being a Hindu."

"And now we are following predictions by ancient Turkish prophets that tell us the world is coming to an end. Is there anybody we left out?"

The two of them laughed together as they finished setting up the equipment. They sat down next to the computer and the recording playback started.

Chapter 78

"This is Clay Barton. It is eight seventeen a.m. on Nargana Island, San Blas, Panama on the nineteenth of September. This is the fourth in a sequence of past-life regression sessions on Sogui Iglesias, subject RB2837-JK3152; soul ID number DF73-7221. I am assisted by Shali Faisal. She will be performing the regression using PLR Protocol 73. The objective is to regress the subject in attempt to locate one or more sets of hidden secret writings. We are also attempting to identify any lives not previously identified for this soul during earlier regressions. The regression will attempt to focus on dialogue with the guide of this soul and avoid flashback experiences due to a difficult and traumatic flashback experience in the previous regression session."

The recording continued for ten minutes of hypnosis and regression scripts by Shali. Afterwards, the guide came out almost immediately.

Shali's recorded voice said, "You previously gave us the location of a large collection of secret hidden writings in Tibet. Do you know that these writings were destroyed?"

"Pity."

"Do you know who planted the bombs that destroyed those writings?"

"Those who are threatened by the truth."

"Who are these people who are threatened by the truth?"

"Those who do not wish for the truth to be known. If it was not them who actually destroyed the writings, it would be another."

"We are searching for another set of secret writings that are also hidden, like the first set. Can you tell us where a set is located and who is hiding it?"

"Which set?"

"Any set. Who has each set? And where are the hidden sets of writings kept? Who are the keepers of the sets?"

"One is kept by those who do not want the truth to be known. The other is kept by those who are afraid to let the truth be known."

As if someone had flicked a switch, the recording suddenly jumped to a humming monotone hissing sound.

s s s s s s s s s s s s s s s s s s s s s s s

The two looked at each other in mutual confusion. Clay immediately looked at the gauges and the laptop screen. He tapped the speakers, thinking that was the problem. But the voice playback scale on the laptop screen had flat-lined. He clicked on the backward arrow to look at the playback scale from the start of the recording. There were jagged bars showing strong voice signals until the moment the guide began to go into detail. The hissing continued.

Clay looked frantic. He shook the speakers and then the laptop. He checked all around the laptop, picked it up and shook it, and then he checked all the wires and cables again. He tapped the case of the laptop, the tapping turned to knocking, the knocking turned to pounding.

Shali reached over, grabbed his forearm and shook it hard. "Clay. Stop. Look at the recording signal. It's not there. Don't hit the damn machine or you might damage everything on the hard drive. Just spin through the recording and see if the signal comes back."

He hesitated with a near-blank stare. Shali gently pushed him aside and moved in to take over the laptop. She clicked the playback button to four-times speed, and then eight-times speed. Five minutes passed, but still there was only a hiss.

They checked periodically, but got only the hissing sound.

Finally after hours of hissing sound, a squeaking chipmunk-like dialogue started again. Shali slowed the speed to normal and rewound the recording to where the jagged lines first appeared on the laptop screen. They recognized Sogui's Spanish immediately.

"Ah. They're beating me! The thorns - ahh, the pain … cutting my head! They are pushing it into my head … I cannot see! Blood in my eyes … it burns! Stop, please stop!"

"Shali, get her out of there. We lost the guide. Sogui's soul is back in the life. She's reliving the life and they're going to crucify him. Get her out. Wake her up… bring her out, now."

They could hear background shuffling noises, and then a chair tipping over, followed by thumping, rustling, splashing water and mumbled dialogue.

"Sogui, you will come out of this life, now! Get out of the life and go to a peaceful place. Sogui, you will now wake up and come back to this present life. You will leave the life of Jesus, now. Leave it now and wake up to the present. On the count of three, you will wake up. Three … two … one. Wake up, now!"

"Aahh! The Roman soldiers … they are nailing my hand to the beam! Ahh … ahh … ahh …

The painful memory was mixed with muffled sounds of the rescue activities in the room. By then, both of them were in tears again. Clay reached over to the laptop and clicked the *stop* button.

Silence permeated the room; neither moved. Clay regained his composure first. He moved the laptop recording back along the playback link. There was more than three hours of flat-line hissing from the time the guide entered the dialogue until Sogui's soul came back into the regression during the crucifixion.

Shali asked, "Are you sure you grounded the shielded the cables?"

"Yes. Exactly as I have for all these years, exactly to the specifications of the PLR protocol. The meters and gauges all verified that everything was connected properly and that the recording was working fine all through the session. I watched the audio meters jumping around throughout the whole regression. It should have recorded; it should have been fine." He hesitated. "Obviously this guide was more powerful than anything anticipated by the protocols."

"But the recordings worked on the first three regressions with Sogui."

"And the recordings worked on this regression, until the guide did not want us to know any more. This one was too powerful and obviously playing a game with us." Looking up in the air, Clay shouted toward the ceiling: "Yeah, you say you gave us the location of both the writings and of Maria's soul ... and then you wipe it all out."

Shali reached over to Clay and rubbed his forearm to comfort him. "It is what it is. Chill out; there's nothing we can do about this. Any ideas on what to do next?"

Clay looked at Shali with a sense of gratitude and then said, "I don't know. But we are not done. If this world is subject to its own destiny, and if it is going to end soon, I'm going to do my part and make life easier for every soul at the end. No disease, no pain, no strife, unlimited energy, perfect health and easy life for all. Let's go back to San Diego. We've got a lot of work to do. We can start by finding the bastards who are trying to kill us. I am taking control of my destiny, on my terms. No damn Turkish oracle is going to dictate what happens to my life."

Shali cut him off. "We'll go back to San Diego and get moving but only after I take you down."

Clay's head reared back in surprise. His face glowed like a boy entering an amusement park, thinking that Shali was ready to break their platonic relationship. She quickly recognized his misinterpretation. "No! Down, as in regression down. Let me regress you and see if we can get a shot at Sogui's soul. If we can get to her, maybe we can still draw out the location of Maria or the other copy of the secrets. It won't to hurt to try."

Clay sat quietly contemplating her request. He then slowly responded, "OK. But stay out of my life … or lives, alright? Just shoot for Sogui. And PLR 73; I want to know everything you poke at."

Without another word, Shali began setting up the rest of the equipment for her regression of Clay. Clay silently stood watching her for several minutes, contemplating if this was a smart move or not. He finally joined her in setting up the session.

She glanced over at him, careful not to catch his eye. "I'll bet you will be the easiest regression I've done."

"Yeah, yeah. Just get to the guide and probe for Sogui's soul. This is unorthodox for the protocols and I've never done it. Her having just died is going to influence any the results, if it is even possible to make the connection."

"We'll see." She pulled the cables back off of the lounge chair and said, "Come on. Jump in the chair; your magic carpet ride awaits you."

Chapter 79

Clay slowly sat down and lay back in the chair looking at her with a cautious air of suspicion. Shali hooked him up to the regression equipment and tested the volumes and pulse strength. She moved back to the console, started the recordings and launched into the regression without any hesitation. "This is Shali Faisal conducting a past life regression of Clay Barton in Panama City, Panama ..." Shali described the session objectives for the recording. She then turned to Clay and quickly walked him through the opening hypnosis scripts of the PLR 73 protocol. She took him directly to the Akashic records library. As Shali suspected, Clay's guide came forth immediately and engaged with her in open dialog. Shali noted the slow monotone voice of the guide, which was quite different than Clay's normal style.

"Would you allow this soul to view the Akashic records of another soul who recently left body of a Sogui Iglesius? This person lived in a place called San Blas in Panama."

She waited five seconds, but after no response she continued. "We have been told that we must reveal special knowledge to all those souls living, now. The knowledge has been hidden for thousands of years. This knowledge is to enlighten the people and to make their present lives easier and without pain or suffering. The soul we seek has information we need to find the special knowledge. This soul lived many prominent lives including one called Jesus Christ who was killed by others and became a popular martyr. Do you know the soul of which I speak?" She pressed the micro-pulse to the Third Eye. Clay's head pushed back into the chair.

"Yes."

"Will you allow us to view that soul's Akashic records?"

After a moment of hesitation Shali got a response, but in a different voice with a tone in alignment with Clay's personality. "Yes, this is quite possible."

Shali smiled. "Am I speaking with the soul of this Clay Barton?"

"Yes."

"Is your guide still with you?"

"Yes."

Shali instructed Clay, "Did you find the records of the soul that I seek?"

"Yes."

"Please open the Akashic record book and tell me what you see."

There was a slight pause until the voice of Clay's soul replied, "There are so many wonderful lives of this person; so productive. This soul is strong and has much experience."

"Can you connect directly with this soul?" She hesitated for several seconds then repeated, "Can you connect directly with this soul?" She pressed the micro-pulse button for a short shot to the Third Eye.

Clay slowly responded in almost a drawl, "Yes."

"Describe what you see and what this soul says to you."

"This soul just floated out of the pages of the Akashic records and grows to meet me. It glows in deep, deep purple color; beautiful purple light is all around … all around this soul's image. This soul comes to me."

"Does this soul say anything?"

"This soul is grateful to me for helping while in the last life lived as this Sogui."

"Ask this soul for the location of a set of the secret writings; the writings that we have been searching for."

Clay pushed his head back and then turned to the side as if looking around. "This soul pointed to the record book. There is a picture; a scene. The scene is alive. It is a large storage room, but strong like a vault; a huge vault. This is just a small part of a large … a large … almost a cave. No just a large stone storage area. The picture is changing, zooming out, out, into a large open square with statues. No, a large obelisk, like in Egypt. This must be Egypt. Zooming out again. A city, large city. This must be Alexandria, but, but, zooming out more. The Coliseum. This is Rome. This is the Vatican. The set of writings you seek is stored in the Vatican."

Shali sat back and grabbed her forehead in utter shock. She sat in silence, finally muttering quietly to herself, "That's a lost cause. The Catholics will never reveal this. There's got to be another copy." She leaned forward and asked Clay's soul, "Is there another hidden set of the writings, and if so, where is it located?"

"She says there is another set but that she does not know where it is located."

"You said the word, '*she*'. Do you see a female?"

"Yes."

"Describe this female image of the soul? Ask who this female image is."

"She is a black woman; very tall and slender and beautiful. Even in the purple haze that shrouds her, she is majestic, proud and a leader." There was a pause. "She said ... she had lived as a Queen ... of Sheba."

A huge grin came across Shali's face as she murmured to herself, "Good thing Clay is remembering this." She thought for a moment then said to Clay, "Tell her that we are also looking for her soul mate when she lived the lives of a man named Jesus Christ and a man named Mohammad. This soul's names were Mary and Maria while living. Ask her for the current name and location of that soul who is living a life, now."

Clay's neck loosened and he rolled his head to one side. "She smiled, but then she turned and walked away. She floated back into the scene in the Akashic record book and is walking away in the scene. The picture has changed. She is walking along a beach, a beautiful white beach. It is San Blas; not Nargana, but in San Blas."

Shali asked anxiously, "Ask her to come back, please."

"She will not come back."

"Ask her again"

"She was just joined by a man. They are walking on the beach together, holding hands."

"Who is the man?"

"He is well dressed. Regal. He has a beard ... and a crown. He must be some kind of royalty."

Shali raised her eyebrows as her eyes opened wide then she sat back in her chair. A blank stare slid across her face as she quietly said to herself, "King Solomon. She missed him." Turning back to Clay she asked, "What are they doing now?"

"They continue walking away, down the beach. Now, they stopped and looked back. They smiled at me. They turned away again and are walking away down the beach. The Queen looked back again. No, it is not the Queen. She is not a black woman, she is an old woman. It is the face of … Sogui."

"Did she say anything?"

A huge smile grew across Clay's face. "No. She only winked at me. The scene is now gone and the book of this soul has closed."

* * * ~~~ * * *

Glossary of Historical Figures

Chapters 1-10

Empress Julia Domna
Philostratus
Roman Emperor Justinian
Catholic Pope Gregory
Plotinus
Ammonius Saccas
Apollonius of Tyanna
Apollonius of Rhodes
Hillel
King Solomon
Queen of Sheba
Aaron
Moses
Miriam
Dr. Sun Yatsen
Mao Ze-Dong
Chiang Kai-Shek
Abraham Lincoln
Ulysses S. Grant
Robert E. Lee

Chapters 11-20

Abraham
Isaac
Ishmael
Pythagoras
Iamblichus
Nestorius
Jabir ibn Hayyan
Rhazes
Avicenna
Ezra Pound
Ptolemy
Philo Judeaus
Jesus Christ
Proclus
Dolpopa

Chapters 21-40
Zoroaster
The Buddha
Confucius
Hypatia
Al-Farabi
Solomon ibn Gabirol
Thomas Paine
Helen P. Blavatsky
Milarepa

Chapters 41-77
Karl Jaspers
Martin Heidegger
Zohar
Karl Haushofer
Albert Einstein
Khadijah
Mohammad
Maria the Copt
Muqawqis
Mary Magdelene

Terms of Interest

Stanford Research Institute
Astral projection
Out-of-body experiences
Remote viewing
Past-life regression
Stargate program
San-Min
Triumvirate
The Cantos
Holy Grail
Kidwelly Castle
Kuna Yala
San Blas
Nargana
The Gathas
The Secret Doctrine
Drukpa Kargyü Buddhist Sect
Potola Palace, Lhasa, Tibet
Shigatze, Tibet
Mount Everest
Kodari, Nepal
Kathmandu, Nepal
Shigatze Airfield, Tibet – 6km long runway
Sanskrit
Axial Age
Age of Enlightenment
Swastika
Ahnenerbe
Nechung Oracles
Atlantis
T4 Explosives

About the Author

Raised on an Iowa farm, Lynn Boston spent his summer afternoons in corn fields daydreaming of adventures in faraway lands. At seventeen, while war raged in Southeast Asia, he joined the Army and graduated from West Point as an airborne paratrooper. But his years of duty were spent staring at Russian machine guns during the Cold War.

He spent his next twenty years as a road warrior for an oil company traveling to every God forsaken corner of the world: Nigerian savannas, Saudi Arabian deserts, Indonesian jungles of Sumatra … and even Bakersfield, California.

Lynn was always known for fantastic storytelling, keeping the entire office intrigued and rolling with laughter from his adventures. He finally ended his travels to bring you The Third Eye Trilogy.

Lynn lives in Phoenix, Arizona.

Connect with the Author Online:

Website: www.lynnbostonbooks.com
email: lynn@lynnbostonbooks.com
Facebook: http://facebook.com/lynn.boston
Twitter: @lynnboston